Legacy of the Lightbringers

Chapter One

Larissa, Edouard, and a couple of his henchmen gazed down upon August's body. Light from the full moon illuminated what could be seen of his handsome face, and he seemed for all the world as though he were sleeping.

"I hope your guard didn't hit him too hard," Larissa murmured.

"Just hard enough. Don't worry," Edouard said, quickly reassuring her. "And I have so much to tell you. But as you know, August Hawthorne has always been a maverick and a wild card, and I need to get him contained and get both of you to safety as quickly as possible. The Order of the Chevron has discovered your location and is riding here as we speak."

He pulled her closer to him. Larissa could smell the scent of clean leather mixed with something more exotic. "I have thought of nothing but you since we last met. Come now, your safety is of the utmost importance, my love."

***

August looked out from behind the gleaming enchanted bars of his prison at the stone wall on the opposite side. What happened? Why was he here in this forsaken place? To his horror on awakening, he had discovered the confiscation of his beloved wand and jeweled dirk. He had lost track of time. Worse, he had no idea where Larissa was. That third consideration drove him to distraction, frustrating himself as much as his obvious captivity.

Still dressed in his own clothing, he only kept from freezing by creating energy auras within the confines of his cell. He spent most of his time testing the limits. Apparently, anything he could conjure up manually for his survival was allowable, but without his trusty wand, he didn't have the added energy to break out of this confounded cell.

He had tried kicking out the bars, as they appeared to be glassine cylinders. To his dismay, their crystalline structure was unbreakable. The food was tolerable. At first, he'd refused it. Hunger got the better of him, and he ate for energy-building purposes. Whenever he felt thirsty, he pulled water from within the rock walls of his prison, opening his mouth so the water dribbled in. That had sated him for a while. Water from rocks was always pristine and cold. The taste and touch of it energized him a bit more.

August knew he was a Magical, but like the Mortals, he wasn't immortal. Another reason he deigned sampling the fares delivered to his cell three times daily. It was always hot, mostly venison, some of it quite tasty, with a few winter vegetables thrown in. A sweetened flatbread he recognized as a homespun recipe known as Witch's Puff tasted fairly good, given the circumstances.

All he knew was that they had been in the middle of a great quest, making headway despite their differences, until a stranger showed up. That much he remembered. The mysterious figure under the elm tree. Did that person have anything to do with his predicament? The more August considered the memory, the more it seemed the most plausible explanation. But why?

A commotion echoed down the corridor. August rose quickly to his feet. The crazy bantering bouncing off the stone walls made it impossible to guess from which direction the people were coming. Without a doubt, a group was approaching. Within seconds, the visitors stood before the cell.

The vision of Larissa robed in a handsome scarlet gown, surrounded by three soldiers, stunned him beyond belief.

"Thank the gods!" August said. As he walked toward the bars, he stifled his other words. From looking at his companion, suspicion kicked in. "You are okay, then?"

"Yes, I am." Her answer came out prim, undisturbed, confident. With one hand, she batted away an errant cobweb floating carelessly down from the archway above. "And how are you?"

Her tone and aloof demeanor irritated August greatly. He answered in a pert manner, "Imprisoned, actually. Have you come to release me? What kind of deal are you making? I can tell by their uniforms that we are the guests of someone powerful. Who is it?" He rubbed his head. "I seem to be a bit fuzzy on how this all came about. Maybe you will be so kind as to fill me in, Princess?"

"Don't call me Princess." Larissa said. Her clouded face clearly showed offense. "And you should know that Edouard Anguis, the second sovereign of the Anguis Clave, has been a most wonderful host."

"Aha!" August pointed an accusatory finger at her. "I should have suspected he was behind this. So he was the one I saw you with. Am I right? And for the love of the gods, where are we? Because I have a sneaking suspicion we're nowhere near where we were."

"Why were you even following me, August?" She shook her head, exasperated. "Then again, why should I ask? You were just being you. And to answer your question, we are in Huigra, Ecuador."

He nearly fainted at the answer. "Why? And what about Willem?"

"Shh!" Larissa lifted a finger to her mouth and shook her head lightly.

Beyond frustrated, August continued, "Are you mad? The Anguis are powerful, yes, but also treacherous to the bone. And, I might add, no friend to the North Strondovan Clave nor the South Hawthorne Clave." The young man shook a lock of hair away from his face. "How naive you are, presuming to negotiate with these unscrupulous traitors."

Larissa stepped closer to the bars. "August, as usual you are brash and unaware that you are not in any kind of a power position. I didn't come to release you, but I have come to make you seem less of a threat to the Anguis. I am doing this as a favor to your grandfather, whom I admire and respect, if you haven't guessed already. It's not his fault that you are a horse's ass."

August tried crossing his arms over his chest, but the chains only allowed him to merely cross his wrists. He'd tried to rid himself from those, too, but had no better luck than dealing with those hateful cell bars.

"Fine. What are you going to do?"

"First this." Larissa whisked out her wand and flicked it over her shoulders, stunning the Anguis guardsmen. They froze in place. "You need to brace yourself, August. I will place a temporary Transfigurator spell on you. Fair warning, you won't like it at all, but it may save your life."

Before August could respond, Larissa waved her wand again. A sharp pain ripped through the left side of his hip. At the same time, the left side of his jaw sagged. An excruciating pain seared through his right hand, creating a sensation of bones being crushed at once.

"Yow! Dammit, Larissa!" he shouted. Looking down, he viewed a withered right hand. It also seemed that one of his legs was now shorter than the other, giving him a permanent limp. On the sagging side of his face, drool slipped out of his mouth.

He stared at Larissa incredulously.

She continued speaking. "Because if you seem like less of a threat, Edouard will likely let you go." She stepped back, smiling, looking pleased with the results of her magical handiwork. "Actually, you make sort of a cute gimp. Anyway, it's the best I can do for now."

August limped closer to the glassine bars. "Whach about you, Risha?" He had difficulty getting out the words from his new, lopsided mouth.

"I will rejoin Edouard and convince him to let you go. I am quite falling in love with him, you know. It seems as though he is in love with me."

Frustrated, August watched Larissa fairly float back down the stone corridor, lighthearted as if she were a fairy who had just granted a wish. He'd hoped for release when he saw her, but all she had done was cause him to be more confused than ever, not to mention she'd turned him into a drooling gimp. He decided he had probably been better off before she showed up.

***

"Beware of snakes, dear girl. Not everyone who invites you into their nest is your friend." Edouard reviewed the words from a copy of Larissa's letter again out loud. He had maintained his own copy once he saw hers during their time together at Tiberinus's last feast. Two grinning young men listened intently as he read.

Daniel and Dennis joined their leader by a fireplace, basking in the warmth and sipping whiskey.

"She's in the nest now, isn't she?" Dennis glanced Daniel's way and back to Edouard.

"I'd say close enough. After all," added Edouard, "we first met here in Ecuador, though not in Huigra. She was with her aunt, Dorenda, and I was with my father. We met in Quito." He smiled and sipped his drink.

"Do you think it was a bit much? The note and all?" asked Daniel.

"Perfect," said Edouard. "Close but still cryptic. And she'll never suspect me. Anguis means snake, though, in case you two didn't know."

"She doesn't suspect us, either." Dennis nodded, staring into the fire.

"We've got her, and that's what matters. I need to woo her over in our direction." Edouard tapped his glass. "We already have her aunt, who has been teaching her magic all these years. Dorenda is the best of the best. Now we get Larissa on our side."

"Have you thought about what to do if she balks in any way? You're extremely persuasive, Edouard, but I like to prepare for anything and everything." Dennis looked doubtful. Both men stared at Edouard.

"It may sound crazy, but I'm really banking on her siding with us, that our feelings for each other will carry her over the line, and then the world is ours."

Dennis didn't say anything but frowned in thought. Daniel clinked the ice in his glass.

"Oh, come on, you two. You don't think it can be done?" Edouard's face showed a trace of annoyance. "My father and Dorenda, who have been friends for years, have been planning this. They brought me on board when I turned of age, so I've been at it a while too."

"It's not like we haven't participated," Daniel said. He motioned in Dennis's direction. "He and I have played the doting lovers."

"And you both did a good job, but now play time is over. We must get down to business because there's not a lot of time left."

"How do you plan on convincing her?" asked Dennis. "When she finds out what we're all really up to, I just have a sneaking suspicion it may not go well."

Edouard considered the young man's words. "It's a delicate situation, but if I can play on her emotions, I think I've got it cinched, and there won't be this big battle we keep thinking about. Don't you think it's better to avoid a fight?"

"Of course," answered Daniel, "but Dennis has a point. Sometimes some of the best-laid plans go belly up, despite our best efforts."

"We cannot fail under any circumstance." Edouard passed a stern gaze over his two men. "She's resting in her room right now. I'm going there now to talk to her. Trust me, it's show time." He grinned at his subordinates. "In the meantime, I still need for you two to keep out of sight while she is here. That's why I have her quarters on the other side of this estate. She doesn't need to know you two are here." Edouard looked thoughtfully at his drink. "And I can't keep her too long, though I'd give anything to do so."

***

Larissa glanced toward the door. "Come in," she called out.

"Ah, my dear, did I disturb you?" Edouard slipped inside and closed the door behind him.

"Just relaxing. I think all the traveling is catching up with me a bit." She smiled.

He sat down on the bed, taking her hand in his. "And I thank you so much for humoring me, coming so far away from where you were." He rubbed his lip in thought. "I'm hoping your other companion won't worry too much. No doubt your sudden departure will leave him in a major quandary."

The young lady considered his words. "We will need to get back to Willem. You know that, don't you?"

"Of course, dear one." He looked into her eyes with feign earnestness. "I only wanted you here with me for a bit so we could talk, catch up, get to know each other again." He stood up and held out his hand. "Let's go for a walk. I want to show you Sulphure Castle. I have another residence in Rouen, France. Perhaps I can take you there sometime soon." He smiled as he watched her slip from the bed and fluff her hair in place.

"I would love to see your estate. Huigra seems like such a charming town for a place such as this."

The couple left the bedroom, walked down a corridor toward the front of the dwelling, and exited out a side door leading to an expansive terrace filled with flowers and plants. On one side, a large stone fireplace had been built.

"Your place is lovely. So cultural in décor." She turned toward him, squeezing his arm. "And elegant just like you."

"I like the change of pace in this town, in this country. Beautiful foliage, interesting people. The area is mountainous, and forests are beautiful. It's my summer home."

They walked through the terrace and ended up on a green lawn, where they made their way through a terraced garden filled with a plethora of roses and other flowers.

"Have you missed me, Larissa, ever given me a thought over the years?"

"Why, yes. How could I forget someone like you? We had such a wonderful time together in Quito long ago. Aunt Dorenda and your father seemed so happy too."

"I noticed the same. Very good friends they seem to be."

"How did they ever meet, Edouard? Aunt Dorenda and I have never discussed that."

"Come to think of it, I've never asked that, either. But they introduced us, and that's what's really important, don't you think?" The young man wrapped his arm around her waist.

"Definitely. I couldn't agree more," she answered.

They walked in silence several moments. The mountains stood poised in the distance, their majesty nearly taking Larissa's breath away. A gust of wind whipped around them. Edouard pulled her closer.

"Larissa, what do you want out of life? What are your wildest dreams?" He glanced at her, quickly studying her face.

"I'm not entirely sure," she answered. "I want to be super skilled in my magical powers. That's one thing. I guess the other would be to perhaps settle down and think about starting a family." She looked at him and smiled. "But the urgent thing right now is solving a family riddle. You know the one. I'm sure you've heard about it."

"You are still on a mission to find something, right?"

"Yes," Larissa answered. "Edouard, what have you heard about the mission August and I have undertaken? I'm sure everyone in the Magiverse knows, but you and I didn't discuss it when we last met at Tiberinus's feast."

He chuckled. "Dear Larissa, we didn't have much time to get into anything in depth. We only got as far as, um, your letter from Daniel. Remember?"

"Yes, and you were so intrigued by it? Why? And did you ever find out its strange meaning?

"Oh, I have not had the chance yet, but I most certainly haven't forgotten. Now that you're here, perhaps you can tell me more about why you and August Hawthorne are traversing all over the world, thither and yon." He laughed. "I've heard that much. Perhaps I can help, share some information, save you some time once I know more."

Larissa eyed Edouard with curiosity. "You seem so sure of yourself. Of course, you always did. I remember the first time we met here in Ecuador. Aunt Dorenda was really keen on us meeting. She seemed so excited."

"And are you sorry she brought us together?" Edouard leaned in closer, breathing in the scent of her hair. "I've thought about you all these years. You were so young, and I not much older."

"Of course, I'm glad she introduced us. And it's wonderful to be back in this lovely country and see a different part of it. I just wish August . . . um, I mean I wish there were more time to explore this area. Just you and me together." She smiled at him.

"You only have to say the word, and it can be done, Larissa. Do you know that together, you and I could have anything we want? Anything. Our powers would be limitless." He closed his eyes and lifted her hand to his cheek.

"How are you so sure about that? What makes you think so?" Her dreamy expression turned sober as she studied his face.

"We are two powerful witches. Your Aunt Dorenda is the best teacher. Not unlike my father. It would only make sense for us to be together. Let's face it. We're the perfect age to pursue a union. Now. Together, our powers would give us the world."

Larissa shrank back a little. She adored Edouard from the moment Dorenda introduced them. His charm and energy had her smitten. She'd had lots of boyfriends as she grew older, but in retrospect, none of them seemed to possess the qualities Edouard had. Wit, charm, and magical skills that were difficult to top. She'd witnessed some of them the first time they met. What she'd seen so far impressed her as well. And his estate in Huigra was astounding. But his push toward something serious as a union seemed a bit fast, no matter how strongly she felt about him.

"It's something we can consider, I suppose, but it would have to wait until I solve this riddle I've been thrust into solving. Edouard, it's plagued me. It's plagued families and the Magiverse."

"Tell me more, dear one. I really want to help you. I think I could."

"You have heard of the feud between the South Hawthorne and North Strondovan claves, have you not?"

"Ah, that I have, and from what I hear, the Glanarium Supremo wants it solved once and for all. Something about bad vibes and all that." He shook his head a moment, thinking.

"It's more than that. As you know, it's now been handed down to August and me, the current selected heirs of our claves, to put this feud to an end once and for all."

"How do you plan to do it?" Edouard asked. "If I remember the story that has been told, it all seems so vague. Something about an item that was stolen by one family from the other. Is that right?" He gazed intently into Larissa's face, hoping he sounded sincere.

"Yes. It was a prized relic of some kind, and no one knows what it is, but I have a hunch."

Edouard's face brightened at the words. "Really? What do you think it is, and how did you come up with the notion of it?"

"I think it was a conjuring cloth that was taken. I discovered the lore of the witch spinners just before I started this quest, and Aunt Dorenda and I have spoken briefly about it." Larissa decided against saying anything about her aunt possibly being a spinner herself.

"Interesting." Edouard lifted his eyes upward in feigned thought. "Who owned the cloth, and who took it, do you think?"

Larissa stared back at her admirer. "It was my great great aunt who owned the cloth. Or at least that's who I suspect; I have no direct proof. And I have no idea what happened. And mind you, I'm just putting two and two together."

"That's good. Nothing wrong with that. In fact, I like your hunch." Edouard squeezed her hand in reassurance.

Larissa sucked in her breath, at once a little sorry she revealed so much. This same feeling that confounded her when she and Edouard conversed during Tiberinus's feast hit hard again. Though she thought he was trustworthy on the surface, something deep inside niggled her, almost chastising, suggesting that again she had been too bold in her revelations. Why was he so intent about a union between them?

"You look perplexed. If I were in your shoes, I would be as well. But what if I told you it's possible that I truly could help?"

"In what way, Edouard? What do you know that I and the others don't?"

"I'm glad you asked. You see, I think I may know some information on your great great aunt."

Startled at the announcement, Larissa stopped walking and stared at Edouard. "How?"

"I have met your Aunt Ciana. As a matter of fact, my clave has been keeping your great great aunt safe for a long time.

Larissa stared at him, stunned. "What? Does anyone know this, like the Glanarium Supremo? That's a mighty big announcement to make Edouard. And I must meet her, talk to her. Can I?"

"It's a lot to take in," answered Edouard, pulling her gently along once again. "I'm telling you because we are here on my estate, where there is great privacy. Now is the right time to reveal all this. We helped protect Ciana because, like your family, she needed allies. We, the Anguis, were only too glad to assist. We even kept it from the Glenarium Supremo." He smiled, feeling that his charade was working its charm on Larissa. "She and my family made a pact to keep this a secret, to wait for the right time. We had to handle this carefully. And yes, you need to meet her. We'll have to make careful arrangements, though."

"Do you know how much this means to me? She has lived a long time, Edouard. She knows a lot. Has she told you anything about herself, who she is and what she does?"

"Ah, there is much to tell on that subject. I don't think we are going to have time right now to get into it in great detail, because you are correct. You must be able to continue your journey. I would never dream of interfering. There's too much at stake. Again, we'll pick a good time for a meeting and see what comes of it." Edouard blinked rapidly a few times, trying to emphasize his sincerity in the best possible way without giving himself away. "But let me assure you my sweet, I can be of valuable service to your mission, and you will benefit greatly. I just wanted to whisk you away for a moment of privacy and tell you so. When the time is right, we will talk more of Ciana. In the meantime, please trust that I have only your greatest interest and well-being at heart."

Chapter Two

Willem awakened with a start and a terrible feeling in his gut that something was wrong. For that reason, he didn't move at first, but carefully listened and scanned the woodland environment that surrounded him. Nothing seemed out of place except it was much too quiet, and he was alone. There was no sign of either of his traveling companions, Larissa or August. And because at least *one* of them, August, was his charge to defend and protect, he was already failing in his sworn duty.

Protecting Larissa was even more important to him, though, for reasons he could never reveal to another soul. He was deeply in love with her. It was an atrocious way to start off the day, because he'd only had *one* job, and he'd fucked it up. He had no idea why he wasn't hearing the usual morning bickering to which he'd become accustomed before he had his first savory cup of coffee.

He stood, stretched, and urinated, trying to avoid pissing on the morel mushrooms growing all around their campsite, hoping to collect a few to take along. Afterwards, he did a turn around the area to make sure they had disappeared and to look for any clues. The only one he found was somewhat chilling. Lying on the ground near the edge of the lookout point, he spied a hefty branch from which the smaller branches and leaves had been stripped. When he picked it up, carefully examining it, he found dark stains that looked like blood on one end.

There wasn't much blood, to be sure, but again Willem got a queasy feeling in his stomach. Someone had been hit, and they might be injured. Time was of the essence. He would have to forego breakfast and be on his way. But first he needed to perform a directional charm. Picking up a sage leaf from the ground, he carefully rubbed it against the dark stain at the end of the branch, until a small crimson stain was transferred to the leaf, in stark contrast to its bright green.

Willem discerned that it was August's blood and relaxed a little. Holding the leaf in his hand, he recited a charm that he'd found handy in certain situations.

"Blood calls to blood, float through the air, guide my path and take me there."

This was all he needed to say before the small leaf moved within his grasp. Now activated, it seemed anxious to be on its way. The leaf made one full turn around him, allowing Willem time enough to pick up his pack and walking stick before it began floating ahead of him in a westerly direction.

Willem frowned, trying to call forth a vision of his destination, but he wasn't yet close enough to create a cloud image of the place. For the time being, all he could call up from the ether, which was the element that contained all connections to spirit, intuition and all planes of existence, was a few flickering images in his mind of what looked like a heavily fortified castle, dark and foreboding, along with the prescient sense that it belonged to a powerful Magical family, and that as massive as it was, it was more or less just a "vacation home."

It was a valuable clue, Willem thought as he trudged along through the forest. He was now convinced that he was on his way to the place where Larissa was being kept. He had a feeling that Larissa had been beguiled somehow into following Edouard. And where the hell was August? August's situation felt even more dire than Larissa's. All he understood clearly at that point in time was that he was bound to locate both of them, and it was going to be a long trek.

Along the way he searched the trunks of the ancient trees for portals. Tree portals weren't as efficient as most, though more stable than sky portals, but they were good for short jaunts, and he often took advantage of them if he wanted to get somewhere in a hurry. For the time being he was content to follow the enchanted leaf compass, traveling along at a comfortable speed and deep in thought over how to handle all the possible scenarios he might encounter when he arrived at Edouard's summer house, wherever that was.

He caught the aroma of a stew someone was cooking in the open air. It smelled delicious. His empty stomach growled. As he continued forward, the narrow path opened into a clearing. In the center of it he saw a dwarf leaning over a huge steaming kettle placed atop a log fire. He still followed the leaf as it went right up to the red-bearded dwarf and hovered nearby. Before Willem could utter a sound, he saw the dwarf turn his head, noticing the leaf. With a quick movement, the dwarf plucked the leaf compass out of the air and tossed it into the stew.

Willem was instantly furious. "Say there, what are you doing? That was an enchanted leaf compass guiding me to my destination!"

The dwarf stirred the stewpot vigorously a few times and then stood, smiling at Willem. Willem's first thought was that the dwarf was rather tall, for a dwarf and wondered if he could even best the creature in hand-to-hand combat. Especially close up, the dwarf appeared rather powerfully built.

"Well, it was a sage leaf and will flavor our stew very nicely," the dwarf told him with a wink. "And the best part of all is that you have contributed to the meal, so you shall have three bowls full, if you so desire. I am sure you must be famished. I can hear your stomach growling from here."

Willem scowled down at the dwarf but didn't dare say anything derogatory. Dwarves were known to be powerfully gifted Magical beings, and the last thing he wanted to do was antagonize him. "Very well, and thank you," he said. He didn't fail to notice his mouth was suddenly watering. "I am Willem Wyndom Wiles, usually referred to as Willem the Wizard. And you might be?"

"I *might* be the King of Sheba, but I am not," the dwarf answered, smiling. "I am, however, Phuctious Hesperides." He bowed lightly. "At your service."

Willem gave a start before asking, "Are you in the direct line of Descendants of the Hesperides?"

Phuctious blushed slightly in pleasure at having his Magical heredity and superiority recognized.

"My great great grandmother on my mother's side. Even diluted, that Nymph blood is a powerful genome to have coursing through one's veins. I credit my mother's side for my Magical prowess! Fresh water immersion transforms me into a Naiad! But enough about me. Let's have some of this delicious stew."

A few minutes later as Willem polished off his third bowl of stew, along with a second cup of steaming hot tea and contemplating on having another, the dwarf spoke up.

"I am curious as to why you are taking this particular path through the Forgotten Forest," the dwarf said. His brow wrinkled with concern. "Especially when any path you take through it will only end you up in one place."

Willem was startled yet intrigued. "Actually, I did have a destination in mind, and it seemed to me that my *former* guide, the enchanted leaf, was doing a great job of leading me there…" Willem trailed off, intentionally cutting his eyes at the dwarf. "I was trying to reach a summer home of one I believe to be owned by Edouard Anguis. Perhaps you've heard of him?"

"Ah, so you were traveling to the summer palace of the Elementals. Let me ask you an important question. Was Lord Edouard expecting you? Does he know that you are coming? The reason I inquire is that he is not one to offer hospitality to strangers, especially those who are not of the Magical Nobility. No offense, but it is obvious to me that you are of the servant class."

Willem sat up a bit straighter on the sawed-off stump he used as a seat. Before him, the fire crackled and sent small whorled cinders and sparks up into the air.

"I am not of the Nobility, but I do serve in the Royal Guard of the South Hawthorne Clave, a noble house. I am pledged to protect and defend both Larissa North Strondovan and August South Hawthorne as the Heirs of their respective Magical Houses as they continue on their quest."

To Willems's astonishment, the dwarf snorted and burst into laughter. After a few moments, he wiped the tears from the corners of his eyes, smirked, and asked, "And exactly *how* is that working out for you? I am asking because I see neither the Strondovan Heir nor the Hawthorne Heir with ye. You seem to have lost your own way, not to mention that if either of them are currently the guests of Edouard, you are in grave dereliction of your duty and should probably be shot!"

Willem put down his bowl and shrugged. "I can't fault your assessment of my situation, and it is beyond my power to explain. As I lay down to sleep last night my companions were with me. When I awakened, they had vanished. I do not even know if it was of their own volition or not. I suspect not, though. I believe they were taken by either Edouard or his henchmen."

"I suggest we do a Flamma Vision, if you like," Phuctious said. "It will take the two of us, especially since the wind is picking up."

Willem nodded. He was familiar with that particular spell, which always required two Magicals to perform. He was anxious to do a welfare check on his former companions. As both stood over the flickering flames of the small campfire, the stew pot having been removed, they held their hands over it. They stared into each other's eyes, intensifying and harnessing the energy between them to create the Flamma Vision. From their lips came the following words:

Magia enim quarere ab aquiline et mari
Ostende nobis
Ostende nobis
Ostende nobis heredes!

No sooner had they stopped reciting the spell than the campfire flame shot up, creating a pedestal table with a perfectly round, flat top upon which an image formed. The first image was of a young man in tattered clothes that somewhat resembled August Hawthorne. His face appeared distorted, and he sat on a stone floor behind iron bars. He wore chains on both wrists. As they watched, the vision shifted to one of a lovely young woman, instantly recognizable by Willem as Larissa. His heart leapt when he saw her image.

But then his heart dropped to his feet as he realized that she was weeping. He clenched his jaw in frustration at seeing her cry and wondered what could have happened to cause such sadness. In the short time he had known her, he had been impressed by her fortitude and determination.

He'd hoped that the Flamma Vision would have comforted him, but now he felt more desperate than ever to save his companions.

"I need to reach the Summer Castle more quickly," he told Phuctious. "I feel that both my charges are in peril. Do you have any suggestions?"

"Yes, I do, but I daresay you won't like them," the dwarf answered without hesitation. "The first suggestion I have is to lose the attitude."

Willem was taken aback. "Attitude? I am not sure what you mean."

"Oh, it isn't really your fault, I suppose," the dwarf told him. "Perhaps a fellow like you isn't even conscious of it. I'm talking about the superior attitude that all Mortals and Magicals have toward those whom they consider 'vertically challenged'. Just because dwarves are a few feet shorter doesn't mean we are inferior in any sense. Our proximity to the earth gives us superior discernment as to what is just below our feet. For example, you are at this moment standing on a cache of gold coins that were hastily buried over a century ago, in this very forest.

"The cache also contains a magical object or two, long forgotten but completely functional. I can see by your expression you are doubtful, even though *everyone* knows that dwarves can smell gold, even if it's buried fifteen feet within rock. Go ahead, now. Start digging directly below where you are standing. I guarantee that you won't be digging long."

Willem made no comment. Squatting down over the space of pine needles covering the ground Phuctious had indicated, he began digging. He'd barely gotten dirt under his fingernails before he broke through the sandy soil and felt something solid beneath his touch. The soil had gotten sandier and much looser. He was able to brush it off and retrieve a small chest from its nest in the earth without too much difficulty. As he lifted the lid, Phuctious said smugly, "What did I tell you, Wizard Willem?"

Willem saw the golden coins shining brightly, as if lit from within. As he poked one finger into the small chest, so as not to upset the contents, he felt other objects, apparently enclosed in small canvas sacks.

"Go ahead," Phuctious told him. "And stop dillydallying! Pull it out. Let's see what it is!"

Willem gulped as he breathlessly hefted it up. Though the chest appeared small, it was a weighty piece. He dumped one of the items out on his palm. It appeared to be a coiled golden metallic rope less than an inch and a half across. As soon as it touched the warmth of his skin, it uncoiled across his palm, and the end of it began to twitch.

"Oh, good one!" the dwarf said in an admiring tone. "That will certainly come in handy. I suggest you use this bit of twine, and as soon as the rope coils back up again, put it through the center and wear it as an amulet."

"Yes, yes, but what does it do?" Willem asked impatiently. Just watching how the end of it twitched and wiggled reminded him of a serpent. He knew it was made of metal, but it seemed half alive.

"It will cause your enemies to become tightly bound at your command," Phuctious explained patiently. "It is a Hindi artifact known as a pasha. You would say "Bandh", which means "Bind", to activate it. It will automatically be able to discern your intention."

The dwarf handed the length of course twine over to Willem, and he awkwardly fashioned himself a necklace so that he might carry the pasha.

"You are very, very lucky. I can see that now," the dwarf said softly. "You must have been born under a lucky star, Willem. This artifact that you have just happened to come across will be extremely useful as we retrieve your friends from Sulphure Hall. That's Lord Edouard's summer home. Now hurry and dig the other one out. Let's see it then!"

Willem had more difficulty with the second canvas-covered object, which seemed to be something round.

"Duh, of course it's round," Phuctious said.

The fact that Phuctious could read his mind startled Willem. "So, you can read my private thoughts?" Willem said. "Why did you not tell me? It might have been nice to know that my thoughts are not my own around you."

"Oh, shut up and unwrap the "round thing", Wizard Willem," the dwarf said crossly. "We need to get going, and you are not quick about anything you do. And as for your thoughts, they are mostly very snore-worthy and centered around your apparent infatuation for Larissa Strondovan. You've been sending her sexy dreams with you yourself featured as the main protagonist, fucking her brains out. That young lady, if she is truly of Strondovan blood, has a high libido and is probably a chronic masturbator without your input. Why don't you leave her alone?"

Willem found himself turning several shades of red and chose not to answer. He had found that not answering often served him better than trying to make explanations. The object within the bag turned out to be a copper cuff with many mysterious markings carved into it.

"Ahh," the dwarf said with approval. "A Restoration Cuff. Haven't come across one of those in a while, I have to tell you. No!" he shrieked.

Willem had moved to place the cuff around his arm.

"Stop! If you place it on your body, it will waste its power to restore *you*, and you are not mortally wounded. Just place it in your pocket. There you go, boy." The dwarf calmed down somewhat. "I didn't mean to scream at you. I just hate to see anything wasted, is all. You may yet have cause to use it to save one of your Magical Heirs. You know? As stubborn as they both are, one is sure to place themselves in peril.

"The Restoration Cuff is used to heal instantaneously, to bring someone back from death's door. You can always tell who was spared by this ancient magic because, especially if they have been gravely wounded in battle, their scars will heal and have a silvery color that looks iridescent in moonlight.

"It is an elegant sort of magic, one that I admire. But as I indicated previously, it is only good for a one-time use. So you should save it for a more fortuitous time, of course."

Willem nodded. He was thinking (and to his annoyance he realized the dwarf was probably hearing his thoughts at that same moment) that it was unfortunate that the cuff could only be used to save *one* of his companions. He was after all in charge of protecting both Larissa and August. If it came down to it, though, and he had to make a choice, it would be no contest. He would save Larissa over the Hawthorne Heir.

"Let's go, Wizard Willem," said Phuctious. He helped gather up the loose items and closed the chest. "We must be on our way to Sulphure Hall—and it's in another country—Ecuador, in a small tucked-away town called Huigra. Odd place for a castle, but then again, I've always thought there's something strange about Edouard Anguis. Oh, and we'll have to locate a Sky Portal."

"How do you know all this?" asked Willem.

"I've been around the block more than once. I know who's who, and where they live and what they do. It's a skill I have. We'll leave it at that." Phuctious winked.

With all the artifacts tucked safely away, and the box of gold coins stowed in Phuctious's backpack (something he had insisted on), the two new traveling companions headed off again. Even though the light was waning there was a full Rabbit Moon expected that night that would light their way; and Willem was too full of adrenalin to sleep a wink.

As they tramped along, looking for a handy Sky Portal, Willem dreamt of encountering the spires of Sulphure Hall. He knew an Elemental as powerful as Edouard didn't skimp when it came to pomp and ostentatious display of property. While they moved, Phuctious sang a song familiar to Magicals all over the globe. It was entitled "The Crescent":

Oh, sing us a song of the full glowing moon.
Sing us a song of the Crescent.
For the vainglorious orb is a generous thing,
Shining tinsel on both King and peasant.

I traveled to black castles in the far lands
By moonshine and starlight luminescent
To rescue a maid that once had I laid
From a Nobleman both rich and unpleasant.

Alas, when I arrived, he had made her his bride.
They were feasting on boar's head and pheasant.
She remembered me not, though I fell to my knees
And she asked for my head as a present!

When they finished repeating the final chorus of the song, the dwarf turned and stared up at Willem in contemplation. Willem became instantly annoyed as he perceived that the dwarf was reading his thoughts.

"What?" Willem finally blurted.

The ginger-bearded dwarf just shook his head. "You are in love with the Strondovan Heir, Larissa," he said quietly. "Ah, but that is a misfortune twice over. I know that you have enough discernment to grasp that you are not part of her destiny in that regard."

"Firstly, stay out of my head, would you? Secondly, it doesn't matter to me what happens, or if she ever professes her feelings." Willem tried to stare down the dwarf, but seeing the sympathy in Phuctious's eyes, he finally looked away. He was not ashamed that he had been calling Larissa to join him on the astral plane in the Desire Dreams. It was the only way to experience true closeness with her. "It matters not whether she returns my feelings. I do love her, and I am willing to sacrifice myself, body and soul for her. All I care about is her happiness."

"Oh, I see," the dwarf said. "I stand corrected, then, although I do also know that you use your magical prowess to hook up with her on the astral plane, and because she indeed is somewhat attracted to you, as well as having the same high libido as her predecessors, she welcomes this. She thinks it is a wet dream, a love fever dream, and she enjoys these little trysts, as I am sure you are aware. So at least you have *that* going for you."

With Phuctious's great skill, the two found a handy Sky Portal a few miles farther from the trail where they traveled. By that time, it was noon, and the tall and twisted spires of Sulphure Hall glinted bright gold in the sunlight, appearing as a crown atop the grey hewn granite stone structure of the castle. All around, tall green mountains and steep rolling hills created a breathtaking backdrop. The weary travelers, having reached their destination, stood still, momentarily taking in the impressive view before beginning their descent.

Above him and the dwarf, Willem clearly viewed a half circle of archers standing on one of the parapets, bows at the ready. He was gratified to see that instead of attacking them, they seemed rather welcoming as he and Phuctious headed toward the main gates surrounding Sulphure Hall.

"You might get your new toys ready," Phuctious suggested. "You are likely going to need them, particularly the Pasha."

Chapter Three

Edouard was frustrated and fit to be tied, and that was dangerous. When he felt that way, people around him tended to die, Magicals along with any unfortunate human that happened to be in his line of vision when his anger peaked. He looked with disdain around the huge stone-

walled room, big as a warehouse. He had converted one of the ballrooms into a factory for spinning the holy grail of Magical artifacts considered sacred by witches, wizards, and sorcerers alike—the conjuring cloth. In the past, he had tried to activate some of the cloths that resembled the one Ciana had crafted but failed.

All of the ladies in this room had been recruited because they contained something of the Strondovan bloodline in their lineage. His theory had been that if even one of them could produce a decent conjuring cloth, he would have a backup in the event he could not entice Larissa into doing him the honor of producing the rare cloth. His chances with Ciana were fading fast.

And now he had Larissa secured under his roof, the one witch who was reputed to have inherited the ultimate gift for weaving them. Whether or not she had tried her hand at weaving or possessed doubts about it didn't matter to him. His inclination was to cut through the bullshit of trying to coddle her and use torture to force her to spin for him. But he knew better.

Such a gift, in order to manifest, must be given willingly, so he was resigned to spoiling her, seducing her, and wooing her in order to secure her complicity. He smiled suddenly, remembering her adoring eyes looking up at him. How stupid women were, no matter if they were human or Magical. They always fell for the dark brooding bad boy, didn't they?

He had a reputation he was proud of and came from the preeminent witch family in the Magiverse. Aside from that, he knew that her closest relative associated with the Strondovan bloodline, her Aunt Dorinda, was approving of her crush on him. Well, why not? He really *was* "Extra" as the expression went.

He approached a girl whose name he didn't care to know, asking her, "What is your name, new witch?"

She looked up at him. She was a comely redhead, as so many witches gathered in the spinning room were.

"I am Corrine, your Grace." The lady bowed as she sat at her spinning wheel, working the treadle and keeping tension on the bobbin thread. "I am thought to be a distant cousin twice removed of the Strondovan line."

"I see," Edouard said, "and how are you coming with your cloth? Which loom is yours?"

He indicated an array of different sized looms in the back of the room. He could see that not many held rows of woven material.

"I work quickly and have already managed a small square of cloth as test fabric," she told him. "I made it using charms and chants from me Great Granny.

Edouard was delighted. Her approach sounded legitimate, though he would never be quite sure. Ciana also refused to tell how she created her cloth. Corrine was brand new and already she had managed to produce something that none of the rest had. Her cloth resembled Ciana's the most.

"Secure the edges quickly and bring it to me," he instructed her. "Let's see what you've done."

Dutifully and with a slight curtsy, she made a beeline to the smallest loom, retrieving a square of material that even in the dim light coming in from the high casement windows seemed to sparkle with both outer and inner light.

Edouard held his breath, filled with excitement. The girl held the cloth out to him with both palms up as though in offering. He fairly snatched it from her and held it up in the air for a moment. Filled with confidence, he recited, "*Capitulum quantum, geminus!*" He inhaled deeply. From the depths of his being, he called on the power of volcanoes to light and activate this cloth to a functioning one. His elemental power was an activating source, and he knew it. The ancient energy surged through him, turning his body briefly into a hot bright orange glow before it shot out through his hands.

The cloth rose upward for a moment and then, as everyone in the spinning room watched, riveted, seemed to ignite, burning in midair until its ashes descended and floated down like lacey soiled snowflakes. There was silence for a moment.

"Well, how disappointing," Edouard said in an even tone. "That I can't get at least one of you misbegotten witches to produce even a *small* sample of conjuring cloth that actually enhances a simple spell rather than turning into a firecracker!"

He turned smoldering eyes on Corrine. "You have disappointed me for the first and last time, and I shall make an example of you!" Drawing out his wand, raised it and called out, "*Pellis!*"

Corinne, or what was left of her after all her skin had been removed, dropped like a rock to the flagstone floor, writhing. She still held her human form but had become a grotesque deep red oozing thing. And the oozing thing was trying to scream, making disturbing high pitched agonized shrieks, interspersed with piteous moans. It took her a full five minutes to die.

"Let this be a lesson to the rest of you!" Edouard announced. Servants appeared to clean up the carnage. "I expect results."

Unknown to Edouard, in the darkness afforded by the deeply arched entranceway to the former ballroom, Larissa stood frozen in place. Burned into her memory for all time were the shocking images of the young girl convulsing in agony on the stone floor, stripped of her own skin from head to toe. Larissa turned and ran down the winding corridor, stopping once to access an outdoor viewing balcony and vomit.

Shock and desperation overcame her. It was obvious that Edouard wasn't who she thought he was. Had she been somehow beguiled? She wanted to leave immediately, but her internal witch of wisdom cautioned against an abrupt departure. A prescient sense told her that Willem was on his way. And to have briefly forgotten about him further confirmed that she must have been charmed or under a spell. Larissa knew that the protective spell she had cast on August for his own protection would only last a handful of days.

"All dark things are eventually revealed," her Aunt Dorenda had always told her. Well, Edouard's penchant for cruelty certainly had been. At that moment, all she wanted was to be reunited with August and Willem and get this quest over with—fast.

Fortunately, at least in her mind, Edouard Anguis was called away for a few days for a Summit of Magicals held at what he referred to as 'The Ruby Sanctum'. Larissa was surprised that she had never heard of it from her Aunt Dorenda in all the years of instruction under her Magical relative.

Edouard had smirked before he left. His smirk was one that Larissa recognized from the day she'd caught him torturing one of his employees. Now that she knew how intensely he enjoyed inflicting pain on others, his very touch made her skin crawl. He didn't seem to notice. He leaned over to kiss her and did so twice, though she could not force herself to respond as she had previously.

"When I get back," he murmured, "I will take your flower, Larissa. I will claim all of your secret treasures for myself. After all, if we plan to marry—it is a tradition in the Anguis, also a line of the South, that the bride be with child on the day of the nuptials. So I will be visiting your baby box soon to make sure we are ready."

Just contemplating a union with Edouard sent shivers coursing through her as though cold water had been injected into her spinal column. He was so handsome it was nearly painful to gaze into his perfectly featured face, his unusually dark eyes that flashed unexpected colors from time to time, and his incredibly trim yet muscular body. At one point in time, she had been so into his thrall that she'd been giddy with desire toward him. Now everything had changed, and she was confused as fuck.

With his departure came relief, for which she was grateful. She began plotting on how to leave, what kind of note she might write to Edouard, explaining her reasons for departing. Most importantly, how she would find her way down to the dungeon level again, on what pretense, and with the needed magical tools to free August from the Anguis.

Larissa paced, a nervous habit that had kicked in strongly during the past few hours, and an activity that she'd tried to curb for her Aunt Dorenda's sake. She felt the granite walls of Sulphure Hall, the Summer Castle of the Anguis Clave, closing in on her. How handy another amplituner would be right now. She desperately wished the one first given by Dorenda had not been used in the Hall of Winds. Afterward, it had vanished, its power consumed. Did she dare risk it to find a way for a successful escape?

She thought of Wizard Willem and stamped her foot in frustration-where *was* he? Surely, he must have awakened and realized that both she and August were missing. Why hadn't he found them yet? Any idiot would realize that the only place to which they could have been taken was the Summer Palace, Sulphure Hall. With his skill, Willem could surely discern that information with a little effort.

Sighing, she decided to prioritize. She gazed out a southernmost window just as the sun was beginning to set, determining that her first move would be to free August, though she still hadn't figured out how. She needed the following spells: Guard Stunning, Time Suspension, and Iron bar melting. While her mind roiled with ideas, she heard some noise outside the window. Peeping through the glass, she saw two figures trudging below on a wide path under the intermittent canopy of the forest surround.

Her heart leaped. She recognized the shoulder-length brown hair and easy gait of one of the figures. It was Willem. It had to be Willem! He had managed to find his way to Sulphure Hall after all.

But who was he traveling with? It was a much shorter character with a flaming orange beard and wearing a peaked green hunter's cap. It could only be a dwarf, she surmised, likely one of the Forest Dwarves. This sight was unusual sight because they moved away from the stony and mineral-filled rich caverns of the mountain ranges and, instead, became expert woodsmen and craftsmen.

Larissa had always had a fondness for Forest Dwarves, mostly based on the many stories her dear Aunt Dorenda had told during her childhood. Cunning and crafty, she knew the Forest Dwarves were highly magical and could become either fierce foes or loyal and staunch allies, depending on whether they took a liking to you or not.

Edouard had given her many gifts during her stay at the Hall. Larissa suspected that they also might serve him as tracking devices. Should she attempt to take them with her when she quit the premises? It would be a sacrifice, since she had become especially partial to a set of black pearls he had gifted her. They were highly unusual. Instead of the usual greenish sheen that most black pearls had, they held an unusual azure sheen to them when held in the light.

Larissa shook her head. What a waste, she thought. Soon a member of the Anguis guard appeared at her chamber. He saluted and announced, "There are strangers approaching from the west. Please advise if you would like us to head them off before they arrive. They are traveling through the valley meadowlands now, the perimeter of the property. T'would be easy for our archers to take them out before they reach the castle itself."

"No!" Larissa said, reprimanding him sharply. "They are my distinguished guests I have been expecting. Please make them feel welcome. Give them something to eat and drink and an opportunity to bathe before you bring them into my presence. I imagine that they are in need of both."

The guardsman hesitated just a few seconds before bowing and saying, "As you wish, Strondovan Heir."

As he walked away, the footfalls of his leather boots echoed loudly in the cavernous stone hallways. The guard ruminated over his conversation. He *could* send a message to Lord Edouard by pigeon, telling him of the new arrivals and asking him to advise what he wanted the guards to do with them.

His patrol had sighted one young man dressed in guardsman garb and also a dwarf. He also knew that the Anguis had no love for dwarves in general, regarding them as lower Magicals and would likely not allow them into the castle. The guardsman could not recall any member of the Anguis Clave entertaining a dwarf as a guest, and he had served the family for a great many years.

Nevertheless, he did remember that Edouard had left instruction that all of Larissa Strondovan's wishes be met while he was away, and so he decided to abide by that. Edouard hated to be disturbed when he was away on business and might not appreciate a pigeon post. The guardsman quickened his pace. He needed to have his men in position and have the staff make ready for the arrival of Larissa's guests.

Ushered in and summarily bathed by servants (which the dwarf enjoyed immensely and Willem resented thoroughly), the red bearded Phuctious and Willem soon found themselves face to face with a very pale and anxiety-ridden Larissa.

After dismissing the servants and guards and making sure the door was completely closed, the first thing she said to them was, "Thank the gods! Get me the fuck out of here!"

Willem was somewhat taken aback by her greeting. "What, no hug?" he quipped. "Where are the Anguis? Don't they own this magnificent edifice? I half expected them to greet us."

Larissa's eyes narrowed. "If they *happened* to be here, I can assure you that your heads would be resting atop platters by now. The Anguis are not especially fond of the other prominent Magical Claves. They accept me only because they know the Strondovan Clave has been disgraced and scattered for many years. We are no threat to them. They have an entirely different attitude toward the Hawthornes and others. I think it is extremely fortunate you came at this time."

"Speaking of the Hawthorne Heir, where is he?" Willem asked. His eyes darted about the room.

"He is currently imprisoned in the dungeons. Edouard has already remarked that August is a loose cannon. I saved him torture by altering his appearance with a spell, hoping he seems less threatening."

Willem answered, "We must go to him as soon as I grab a few things."

Without warning, much to Willem's surprise, Larissa jumped on him, hugged, and kissed him thoroughly.

"It took you long enough." she said, fussing with his hair. "I expected you a day ago at the latest!"

Willem's lips still tingled from Larissa's kiss, an enjoyable sensation he wanted to relish for a few more seconds and not be interrupted by speaking. He told her, "It was complicated. I did have help getting here, and I need to introduce my newest friend and traveling companion, Phuctious Hesperides. Phuctious, this is Larissa North Strondovan, the Strondovan Heir."

Larissa's eyes beamed with pleasure, impressed. Offering her hand she said, "I am honored to meet a Magical with Nymph blood in his veins. This is a first for me. I and my clave are at your service, Lord Phuctious."

The ginger-haired dwarf looked pleased. Taking Larissa's hand, he kissed it and bowed. "And I am at *your* service, my Lady. I have always felt that your clave was unjustly blamed. I was raised to hold the Strondovans in as high a regard as any other Elemental Clave."

Willem took all of this in without speaking. Apparently, Larissa was very knowledgeable in the family lore of the most prominent Magicals, more so than he was himself, although he had studied the different family trees and lineages ad nauseum.

"Well, great," he said, "can we please have something to eat and then go release August and leave?"

Larissa turned, and grabbing fruit from a nearby bowl, threw Willem an apple and offered Phuctious a ripe deep purple juicy plum. "This will have to do. Did you not hear me say you are late? The Anguis could return anytime. We might get a three-hour head start if we leave now."

She pulled out her burgeoning traveling bag from a lower cabinet and hoisted it over her shoulders. She also grabbed a capelet with a hood from a hook on the wall and looked at the other two brightly. "Don't worry. I grabbed some bread and cheese from the kitchens earlier to have later, after we have put some distance between ourselves and this godforsaken castle. Come now. There is no time to waste. We must get to Derestney Downs and see a man about a horse!"

Chapter Four

In a glorious chateau, situated in Rouen, in the Normandy region of France, Ciana sat in her sparse room. As beautiful as this dwelling was, she had been allowed no enjoyment of it, relegated to an isolated room in the lowest part of the home. While hours dragged on incessantly, her mind often reflected on the glory days of her youth, enjoying life strong and carefree in days much kinder than they were today.

In games of chase and hide and seek, she outran her siblings, leaving them chasing a whirlwind at best. On full moon nights or times when planets and hours slid into corresponding alignment, they practiced their magic. Their powers strengthened over the years. The North Strondovan line had become a formidable force—until that fateful moment it all came crashing down.

Ciana was no witch like her Magical siblings. She was one of the few Nephilim who walked the earth, part human, part angel, or so ancient lore described it. This fact was no small detail that made up her divinity. However, her inherited traits stemmed from a mating between her mother and one who came to Earth from the stars and not an angel as noted in written history. Those so-called fallen angels noted in lore were described as those who had rebelled against the almighty Creator.

This was a half-truth. Those fallen angels were merely highly advanced beings from other worlds and dimensions, who wanted to mingle with the sons and daughters of Earth, teach humans what they knew—reproduce with them so they could create more powerful offspring. Their powers, knowledge, and technology appeared magical, god-like, angelic. The Nephilim, progeny stemming from mere Mortals and those from the stars, knew things beyond regular humans on Earth. An inner knowing wove its way into their DNA.

Though they were not imbued with capabilities like Magicals, they could still develop their inner power and do astonishing works, fully in accordance with cosmic and natural laws. They were known for their ability to run with such extreme speed that once released, no one could catch them easily. This special group rebelled against an establishment that sought to control and obscure the wisdom that was really everyone's birthright, regardless of the product of any union. And an evil establishment was the very thing Ciana was attempting to fight.

Margaret, Ciana's mother, couldn't resist the powerful charms of the alien ruler who had come to Earth from another universe. These beings often did that, keeping their identities hidden before revealing themselves only to worthy ones. Before she passed, her mother told Ciana the truth. Her real father bore the resemblance of an angel, with fine ethereal beauty and power that ranked high on a Magical level, though his kind were merely advanced beings and not Magicals such as her brother, Desmond. Margaret had kept her union secret from Nicholas, passing off Ciana as his for the duration of their marriage. Ciana's father had returned to his original star system, never to be heard from again. But how her mother smiled when she recounted their history. This otherworld creature had possessed her during their lovemaking, sending her body into sensations that Nicholas simply could not do, though he was a formidable lover in his own right.

Only one window in her room allowed in the light. Levitating to it allowed her a view of the more scenic parts of the estate. She had spent time gazing out that window, thankful for the view of a brilliant carpet of green dotted with shapely trees and a backdrop of forests in the distance. Being confined had drained her energy immensely, leveling it to a little above neutral at best. Through sheer will, meditation, and practice of her divine skills, she managed some semblance of power.

The owners had given her the basics. A bed, which was comfortable enough, considering they could have done worse. A bureau to keep her belongings, as if she had anything else but the clothes on her back when the ancestors of the current family residing here kidnapped her over one hundred forty-five years earlier. A large cushion sat in a far corner. This item was a courtesy extended to her because one of the family members decided they were in a good mood one day and managed to convince the head of the household that it needed to be given to her.

Looking up at the window, she spied the moth fluttering near the sill and smiled. "You found your way here, didn't you?" Ciana held up a hand. The moth, as if on command, flitted down and landed on the tip of her finger. She eyed the creature, studying all its features with the astuteness of a biology scholar.

"Are the others like you hiding somewhere else? Don't let them catch you. Never let them suspect a moment what you are, for without you, I could not create the cloth. You provide the thread substance. I say the words. The ether is the power source, or most of it, anyway." The moth appeared to look at her, moving ever so slightly.

Ciana admired the wings. To the casual eye, one only saw a white moth. On closer inspection, one might see the iridescent sparkle in the wings if the light shined at the correct angle. She knew their full beauty when they were in the midst of doing what they were created to do—spin on command for the one who uttered the spell. As they released their silky threads, the moths' wings would light up in a twinkling of soft colors, pink, lavender, yellow, blue, pale green. The amalgamation of colors reminded one of cotton candy when pastel shades had been swirled into a cohesive delight. It was up to the spellcaster and activator to determine how the finished product would be used.

"I'm so sorry. It's not time to create another cloth. I will call on you soon, though. A little more time is needed. Go. Be safe with the others." She stretched out her hand once again, watching as the moth flew up to the window, disappearing into the pale light. Ciana sighed and sat on her bed. Seeing the moth was like seeing an old familiar friend. The last cloth was made right before Clement had died. Since that time, she hadn't created another.

The moths were as eager to spin. Why else would they seek her out here? As long as the current cloth remained in the wrong hands, she'd never activate it. Yes, the one who lorded over her may possess it. Yes, they also had the power to ignite it. But they were not the designated one. Clement was. And that honor had been snatched away from him without a care by the very ancestors of the one who held her captive now.

The Anguis clave stemmed from the elemental fire families, just like Clement Hawthorne's. Only the Anguis's fire source was volcanic, and the Hawthorne's was the sun. Neither source was good or bad, in and of itself. It was merely intention that convinced her that the Hawthorne clave would be the choice for activating her precious cloth. That family had shown a long history of strong, skillful, and courageous witches throughout time. She'd heard of their history and seen it.

It had been shown to her that the line of the Anguis had taken a completely different path altogether. The clave hadn't always started out that way, but as time progressed their behavior had become more insidious, creeping ever so slowly but surely toward the dark ways. A hunger for power over everyone and everything. Like the Hawthorne's, the Anguis also had fine enchanting skills. They needed it, to pull off the stunts they did to hide their ugly deeds.

Their transgressions weren't really any worse than most Mortals or Magicals could commit, but when the intent affected the world, bad deeds compounded themselves. Ciana got up and headed toward her beloved cushion in the corner and sat down on it in a lotus position. Closing her eyes, she prepared herself for reviewing the history of the Anguis. The truth was no more than one might hear in fables. The truth was that most stories stemmed from facts or a form of them, anyway. She'd always known this, and the tale of how Edouard Anguis came to power just proved her point.

Though she had dearly wanted to share the knowledge of creating a conjuring cloth with Dorenda Soltaro, and even showed herself to Dorenda in a dream, the latter's behavior after that long-ago dream forced Ciana into a different direction. Showing Larissa Strondovan's beloved aunt ancient knowledge would have been a delight, for the woman was an exceptional witch. Instead of helping Dorenda with transcendence and expansion, the goal now had devolved into one of entrapment and she, Ciana, would be the one to do it. The wayward aunt would pay for her lust, for it had created a monster that would destroy the world.

Not so much for lust alone, because many a witch had succumbed to lust, but for supporting the dark side from which she should have walked away ages ago, regardless how the personal transgression turned out. She would no more show Dorenda the arcane knowledge of cloth conjuring any more than she'd cut off her right hand. The aunt had gone too far, and there was no forgiveness or turning back. Ciana took in several deep breaths, opened her psychic third eye, and in a deep meditative state, tuned in to the history that was imprinted in time and space . . .

"He's ugly," Malevolinda whispered to her sister.

Carnetta replied, "It will take some high-level enchanting skills to make him appealing, but he seems rather bright. So he has that going for him, at least."

"I can't believe we're just now learning this, that he's our brother. How come Mother never said anything before she died?"

"What I want to know," stated Carnetta, "is why Father would send our brother off to live with Grandfather Clavius? I mean, Edouard may not be the best-looking witch out there, but as you said, enchanting spells on his appearance would solve that problem. I mean, he couldn't help his stroke of genetic bad luck. Physical disfigurement can happen to the best of witches. I think there's more to this story. Why the secrecy?"

Malevolinda nodded. At once, she and Carnetta straightened up in their seats where they conversed in the morning breakfast room, putting on the most natural expressions they could muster.

"What are you girls talking about?" Eustace Anguis, their father, had entered the room.

"Just talking about how shocked we are to learn about Edouard. Nothing more." Malevolinda briefly exchanged glances with her sister.

Eustace's eyes narrowed. "I'm not sure I believe that. Besides, I heard the word ugly."

"Oh, Father," said Carnetta, "we didn't mean anything by it. It's just that Mother was noted for her great beauty. And I've heard other women, both Magical and Mortal, talk about how striking you are. That's all."

The father sat down at the head of their handsomely carved rosewood dining table and stared across its length toward his daughters. "You'll do well to embrace your brother. Your new discovery makes no difference to me. The time had come for me to tell you, and your mother's passing only made it convenient." He feigned wiping a tear from his eye while the daughters looked on. "The truth is, your mother was greatly ashamed of him, and we both agreed that he should live with your grandfather. I'll not bore you with the details."

"We're not bored at all," said Malevolinda. She discreetly kicked her sister's ankle under the table and leaned forward, chin propped in her hands. "Is there more you'd like to share with us? I mean, was Edouard kept in the dark as much as we were all these years? You, Mother, and Grandfather passed him off as someone adopted from another witch family who couldn't take on another child. That's all we've ever heard."

"Until now," said Carnetta. She glanced at her sister and back to Eustace. "And to think you passed him off as nothing more than an orphan when he was really our brother. What are we supposed to think?"

"Don't think," said Eustace. He glared at his daughter. "Your grandfather, mother, and I handled things the way we wished, and one thing we do not wish is to detail everything to you ladies, though we love you greatly. It simply means nothing to you. He is the heir and will be the head when I pass." Eustace poured himself a cup of hot coffee from an ornate Chinese-style coffee pot. "Besides, it's not like he's a total stranger. What does it matter where he spent his time growing up? He's with us now."

The two daughters, realizing that they would learn nothing more, politely excused themselves and left the room, leaving Eustace to his thoughts. He sat back in his highbacked chair and inhaled the aroma of the coffee steaming from his cup. His wife's untimely death couldn't have been more convenient. Make no mistake, her passing was lamentable; her presence was deeply missed. But Edouard's coming of age the day before had presented him and Clavius with a dilemma.

They had no choice but to come somewhat clean with what had happened, except for one small detail. Revealing whom his real mother was. Only Eustace, Clavius, and Dorenda would know the truth behind Edouard's birth.

Eustace had always thought highly of Dorenda Soltaro. Had it not been for a pre-arranged marriage between himself and Priscilla by their families, he might have asked Dorenda to marry him. Since that was not possible, frisky romps and trysts were his only ways to be with one he truly loved. And he not only admired her magical expertise, he admired her as a person. Her cool, collective manner calmed him when he needed a level head.

She possessed warmth and vitality. In bed, her love-making skills knew no bounds for creativity and contained an openness that made a lover of even his caliber blush. Together they would have made a formidable couple on the Magical world stage, if given the opportunity. He believed this more than anything. When he learned from her confession eighteen years prior that she was carrying his child, he could not imagine doing anything else but step in and help her.

This child was the tie that would bind him to her forever. Because she had been associated with the Strondovan family through Eleanor's marriage to Roman, keeping Edouard with her was too dangerous.

Clavius gladly helped his son and accepted his grandson, promising to give him the best education, in both Mortal and Magical school systems. Edouard, like his mother Dorenda, was a quick study, learning aspects of magic with speed and topnotch execution . . .

Ciana opened her eyes and grimaced. There was more to the history than what she had tapped into at this moment. Her years of entrapment had given her much time to attune with the great spiritual library of knowledge. Of great concern to her was that the adult Edouard was being given the reigns of the family and all the darkness with it. She sat up. The knock at the door shattered her privacy.

"May I come in?" Eustace Anguis entered the room.

"As if I have a choice." Ciana wrinkled her nose and lifted her face toward the ceiling, avoiding his gaze. His feigned pleasantry, the greeting, the forced smile on his lips irritated her beyond words.

"I'm just coming to visit, see how you are. You are a guest, after all."

"Oh, please. I'm a captive here, and you know it."

"Now that's your choice." Eustace forced out a chuckle. "It has always been your choice, Ciana. You and the rest of us know that."

"How many times do I have to keep saying it? I will never tell you how to activate the cloth you stole from me. Your forbears killed my darling Clement, and you've allowed everyone in the Magiverse to believe innocent Desmond Strondovan did the dirty deed. Luckily, the Glanarium Supremo showed mercy and have been allowing the families involved to try and work it out."

Eustace stifled a yawn, pretending to listen with a semblance of interest.

Ciana continued, "Unfortunately, the real family behind all this isn't named anywhere, and their only involvement is to create more trouble. And that would be your family, Eustace." She scowled at him. He had ventured closer to her.

"Look, dear Ciana." He stretched his hand toward hers, hoping to soothe her anger. She bristled. "We were only trying to keep you from making a huge mistake."

"I don't make mistakes when it comes to conjuring cloths." Her lips tightened with rage. "And you keep sending that bastard son of yours in here to threaten me."

The man's eyes matched the indignation in hers. "We may have our disagreements, but you'll not talk about my beloved son that way. Do you understand me?"

"I understand that I have no intention of giving you what you want. Ever." Ciana crossed her arms, staring at Eustace with a killing stare.

He moved toward her until they were nearly nose to nose. "You can be destroyed forever. Don't think we won't consider that once we throw our hands up and tire of you." He chuckled and stepped back. "If you won't help us at some point, we might be inclined to torture you until you pass away naturally. And from what we know, Nephilim can live for quite a while longer than you have already."

The lady remained still, arms crossed. Her jaw had tightened with resolve.

"Have it your way, Ciana. I don't have the energy to trifle with you today. Edouard has tried to convince you. I've tried. Carnetta and Malevolinda have also." He wagged a finger at her. "Time is running out."

With those last words, he turned and left the room. Ciana winced as she heard the key turn in the lock. Trying to pick or destroy a lock was one thing, but Magicals had one thing neither she nor Mortals had. True magic. The kind only true witches weaved. The ones who transcended time and space. The ones who truly broke through blocking and protection spells, rendering them useless.

Over a hundred years she had spent in this room, only allowed outside three times a week for about an hour, and it was with strict supervision by one of the Anguis family members. The girls were more bearable than the men. At least they tried talking to her and acting like they were interested in communing with her. But they all knew very well the blurring speed of Nephilim. If she ever managed to break free from the chain on which they had her bound, she would run so fast no one would ever be able to catch her again.

Like it or not, she agreed with the man who just left the room. Time was running out, not only for her, if that horrible clave decided to do something with or to her, but for all Mortals and Magicals. The powerful Anguis clave had rallied allies to their side, those select elite who reveled in greed and power, though Ciana knew all too well that the Anguis had enough of that within their own group alone that they wouldn't have needed any help.

But like attracts like. And what better thing to have than others who help do your dirty work even faster. She also knew that spiritual truth all too well. Ciana twiddled her fingers a bit and gazed around her room.

Chapter Five

In Nepal, Jove sat in his control room at Katharta castle, the stronghold for his South Hawthorne clave. This clave was a renowned elemental from the fire source. They handled issues of passion, purification, and creative ventures with flair and vigor. August's quest with Larissa North Strondovan fit in quite nicely with their element, as his grandson usually contained a fiery boisterous spirit for adventures and an opportunity to try anything new—until he learned he'd have to try the something new with Larissa, heir of the hated North Strondovan clave. How he'd pitched such a fit. If only they'd cooperate long enough to finish their assignment and help bring the families together again.

The only truth that saddened Jove was August's lack of spirit for honing his magical skills. A crystal sphere chat he'd had recently with Tiberinus, Lord of Lakes, sent his spirits soaring. Some may have thought the Lord of Lakes blustery and outright nosey at times. Jove chose to call his good friend and confidante ever watchful, for Tiberinus kept his eye on things, even though his world rested mostly underground.

"He slayed Svapada, head of the Devoratrix! Can you believe it?" Tiberinus laughed when he connected spherically with Jove. "Let me show you."

Jove shrank back, eyeing the taxidermized kill with impressed horror. Two dusty green colored heads held two sets of eyes, which had been replaced with a beautiful glass likeness. They stared back with unbridled hostility, the yellow irises and cat-like pupils reflecting anger, even in death. Svapada, a cojoined necromancer, came riddled with a history of having a voracious appetite for human flesh. Years of stories told horrific accounts of how he preyed on innocent people, tormenting them unmercifully before devouring them in the end.

"August did that? All by himself?" Jove asked.

"He and his quest mate, Larissa North Strondovan. Just the two of them. Those Devoratrix are hard to get rid of. Now, he didn't wreck the whole lot of them for good. They're still some groups of them out and about terrorizing Mortals and Magicals, but the two managed to put a tremendous dent in their operation by offing Svapada the chief, whose head I still enjoy looking at on my prize trophy shelf."

"Simply dumbfounding," murmured Jove. "I wouldn't have thought my grandson had it in him."

"Ah, my friend," said Tiberinus, "our children surprise us at times, and this was one of them. I knew they would either be consumed themselves or find a way to win. And win they did!" Lord of Lakes turned and placed his treasured head back on the shelf behind him. "Make no mistake, my good man, the Anguis have their clave claws in this group. They control them. And what better ally to have if you want your way with people or witches."

"The Anguis? Surely you're joking." Jove sat back, stroking his chin. "I've heard of many things, but how did I miss this piece of information?"

"Sad, is it not? And the Anguis could have been so good, if they had not turned away and pursued a path of darkness."

"Exactly why did they do that? And when?"

While he thought, Tiberinus sucked on a long pipe and blew out a stream of perfectly rounded smoke circles, watching with mild interest as they floated in the air. "I believe it was sheer narcissism." He looked directly at Jove, raising both eyebrows.

Jove squinted, trying to make sense of what his friend said. "That's it?"

"Dear friend, such a character disorder can lead a person to utter destruction. The sense of entitlement and desire to have everything about me, me, me—you know the type. They think the world revolves around them. In case of the Anguis, they think the world is theirs, that it's owed to them."

The two stared at each other in silence several moments, Tiberinus taking a brief reprieve to tap out the ashes from his prized pipe and fill it again with his favorite smoked cherry tobacco. Jove brought a silver ornate goblet to his lips and sipped an exclusive wine given to him by a master vintner.

"And here's something almost no one knows." Tiberinus tightened his lips with a knowing look on his face. "Edouard doesn't belong to Priscilla the Beautiful."

"What?" Jove's mouth fell open. "Well, to whom does Edouard belong, then? And how do you know this as fact?"

Tiberinus smiled and rested easily in his over-stuffed cushioned chair. "I held a feast not long ago. Had many guests, and among them were the Anguis clave members. Only Edouard and his sisters Carnetta and Malevolinda. Eustace declined courteously, stating his regrets and having other commitments."

"Why did you have this feast? And why wasn't I invited?" asked Jove. A flash of indignation shot through him. He and Tiberinus had been friends for as long as he could remember.

"Don't get all up in arms, my good friend. I only held this gathering, if you will, so that your grandson, the lovely Larissa, and the Anguis could get acquainted. In Larissa's case, reacquainted with Edouard. I wanted to feel everything out, see if I could hear something, see something. You know, a scanning operation, if you will. But there's more to the reason I held this feast." Tiberinus paused, taking a few puffs on his pipe.

"What was the reason?" said Jove.

"A visitation I received," answered Tiberinus. The wizard grinned at the contorted look of puzzlement on Jove's face.

"I'm so confused, Tiberinus. Why on earth would that lead to a feast?"

"I'm glad you asked that. It was because of Priscilla, Eustace Anguis's wife."

"And she came to you . . . why?" Jove drummed his fingers on the arm of his chair.

"Why not? I'm well-known throughout the Magical world, and I'm looked upon as sort of a confidante by many. I can't explain it. You know how that goes."

"No, I really don't, but don't let me keep you from your story. I'm really interested in why Priscilla wanted to talk to you."

"You know she's been dead for many years. Died before Edouard became of age."

"Ah, so it was a disembodied visitation. I didn't know she had passed." He wagged a finger at Tiberinus. "For an underground, cantankerous old wizard who rarely sees the light of day, you sure seem to know and get around a lot." Jove chuckled.

"And I'm surprised you don't know more than you should, but I won't hold that against you." Tiberinus threw back his head and laughed.

"So on with it. Tell me all the juicy details."

The old wizard took one last draw on his pipe, blew out more rings, and said, "Sit back and enjoy the tale . . ."

The movement of his bed covers in the inky blackness of the bedchamber woke Tiberinus with a start. He sat up straight, glaring into the darkness. It came again, a solid yank on the linen cover, so hard it left him exposed in his striped nightshirt.

"Who's there? Announce yourself!"

A soft chiming, tinkling sound filled the room. At once, the darkness changed to eerie luminescent soft green. It was then the wizard saw the faint bluish white outline of a woman standing at the foot of his bed.

"How did you get in here, and who in the hell are you?" Tiberinus, annoyed that his sleep had been disturbed, jerked the cover back over him.

"No need to hide from me, you silly old wizard," said the voice in a rather familiar teasing manner. "And no need for such harsh language. I'll be glad to tell you who I am, though you should know well enough. I am Priscilla the Beautiful, late wife of Eustace Anguis."

"Late wife, is it? My condolences. Last time I heard, you were still alive."

"Ah, I wish it were true, Tiberinus. My time on this earth was far too short." Priscilla floated over close to the side of the bed where he slept. "I came for a favor."

"A favor? Ask away, my dear. I'm only too glad and honored to help someone as yourself. You were quite the lady back in the day. Classiest of them all." Tiberinus smiled toward the glowing figure.

"Thank you. Little do you know how fond I was of you. Still am. You may be gruff, but anyone worth their salt knows you are a fine wizard and upstanding to boot."

"What would you have me do?"

"I must tell you a secret." Priscilla stretched out a ghostly hand toward Tiberinus's shoulder. He flinched away and pulled the cover tighter, trying to quell the stream of chills pulsing through his body. "Somebody else other than the ones involved needs to know. The information may be needed someday, and I wanted someone like yourself to be in possession of this knowledge."

"Do tell, please. I'm listening and will gladly help you."

"I didn't accidentally slip and fall down the stairs in our home and break my neck. Someone pushed me that night, and it was Eustace."

Tiberinus stared at Priscilla with alarm. "He pushed you? Whatever for?"

"The secret I knew about him. He thought I could be fooled, but my recorder crystals noted everything. I tapped into them after I felt like I'd given them enough time to gain information, and I was disheartened by what I learned."

"Oh? Again, what was that, Priscilla? Out with it." Tiberinus tugged at the covers of his bed. His impatience grew each second Priscilla hedged.

"He's a philanderer. Everyone knows it." Priscilla's ghostly glow changed from whiteish blue to crimson and back to the original hue when she first awakened her friend. "My husband was being unfaithful. Perhaps others knew of this, but no one whispered to me about it."

"But men are unfaithful all the time," said Tiberinus, "but they don't go around murdering their wives. What would have driven him to such extremes?"

"Tiberinus, you must listen to me. Heed what I say. Eustace had been practicing baneful magic for a while, and it wasn't for good purposes like someone can often use it. While the years passed, he became obsessed with power and garnering it for himself. He had finally coaxed her into it too."

The wizard stared at Priscilla, perplexed. "Her? And for the love of all the gods, who is this mysterious woman?"

"Dorenda Soltaro. Sister of Eleanor North Strondovan."

"You surely must be mistaken, dear Priscilla. Dorenda is a fine upstanding witch."

"Wait. There's more." Priscilla's effigy changed back and forth from one color to another as her excitement mounted. "Edouard is their son. Eustace and Dorenda."

"No!" Tiberinus sank back against his pillows, flabbergasted at what he heard. "How could that have been kept a secret all these years? How were you able to keep quiet?"

"I kept quiet until the night I died. I was going to my sanctuary to work some magic of my own. He was having none of it. Eustace is a powerful witch. He was simply quicker than I was. And to think that he tried fooling me with having Edouard live with Clavius, my father-in-law, all these years. They passed him off as belonging to another Magical family who needed help." Priscilla's lips turned up into a smile of triumph. "Edouard was born with a facial disfigurement. That was my greatest joy. To know that the offspring of my husband and Dorenda Soltaro was a less than desirable-looking witch." She stifled a laugh.

"Oh my." Tiberinus glanced around the room, trying to mentally digest everything Pricilla had told him to this point.

"I was going to confront him and Clavius, out that little bastard Edouard for what he really was, and let Eustace, Clavius, and that tramp Dorenda have it for all it was worth." Pricilla lowered her face. Whiteish blue tears fell from her eyes, bursting into mist and evaporating when they hit the floor.

"There, there, Priscilla my lovely friend. Please don't cry." Tiberinus reached out to touch her in consolation but stopped short. He knew touching the vision of one deceased was a huge no-no in the Magical world. The act, though well-meaning, scattered the departed soul's energy, causing it to lose a part of itself.

"Anyway," said Priscilla, "I need your help in doing the last part of my work for me. The Magical world needs to know this story. Eustace and his overreach need to be stopped, and that pompous Edouard needs to be seen for what and who he really is. And Dorenda . . ."

"Yes?" Tiberinus almost dreaded hearing this part. What would Priscilla have him do? Could he oblige her wish?

"I want you to out that whore for what she is too. You do know that she is all wrapped up in Eustace's lust for power. What she doesn't hold between her legs, she spends time doing baneful magic in private. Sometimes with Eustace. They manage to either connect in the physical realm or astrally when they're in a hurry to speed things along."

The wizard huffed in dismay and tugged the covers tighter over his body. "I'm not sure how to do that, but I'll think of something. I can get creative when I need to."

"Oh, for heaven's sake, Tiberinus. You're a wizard, and none too shabby. It's not like you've never gotten creative before in all your years of living." Priscilla leaned in close to his face. He shrank back, barely avoiding the smashing of her nose against his. "Think of something. Better yet, have that delightful little stud, August South Hawthorne, do the dirty deed. He has every reason to be involved. Dorenda is too close to the North Strondovan clave, and even if it's through her sister's marriage, it's still too close."

"This is quite a conundrum, my dear." Tiberinus scratched his head in thought. "I mean, we must consider that it has been Dorenda that has taught Larissa all she knows where magic is concerned. And that young lady is quite a whipper snapper from what I've seen and heard." He chuckled.

"She's grooming her, you silly fool. Don't you see it? Dorenda wants Larissa to join with Edouard so they are a formidable force and can rule the world. I know so because I've overheard Eustace and Dorenda talk about it. Or rather, my crystals did. I got that much before that creep husband of mine finished me off." The floor misted up again with the new round of tears falling from Priscilla's face.

"I'll figure something out. Not to worry." Tiberinus tried showing a smile of reassurance, but the inside of his head was a whirl of thoughts that wouldn't stop.

"Oh, thank you, Tiberinus. I knew I could count on you. Say it again that you'll help me. Call out that motley crew for what they are."

"I'll help, Priscilla. You have my word." Tiberinus raised his right hand toward her and made the sign of his sigil for keeping promises, a circle with the closing stroke slicing through and ending below it.

Priscilla vanished without a word. A cold blast shot across the bed, knocking Tiberinus solidly back on his pillow. "Dammit! That was one hell of a visit."

Jove sat, entranced, saying nothing as his friend finished what was a strange tale, indeed. A nasty secret that leapt from the grave and demanded justice. But he had not missed the suggestion of soliciting August to deal with Dorenda, and that part troubled him greatly. When the aunt and her niece, Larissa, had visited him for the first time at Katharta Castle, he had quickly taken quite a fancy to the older woman. She had a haunting beauty and an amiable nature. He most certainly held a soft spot for Larissa. Maybe he could coax August into using his enduring hate for a good cause.

"So what did you find out from your feast?"

Tiberinus grimaced. "Larissa is love-struck over Edouard. Nearly giddy like a schoolgirl over him. And let me tell you something else. I don't think your grandson liked seeing that at all." The wizard stroked his chin and stared at his friend. "You will talk to August, won't you?"

"Um, yes. Of course." Jove shook his head. He had to be careful. His old friend could put on his telepathic hat and burrow into his thoughts if he took a notion. "I'm sure my grandson would love nothing better than to have a legitimate shot at a Strondovan, even if it's only close to one. And I'm not sure he'd mind hurting Larissa over it, either." He lowered his gaze, staring into the goblet of wine he held.

"Maybe, maybe not. That young woman has no idea about her aunt." Tiberinus frowned.

"Not a clue, from what I saw when they visited me. They seemed quite close. Would surprise me greatly if she did."

"Listen, Jove, you and I will work together and figure this out. It can be our contribution to the cause. Besides, if we don't try and influence this horrible evil shift that's happening due to Anguis greed, we'll be in trouble. I don't want to spend time kicking myself in the pants because I was too timid to do a dirty deed when it needed being done."

"Got it." Jove tipped his goblet to his lips and let the wine burn a sweet hot path down his throat. He swallowed hard, wishing more than anything a buzz would kick in hard and heavy. He exhaled loudly when he finished his drink.

"Don't worry, my friend. I'm always around if you need me. Gotta run. It's near dinner time here." The wizard smiled and winked.

Jove waved to his friend as the crystal sphere darkened first before resuming its former clarity. He placed the ball on a sterling stand and sat back in his chair. Getting in touch with August was of paramount importance, given the news he'd just heard. But most important of all, he wanted to see someone else first. There were questions that needed answers, and he had a surefire way of getting them. He may have been much older than his handsome, virile grandson, but where else would August have inherited his sexual finesse?

"Time for a visit to you know who," said Jove.

Within minutes, he stood before the altar in his bedroom. Two candles at either side lit up at the snap of a finger. The mirror hanging on the wall reflected bright lusty eyes and a small grin. This reflection, however, did not show lust for a lover. It did reflect lust for knowledge of the truth. Tonight, he would get that truth and knew a near fool-proof way to get it.

Taking slow deep breaths, he eased himself into a trance-like state. His right finger traced a symbol on his left wrist. To a casual observer, the insignia would look like meaningless scribble. To him, the two squiggles and a jagged line signified his desire. Jove winced as the insignia, the size of a quarter, burned into his wrist. The stinging stopped. He smiled. Now for the next step.

In the glow of the candlelight, he loosened his trousers, slipped his right hand between his legs, and grasped his balls. With manipulations and gentle squeezing, he let out a light groan. A tingling sensation filled his balls. He twitched as they took on heat, itched a few seconds, and stopped. Grasping his cock, he worked himself and muttered an age-old incantation, modifying a few words to fit his current needs. At the height of orgasm, he stared at the sigil. A brief shot of pain flared through his left wrist. He knew now that his sigil was charged for the upcoming task.

***

"Jove, you should have told me you were coming. What if I'd been out and missed you?"

"Ah, my dear, I would have waited. All I know is I couldn't wait another minute to see you again."

Jove picked up Dorenda, kissed her on the lips and placed her back down. She laughed and clapped her hand over the bun she'd neatly set in place. Always caring about her appearance no matter whom her guests were, she cared even more when it was Jove. They'd instantly connected when she and Larissa visited Katharta Castle for the first time.

How gracious he had been, offering sleeping quarters and meals fit for royalty. And that was exactly what Larissa was, even if August nearly held his nose at the idea of even thinking about it.

"What brings you here tonight?" Dorenda fussed with his hair and collar as he answered.

"You came to Katharta last time. I thought it was only fair that I come to you this time. Don't you think?" He chuckled and kissed her again.

"I think so. Have you missed me?"

"How could I not? Our last time was . . . how should I say it? Delectable, that's what."

The older lady grinned. "That's what I'd call it. And you really were a naughty boy, with all the things you did." She grinned.

"Oh, I've got more where that came from." Jove raised his eyebrows and showed a winning smile. Part of him cringed inside at the pretense of it all. Deep sadness filled him. As much as he hated admitting it, this meeting would most likely be their last. And he had so enjoyed his times with this lady. No wonder Priscilla's husband liked her so much.

"Shall I pour us some wine?" Dorenda loosened herself from Jove's arms and headed toward a cabinet.

"A little wouldn't hurt. Might help us warm up a bit."

"I hardly think we need warming up, but I have a special bottle I've been saving, and I say we tear into it now. No reason why not." She took out two vintage crystal wine glasses. While Jove looked away, entertaining himself with the books in her bookcase, she slipped out a tiny green bottle and poured some of the contents into Jove's glass and filled the remainder with wine. For herself, she poured wine with nothing else added. She wanted a clear mind tonight, and they would be between the sheets before any intoxication set in on her part.

Dorenda handed Jove his glass. "Shall we toast to us?"

"Wonderful idea. Let's do it." Jove raised his glass and touched it to Dorenda's. "To our love and genuine affection. May it remain as perennial as the grass that grows."

"How beautiful," said Dorenda. "I'd like that very much."

Jove sat down in the armchair opposite hers. "Have you heard from Larissa?"

"I have heard very little. We tune in every now and then, but I know they are quite busy."

"Mmm, I see." Jove nodded and sipped his wine. There was something in Dorenda's countenance that didn't seem right tonight. A certain hint of distraction emanated from her. He knew there was more, but she wasn't saying anything. And the wine, there was something in the taste that hit him in an uneasy way, and he couldn't quite decipher the reason why.

"Is something wrong?" asked Dorenda. She eyed Jove with concern. "Can I get you anything else, perhaps something to eat?"

"No, my dear. I could be a bit fatigued from the ride here. You know how trips in the Vanishport are. You never know." He laughed.

"There are Magicals who get quite woozy in them. Your wine should help ease whatever it is you have going on. It's from a good year."

"I see." The older man considered her words. "I'll just have to drink up, won't I?" He returned her smile. In no way was he going to drink the rest of this wine. Instead of magic, he decided to use a simple trick of illusion to make it seem like he was drinking the wine. The glass would appear less full each time after lifting it to his lips. Dorenda shouldn't suspect a thing. And it would be much simpler than spell casting and take a lot less energy. The South Hawthorne clave was a dynasty known for their enchanting skills. But they also had family members who had handed down the art of illusion throughout time. He was one of the lucky ones who learned it.

"Do you think," asked Jove, "that August and Larissa are getting along any better? They really must do that to accomplish anything."

"I hope so. The times I have seen them when checking in they appeared mostly okay. Not a whole lot of tension that I noticed. But then again, anyone can be civil for a few moments." Dorenda nodded in Jove's direction.

"Yes, that's true." Jove pretended to sip again from his glass, satisfied that his illusion trick was working. The glass appeared less full than before, and best of all, he still retained his faculties. "You look beautiful tonight, Dorenda, but you always do. I often wonder why no one has snatched you up by now."

"Sometimes, a woman doesn't necessarily need to be snatched up, but be left to enjoy and be enjoyed when times are right. Don't you think?"

"I think that works in many cases," answered Jove. "I'm lucky I can enjoy you. You're such a delight."

"As you are, dear Jove."

The gentleman cocked his head and gazed at the lady before him. His lips pulled into a light easy smile.

They spent the next several minutes making small talk, each one partaking from their glass until both were empty.

Jove looked at his hostess. "Shall we?"

Dorenda smiled. "Let's. Follow me."

Her bedroom's simplicity always left him in a quandary. Charming but slightly cold. To be fair, the opulence of Katharta Castle would leave most settings in the category of mere charming, if not less.

They both pulled the sheets back, revealing fresh white bed linens. Dorenda lit the sets of candles on the nightstands. The room filled with a warm glow. A creamware pitcher on the bureau left a scent of fresh flowers wafting through the room. Jove quietly removed his clothes, as did Dorenda.

Jove watched as her naked form came into view in the candlelight. He loved the shape of her breasts, her rounded hips, the length of her hair when she released the sterling hair pin from her locks. She viewed him with the same interest. He knew how his appearance filled her with an inner hunger. For an older Magical, Jove still posed a rather striking figure, and the flesh between his legs didn't disappoint, either.

He waited as she climbed into bed and settled on her back. As she bent up her knees, resting her feet flat on the sheet, he eyed the crimson, red-painted toenails and the gold ring adorning one of her dainty toes. Even her feet were pretty. Jove now sported the makings of a hard-on. Silently he slipped into bed, and as much as he wanted to savor the moment and think of nothing else tonight, he couldn't.

Dorenda's breasts held two plump nipples, which Jove feasted on, taking turns licking and sucking one while massaging and squeezing the nipple of the other. She let out a sigh of pleasure. When he lifted his head, she gently lifted her hands to his chest, fondling his nipples. Jove lowered his lips and kissed hers. Without wasting another moment, he placed his hands on her knees and pressed them apart. She obliged, opening wide.

Jove gently inserted two fingers inside her. She was more than ready, but for the sake of appearance, he decided to stall just a little. The more she had extra pleasure, the more the charm would work for him. Inserting his thumbs into her slit, he spread her nether lips apart and landed his tongue on her clit. Dorenda gasped, followed by a groan as he licked in slow firm circles, up and down, and back to circles. After a few rounds, he sucked at her softly at first, ending with a harder one that sent her body bucking. She let out a moan.

Between his thighs, Jove's balls had started aching. They held the same tingly, itchy sensation he'd felt earlier when he charged everything before this moment. His cock raged, flesh straining. He settled easily between her legs and slid in, feeling her walls hugging firmly around him. For someone so bad, she felt good. He savored the moment. As he moved rhythmically in and out, her chest heaved with the passion mounting with each thrust.

Time was running out. Jove couldn't hold back much longer. Whatever he had to do in making this brief convergence a success, he'd do it. He panted while rotating his hips in a circular rhythm, ending with a few quick thrusts. Dorenda closed her eyes and moaned with pleasure. Inside she'd become wetter, accepting every movement with enthusiasm, face drawn up in the heat of the moment.

It was time. Jove let out a loud groan, delivered one hard, final thrust and held himself in place. His lust released inside her. He felt the heat, its power, and smiled. In the throes of ecstasy, he turned his left wrist enough to glimpse the sigil he'd traced. It glowed bright gold. A sharp burning sensation bore straight through him, and he shouted with pain and joy. Dorenda's eyes flew open as if someone had delivered a shock to her flesh. She panted, letting out a couple of sharp cries. Her gaze locked upward a moment.

"Eustace!" she cried out.

Jove immediately dropped his gaze, studying her face. "Yes, my darling. I'm here." Jove whispered the words, feeling no shame impersonating the father of her child, Edouard Anguis, who was not the son of Priscilla the Beautiful. His voice took on Eustace's rich timber. "Shh, my sweet. You are so delicious, so divine." He traced around her ear with his tongue.

"Oh, Eustace. You are my true love. There is no other. You and I should have been together. But we have our precious Edouard as the tie that binds our union. For we have a union. Priscilla was of no consequence."

Jove stared down on her face once again. Her eyes still showed an absent stare, like one in a deep trance, conscious, but not conscious of the present and with whom she truly shared her bed.

"True, my pet. He is the living, breathing, incarnate gift from our loins. And you have always been my heart, the one I live for. And the one I will die for." Jove enunciated the last words clearly in her ear.

"My darling," Dorenda sighed, "I must sleep. I am so tired." Her eyes took on a brief clarity of mind and finally closed.

The feel of her body totally relaxing and sinking deeper into the sheets satisfied Jove greatly. His spell had worked. In the morning, her mind would be foggy at best in trying to fully recollect this night.

Chapter Six

Dorenda sat the next morning alone at her kitchen table. Her head throbbed. The fact that she had awakened alone in bed puzzled her the most. It wasn't like Jove to slip out in the middle of the night, leaving her cold and all to herself. They usually enjoyed breakfast together, and sometimes lunch, before one or the other returned home.

She lifted a hand up to her temple and massage the area. Why was her mind so cloudy today? That was unusual too. An urge set in to contact Jove. Maybe a brief conversation would answer the questions she had. Perhaps something came up, and he had to make a quick getaway. What alarmed her the most was the tightening in her gut. Something simply wasn't right. Though she struggled to remember the events from the night before, when he first came inside her home, it didn't leave her mind that he didn't seem to act as he usually did.

He seemed warm as always, but his mannerisms teemed with a certain something else she couldn't grasp. Dorenda snapped her finger. Ah, yes. And that's why she'd given him the "special" drink too. Of course, that was her plan all along. Give him the special potion the next time they met. In her dreams, she had received ominous warnings.

At the time, she couldn't readily make sense of them, but one thing she did remember was seeing Jove in the shadows. The messages loud and clear in the dreams were to use caution when around him. Following her intuition, she concocted a potion, using the finest herbs and other ingredients, crafting what she thought was a most refined protection tincture.

She had taken great pains to create it, using the power of Saturn, selecting the hour when the planet ruled the strongest, and on a Saturday, the ruling day of Saturn. Foolproof, in her estimation, the liquid should have banished from his mind, any intent to harm or trick her in any way. He drained his glass. Her eyes didn't mistake that. So what happened? Why did he leave her alone now and in a foggy haze?

Just as Dorenda got up to fetch her crystal sphere, she dropped back down in her chair, defeated. There was no way she could ask Jove about why he left. It would be so unbecoming of her to do such a thing. Speaking to Eustace was out of the question. It would only incriminate her. They had all but vowed to be just the two of them in any physical union, though there had to be an exception made for him already being with Priscilla. She took a quick sip of hot tea, hoping the strong peppermint would soothe her.

Not remembering clearly what happened after they had bedded together troubled her greatly. Anything she said or did could be used against her, at this point. Jove, it appeared, may be no exception. Dorenda suspected nothing good could come from the situation in which she found herself now. The older lady held her head, closed her eyes, and tried to let her weary brain rest.

***

In his compromised state, August tried sleeping in his cold, dank cell in the bowels of the Anguis castle. As he fell in at out of a fitful sleep, he wasn't sure whom he hated most, Edouard or Larissa. This whole thing reeked with an unsavory feeling to it all. He didn't trust Edouard, and he swore at Larissa in his mind for falling in love with such a witch as Edouard. He despised even more the gimp spell Larissa cast on him.

Desperate, and for the first time ever, he invoked the deity of Athena. As the goddess of wisdom and justice, she was perfect. Mustering up his most sincere mental state, despite his deplorable situation, he spoke softly under his breath, just loud enough so only he could hear, with the best pronunciation possible:

"O wondwous, powerful goddess Athena, I invoke your energy. I call on you, your bwilliant mind, insight, and bwessings, that you may fill me with knowege and power, that I may weave here safewy and soon vanqish the enemy."

A bright light filled the cell, warming it by degrees for a few moments. Softly, from the depths of the prison walls, August swore he heard a female's voice:

"I hear your call, O August South Hawthorne, one who grapples with love and hate. One who has hidden boundless power that longs to be unleashed. Valuable information shall be revealed to you. This knowledge will help you greatly in achieving what you desire. Knowledge and connections will set you free. You who have called on me with great sincerity and humility shall have your petition granted. So it is done."

The cell went dark. August's heart pounded at what he'd just experienced. Had anyone heard? Would the guards come for him and end his life? Did he really just hear the voice of a deity answering his call? He let out a shout of surprise. In the darkest corner of his cell, where the rock water tended to pool, he heard another voice, that of a male. If he listened closely enough, it sounded just like his grandfather.

He struggled to a standing position and limped over to a small puddle of water. In the reflective sheen, he saw Jove's face bright and clear.

"So you're into using water for scrying, are you?" Jove's face showed some amusement and more worry. "Where in the hell are you? I can barely make you out. Come closer."

August struggled one last bit to inch his face toward the center of the puddle. "This is the best I can do."

"What happened to you? Your face . . . your . . .?"

The younger man shook his head in defeat.

"Unbelievable!" Jove cried out. "Who did you piss off this time?"

"I'm a pwisoner of Edouard Anguis." August dropped his gaze in shame.

"The Anguis, eh? From the looks of everything I see so far, I don't need to know much else but that you're in trouble, and you better hope that smart companion of yours, Larissa, saves your hide. Because honestly, if I could, I'd kick it to the moon and back."

"Gwandfathew, pwease."

Jove showed a facial sign of disgust and continued, "Come even closer. I have something to tell you, and I don't want anyone hearing it but you."

Grunting and groaning his way into a position where he could hear the best, August finally scooted himself in place to his grandfather's satisfaction.

"Pay attention, son, because I'm about to give you an earful that could blow the nuts off this quest. And if you play your cards right, it will all be in your favor."

"I'm wistening, Gwandfathew."

"Just shut up. Here I go."

For the next several minutes, which to August seemed like an excruciating eternity, Jove revealed the information Tiberinus had shared in their earlier conversation. He also mentioned meeting with Dorenda but refused to go into detail on how he'd confirmed her input.

"Just trust me on this and use this tidbit to your advantage. You have no choice but to rid that Edouard and his clave from the planet. And as much as I hate like hell saying this, Larissa's aunt may have to go too."

If he hadn't been in such a physically compromised state, August would have danced a jig. The fantasy of bursting Larissa's arrogant pretty ass bubble thrilled him to no end, and that proposition alone made him feel much better and more hopeful.

"Son, do what you have to do to get out of that damned wherever-you-are and back to business on this quest. Time's running out. The Glanarium Supremo won't wait forever."

August merely nodded. Jove's face faded from the water, leaving the young man in darkness once again. But he had another idea. What did this suave imposter of the good looks, Edouard Anguis, really look like? He was filled with a burning desire to know. But his energy was sluggish at best. It had taken a lot out of him to first summon Athena and after that to hear his grandfather. "I need more help," he moaned.

It occurred to August that if he succeeded at invoking a goddess, he might get lucky again this time and secure the services of a demon. And this situation of blowing Edouard's cover needed an entity that would not only chew gum and take names, but would kick ass for all it was worth. After all, demons were heavy hitters and kicked where it hurt, if need be.

After finding his way back to a wall where he could sit somewhat comfortably, he spent several minutes thinking. He needed to choose the most appropriate demon for his cause. He also needed some information to do this conjuring properly, or it would fail miserably. Using the water puddle might have been the best place for this ritual, because he could use it as a means of scrying, but he simply didn't have the energy to crawl back to it. He rested his head on his thighs, nearly in tears, and thought hard. The book of Demon Magick is what he needed because it had all the sigils and ritual instructions. Jove had used it many times when he required extra help on a project.

August closed his eyes and thought hard. Perhaps he could bring the small pool of water his direction, if he had the mental energy. He stared in the direction of the puddle. Fortunately for him, the flaming sconces along the hallway walls helped with some visibility. He thanked the gods for that small fortune.

Concentrating hard, he willed the water to flow in his direction and land in a hollowed-out dip among the cell floor stones. When he collected all the water, he gazed into the pool and focused on the book he needed. The tome came into view. Relieved, he reviewed the sections he needed, followed the ritual and waited.

A soft breeze filled the cell, gathering in sound until it became a full hissing noise in his ear. Soft gray starlight surrounded him. At once he felt a pull, like something or someone tugging him forward. August shuddered. Inside his mouth, he tasted what seemed like fermented fruit that was in its last days before it turned to rot.

"I am Andromalius."

Startled at the sound, August glanced around the cell, trying frantically to see from what direction the voice came.

"Never mind trying to see me. You have performed the rituals and viewed the sigils that call out to me. I am here. How may I be of service?"

August shook his head and tried to order his mind into something that functioned, swearing that if he survived this ordeal, he'd have a week-long drinking binge. "I want to see what Edouard Anguis reawy wooks wike."

Andromalius didn't answer immediately. August winced and glanced around, fearful the demon may have decided to quit on hearing him speak. He cursed Larissa for the millionth time.

"I think I understand what it is you are wanting," the demon finally answered. "Gaze into the water, and I will show you what you ask."

Without further persuasion, August stared into the water. The surface rippled, turned red and soft grey. In the hazy film, he saw Edouard. It looked like he was talking to a large group of people. Behind him was a strange logo, a golden circle with serrated edges. What was interesting was that the edges changed from golden to dark red and back again. Beside it he read the following: The Ruby Sanctum.

"The Ruby Sanctum? What is that? I've never heard of it before. Do you know, O demon, Andromalius?"

"My good man, August South Hawthorne, this group intends to bend the world to its will, reap all the rewards, see that their creations and intent rule all, come what may. Please keep your eyes on the water. There is more."

From the hazy surface of the water, August watched as Edouard talked and how everyone in the room seemed so agreeable to whatever he said.

"My good people, we are so close to achieving what we want. The world is within our grasp and the poor fools who are not one of us shall do our bidding. You have come from many countries and other dimensions to help participate in the great takeover. We have only one more piece of the puzzle to solve before achieving our goal. I am working diligently on that myself. It's a very delicate situation, and I won't elaborate here . . ."

The sound faded away and the scene in the water changed. This time August viewed Edouard alone in what looked like his private quarters, wherever that was. He was undressing for bed. His face turned up as if viewing a camera lens head on. August gasped, first dumfounded and in the next few seconds filled with glee. Edouard Anguis's face showed below average looks, by any standard, Mortal or Magical.

His nose was wide, a bit crooked, and with a small hook to it. A set of large ogling eyes gave him a continuous bug-eyed look. Inside a crooked mouth were a set of teeth, with some that could have benefited from Mortal orthodontic work or a Magical with better spell-casting skills. His skin tone had a rather ashen cast that dulled his ebony features.

"Have you seen enough, Mr. Hawthorne?" asked Andromalius. "Your time with me is coming to a close."

"How does he keep his looks? I've seen him before, and he doesn't look anything like that."

"Mr. Hawthorne, have you forgotten glamour magick? Our person of interest, Edouard Anguis, works harder at it than most. He has learned his skills from his grandfather and father. Every day he performs certain rituals and engages in enchanting and incorporating special sigils to maintain his looks. It's quite an ordeal. It's not the usual routine for most Magicals or Mortals, that much I can tell you."

"Anything else you'd like to share before you're gone?" August asked.

"He's trying to get your girl, Mr. Hawthorne. If you're not careful or don't make a change soon, you could lose her. Oh, and I will give you this." The demon snapped his fingers. "Check the pocket of your clothing, Mr. Hawthorne. Keep what I have given you safe, as it will serve you well."

There was a sudden pop, like a loud ember bursting in a fireplace. The puddle retreated to its original location across the wall where August sat. The starlight in the cell flicked off, leaving the young witch sitting in a darker cell with only the distance sconces giving off some light.

He reached inside one pocket of his trousers and pulled out a thin shiny golden disc. It was not a gold coin, but a carrier of information. Something had been recorded on this disc that he and his companions needed to hear. August slipped the item safely back in his pocket and thought once again on what the demon had showed him.

"I'll be damned." August chuckled. "Edouard Anguis is an ugly bastard and has been all along." He slapped his knee in laughter, quickly yelping at once because it was with the hand Larissa withered down to half its size. "Get my girl? Hmm. I know one thing, with all the information I've learned today, I'll kick your ugly ass to the outer dimensions and back. Just you wait, Edouard Anguis. You and your clave will be mine."

Chapter Seven

August was playing a game, one of many he had invented since his imprisonment. While he racked his brain to select a ritual on how to get him and his companions out of Sulphure Hall, he busied himself luring out of its hole one of the many rats that kept company any hapless prisoners of the Anguis.

He had managed to unravel some thread from his torn cloak and had tied a piece of stale bread to it, placing it outside one of the promising rat holes in the flooring of his stone cell, not so close that the rat could dart out before he moved it closer, but close enough to attract attention.

He wasn't sure what he would do if he caught a rat. He was fairly sure he could roast it. For some reason his ability to create a flame at the tip of his index finger hadn't been hampered by the warding spells that permeated the dungeon, but he wasn't sure he wouldn't be interrupted by guards if they smelled meat cooking in the austere underground place.

He startled and looked up at the commotion of feet tramping toward his cell. Just as he looked away from the hole, an inquisitive rat appeared. August had loosened his grasp on the string tied around the piece of bread, and the rat dragged both the bread and attached string back into his lair without difficulty. By then August was at the bars.

"Leave us!" Larissa shouted.

August heard heavy footfalls departing down the corridor. In seconds, she was there, looking at him in contemplation through the enchanted bars. With her was not only Willem, who was a welcome sight, but also a ginger-bearded dwarf who seemed taller than usual dwarfs.

"Hello, August," she said briskly, "you need to stand back for a minute. We are on a tight timetable, and I need to remove your gimp spell. Oh, Willem and Phuctious, this is August. August, this is Phuctious. I think it best if you come out here for a minute with us, in fact."

There was a bright flash that appeared as an arcing electrical current, which temporarily blinded August. He felt his distorted features and twisted limbs snapping back into place. Immediately afterwards, a huge swirling hole appeared in the center of the bars. He felt himself yanked through it by Larissa's spell.

She looked up at him with disgust. "Don't even think of hugging me, August. You stink!"

August nearly laughed. Her rudeness was so welcome and familiar, and he was so ecstatic to see her and Willem again.

"Go ahead," Larissa said to Willem and Phuctious.

As August watched, both Willem and the dwarf stepped inside his cell and, working together muttering enchantments, they opened a hole in the back of the cell that blasted both the stone wall and the surrounding earth aside. When they finished, daylight was visible. All of them heard running feet. Guardsmen rushed down the passage, but Willem used his golden Pasha to detain them so that the foursome could have time to escape.

The first breath of fresh air August inhaled as he hoisted himself up and onto the hillock outside the hole was the most delicious he had ever experienced. They rushed for the canopy and seclusion the forest provided. All of them hurried to put distance between them and Sulphure Hall. Eventually out of breath, they slowed their pace when they no longer heard the cacophony they caused after creating a gaping hole in the dungeon wall.

It was time to smile at each other. In her vast relief at having successfully rescued the stubborn August Hawthorne, Larissa started to fall into his outstretched, welcoming arms for a hug when she again caught a whiff of him.

Always attentive to Larissa's reactions and moods, Willem said, "Wait, let me handle this. You might want to turn around for a minute or two, Larissa. August, get those filthy rags off quickly before we all start retching."

For once, August didn't argue. He shucked off his stained, smelly prison garb, which Phuctious immediately incinerated in midair. Willem foraged around in his pack and brought out suitable replacement clothing.

"None of this is velvet or fur-lined, of course," he said with a tone of apology, "but the shirt is my best one, pure ecru silk. The breeches are suede leather. You are welcome to them, Hawthorne Heir."

"But I don't see any water to bathe in." August stood naked and slightly disgruntled.

"Close your eyes," Willem told him, grinning, "I feel a storm coming in. Oh, and take these soapwort blossoms and leaves to bathe with."

August heard a small rumble above his head. Looking up, he saw a small, puffy purplish cloud forming. Quickly he closed his eyes, saying, "I see now why you are called Willem the Wizard. I haven't seen a mini cloudburst conjured since I was a kid."

As the cloudburst rumbled again, this time a bit more loudly, rain poured heavily down on August. He stopped talking and rubbed himself vigorously with the soapwort. It had a very pleasant smell, one of clovers and bouquets of field flowers. Within three minutes, August had soaped up and rinsed off twice. He nodded to Willem, who quickly reversed the conjure. The small thunder cloud shrank and finally disappeared with a last watery burst.

There was nothing to dry off with. The gentle breeze blowing that day proved helpful. Soon August was back in form, sneaking up behind Larissa where she stood impatiently waiting for August to be hosed down. She yelped as he spun her around and lifted her up off her feet in a bear hug.

"Put me down!" she finally said, brushing the dampness from her clothing. "Well, at least you don't smell like cattle now. We still need to be on our way." Turning to Willem and Phuctious she said, "I thank you both for your assistance. I do not think I could have traveled another yard downwind of August in his unwashed state."

"At your service, Strondovan Heir," Phuctious told her.

Larissa looked at Willem with tenderness in her eyes. Throwing her arms around him she said, "And *you*, Willem, have redeemed yourself. I couldn't understand why it was taking you so long to come after us, but I realize now that you were under the influence of something unanticipated. I believe it kept you asleep for a long time so that you would not awaken and follow us right away."

"Yes, I came as soon as I was able," Willem said. "And I was fortunate that I encountered Phuctious Hesperides. He is an astounding Magical and a stout fellow."

Larissa turned to the dwarf. "I am so grateful for your assistance. I hate to ask but I must. Would you be willing to accompany us to Derestney Downs? It would be an honor. I feel there is some danger to this place, and I have never been there before."

To her vast relief the dwarf nodded and bowed slowly. "Your intuition is correct," he said. "Derestney Downs has a reputation for both its wholesome atmosphere and also for suspiciously being a place where travelers tend to disappear without a trace. It does not serve any traveler well to spend the night there, no matter what accommodations are offered them, for they will not live to see the light of dawn, according to the legends."

August, Larissa, and Willem grew silent as they digested this piece of information.

"I am happy to accompany you all," the dwarf continued, "though I must ask for one small favor in return for my time and talents."

"Of course, anything." Larissa replied quickly. "I have gold with me, if that is what you are asking."

"No, no," the dwarf said in a mild tone. "I will instead require your first-born."

"Excuse me?" Larissa forced out the words, speechless and taken aback.

"I said I will require your first-born child in exchange for my help in your grand quest," the dwarf said mildly. "I didn't stutter. F-I-R-S-T-B-O-R-N. Capiche?"

There was the most uncomfortable silence possible before the dwarf burst into laughter, slapping his knees in merriment. When he finally caught his breath, he said, "You should have seen your face, Strondovan Heir. I was only joking. Dwarf joke. Get it?"

Larissa composed her face and tittered politely, while August resisted an impulse to grab the dwarf up by the collar, dangle him in midair, and tell him that his attempt at humor sucked. But looking over at Larissa he thought the better of it. Willem, too, looked perturbed, as if he were thinking that dwarves had a really odd and inappropriate sense of humor— or maybe just Phuctious.

***

Onward they moved, until they found a Sky Portal that took them back where Willem had met Phuctious. From that point, they trekked onward toward Derestney Downs. At last, they felt comfortable enough to take a respite. Larissa quickly brewed a fragrant pot of coffee over a fire and unwrapped a cloth in which she had stored two loaves of crusty bread and two round cheeses.

Coffee was served and everyone ate their fill. Even though August had been half starved in the Anguis dungeon, he started to complain about there being no soup. In his opinion a nice hot soup would round out the meal, even if it were made from random wild carrots, wild parsnips, and the tiny fingerling potatoes that grew in the region.

The moment he started to gripe, Larissa silenced him with one fierce look. He never even had a chance to verbalize his complete thought before he went silent, much to the amusement of both Willem and the dwarf. August waited until she was tidying up and the others were distracted before speaking to her again.

"Excuse me, Larissa North Strondovan," he told her in a terse voice. "I wonder if I might have a private word?" When she didn't answer, pointedly ignoring him, he continued anyway. "I have no idea why you are treating me like shit. I thought we had learned how to get along, in spite of the fact that our philosophies and personalities are polar opposites.

"At any rate, I need you to treat me with some degree of respect and stop talking down to me like I'm a naughty schoolboy. In exchange, I will agree to do the same, which by the way, I always have done since the beginning.

"I *do* have skills, but unlike you, I do not torture other Magicals later with the fact that I was of assistance. I do a lot of spell casting behind the scenes to benefit our quest, especially to protect you from a barrage of spells that seem to be coming toward you from some undiscernible source. I couldn't quite get a handle on it in the beginning. However, trust me when I tell you that I now have information and know full well the energy moving in your direction.

"To gain more information, it took every bit of my wizarding power in my bag of Magical Anticasting Spells to learn and confirm the web of lies and spells used by both your Aunt Dorenda and Edouard to make you fall in love with him. You're welcome!"

August paused a moment for a quick breath. He knew his sermon contained a little exaggeration but wasn't far off. When Larissa didn't answer right away, he continued,

"You've been a fairly blindsided Magical moron for months now. Not yourself at all. Oh, yeah, and believe me when I say there was a big web of delusion making you see Edouard as more handsome than he is."

August finished with a cocky smile, "I don't need any magical enhancements. I am *damn fine* without them!"

Larissa looked at him for the first time since he'd started speaking. She stared, coolly appraising him. "Oh, thank you, Hawthorne Heir!" she said in a mocking tone. "I can't think what we'd do without *you*! And for your information, Edouard Anguis is a very handsome man. And very rich. Unfortunately, he has some wretched and toxic personality disorders, ones that I only recently became aware of. Is that enough accolades for now? For *you*, I mean?" She inched up close to him, her cheeks scarlet, teeth clenched. "One more thing, don't slander my Aunt Dorenda. Ever."

August stared back at her for a moment in disbelief. It seemed to him that every single time he proffered an olive branch, Larissa managed to somehow beat him over the head with it. To totally diss the information he'd worked so hard to learn and finally shared with her, frustrated him completely.

What she really needed was a good spanking. He was sure that she had never been disciplined her entire life. But knowing she would hate being kissed by him even worse, he decided to go for it. He swept her up easily in his arms and planted his lips firmly over hers. It was an angry kiss, but strangely, as soon as their lips touched, his feelings began to change.

There apparently was some electricity between them. With a mighty shove that sent him reeling backwards, Larissa extricated herself from his grasp and slapped him soundly across his handsome face. He was so surprised by the lingering sensations from their lips touching that he mentally dismissed the sharp sting on his face. Instead, he smiled. Larissa moaned with disgust.

Willem, attracted by the sound of Larissa's slap, immediately stood beside them. "You know, it might be great if all of us refrained from hitting each other," he said mildly. "Particularly because we have some distance to cover, and we need to conserve our energy."

"Tell him to stop kissing me!" Larissa said. Her face colored with anger. "Or he may find himself missing a limb—or possibly his favorite appendage."

Willem worked hard not to smile. He turned to August. "Stop kissing her," he said.

"Sure, at least for now," August answered agreeably. He sauntered off to collect his gear.

Refreshed and renewed by their simple repast, they had just started off again when Willem noticed a small sack sitting on a stump in the same clearing where he and Phuctious had first prepared their food.

"What is it?" Willem wondered aloud. He turned to the others. "Do you think it might have been placed here by some kindly Magical to assist us on our quest?"

"Don't touch it!" Larissa said, cautioning him. "It might have been placed here by some of our many enemies to detain or distract us."

"I think we should open it and find out," August said. "If the rest of you are too fearful, I will do the honors myself."

Phuctious remained oddly silent during the exchange, although Willem thought he saw the dwarf's eyes flicker with merriment. August strode over toward it, Willem following closely behind. As the bag sat perched on the sawed-off stump, August reached forward, without actually touching it, and gingerly untied the twine at the top, using a small twig to untie the loops.

The bag unfolded, revealing two molar teeth sitting in a pool of ooze. Willem rocked back on his heels. A curious expression covered August's face. He opened his mouth and felt around with his tongue. His expression froze. Larissa looked on, noting that his eyes got wider until his face took on a frog-like appearance.

August gasped through spittle-covered fingers. "My back molars!" "Oh my gah," he garbled, "They awe gone! I nevew felt a thig."

"You can take your fingers out of your mouth now," Larissa told him. "I don't think they're coming back. And here's a tip for both of you. Never open a bloody sack."

"Even if it's small?" Willem queried her.

Larissa let out a sound of disgust. "Especially if it's small." Her voice raised in a short high-pitched shriek of frustration. "I believe what you just encountered is an enchanted sack of Fairy origin. It is called a Subtraction Sack. It always takes something from the person who opens it."

"Fairies are tricky beings, and they love to fool other Magicals. You are damn lucky it didn't take one of your limbs, August. And I am extremely disappointed in you, Willem. I thought you would have known better than to follow the lead of the feckless Hawthorne Heir. When has he *ever* been right about anything?"

She was getting tired of being questioned, especially since she had proven during the course of their journey that she was right ninety-nine percent of the time. Just her luck to have been paired with two impossibly slow learners.

Just when their legs were about to give out, they heard music up ahead. The dark woods had grown uncomfortably full of glowing orbs. She half suspected that they might be spies sent by the Anguis or others to track their progress.

Chapter Eight

Larissa had almost uttered a spell to send them back where they came from when the gloom of the forest opened up to a panoramic view of meadowlands, with a village in the distance. Unsurprisingly, the lilting sound of flute music reached their ears. Part of the charm of Derestney Downs was that all the inhabitants were taught to play the flute at an early age so that there was a constant fairground atmosphere that imbued the town streets.

The melodious, intermingled tunes lifted the spirits of the travelers. Even Larissa found her mood improving, and she smiled over at her companions, asking, "Are we ready for this? Phuctious, do you have anything more to tell us about this place? For not being a habitable place to stop over, it certainly seems a merry one."

"Yes. Well, it would have to be appealing, wouldn't it?" Phuctious half grumbled, almost as if he had forgotten his companions and was talking to himself. "Like a Venus flytrap, it must have an allure, a promise of gaiety and amusement, to attract its prey. I can't tell you how many thousands of travelers who have come before you through the ages have been lulled into thinking they wouldn't mind staying here forever. And many of them did end up staying. Forever. Or at least their bones did, after they met their demise."

Something in Phuctious's voice made them all shiver momentarily.

"We will certainly keep your warnings in mind, Hesperides Heir," Larissa said politely. "As for now, we have business that must be attended to."

They walked across the meadow toward the colorful and quaint town buildings, noting a flock of fluffy sheep on the hillside and a boy with a peaked, slouchy hat and bare feet playing the flute as they walked.

"It seems to have gotten much warmer," August remarked.

"It is always midsummer in Derestney Downs," Phuctious said in a dreamy voice. "Or at least it always appears so. I would keep my boots on if I were you. It may all be an elaborate illusion, conjured by the Dark entities that are the Lords of this town. I have heard stories of travelers who only stayed a few hours, walked around barefoot and halfway to their next destination, and found that they had contracted frostbite. Keep your cloaks around you too. All this Summer beauty and trout fairly leaping out of streams and…"

The dwarf stopped speaking. Within a few seconds, all of them knew why. The tantalizing aroma of fresh baked bread and cakes permeated the air the closer they got to the nearest building. On the side of it they saw a sign swinging in the breeze that read *Bygones Bakery and Bistro*.

"And the aroma of home-baked bread," Phuctious finished his sentence with a dreamy look on his face. "Keep in mind that anything you eat will increase your sensation of hunger after we leave this place. It won't poison you or anything, but it's good that we have our own bread and cheese. Do *not* stuff yourselves or you will be sorry later."

Despite the dwarf's words, the other three found themselves unable to walk past the bakery without going in. Phuctious reluctantly held the door open for them. The rich fragrance of pastries and yeast-raised rolls met them as soon as they were inside. The aroma was so delicious that they felt they could almost take a bite of the warm delectable air around them.

Walking up to the counter, Phuctious nodded, and they each picked out their favorites from a glass showcase burgeoning with goodies. Larissa chose a napoleon, her favorite. She loved this pastry with its many flaky layers covered with a rich custard. On top, icing of vanilla buttercream topped with rich dark chocolate squiggles.

Phuctious selected a giant crueler with raspberry filling. It was nine inches long and covered by powdered sugar on the outside.

August picked out a lattice-topped tart with a rich lemon chess filling and meringue on top. Willem chose a half dozen plain buns with plenty of butter on the side.

The dwarf paid with one of the golden coins that he and Willem had discovered. Larissa was aware of an overall relaxing sensation. Even though she had to admit that the napoleon pastry was the best she had ever tasted, she remained on alert, thinking Phuctious was right about the "allure" of Derestney Downs. It seemed seductive and beguiling, so much so that she believed him when he said it was basically a trap in the shape of a most charming town.

"We have to get going," she said, shooting up out of her seat.

The afternoon was wearing long, and they seemed like they were completely forgetting their mission. Once on the street outside, Larissa realized that her head felt much clearer. As she looked around, she saw the same look of recognition in the eyes of everyone standing there, but Phuctious.

"I see what you meant," August said to the dwarf. "I was perfectly full when we went into the bakery. Now I am starting to get hungry again."

"Yes, tis always so," Phuctious said sadly. "Good thing none of you stuffed yourselves to the gills, or you'd be starving right now."

Larissa was swivel necking, looking all around at the shops in the village. She wasn't sure where the man with the horse was located and was looking for clues. They had entered town from one end of the main thoroughfare. Shrugging, she gestured for the others to follow her lead and continued down the street.

There were sidewalks on both sides. The main street in between was made of cobblestone. Larissa found herself admiring the old-fashioned charming craftsmanship. Even the store fronts, with their ornate beautifully painted signs and gingerbread storefronts, looked like something from a fairytale. With one exception.

As they walked up the street, they came upon a lot on which was situated a dilapidated-looking older building that housed several bays in front. They could see from the street that inside that one of the bays had hay over the weather board flooring, and on it stood a huge dappled gray horse.

"This has *got* to be it!" she told the others. "You agree, Phuctious?"

Phuctious held out an object he had been consulting while they had been walking through Derestney Downs. It was about the size of a large pocket watch. At the top were the words Travelscope. On one side, a window indicated that it had been set to Derestney Downs, and the small window underneath it read See a man about a horse.

Finally, Larissa saw that on the bottom a small green light was blinking by the inscribed phrase You've Arrived! She chuckled. Apparently, the dwarf knew where they were going all the time and had them covered. She glanced upward at the swinging sign over their heads. Beneath it was a bell on a rope that looked like a miniature version of an old-fashioned school bell.

The sign read, in ornate and gilded lettering: SEE A MAN ABOUT A HORSE HERE. Directly below that, in smaller lettering: All Questers (Including Witch Questers) DISCOURAGED. Below that: SHIRTS AND SHOES REQUIRED!

"We're not just any witch questers!" August said bitterly. "How dare they?"

"Shh," Larissa answered. She spied a figure emerging from within the dark interior of the open barn. "I think someone is coming."

A figure emerged, wearing a plaid shirt, overalls, and a plaid Scottish flat cap with a pom pom on the top. It looked like the golfing hats the Scottish were known to wear traditionally.

"May I help you, witchfolk and dwarf?" He looked them up and down, accessing each one.

Suddenly he gasped, "Heirs! Heirs! I apologize, I did not recognize you at first. Please forgive me."

"Of course." Larissa smiled broadly, happy to be recognized for once. "Sir, we were advised some time ago to come here and see a man about a horse. We are hoping you can tell us why it was important for us to journey here. Scant information was given as to what we should hope to find."

"Of course, of course," the man said, nodding. "Tis always the way it is. Vagueness is employed as a sort of warding for your own protection, you see. But I find that all those who are destined to seek myself and Arion manage to find their way here anyway, including a lot of pesky teenybopper witches. Apparently visits to "see a man about a horse" in Derestney Downs are trending or something. It has been a constant nuisance, I assure you, hence the additions to the sign."

"We accept your apology and are anxious to be formally introduced to your steed," August said, speaking up. As a long-time student of legend and lore since he was a child, he had gotten excited at the mention of the name Arion. Although a horse, he had been descended from gods, was likely a demigod, and most importantly had the ability to foresee the future.

August turned and exchanged a look with Willem, who smiled, indicating he was thinking the same thing as August.

"Very well," said the man. "I hate to mention this, but both myself and Arion have to eat and maintain our buildings. Gratuities are not required, most especially for you Heirs, but would be *greatly* appreciated."

"Absolutely," Phuctious said. He stepped forward and retrieved several golden coins from the treasure sack. "There you go, my good man."

"Most generous of you, I am sure. My name is Cosmo Caster, by the way."

"I am Larissa North Strondovan," she told him. "And with me are Phuctious Hesperides, August South Hawthorne, and Willem the Wizard, our escort and guide for our quest. And you are definitely the one we need to see. You and your horse."

After introductions and half-bows in deference to each other, Cosmo led them over to the massively tall but placid animal residing in one of the foremost stalls in the open barn. He surprised everyone by addressing the horse with a slight bow. "O Arion, noble steed, I would like to introduce Larissa North Strondovan and her party of sojourners who have come to seek your counsel."

The horse nodded and lifted his head as though to sniff the air. "Do I also detect a Hawthorne Heir, a Hesperides Heir, and then a garden variety wizard in the party?" it asked.

All of them were taken aback at how deep and resonant the horse's voice was, and also how perfect his diction.

"Yes, honorable Arion," August answered. "You are completely correct."

August knew that this must be one of the original War Horses owned by Achilles, and wasn't too surprised, since the original pair of horses were Immortal. But he had to wonder why the horse was now alone, and also why such a legendary figure would be residing in a small town like Derestney Downs. Within the next minute, as he looked more closely at the fine tall steed, he suddenly knew why.

It was obvious that Arion was blind. The horse's eyes looked opaque, pearly, nearly opalescent.

"I might not be able to see you as clearly as I once was able to," Arion told him, "but I am more than prescient enough to tell you exactly what you look like. I can see in my mind, although my eyes are no longer functioning as they were when I was a Battle Horse."

"But how…?" Willem started to ask a personal question, but he stopped, thinking the better of it, not wanting to be considered rude.

"A witch took my sight. A very powerful and wicked witch from a once lauded elemental clave. She took it because she came seeking me out as one of the most sought-after oracles in the Magiverse. Yes, she sought me out to find out the truth about her nefarious plans, specifically to be told if they would succeed or not.

"As an Oracle I could only tell her the truth, and she became so enraged upon hearing it that she attempted to kill me. But I am not as others, and my immortality prevented her Occidere Incantation from working, not to mention I had discerned what she was going to do a few precious seconds before she cast the spell and refracted some of the killing energy back to her.

"She didn't die, though. I did hear that, though she was still a young woman at the time, it turned her hair completely white. I'm sure she dyes it now."

The entire party was silently taken aback and filled with different emotions. Larissa felt scandalized that Arion would have had to go through such torment because of a highborn and diabolically ambitious witch.

August was quiet. Willem shed a tear. He wanted to reach out and pet the horse on his muzzle. He was only thinking it when Arion startled him by saying, "You may go ahead, Wizard Willem."

Willem tenderly petted the horse down the length of his muzzle and then remembered that he'd stuck a few of the wild carrots into his jacket pockets. He retrieved one and Arion snorted in approval and quickly chomped it down.

"Ah, thank you," he told Willem. "I haven't had a wild carrot in quite some time. I think they are the sweetest, don't you?"

After Arion finished the carrots and had some water, he felt refreshed enough to deliver the Oracle message he had discerned. All who were present remained silent, awaiting his message. Because he was a demigod, he received information directly from the gods.

"First, you must know that one of you will die. This is fated and inevitable and inescapable. This person will have pre-knowledge of their death, but because they are committed to your cause will not run from it but rather, run *toward* their demise.

"Secondly, and I am sure you have felt this, a storm is coming of such great magnitude and import that it will affect all life on earth for a millennium to come. This is not an ordinary storm, but a storm of souls, in which the very elect agents of both good and evil will be engaged in a life-or-death struggle. Thirdly, a child born to rule all the Magiverse will be conceived before the final battle even begins."

All of them waited for more. When it appeared that Arion was finished speaking, Larissa asked, "But who will *prevail* in this battle? Can you at least tell us that the Light Bringers will ultimately *win*?"

The horse snorted and stepped back. "I know you are thinking that to know the outcome of such a decisive and epic struggle would increase the morale of the Light Bringers, but I assure you that any foreknowledge of the outcome would only prove confusing. Anyway, I am *forbidden* to comment on it, per the deities.

"Think about it for a moment. If you knew everything you did were to be successful, would you try as hard? False confidence and your fallible human natures would dictate that you might slack off, thinking that no matter how much effort you put into it, the outcome is certain.

No, the stakes are much too high for that! And that is why even though I know, I will never reveal the outcome to you, Strondovan Heir."

Larissa flushed, a bit shamefaced, and stopped short of apologizing for asking the question. Although she had to concede that Arion had a point, she hadn't liked his answer.

"Thank you so much, O Arion the wise one," Willem said. He wanted to change up the heavy atmosphere that the horse's predictions had caused within the confines of the weathered building.

"Yes, thank you so much," August added.

Phuctious chimed in too. Larissa was the last to add her appreciative words.

The proprietor, Cosmo Caster, appeared as if out of nowhere and went up to Arion, looking the steed in the face for a moment. "Aye and I am afraid the Oracle is very depleted of energy at this point and must rest. I will be happy to show all of you fine folks out."

"Stop!" Arion said in a loud commanding tone. "Two more things. First, I wish to have a private word with Wizard Willem for a minute before your final departure. Secondly, do any of you happen to have a spare lump of sugar?"

August, Larissa, and Phuctious waited outside for no longer than a couple minutes before Willem joined them. His expression was unreadable.

"Well, good news or bad news, Wizard Willem?" August asked. He tried to sound conversational. "Something good, I hope? Like where you and I can find a bawdy house in this town to have a few drinks and get laid?"

"Hey, believe it or not I like to get laid too," Phuctious said indignantly to August. "Everyone is the same height when they're lying down. And I never knew a lassie of loose morals to refuse a gold coin. I assure you I see plenty of action. You don't want to compare peckers with me. Mine is so long that if I get tired of walking, I can use it as a pogo stick."

All of them, Larissa included, had a laugh at Phuctious's comments. The dwarf winked at Larissa, and she realized that he had made the joke to ease the tension at that moment. As soon as Willem had emerged and joined them, looking perfectly calm, she had the distinct impression that he had gotten some bad news from the Oracle. Her impression had been that a deep unspoken sadness emanated from the usually upbeat Willem.

But he kept his own counsel as he usually did. Larissa felt it would have been invasive to ask him about it, but her heart went out to him. He really was a good guy, a stalwart soul, and if they had met under different circumstances, she might have been able to seriously consider him as a suitor. She'd always known that he carried a torch for her. Perhaps Arion had told him that his love for her would never be.

As he walked along, Larissa caught up to him and slipped her hand into his. "My hand feels a bit cold," she said, smiling up at him. "I hope you don't mind."

The smile he showed was so warm and genuine it immediately melted her heart. "Not at all," he told her.

She realized at that moment that her hand really had been cold. Enclosed in his warm one, she found herself enjoying the cozy sensation of holding hands with him. Only once did August, who was engaged in some in-depth discussion with Phuctious, turn around and glance back. She noted that he had homed in on the fact that she and Willem were hand in hand, and that he frowned momentarily before turning around again. His reaction made her smile, because she knew that her holding hands with Willem bothered him more than a little.

They soon came to a promising-looking tavern. Phuctious and August exclaimed their pleasure at seeing it. As they swung open the door, their noses were accosted by the aromas of stale beer, juicy roasted beef, and the specialty of the house: a very finely brewed single malt scotch.

Phuctious turned to Larissa. "You needn't worry," he told her. "This place serves *real* food, delicious by slow brewing and slow cooking and in no need of enhancements of any kind. You may indulge yourself without concern."

They had a delicious oat bread the establishment served with meals, not to mention the giant yeasty hot pretzels they served with beer. As soon as they found seats around one of the few remaining tables, Larissa ordered both the local beer on tap and a bowl of beef stew. The others quickly followed suit.

August would have preferred a booth. He had the strangest feeling that although none of the other patrons had said a word to them that they were somehow listening to everything the group said. He leaned forward, saying in a low voice, "Watch what you say in here. The walls have ears, I believe."

Phuctious cut his eyes upward. All of them tilted back their heads to regard the rather low, rough-hewn open beam ceilings. Located randomly along every beam were replicas of human ears carved in the wood. Although made of wood, they looked realistic enough and seemed to move slightly, tilting in one direction or the other as the volume of different conversations picked up.

"I see what you mean," Willem said, nodding at them both.

Now aware that they were at least under auditory surveillance, their delicious meal was fairly bereft of conversation, other than asking each other to pass along condiments. Afterwards all of them pushed back from the large round table. Phuctious ordered a round of Scotch whiskey, served neat.

Next to one of the corner fireplaces, a fiddler struck up a tune. Well sated and feeling no pain, they all joined in a chorus of "The Box of Heads":

I once meant to travel to London,
But traveled to Bristol instead.
At a Wayfarers Inn I was welcomed right in
By the owner who wanted me dead.
"I have such a fine collection
Of Sojourner's heads you can see.
If you stop for the night,
I'll have your head by daylight,
And a new head would really please me!
I promise that you will feel nothing.
I am skilled at head removal.
And I'll make sure the rest of you gets
The best burial yet,
If I can only obtain your approval!"
But sadly, I had to decline him.
I was fond of my head you can see.
Told him he'd have to wait.
I would be on my way,
And his collection box couldn't have me!

At the end of the song, it was traditional for each guest of the establishment to slam their glass of whiskey or beer on the table pursuant to draining it completely with a collective "whoop!" It was a fun drinking game, and by the time it was finished, all of them were drunk but Phuctious, who could hold immense quantities of liquor, despite his smaller stature. He had been too amused watching the others become inebriated and didn't remember to stop them.

It was nearly half past eleven at night before they stumbled out the door of the Tavern. In the crisp evening air, Phuctious realized that his Sobriety Spells were having little effect on his companions who were bumping up against each other and laughing like fools over nothing.

"See here!" he told them in a stern voice. He wanted to discuss their lack of delayed gratification.

"Oh, please don't be annoyed with us, Phuctious," Larissa said with an imploring tone. Tripping forward, she quickly darted closer to the dwarf and planted a kiss on his cheek. "I kissed the dwarf!" she said gaily, "and his beard tickled me."

Phuctious was shocked that the usually strait-laced Larissa had kissed him. She was gorgeous, and her peasant blouse that had been tied up to her throat had the ribbons undone to the point of showing a great deal of previously hidden cleavage. As he gazed on her creamy bosoms, he had an impulse to show her how much more his red beard would tickle when he was between her lily-white thighs. However, he knew there would be hell to pay if he took advantage of an Elemental Heir.

"See here," he continued in a gruffer voice. "None of you are in shape to continue our journey. We are, therefore, in a pickle. Did you not hear me when I said that staying the night here in Derestney Downs would be dangerous, if not fatal?"

"I did hear you Hesperides Heir," Willem told him. "And I truly apologize . . ." Willem could not suppress a belch at the end of his statement. August and Larissa collapsed against each other laughing.

Phuctious's eyes gazed upward in a sign of disgust. If even the level-headed Willem the Wizard was three sheets to the wind, they were doomed. He knew they needed at least a few hours of rest. Perhaps if they sought refuge at the barn, Cosmo Caster would give them permission to sleep in the clean hay near Arion.

"Follow me," he said. The dwarf resigned himself to the fact that he would get no sleep that night. But sleep was optional for most of his kind. He resolved to make sure the others rested while he would stand watch over them until the first rays of dawn appeared.

***

Phuctious sat on a low milking stool with his back resting comfortably against a pole inside the barn. His party had gotten the reluctant permission to sleep in the barn with the understanding that Cosmo Caster would not be responsible if anyone was harmed.

"I wish you will not bestir myself to come outside my little hut, even if I hear you all screaming," he said in a forewarning tone. "I mean it. If they come for you all, they can have you."

The man was so nervous he was shaking slightly. Phuctious cocked an eye at the man. "And pray tell, what is it that stalks the streets of Derestney Downs at night seeking travelers?" he asked the man. "What manner of creature?"

Cosmo answered, "The Ghouls, of course. I'm surprised you couldn't guess. I believe they are joined by a few wraiths from time to time, but the dead have been an integral part of the population of Derestney Downs for centuries."

Phuctious suddenly remembered some of the lore he knew about Ghouls and countered, "But Ghouls do not consume living flesh, just corpses."

"Precisely my point, sir!" Cosmo Caster removed his cap, wiping the sweat off his forehead with a large kerchief. He looked around frantically to make sure nothing was heading their way. "They will kill everyone, drag them off to the seasoning cave, which is just a place to let fresh corpses rot to their liking, and then have them when they are ripe. Now I must leave you. I am nearly certain they will come for you people. All the other travelers had the good sense to skedaddle out of town and clear the city limits before midnight."

"I am not tired, and I intend to keep watch," Phuctious told him. He sounded confident. "Do not worry. I have many magical weapons at my disposal."

Cosmo Caster departed. Phuctious resumed his comfortable perch, which gave him a clear view into the open stall filled with clean-smelling hay just opposite of where he was sitting. Not four feet away he could see Larissa Strondovan in the middle of August and Willem, sleeping solidly with one arm above her head.

As she breathed deeply, her chest rose and fell. One of her breasts had worked its way completely out of the confines of her blouse. It was a glorious view, Phuctious thought to himself. One he was happy to enjoy for many hours. He felt privileged. He would wager not many had ever gotten to see the naked tit of the Strondovan Heir.

August and Willem were unconscious as well. Willem snored softly. August snored loudly enough to wake the dead, or at least loudly enough to attract the attention of any ghouls roaming the now deserted streets of Derestney Downs.

Phuctious could have kicked himself, because he meant to ask Willem for the Pasha before he had bedded down for the night. It might have come in handy to subdue any creature attempting to do them harm. He comforted himself with the thought that he knew a great many blindness spells, and even had a small sack of Caecus Powder, a rare concoction obtained from the Carrion flower. This plant, also known as the Starfish Cactus, grew naturally in South America. He had paid a pretty penny for it, so he was half hoping he wouldn't need to use any of it.

The dwarf felt well-fed and was delighted at being able to listen out for interlopers while staring at Larissa's errant breast. He sighed with contentment. And then the unthinkable happened: he fell asleep.

Phuctious awakened to pure chaos: screaming, shrieking, and the wild neighing and outraged snorting of Arion.

He jumped up, realizing that he'd been ignored by sheer luck. Frantically, he muttered an incantation as he poured onto his broad palm the instant Blindness powder, which he blew in the direction of what seemed to be a horde of creatures.

Some were hideous in appearance, six limbed and crawling like insects over the floorboards of the barn. Others stood upright and displayed on their front side the normal looking appearance of a regular person, while on their backside they had dark twisted bodies and satyr's faces. It was a mess, Phuctious decided as the magic powder he released instantly blinded the front line of attackers.

Some of the other ghouls ran off when they observed their comrades being blinded and shrieking in agony. Larissa brandished a sword. Phuctious noted that the poor dear still had one breast mostly exposed. At her feet he saw three hideous heads she had, with a powerful blow, managed to disconnect from ghoul bodies.

August had done something unexpectedly clever. He apparently had worn enchanted boots, and the spikes protruding from the front had pierced through and eviscerated several attackers who lay on the floor writhing in their death throes.

Willem had a spiked ball flair that he arced through the air while landing blow after blow to some of the half-dead, all in an effort to finish them off.

A diminutive troupe of ghouls no bigger than large rats, and kind of cute in their own way, were also blinded by Phuctious and finished off by the others. Finally, all the travelers stood braced for another attack, but the night became silent again.

Arion had stamped on several of the attackers, rearing back and stamping them with his powerful front hooves. Larissa and Willem went to him, thanking him for his assistance.

"I was a War Horse, remember?" He chuckled. "I still remember a few tricks when it comes to defending against a sneak attack. Nevertheless, it would behoove all of you to be on your way as soon as possible. It will be dangerous for you until you reach the town limits. But I can assure you more will be coming to seek you out.

"They operate with a hive mind, you see. By now all of them know that you have killed a great many of their number and they will be out for your blood. You are within mere minutes of the first light of dawn, but I would recommend you be on your way. As the sun comes up, they will either slither off into their caves or revert to their human form and resume their duties at the various establishments here in Derestney Downs."

"Some of them appear in human form during the day?" Larissa asked.

"Yes, and there will be several signs hung out today advertising for help, since some of them have been killed by your fine selves this very night," Arion answered. "Don't look so surprised, and don't take it personally that perhaps the waitress that waited on you last evening may have shown up to kill you and carry off your bloody corpse. They are ghouls. They are just following their natures."

Willem, Phuctious, August, and Larissa hastily gathered up their belongings and headed off. Larissa felt grumpy and out of sorts. She not only had the rudest awakening ever, but she was sure that her hair looked a fright. There hadn't been time to brush it. She did, however, finally notice her wardrobe malfunction and laced up her blouse again. She'd hoped that in the confusion of the attack no one had noticed her unintentional partial nudity, but of course all of them had.

The mood of the group was tense. Larissa, with her longsword still out, and Phuctious were in the lead. Willem and August guarded the rear, walking backwards periodically to make certain that the group wasn't being followed.

They had almost reached the end of the city limits and saw a sign that read: You are now leaving Derestney Downs. Hope your visit was pleasant!

"I wonder how many souls that dared to spend the night in Derestney Downs ever actually got to read this sign?" August remarked. "I wager not very many."

Willem was about to agree with August when both became aware of a commotion in the duskiness behind them. They turned and were instantly horrified. It seemed as if the entire population of the town was galloping up the avenue behind them. Some slithered, while some crawled so quickly their eyes could hardly follow. Some were in human form. All of them had murder in their eyes.

"Run!" August shouted.

All of them took off, aware that every second counted. Phuctious was out of the Blinding Powder. All four prayed to reach the town limits. They reached the end and entered the shelter of the tree line just as the first rays of the sun burst upward from the countryside, filling the sky with light. Anguished shrieks from the ghoulish hoard filled the air.

Larissa almost made it through the trees when she felt something violently jerking her head backward. Two seconds later, it was released. She turned in surprise and saw August.

"So sorry, Larissa, he said, "it was the only thing I could think to do!"

Horrified, it dawned on her what happened. The side of her head where her hair had been jerked still hurt. She reached up and discovered that her long hair had literally been hacked off to above shoulder length. The other half was still its current length. This was the second time her companion had whacked off her hair during this quest.

August waited for a diatribe that never came. With an air of injured dignity, Larissa took out an elastic hair tie and fastened her locks back in a low, uneven looking ponytail.

Willem tried to catch up to her as she indignantly strode off. "I might know a restorative spell for hair loss," he said. "Of course, I'm not exactly sure whether it would restore the length or just make your hair generally thicker."

"Shut up, Willem!" Larissa said between clenched teeth.

Willem, who was quite familiar with her and her famous Strondovan temper, did just that.

Chapter Nine

It was another small town that Phuctious assured them was nothing like Derestney Downs.

"Meaning what, exactly?" August said.

"Meaning this small village in the area called "Walnut Grove" is full of walnut groves and isn't cursed," Phuctious replied. In his mind, this latest bit of information was something August should have already known.

All of the others looked surprised.

"That might have been something you'd have thought to alert us to before we set one foot in Derestney Downs," August retorted.

Phuctious looked at him obliquely and shrugged. "What difference would that have made?" he countered "You had to go there anyway. No choice. Oh, wait. There was some choice about how inebriated to get on our final evening there, and all of you made the wrong one with unfortunate consequences, I might add."

"But we got out alive . . . ." August stopped, seeing Phuctious nodding in the direction of Larissa, who was keeping pace with Willem in front of the other two—and who had a very lopsided looking ponytail.

"Oh, right." August finished his thought, remembering that Larissa had a new hairdo, one that she probably did not appreciate, even though he'd saved her life. He hadn't expected that she would thank him for it, and she never had.

"Well, Larissa noticed some diminished capacity as far as her spell casting, and the foremost expert in such repairs happens to reside in Walnut Grove," Phuctious said smugly. "I suggested she see someone, so she made an appointment."

The atmosphere in the town of Walnut Grove was completely different than it had been in Derestney Downs, which all of them felt might be a good thing. The rarified air seemed delicious to breathe, with warm and gentle breezes, perfect temperature, and best of all, it seemed as though all their fatigue from journeying for so long had evaporated.

The townspeople they passed greeted them with beatific smiles and nods and greetings of "Cheerio!" All of them appeared happy, content, and welcoming. Everywhere, baskets of free walnuts were set out with little signs that read, *Take one*. The abundance of walnuts was evident in that many of the advertised food items sold in the shops seemed to incorporate the tasty nuts into their recipes.

A fragrant aroma of cinnamon walnut buns permeated the air along the main street. They reached a place called Magicianeers Shop, which had a main door that led into a waiting area. Beyond that point, the travelers could see small bays on both sides where repairs were being made on individuals. It was hardly private.

A staff member came to the waiting area and called out, "Next?"

Phuctious gently pushed Larissa forward, much to her annoyance. Before she could protest, the tech's eyes locked on her.

"This way, please," he stated.

Inside a vacant bay, Larissa followed the man's instructions and stood still, holding out her arms from her body. The Magicianeer tech waved a broad wand, emitting a laser grid of light blue dots over her, taking his time. Lust wafted off the sweaty man in waves. Just being close to him caused a wave of nausea to rise in her throat.

"Are you finished now?" she finally said, more sharply than she'd intended.

"Hmm," he answered, "not quite, but . . . there. That should do it."

"Well?" she answered.

He finally and blessedly stepped away. "What is your diagnosis? Power loss of unknown origin, obviously."

"I told you that!" Larissa retorted. She was thoroughly out of patience with the man. "Tell me something I *don't* know!"

"You might be able to supplement with an amplituner," he said. His eyes remained fixed at the cleavage peeking out from the top of her blouse. "I mean, temporarily. These dips happen frequently to witches who are away from their power source and oftentimes correct themselves without outside intervention. You might consider combining resources with an associate witch in the meantime."

"Nothing you've told me is at all helpful," Larissa told the Magicianeer between gritted teeth. "Is that all you've got in the way of insight or recommendations?"

"We do have a line of Cursus Boosters," he said. "There is a display at the checkout counter, if you're so inclined, Miss."

Her haughty tone grated on the technician's nerves. His grid search had the added bonus of showing the "hot spots" on the human body and their sensitivity. Among the other things his analysis had revealed is that she had an oversensitive clitoris and overactive hormones. He bet she found herself "ringing the Devil's doorbell" a lot. Looking at her face, he decided to make his exit before she exploded.

Although the town of Walnut Grove was small, they did have a single inn, *The Downy Duck Inn*, for travelers to stay. Sick of sleeping on barn floors and in the woods, Larissa insisted they procure rooms for the night. She was surprisingly happy at the quaint comfort the inn offered and was agreeable when all of them decided to turn in early in order to get a jump start in the morning.

That night, Willem came to her in a dream, or rather, he sent her a dream, one of the stress-relieving ones that made her feel as though they had been intimate, but in reality, they had not. In this one, which was particularly vivid, she could see his brown head bobbing slightly up and down between her legs as he opened the petals of her vagina with his lips, sliding his tongue up and down between them.

At last, he concentrated on her clitoris. She involuntarily opened her thighs as wide as they could go.

"Please, Willem, please," she told him as he sucked and nipped at the sensitive nub of flesh radiating with pleasure from her core.

She came and came again. He seemed happy to receive her gush of fluids on his face.

"Goodnight, sweetness," he said to her. Willem, and the dream that he had sent her, faded softly away. She floated downward into velvety and relaxed oblivion.

The next day, the travelers were awake before dawn and had a sumptuous breakfast in the restaurant of the Downey Duck. All of them stuffed themselves on hot buttered biscuits, walnut muffins, thick slices of bacon, and scrambled eggs.

After all the men belched a few times, to Larissa's supreme disgust, they took off on foot again. Phuctious studied a map as he walked along. He looked concerned.

"We have to navigate through the rain forest in order to get to the Crystallo Waterfall," he told the others. "It's quite a trek, and we should be on our guard." Phuctious cleared his throat and addressed Larissa specifically. "Strondovan Heir, I hope you have some other clothing to change into. If not, you might need to borrow some pants from your traveling companion, Willem. I would offer a pair of my own, but I'm afraid they might prove too short."

"I do have some extra clothing," Willem said. He immediately pulled off his pack and retrieved a pair of baggy-looking cargo pants. "I'm afraid you'll have to pin them at the waist, though."

"Thank you," Larissa told him. She took the garment with an air of distaste. "I have some safety pins and can make an adjustment."

"What do we need to look out for, Hesperides Heir?" August wanted to know. "What kind of wild animals live in the rainforests?"

He tugged at his red beard, wrinkling his brow in thought. "First up, I would say keep your swords at the ready. Other than that, hmmm, giant wandering spiders, green anacondas, giant centipedes, poison dart frogs, bullet ants, huge alligators in the swamps, jaguars, pit vipers. Not a complete list by any means. Be very careful where you step. Also, don't forget to look above you, because some of these predators attack from the trees. A complex and rather diverse ecosystem, but I am sure we can manage."

Larissa was silent at Phuctious's answer.

"And why must we get to the Crystallo Waterfall?" August again wanted to know.

"Well, we are close, and it's always been on *my* list of must-see attractions when I find myself in the general area," Phuctious said cheerfully. "And believe it or not, the rest of the *main city* is hidden behind the waterfall. We've only been on the outskirts. We will need to find a very powerful being who resides in the city and considers himself politically neutral, kind of like Switzerland.

"Our task is to convince him to join the Lightbringers in the upcoming struggle. It will take all our good graces and persuasive powers to form this alliance, and possibly quite a bit of gold as well. I heard that he is very fond of gold. I only hope we get to him first. If the Darkness Dwellers have already recruited him, he might capture us and turn us over to them."

The travelers neared the Crystallo Falls and started counting their blessings that they had not encountered the creatures that Phuctious had warned them about. But disaster struck in the form of a Margay. The creature was a smaller version of an ocelot, and it jumped down from the trees onto Willem's shoulder, sinking in its fangs.

Before anyone could react, August drew back his arm and directed an Extergimus Spell toward the small but ferocious cat, picking it up and tumbling it over Willem's shoulder, sending it many feet through the air and into the forest, as though it had been catapulted by a small hurricane.

Larissa was outraged. "Why didn't you just *kill* the thing?" She glared at August. "It could come back!"

"It's a protected species, Strondovan *brat*!" he said back through gritted teeth. "And you're just mad because I was quicker than you."

Larissa was about to come back at August when she heard Willem, who had gone very white, let out a small whimper. She stood back and gasped. Blood ran down the length of Willem's arm, ostensibly from a shoulder wound hidden under his cloak.

"You're a freebleeder," she blurted out before she could stop herself. "Why didn't you tell us you were a freebleeder?"

Willem flushed. "How observant you are, Larissa," he said. A sarcastic snarl edged his words. "Have you always been this observant?" He looked immediately shamefaced as soon as the remark left his mouth.

"Thank you for saving me," he said to August.

Larissa immediately went into Florence Nightingale mode, shoving his cloak aside and dressing his wounds, which turned out to be minor.

"I think I need a break after that," Phuctious remarked to August. "Care to have a smoke with me? I think we can trust Larissa to doctor Willem's wound well enough."

As soon as the other two were out of earshot, Willem addressed Larissa once more.

"I'm sorry," he said. His luminous eyes met hers. "I didn't mean to go off about it, being a freebleeder, I mean. But it vexes me. Even though it's considered a disability among witches, I have never let it stop me from doing what I need to do.

"I know I am oversensitive about it. Truth be told, if I had confessed it to Jove, I would never have been accepted into his Royal Guard. It is my darkest secret, I suppose. Or it was until today. But I never should have gone off at you, Larissa. Anyone but you! Especially because . . ."

He stopped for a moment. His gaze remained fixed on hers, never wavering. Willem plunged forward in desperation, hoping that his body, having been so long repressed, might articulate the overwhelming feelings that had surged to the surface like an eruption.

He drew her to himself, placing his lips over hers. She did not resist. They clung together, their tongues dancing, searching for the passion and trust that existed between them and finding it.

As Larissa melted into him, she knew why she loved him. He made her feel safe, even though he wasn't as strong as Prince Elek or as muscle-bound as August or as aggressive as Dennis. She found a haven and an unexpected fire in his arms.

He aroused her deeply. She felt a hollow insistent ache between her thighs, and realized her body wanted to lie with him for real, to experience an intrusion of his flesh into hers, to give herself over completely. The oddest thing about it was that she thought Aunt Dorenda would approve. Willem would treat her like a queen and value her pleasure over his own. Always.

It was daunting, fighting through the last of the thick rainforest foliage to reach the falls. Despite Willem's injury, the sweat pouring off them, and the dangers, nearly everyone in their party agreed that reaching the Crystallo Falls was worth it just for the spectacular view alone.

It was the kind of symmetrical beauty impossible to find occurring naturally in nature. There was no less than one main fall, surrounded by four tiered smaller falls on each side for a total of nine altogether. The water was pristine, foaming, cool, and alluring. August, Willem, and Phuctious all stripped down to their underwear (Larissa noticed with a smirk that August favored a leopard print) and plunged in to clean off the grime from the journey.

Larissa sighed and did the best she could. The hem of her tunic covered her thighs, so she wore it into the water, not wanting to reveal any more of her body than she needed to. She left the pants on the shoreline. Even though she resented having to wear more clothing than the others, she still found herself laughing, enjoying the sensation of buoyancy in the lovely cool water around her.

Willem, with a mischievous look in his eyes and curly hair hanging in wet ringlets, popped up suddenly and splashed her. She sputtered and splashed him back. At once, all of them were splashing and dunking each other.

After what seemed like too short an interval, Phuctious reminded them that they had best put their clothes on again and resume their travels. As the others headed to the shoreline, Willem came up behind Larissa one last time, dragging her down and quickly flipping her around for an underwater kiss.

Larissa came up from the water blushing, glad that neither Phuctious nor August seemed to have noticed. They walked along the edge of the river basin up to the main waterfall, navigating the tricky climb by dexterously using a series of little ledges as steps to help them ascend. Phuctious assured them that behind those falls lay the hidden main city of Walnut Grove.

When at last they all stood on the widest ledge outside the large waterfall, Phuctious moved past them to assume the lead position.

"Follow me!" he shouted. The magnitude of sound emanating from the rushing water nearly drowned out his voice. He motioned with his hand. They all followed. The ledge had grown narrower, forcing them to walk single file. They stopped and waited, watching Phuctious disappear into the rock wall behind the massive, gurgling torrent of water.

"Hey, what's the holdup?" August shouted.

Both Larissa and Willem turned and frowned at him.

"Hold your horses, you old dunderhead!" the dwarf screamed back. "It takes an incantation, boy!"

August colored such a deep red that even his ears flamed a deep scarlet. He did not tolerate correction well, including the mildest form, and was especially averse to being called stupid by anyone. Eventually, the passage opened to admit all of them. After a short walk, bent over through a narrow tunnel, the far opening appeared and fairly spit them out onto a wide ledge as expansive as an outdoor castle terrace. It was bright with sunshine and showed a panoramic view of what seemed like a completely different landscape.

And so it was. Instead of the rainforest with its constant mists, overgrown vegetation, and low-hanging clouds, this appeared more like a bird's eye view of an English countryside. They looked up and saw the sky again, which puzzled them.

"This place was first formed in the crater of a long-extinct volcano," Phuctious orated in a sanctimonious voice. "It appears to be lower but is really set in a higher elevation than the rain forest. It also has different weather patterns and its own rare atmosphere."

"Rare atmosphere?" Willem echoed the dwarf. "How?"

"More oxygenated," the dwarf replied quickly. "Increases energy level, improves mood (at this point the dwarf cut his eyes in Larissa's direction), relieves stress, and promotes sleep.

"But try not to fall in love with the place. They adhere to a very strict population quota. Only a handful of applicants for citizenship are allowed in each year. And you must be related to someone who already resides here."

All four of them agreed that they already felt more refreshed than they had in weeks. A set of winding steps stretched down to ground level, and the group made their way to a building labeled, *VISITOR CHECK IN.*

After filling out forms indicating the reason for their visit, they were each given a temporary visitors pass that allowed up to a week of visitation. Earlier, August and Phuctious had discussed in more detail about the influential person the dwarf wanted to find, and to August's delight, it was none other than his second cousin, Tempest Oleander Hawthorne, who also lived in the area. The clerk checking them in smiled broadly when August mentioned his relative, and for good will, gave him an added week.

Though none of them, including Phuctious, planned on staying that long, each one was curious to see the sights this amazing town had to offer. They were all in such good spirits that everyone agreed to make a little vacation of it.

After asking directions from the clerk—and finding out that Tempest, who was only a decade older than August and lived just a few blocks away—they stopped in at a nearby patisserie and grabbed coffees. Nothing had ever smelled or tasted as good as their first sips of the aromatic beverage. August selected a large cheesecake to take as a present to his cousin.

"Cheesecake seems like an odd choice," Larissa sniffed. "I should think a flan would be more appropriate."

"I have never met a member of the family who could resist a cheesecake, though," August told her. "Personally, I could eat the entire shop."

He ordered a huge sack-full of chocolate croissants, and all of them munched as they navigated the charming streets of Walnut Grove. Every other tree was a walnut tree, and in the distance, they saw several orchards. Tempest resided in the strangest house they had ever seen, quite different from the standard issue homes of his surrounding neighbors. It was lavender colored, cube-shaped, and set on one of its points. The point, of course, had been flattened in order to make a small set of steps going up to a porch with a striped awning over it.

"Ingenious," Phuctious remarked, looking around.

August rang the bell, hoping his cousin was up for company. He hadn't seen him since he was a small boy and his cousin already a teenager at the time. They heard someone walking to the door. A handsome man answered. He wore an embroidered smoking jacket. A turban covered his shoulder-length black hair.

The man cried out, "Cousin!"

He immediately wrapped his arms around August, who kept patting his cousin's back and gritting his teeth as he tolerated the embrace. The others watched. They could tell August wasn't really a hugger. He never hugged men unless it was his own grandfather, and he was leaving on a quest. After introductions were made all around, Tempest Hawthorne seemed to fixate on Phuctious.

"I don't suppose the dwarf could wait on the porch?" he asked in a hopeful tone. "I mean, I really am not in the habit of having dwarves in the house."

His face instantly reddening, Phuctious started to speak, but August cut him off. "This is the Hesperides Heir. You have no doubt heard of him. He brings both good luck and prosperity into every home he enters, Cousin."

"Ah, I see," Tempest said in a doubtful tone. "Well then, all of you come into the kitchen. I will have my cook prepare a quick repast."

As August and Tempest made chitchat, the others gratefully dug into some fresh and delicious food. They couldn't help but notice that every single recipe contained walnuts in some form or another. There was a salad of endive, arugula, buttered lettuce with cranberries, candied walnuts, and a raspberry vinaigrette dressing.

Glazed chicken breasts were rolled in crushed toasted walnuts. Mashed parsnips had walnuts and haricots verte with bacon and walnuts thrown in. Dessert was, of course, walnut pie.

After everyone had finished eating and was enjoying a dessert coffee, Tempest remarked at last, "I assume you have some urgent business to attend to here, or else you would not be in Walnut Grove. Is there some way I can be of assistance?"

August cleared his throat, knowing that he was about to give the sales pitch of his life to a confirmed bachelor who apparently enjoyed living in a very out-of-the-way place as a virtual recluse.

"Cousin, do you happen to have Internet here?" August asked. His abruptness surprised the others. Larissa was particularly surprised, since she hadn't seen any modern technology at all since they'd entered the tastefully decorated house.

"Of course," Tempest grinned, showing at least two gold teeth. "We are up high enough so that we have great Wi-Fi, even though we are surrounded by rainforest."

"Great. I need to show you something that will provide proof of what I am about to tell you."

A few minutes later, they had all moved to what could only be described as a media room. They found themselves surrounded by all the technology that had been missing from the rest of the house.

"Cousin, I know we haven't seen each other for quite some time," August began, "and I apologize for not keeping in touch. But a matter of much gravity and great concern is brewing, and I have come to enlist your formidable skills and your assistance."

Tempest held up one hand. He was already shaking his head, his lips set in a firm line. "Let me save you some time, dear Cousin," he told August. "I have lived all these many years happily because I refuse to pick sides. When I was younger and more involved with the outside world, I saw that the conflict, particularly the conflict between so-called good and evil, especially between the members of the Elemental Claves, which are never ending.

"When I retreated to Walnut Grove, it was more than a choice of lifestyle, it was a statement. I do *not* wish to be included in any defense of Hawthorne family honor, no skirmish to establish superiority of South over North. *None* of that!

"Look at what the last conflict did to the Strondovans of the North," he said, pointedly staring at Larissa. "And while I am at it, not to be rude, but why are you in the company of Larissa North Strondovan?"

August seemed calm and collected, despite what appeared as an early rejection of his proposal. "The fact that we are united and seeking to recruit more allies to our cause should alert you, and hopefully alarm you, as to the precarious position we will all be in, in the very near future."

Reaching into his pocket, he retrieved the small thin golden disc given to him by Andromalius. "You have a Slipdisc player, I trust," he said to Tempest. He handed over the disc. "I believe what you will hear in this recording should be of great interest. I personally think this has something to do with the Dark Powers and may speak to you of the dangers we are facing."

Wordlessly, and with a look of incredulity, Tempest took the small disc and inserted it into the Slipdisc player he retrieved from a small drawer in the same room where they all sat.

Immediately an image, grainy yet visible, appeared on the screen. It was obviously an assembly of entities, all wearing dark cloaks and with masks over their faces. Yet the sound quality was excellent, and they could be heard speaking.

"You might want to forward this a bit," August said, "perhaps to about the twenty-one-minute mark. That is the part you need to hear."

Tempest did just that and turned up the volume.

"Now the matter of Walnut Grove." The speaker at the head of the table looked fearsome, giant in stature and wearing a medieval plague doctors mask. He spoke in a sonorous tone. "We are considering using it as our official headquarters after our victory over the Lightbringers. It will be one of nine domed cities for our Darkness Elite after we enclose the world in our Shroud of Night.

"Naturally, we will have to exterminate the population of Walnut Grove first. The Ghoul Army should enjoy that assignment very much, I believe. By the way, we have already recruited the Ghouls from Derestney Downs. They have sworn their fealty and pledged to serve us."

"Stop!" Tempest shouted. He jumped up. "I want to hear that part again!"

August noticed that his cousin was shaking and seemed to be half in shock. Inwardly, he smiled. Tempest was a very skilled Magical set in his ways, and August had known instinctively that there was nothing that he could offer him this side of heaven that would be a big enough bribe to get him to join the Alliance of Lightbringers.

Only the possibility that everything, his beloved town of Walnut Grove, his oddly shaped cozy little home, and his very life would be taken from him if he didn't fight, would be enough of an incentive to get Tempest on board.

After reviewing the captured, covertly filmed Slipdisc recording again, Tempest agreed to join the Lightbringers. Not only that, but he surprised them all by declaring, "Not only will I bring all that I have in the way of powers to the conflict, but I promise you that I will gather the heads of all of the conniving Magicals present at that meeting. I know I recognized the voices of two Anguis. I am determined that they will die at my own hand."

Satisfied that they had obtained, with August's clever strategy, what they had come for, the questers reluctantly bid farewell to their stalwart and determined host, and to the veritable Shangri-La of Walnut Grove.

Chapter Ten

Roman Strondovan stared in disbelief at the notice he had extracted from the War Pigeon's foot. When he first saw the bird outside his open window, he didn't know whether to be happy or scared. He strode to the kitchen table, sat down, and unrolled the parchment:

Esteemed Roman Armand North Strondovan:

It is by order of the Glanarium Supremo, the highest council of witches in the Magiverse, that you mobilize now. Your clave has been dispersed by your enemies, but the time has come for the great reunion. We have seen the signs.

Make haste, for the time to fight will soon be upon your illustrious clave and those who support you. Guard your life and those of your loved ones. Gather the best tools. Bolster your power with the strongest magical skills at hand.

You must rectify the wrong, clarify the misunderstanding between your clave and that of South Hawthorne. Failure will continue division among witches in the Magiverse, for there are those who desire your family's complete destruction, and those who wish for your success. The dark forces have already fed on this division, seeing it as an opportune moment to band together, grow in power. They continue growing stronger. The aim is to keep us in darkness and ignorance, obliterate our heritage, and rule the world in accordance with their own wishes. Their triumph will be everyone else's despair.

The two rightful claves, North Strondovan and South Hawthorne, must reunite and take their rightful honored places in the Magiverse. It is always with a watchful yet kind eye that we send you this message.

Glanarium Supremo

He read the writing one more time and brought the parchment to his lips. Upon bestowing the kiss of joy, parchment and words vanished. The Glanarium Supremo had sent their long-awaited message at last. Had his wife Eleanor, his brothers and sister, nieces and nephews also received a similar notice?

During the exile, it had pained him to be away from his wife, the love of his life. It had pained him more not seeing his beloved daughter, Larissa, grow up. He cursed silently to himself. He had missed the most wonderful years of her life. Thinking about this during times of solitude, especially with a drink in hand, usually instigated a cascade of bitter tears.

He sat back in a stout wooden chair and gazed around the simple decorated humble abode he'd called home for many years. Tucked away in the charming town of Cuenca, nestled in the country of Ecuador, he considered himself lucky to be near Brazil. Everyone else in his immediate family had scattered themselves to the four corners of the earth, it seemed. At least that's what Quri told him. Quri was one of the best practitioners of *limpias espirituales*—spiritual cleansings—in all of Cuenca. Did she know about the letter first? Would she tell him it was time to head back to the super seven crystal cave in Brazil?

Roman and his wife, Eleanor, hadn't made their home in Ecuador. After living here for a while, he wondered if they hadn't made a mistake. After all, relatives stemming from his father's side had been born and settled in this beautiful country. Ecuador had its own magic, much underplayed by other witches in the Magiverse. When he and Eleanor married, they had set up residence in New Orleans, Louisiana, the hottest place for magic in the States. When his family came under attack by witches intent on seeing him and his clave wiped out completely, he quickly leased out his manor dwelling in the French Quarter and fled the country.

He and Eleanor agreed that neither would tell the other where they were going. It was safer that way. With the help of worthy allies, they entrusted their beloved Larissa to be adopted by a loving family. But now he needed answers. After donning a Panama hat, he quickly got up and headed off to find Quri.

It was Friday, and the marketplace of *Mercado 10 de Agosto* was just getting into the swing of its usual rhythm. Vendors came and set up like they always did, selling a variety of products, including produce, meats, raw milk, fruits, and chocolates to name a few. The upper level served as home to many eateries, with food so tasty that it fed the soul as well as the stomach.

Roman looked all around at the men and women behind the stalls. The women wore traditional South American clothing while the men wore western, modern garb. He studied their shorter stature, the browner skin smooth with youth or showing hardened lines from old age and hard work. Thick black hair covered their heads, and their faces showed a haunting intensity and inner knowing that touched him deeply. Many of these people represented the indigenous folks of South America.

Their history was a pedigree of survival, endurance, and cunning, one that should have made any of them proud of their heritage and ancestry that scanned at least eleven thousand years. They understood the land and nature and how to work in harmony with it. Sadly, they were often seen as nothing more than inferior peasants by those in the upper echelons of society.

He walked to the bottom floor and headed toward a group of women who had already started their work. Taking in a deep breath, Roman closed his eyes and inhaled the rich scent of the market. Where was she, the lady he always saw each Friday? She was late, an unusual occurrence.

"I did not forget you," a throaty voice filled Roman's ear.

He opened his eyes and saw Quri, a short strongly-built woman with a large, wrapped bundle on her back. The white parcel held the tools for her spiritual cleansings. Today, she wore a bright pink dress with a blue checkered apron. Pockets at the bottom held the funds collected from clients.

"I was about to select another healer." Roman smiled, teasing the woman.

"You wouldn't dare." Quri laughed. "I have been guarding you all these years. It is I who reveals to you what is permitted."

"*Por supuesto*—of course. But why are you late?"

"Never mind." Her eyes glittered as a wizened smile crossed her lips. "*Vámonos*—let's go. I have much to tell you."

Narrowing his eyes, Roman followed her in silence and great curiosity to the place where the other women did their *limpias*—cleansings—to eager, paying clients.

Quri walked down to the far end of the line of women and motioned for Roman to sit in the vacant chair. This was her designated workspace, separated several feet from the others. She confided in him that a spell had been placed around it. If anyone tried to use her spot, an overwhelming sense of anxiety and a feeling of discomfort filled the intruder and they simply moved elsewhere.

She removed the bundle from her back and quickly set up the workspace around her, lining up a couple of glass cups, a bucket of eggs, a bag filled with flower petals, bundled herbs, water, and two bottles filled with a liquid concoction so mysterious that even a seasoned witch such as Roman had scratched his head many times, trying to guess what made up the sprays and pours Quri used.

The healer finished with her prep work and faced her client. "You got your letter. How do you feel?"

Roman smiled. She knew. "I—I can hardly believe it. I have lived here for years, trying to create a life for myself in a foreign land, always longing for this day, waiting, questioning if it would ever come. Now that it has, I still don't believe it."

Quri's face grew solemn. "The Glanarium Supremo has decided on the right moment. The members reviewed history, current events, and made their decision. Now it's time for action." She placed her face within an inch of his and whispered, "Roman Strondovan, no more feeling lost and helpless. You and your family will rise again."

He gazed at her. "You have been my source of comfort and wisdom from the first day you made yourself known to me. Had it not been so, I would have gone mad, most likely." Roman turned his gaze to the floor.

"My job guarding you," said Quri, "is to be a source of knowledge and a beacon of light—and to keep you safe. It is an honor serving you." The lady bowed slightly. "I shall miss it, because you cannot remain here in Cuenca much longer."

Roman knew that as a Remnant, one of the remaining few of what was once a long-reigning clave, his family had been provided overseers by the Glanarium Supremo. It was they who reported back to the highest group of witches. The old feud between the Strondovans and Hawthornes had been long-standing. What really happened between the two claves? He had heard nebulous stories. No matter how much magic he'd used, the answers wouldn't readily come.

"The answers you wanted were meant for others. Your time for learning is now." Quri eyed the man with a knowing look and picked up an egg from her bucket. "Ready?"

Roman prepared himself for the cleansing. Maybe answers would come today, unlike the cleansings before. But as the older woman suggested, perhaps the former *limpias* were never meant to be a revelation in the way he was searching. They only told about himself, instructed on ways to keep sane, maintain his magical skills, and begin a plan for resuming life again with an intact family.

With deft speed, Quri tapped the egg on each of Roman's shoulders, arms, chest, back, and head. Following the tapping came the vigorous rubbing of the egg over all his body. Each time he'd held his breath, fearful she'd break it, leaving him a sticky mess. It never happened, but there was always a first time.

The older woman finished and sat next to Roman. "Now we see what the egg reveals." She filled one of the glass cups with a small amount of water. With one crack, the contents of the egg filled the bottom part of the cup. Quri eyed everything, watching intently the way the white part spread out in tendrils, how the yolk looked. In an instant, the yolk ruptured, creating a pool of yellow.

"Mmm," said the woman, pursing her lips in curiosity. "You need to see this, for it is not I who will diagnose this time."

Roman leaned over and took the cup Quri pushed into his hands. This was never done. Not that he'd ever seen. He gazed into the glass just like he would into a scrying sphere or smoked mirror. At once, he saw her. The face of his beloved bride. Eleanor looked older but every bit as beautiful. She looked directly at him and smiled. His heart raced. Just as he dipped a finger toward her face, the image disappeared. Inside the cup, everything immediately hardened, transforming into a citrine crystal with several points, all resting on bed of quartz.

Roman looked at Quri with surprise. "Has this ever happened before to people you've cleansed?"

"No. You aren't like my other clients, either. Remember that." She took the cup from him and emptied the crystal formation into his hands. "Keep this with you. A very good sign, I might add. Citrine dispels negative energy and transmutes it to positive. There will be joy in your life now."

"She's coming. I'll see her again soon. Very soon." Roman kissed the stone and held it momentarily to his chest.

"All is being revealed to you now. You were kept in darkness for safety." Quri placed the empty cup by her supplies and grasped one of her bundles of herbs. "Breathe in."

Smelling the bundles sent many clients gasping for breath or stirred up a bout of coughing. The aromatics Quri sprayed on them were strong and sent one's nostrils into a burning frenzy. Roman had grown used to it, had hoped each time the aroma would trigger insight into his family. He breathed in the scent from the bundle pushed against his face. His eyes watered. The breath hitched in his throat. Again he closed his eyes, squeezing them shut.

A silhouette of a girl appeared in his mind's eye. He noted the slender outline of her face, long hair. This person he'd never seen, yet something felt familiar about her. An instantaneous longing gripped him. Who was she and why was she appearing to him now? Quri shoved the bundle of herbs against his face again.

"Breathe deeper."

Roman coughed. He'd had enough and pushed the herbs away. The older woman rubbed her hands over his face and through his dark brown hair. "What on earth is in that scent?" He sputtered the words.

"My secret. I've kept it quiet this whole time. I'll not reveal it now." Quri smiled. "We've just begun." She tapped the herb bundle over his body, just like she did with the egg. Roman braced himself. Now came what felt like a mild thrashing. The woman whipped and brushed the bundle all over him, slapping at his arms, back, shoulders. She even lifted his shirt to make sure her herbs had touched everywhere.

When Quri finished, she grabbed up a couple of bottles and sprayed Roman with a round of other strong scents, but not before making him inhale the aroma of them directly from her hands. He coughed some more, nearly reeling.

"Did you make your concoctions especially strong today?" Roman managed to ask between breaths. "*Dios mio*—my god—these are strong!"

"Just keep concentrating." Quri put the bottles back. She filled her mouth with some water and blew it all over him. Roman flinched. This part always caught new customers off-guard. The next part was better, when the woman took a mouthful of flower petals and blew them all over him. He sniffed the scent of roses and a hint of wildflowers. That was at least bearable. But she wasn't quite finished yet. She spent a few moments adjusting his neck, never minding the cracking sounds.

"Relax. I've not broken any bones, yet." She smiled at him.

"I'm just waiting for my luck to run out."

Quri let out a short laugh. "One last thing and we're done. You know the routine."

Roman nodded. The first time she had done this to him, he almost bolted from the marketplace. From a small jar, she dipped in her finger and removed a small amount of a special salve she'd made. Again, she refused to share with him the ingredients. He gritted his teeth. This part he disliked the most. Quri remained serious as she applied her salve-laden finger to his navel and at the top crack of his buttocks, taking a few seconds to rub everything in.

"You're done. Pay very close attention to any visions or strong intuitions today. They will come. Try to understand their meaning. Be prepared to follow if you feel directed or led to do something."

"Will do. But I have a question. I saw another person, a girl, during the cleansing. I don't know who she is, but something about it all seemed familiar on the most primitive level."

"Perhaps she was your beloved daughter?" Quri's gaze met Roman's.

"Do you think she's okay? Do you know what she's doing now, where she is?"

"You have a lot of questions. All will be revealed in good time. For now, we are done. Be gone and get ready for the rest of your life. I will miss you, my friend." Quri patted Roman's shoulder.

"And I will miss you. Thank you for everything." Roman got up and hugged her. "What will you do now? Will I ever see you again?"

"I go where the Glanarium Supremo sends me. For now, I've decided to stay in this charming town." She smiled. "As for meeting again, it is always possible, depending on the events. Blessings to you and your family." Quri pushed Roman lightly away. "Now go. There is much for you to do."

Roman turned on his heel and headed out of the marketplace. Emotions ranged from sadness on leaving Quri and Cuenca to excitement on seeing his family again to pure anxiety on what might happen next.

***

The Tomebamba River flowed through the middle of the city. Currents rushed over rocks, having started from the Cajas National Park, and sailed their way on down to the mighty Amazon. Like he often did, Roman sat down on a grassy patch and stared at the rushing, crisp water. Bikers rode by, couples dotted the bank. Sitting in this area always brought an immediate peace. After his meeting with Quri, however, he didn't feel the usual peace.

His solar plexus area clenched. The nerves in his body perked up. An unexplained anticipation gripped him with a force that made him pay attention. He tried easing an overactive mind and sipped a beer, focusing on the river, determining his next move. The citrine crystal inside his pocket at once sent out a tingling sensation against his leg. Roman removed it. The amber points glinted in the sun. Mesmerized by its beauty, he gazed into the center of the stone.

Would she come again, his beloved Eleanor? He had to communicate with her some way. Now that he'd received the green light from the Glanarium Supremo, reaching out to his family was expected. Wasn't that what was meant by the great reunion?

It could be nothing else. Roman shifted his gaze from the stone to the water, at once curious at the mist rising from the middle of the river. On closer inspection, the condensation appeared to be taking on the form of a woman. When he concentrated harder, it all dispersed, with nothing but the currents moving on as if nothing happened.

"Are you hungry, my love?"

A woman's voice rang out where he sat. Roman thrust the crystal back in his pocket, looked up, and scrambled to his feet. He gazed several seconds, studying the person's features. Age always took its toll on Mortals. Though witches aged, they seemed to battle time much better. She wasn't the young one he'd married years ago, but the face was still just as smooth and pleasant to behold.

"Eleanor, you've come!" He stood entranced, breathless, hardly able to comprehend reality.

The woman placed her picnic basket on the ground and fell into her husband's embrace. "How I've missed you!"

Their lips met. He didn't care if anyone saw their display of affection. Nothing else mattered. His beloved had come all the way to Cuenca to meet him. She was real, from the feeling of her body pressed against his to the smell of her hair and a light fresh floral scent of perfume on her skin. He kissed her on the lips, cheeks, forehead, and back to her lips. Her fingers ran through his dark locks. His fingers laced through her ginger ones.

"You changed the color of your hair!" Roman stepped back and studied his wife. "Where have you been all this time, and how did you get here?" he whispered in her ear.

"Remember the Vanishport, or have you become that rusty in magic? Being half witch from my father's side, I have the capacity to indulge in the higher magical conveniences." She kissed him again. "Have you forgotten after all these years?"

"Perhaps time has been a culprit. But I think mere excitement of having you again has clouded all my knowledge for the moment."

"I changed my hair color as a disguise. Where have I been all this time? Cloistered away in an abbey in Austria."

"An abbey?" Roman laughed. "That seems almost sacrilegious."

"Not at all, dear. I can make a convincing case that I am a person in need of sanctuary. The sisters took me in and treated me with great kindness."

"Why an abbey, of all things? There are so many quaint dwellings in Austria. The country alone is magnificent. And you couldn't see any of it?" Roman wrinkled his brow at his wife's story.

"Trust me, I had ways of sneaking out and returning with no one noticing. I have ways of creating an illusion of my own image and fooling the best of Mortals. I had to have a lifestyle that would keep me in a certain rhythm and occupied during the day, or I would have gone mad. I missed you terribly. Worse, I missed our daughter. I didn't even have a baby picture I could tuck away in a special locket and gaze at her when I wanted."

"To do so would have been dangerous. You know that," Roman admonished his wife gently, holding her close.

"True, but danger doesn't strip the longing away. Instead, it fires the flames of a mother's love. Did you not feel the same?"

"If I had a gold piece for every hour I've wept for her, we would be rich beyond belief. I'm a man with a father's love. No less than yours." He squeezed her arm lightly.

"Of course. I didn't mean to be thoughtless." Eleanor stared out across the water. "Why did you choose this town, and all the way in South America?"

"The same reason you chose Austria. We all needed to be far apart. Scattered. Besides, I have cousins in Quito. Remember?" He smiled.

"Ah, I had forgotten. You've never met them, have you?

"No." Roman gazed toward the river in thought. "It will be time to meet them, though. I'm just not sure when." He looked into Eleanor's eyes. "We could use their help, you know."

She nodded.

"Let me show you around Cuenca, and then we must plan our next step."

"We eat first," said Eleanor. She pointed to a basket and sat down beside her husband.

***

Roman and Eleanor shielded their eyes as they gazed back at the *Cathedral del Inmaculada*.

"What a magnificent structure," said Eleanor.

"The architecture here is magnificent. Reminiscent of olden times. The styles in this town show styles that are Romanesque, Gothic, and Renaissance."

The New Cathedral, as it was commonly known, had tours where people could climb to the top of its towers. Being a witch hadn't stopped Roman from indulging in a tour and climbing too, when he first arrived. He'd always admired the bright blue domes on top. He and Eleanor had just descended and stood near the flower market, which added color and a vibrant energy. Customers surrounded the stalls.

"Will you buy me some flowers?" She smiled and laced her arm through Roman's.

"I would be delighted to buy you anything you want." He led the way, and the couple spent several minutes browsing before coming away with a wrapped bouquet of brilliant-topped stems she had chosen.

"Let's have a drink and celebrate." Roman led his wife to a window on the side of the cloister.

"*Dos Aguas de Pitimas*," he said to the woman inside the window. "You have to taste this." He paid and led his wife away.

He handed Eleanor a cup filled with a vibrant, pink-tinted drink. She lifted the drink to her nose, sniffing with curiosity.

"A most unusual drink," Roman added. "Go on. Take a sip."

Eleanor followed as instructed. "Oh, my! Tastes like I swallowed a field of wildflowers."

"This drink is made from dozens of flowers and herbs. No one knows what's in it."

"It's very relaxing." Eleanor took a longer drink and closed her eyes." She opened them after a few seconds. "Did you see her?"

"Who?"

"I just saw the darkened image of a girl in my head. It must be this." Eleanor pointed to the drink.

"I think I saw earlier today what you just did. It was on inhaling a drought of some mysterious liquid when I was in the marketplace."

His wife gazed at him in curiosity. "I sense so strongly it's our daughter. We have to try and reach out to her some way."

"Let's go home," Roman said.

From across the flower market, a lone male figure stood hidden in the shadows. He held what appeared to be an ordinary newspaper in his hand. He'd seen the couple with the flowers and drinks. Quickly, Daniel typed a code on a blank space where a picture would be. *"I have seen them. Together. It's all starting. We must prepare."* The young man disappeared in the shadows of a doorway.

***

In the countries of Germany, Australia, and Canada, Roman Strondovan's siblings, Brendan, Henry, and Andrea prepared for their journeys. They too had to leave. From other parts of the world, their children also headed out from where they had been in hiding for the last several years.

Chapter Eleven

Roman and Eleanor sat at the table, viewing an Egyptian papyrus while they sipped hot herbal tea. Roman held a magical brush pen, the companion to an equally magical sheet. A few seconds earlier, the couple's attention had been drawn to a drawer in a cabinet. They looked on as the drawer rattled at first, and finally shot open, loosening the papyrus and matching pen to its rightful owner.

The couple watched, wide-eyed. A message in sepia-colored writing flashed across the sheet:

pass code

Roman squinted his eyes, reading and thinking. This message was as important as one from a war pigeon. More so because of the manner in which it was sent. Many witches possessed a magical sheet and pen of their choice used for far more secret messages. Another witch could see a war pigeon, but sheets and pens were more personal.

The fact that the message had no name or secret username preceding the request for a code intrigued him most. That was always the way messages like this were sent and such communication started. But who was writing to him? It could be none other than one of his family members, and it surely wasn't from Larissa. That much he felt sure of.

He had to rack his memory for the passwords he used with his siblings. There was one the entire family used for general communication but private, nonetheless. And there were ones used privately between any two people. The problem now, which sibling and which pass code to use—or use the family one?

"Do you know it?" Eleanor rested her hand lightly over his.

"What a hellacious time for using this." Roman scowled.

"Hurry up, dear, before the message disappears. Remember, there are time limits on whatever is being sent."

"Yes. All for security, I know."

She tapped his shoulder, urging him to focus.

He took up his brush pen and wrote on a blank space the code for the family. A red X flared over what was written. Roman tried one of his sibling's codes. Same red X.

"Damn!" He grunted in exasperation. It was the code for his sister, Andrea. She had always been the organizer among them.

"Perhaps it's Brendon? After all, you were always closest with him."

Roman grimaced and quickly wrote the code for his sibling. Just in time, too, because the countdown numbers popped up at the top of the sheet, almost running out before the sender would have to try again or give a hint. It worked:

Where are you, my brother? It is time we meet. Where?

Eleanor gazed at her husband. "We were just talking about this very thing. Where should we meet now that we've been given the go-ahead?"

He took up the pen and quickly wrote:

In Ecuador. Where are you?

A question mark popped up in reply. The following message appeared afterward:

Left Germany. Spending night in another small town. Do we meet in Brazil? *smile*

Roman answered:

Best place so far. You know where.

Brendan replied:

Yes. Will contact Henry and Andrea. They will tell their children—you tell yours.

As with each message, the letters vanished in a sepia-colored cloud. One last message of bye from Brendan, and that was it. The papyrus floated up from the table and properly returned itself to the drawer, followed by the pen. The drawer shut with a loud thud.

Eleanor sat back in her chair, sipping from the earthen mug in her hand. "How do we communicate with her? What do we say?" She looked over at her spouse.

"Rather strange to be communicating now, isn't it? It's been so long. The Glanarium Supremo had forbidden any attempts at familial communication for our safety. The children were young when they were sent away."

"And to think now that they are adults with their own minds." She watched as her spouse poured more tea into their mugs. "When do we reach out, Roman? Do you have a certain feeling on this? We all need to meet in the same place, create a game plan."

Roman narrowed his eyes and glanced over at his wife. "What about your sister, Dorenda? Have you completely forgotten about her?"

His wife sank back in her chair, staring out the window. "Mind if I borrow your papyrus and brush pen?"

With the snap of his fingers and a quick incantation, the items issued forth from the drawer and landed easily back down on the table once again.

"Here I go. I'll send her a message." Would Dorenda remember her username and code? Eleanor picked up the brush pen and began, being more revealing than her brother-in-law:

ravengirl
pass code

She waited several seconds with bated breath, heart racing in her chest. There had been no good-byes between them. Through the years she had wanted to talk to Dorenda badly. Though her sister was not of Strondovan blood or married into the family, she could still be a target for ill will since she was related to someone connected to Roman's family line.

With a sigh, she gazed up at her husband. "What if she's—?"

"Wait, look!" Roman pointed to the papyrus. "I think she's writing something." The message read:

Dear sister! Is it really you? Can we see each other first before sending messages? I want to see your face."

Roman and Eleanor stared at each other with questioning looks.

"You could talk to your sister via scrying, but I would keep it brief. Someone could always hear. Give no specific information. I would continue the specifics with our papyrus and pen."

Eleanor penned back:

Let's crystal talk for a moment.

Within seconds, Roman retrieved his prized crystal sphere and placed it on the table. He quickly closed all blinds in the windows and lit a large thick candle. When finished, he seated himself beside his wife. "Ready?"

She nodded and turned toward the sphere, rubbing her hands on it's smooth surface. Concentrating hard on her sister, she focused on Dorenda's name and the last memory of her image. It was the best she could do since being away for so long. Dorenda's face appeared in the sphere. A smile pulled across her lips.

Eleanor wiped at the tears welling in her eyes. "Sister, is that you? I've missed you so much."

Dorenda's lips quivered. "Same here. I have waited so long to hear from you and wondered if I ever would. My biggest fear was that perhaps something had happened."

"As you can see, I'm still here. There will be lots to talk about. Now that we've seen each other, can we continue talking our other way? It would be safer."

"Agree," said Dorenda. "I only wanted to see your face again, hear your voice, if only for a moment."

"And I you. I will send you a message and we'll catch up on the details."

The sphere went back to its natural clear quartz state, and Roman placed it back where he kept his magical tools. For the next several minutes, Dorenda apprised her sister of how she had guarded and taught Larissa from a tender young age until the moment she was called on by the Glanarium Supremo to team up with August and begin their mission. She shared how Rick and Amy Martin were loving and kind parents, and how it was difficult informing them of what happened—without revealing too much. Dorenda suggested the following, a message that also appeared on the magical papyrus:

You should try and reach out to your daughter. Now is as good a time as any. She's smart, intuitive, and she wants her family back, to know who her true parents are.

Eleanor responded:

And August? Is he truly to be trusted?

Roman nodded in approval at the question. He'd silently been watching everything and mouthed to her about August during the communication. His wife smiled back after she wrote the question.

Dorenda responded:

They seemed okay when I spoke to them last. Didn't start out that way, though. They must come together. There is no other way.

Eleanor wrote back:

True. The feud must end, and no more hiding. Nothing good coming from it. I must go. We will communicate more.

Dorenda wrote back:

Please keep in touch. Remember that I love you and have never forgotten you. I have been lighting candles and performing rituals for your safety since we parted. Be well, my dear sister.

The words dispersed, and both papyrus and pen returned to the drawer.

***

Dorenda sat back, grinning. Good. Her sister had finally reached out. This occurrence she had been expecting lately. Communication with Eleanor was bittersweet at best. She had missed her sibling terribly over the years, that much was true. But life changed along the way. Time marched on, and other opportunities had made some grave shifts in her personal goals. She glanced at the visitor in the corner who had overheard the conversation but remained out of sight. He had also reviewed the exchange of messages.

"Wasn't I correct in saying that your sister would be contacting you soon?" Daniel smiled.

The older woman remained silent. She knew the biggest battles were about to ensue. Power and greed not only held Mortals in a tight grip, it did the same with witches. A fight for ruling over others. A race to gain the most resources. A contest to see who used them the best. A desire to bend one to another's will. Age-old ideals for age-old battles.

Daniel tapped his fingers on the arm of his chair. "Are you any closer to spinning a complete functioning conjuring cloth? You've been at it for some time."

Dorenda shook her head. "I'm still working on it. There's something I'm missing, and I can't for the life of me find out what it is." She sighed and stared at her hands in thought.

She hadn't lied to her niece, Larissa, when she said a beautiful being informed her in a dream about creating the cloth. According to Magical lore, creators of the coveted conjuring cloths were half human, half angel. Dorenda had contemplated this subject a lot. Based on her studies of these beings and their place in history, they were dying out long before the final destruction of Atlantis, which resembled nothing compared to the first glory days when humans walked among deities.

By the time both continents of Atlantis and Lemuria lay submerged on the ocean floors, Nephilim surely ceased to exist—unless there were descendants along the way. Were there any spiritual beings in the cosmos that would deign to mate with a human this day and age, or even a hundred or couple hundred years ago? When Dorenda learned that Larissa's great great aunt, Ciana, was a Nephilim and still alive, the ancient lore concerning witch spinners became a full-fledged reality to her.

But was there more to the lore? Were Nephilim the only beings with the ability to create conjuring cloths? Dorenda always asked herself this question. Nephilim held angelic qualities, for sure, but divine knowledge had mostly been imparted to Magicals and Mortals alike all throughout history, especially to those who so earnestly sought it. Surely, it was not randomly selected creators who could weave such a wonderful powerful cloth. Perhaps those who sought knowledge and wanted to learn the craft could do so as well. And knowledge such as this would only be shared with a select worthy few. Why else would Ciana have visited her the first time?

Daniel broke the momentary silence. "If you want to remain useful to our cause, you'll need to find out the missing pieces soon." He leaned forward in his chair. A sober expression covered his face. "Edouard is running out of patience, and he won't rule out the possibility of extinguishing you altogether, if the mood hits." He rubbed his lower lip. "I only say this not to be harsh, but as a friend warning another."

"I'm perfectly aware of the risks." Dorenda fought back a wave of agitation consuming her. "Maybe I need a new approach. There has to be more. I'm simply too close."

"Just remember, at some point you will need to deliver." With that last statement, Daniel said his goodbyes and left.

Outside the rain poured, tapping drops against the windowpanes. For what should have been such a glorious day communicating with her long-lost sister, the day couldn't be drearier. But the truth cut through Dorenda's heart the most. She and Eleanor would not be picking up where they left off the moment the two were parted by ill-fated circumstances. Other deals had been made. Temptations had won her over, and like others, she had fallen helplessly into the deep well.

And what of Larissa, her beloved niece? The older lady rested her head back and closed her eyes. She truly loved her niece. Unfortunately, she had come to love other things more. The beauty of teaching Larissa just about everything she knew is that she knew everything the young woman could do. Building up one for success could easily be shifted into reverse, leading to a tearing-down little by little or in one big swoop, a wave of a powerful wand or perhaps a strong spell.

A very delicate situation lay before her, and for a moment, Dorenda considered possibly stepping back. To betray her family suddenly seemed unpalatable. The ugly truth, she may have gotten herself in too deep. There could only be one way out of this, and it might be risky at best. If Larissa could communicate with Ciana, why couldn't she? After all, Ciana appeared in a dream before her niece even knew of witch spinners. Dorenda grinned, eyes sparkling. The answer had been so obvious. With some finesse, maybe she had a plan that could get her out of a huge predicament. And surely dear Edouard wouldn't be so unkind to her as Daniel suggested. One thing she knew for sure, regardless. Failure on her part was not an option.

***

Larissa awoke from a fitful sleep. The travels from Walnut Grove and all the other heightened activity before that had left her exhausted. The fact that a sound slumber failed her created a bout of irritation. Her dreams had been veiled and hazy the last few days, and tonight, sleep wouldn't come easily. Something was changing. Her solar plexus area tightened to the point of creating a dull ache that nearly drove her to irritation. She sat up and stared out. Obviously, her companions felt nothing. They were out cold, snoring away, oblivious to everything right now.

Tonight they rested in a zone of woods, heading for nowhere, it seemed. All had reached a blank in their plans. Not sure of how to proceed next or where to go, they all pitched camp under an old sprawling oak and had eaten a light dinner from some of their food rations. No one had advised of anything unusual. She hadn't heard from her Aunt Dorenda lately. Surely, August had to be bluffing about her aunt and web of lies. The thought of such possibilities cut her to the core. If she couldn't trust her beloved aunt, then whom could she trust? She had trusted Edouard once, but now that notion was dashed to smithereens.

Somewhere deep within her being, a longing overtook her, so bold and decisive she almost gasped like one fighting the effects of a slow suffocation. At once, she wanted her mother. Not Amy Martin, the only mother figure she'd ever known, but the biological woman who birthed her.

Where was this feeling coming from? What drove the sensations? It wasn't normal. Yes, she wanted to know her biological family, once Dorenda told her she might have one, if they hadn't all been totally wiped out by now. Something told her intuitively that they still existed, yet she had nothing to substantiate the thoughts.

Should she discuss it with Willem? He surely could tell her the reasons for such an onslaught of emotions. Except for a couple of stressful moments, they got along so well. Much of the time he seemed to have his finger on the pulse of delicate situations. His kindness and input always amazed her.

Quickly, she rummaged through the bag carrying her magical tools and withdrew a palm-sized clear quartz crystal sphere. She slipped out from her sleeping space and into the night. The chill hit her skin. She gripped the edges of her cloak and wrapped it tighter. There was no sound but the rush of the night breeze through the grass and trees. Tonight, the moon wore a hazy soft white veil.

Larissa walked across the grass and sat under an elm tree and gazed across the field. Her eyes strained in the darkness, trying to discern any shadows, and if they were real or merely imagination. She wanted answers and the next direction in her quest with August and now Willem, who showed up one day and stayed with them ever since. Yes, maybe she should discuss her feelings with Willem. Being the competent wizard he was, he could surely shed some light on her troubling thoughts. No matter how hard she wanted a confidante, the nagging decision needled her. She needed to discover answers on her own.

She held the small sphere in her hand, said an invocation to activate its powers, and sat still, gazing into its depths. The ball immediately lit up, turned cloudy, and returned to its former clarity. Her pulse quickened. The speedy activation stunned her. Someone or something was intent on communicating with her. Larissa sat up straighter and peered closer into the ball. Two faces morphed into view, those of a man and a woman.

The woman spoke first. "Is it you, Larissa North Strondovan?"

Larissa's gut tightened with a mix of excitement and a twinge of dread. "Yes." Her words bore a trace of uncertainty. "Who are you, and what do you want?"

"We are your parents, Larissa."

The young woman's eyes shot wide open. She took in a deep breath, steadying herself from nearly falling over in shock. For the first time, she heard the voices of her biological parents. Her mouth refused to move.

"Did you understand?" Eleanor asked. "This is sudden. We found a connection by way of your crystal sphere. We were searching for just such a way. Perhaps you were searching for us, too?"

Larissa shook her head, trying to ward off a wayward strand of hair the breeze had carelessly tossed against her face. Tears welled up in her eyes, and she cursed the lump forming in her throat. "I felt you. That's why I came out here. I couldn't stay still any longer. I wanted to see both of you so much." Unable to contain her emotions, tears streamed from her eyes. Her lower lip trembled and she choked back a sob.

"Are you happy or distressed?" Eleanor's face clouded with a flash of momentary worry.

"I'm just overwhelmed, I think." Larissa sucked in a throatful of crisp night air. "I was not expecting this. You came. I wanted you, and you came."

"Parents want their children as much as they want us." Roman smiled. "You're beautiful, just like I saw you in my visions and in a special crystal I have."

"You've seen me before?" Larissa relaxed a little. "How come I've never seen you?"

"It wasn't permitted. Too risky. It took everything I and your mother had within us to stay still."

Eleanor chimed in. "But all that has changed now. The risk must be taken. The Glanarium Supremo said so."

"I've received nothing from the Glanarium Supremo or a war pigeon or any other message."

"It was us who needed to reach out to you first, when we knew the time was right." Eleanor smiled. "Your father is correct. You are truly beautiful, and it grieves us to the quick that we missed all the younger years of your life."

Larissa gazed at her parents, taking in their features. Dorenda was right about the resemblance with her mother. And her father was as handsome as she had heard, with his dark hair and intent eyes.

"I guess this wasn't the way you thought we'd be introduced. Quite a surprise, eh?" said Roman.

"It's the best surprise in the world." Larissa smiled. "Can I come home now, wherever home is?"

"Home is not in Kansas, that much we can say." Eleanor chuckled. Her eyes sparkled like diamonds, and Larissa noted her mother's remarkable beauty, the kind face and flowing hair.

"I'll go to the ends of the earth, the outermost dimensions; anywhere you are, I'll go." Larissa's words spilled out with the urgency coursing through her body. "Where are you now?"

Roman spoke up. "We need you to come . . ."

Waiting for the anticipated instructions, Larissa's heart sank when the sphere's light shut off, leaving nothing more than a smooth polished orb glistening in the soft hazy moonlight. She glanced around and saw a figure walking toward her. Quickly, she wrapped her ball within the folds of her cloak. Much to her relief, it was Willem making his way toward her.

"Ah, so you're here." He seated himself next to Larissa and took the liberty offered by the darkness to wrap his arm around her.

"You were looking for me? Is everything okay?" Larissa asked. "Surely we're not being attacked by god knows what."

"No." He nuzzled against her face. "I tried reaching out to you in a dream, and you weren't there. I did some deeper searching and found you out here. Why are you up?"

"I'm sorry I missed the dream. You know I look forward to those, don't you?" She nuzzled him in return.

"As do I. But again, why are you up?"

"I just had some things on my mind, that's all. Too deep to get into at this hour." Larissa determined that the next opportune time that came around, she'd talk further with him about what she just learned. Part of her wanted to make their dreamtimes a reality and do him right here under the moon and the old tree. A greater part of her barely contained the excitement bubbling inside. She had just met her birth parents under the most unusual of circumstances, and it was all she could do to keep from screaming with joy.

"What's really going on, Larissa?" said Willem. "I sense a strong energy coming from you, something different that I've never felt before." He gazed at her intently. "You seem almost electrified, like something has wound you up so tight that you'll burst or explode if you don't release yourself."

"You know, Willem, sometimes the way you just described me is the way I feel about you many times, though I don't let on." She landed a light kiss on his lips. "I think I have an idea on how to release this electrified energy you mentioned."

Chapter Twelve

The early morning shone through the dining room window of Roman's house. He and Eleanor had arisen together after neither could go back to sleep.

"We must speak to them, my cousins here in Ecuador," said Roman. He stirred his cup of steaming coffee, thinking, as he sat back in his chair.

"You've never met them. How do you go about an introduction followed by an intense discussion of what we're up against?" Eleanor raised a coffee cup to her lips and gazed at her husband.

"We've contacted everyone we need to right now. My brother, your sister, and our most beautiful daughter." He closed his eyes and smiled. "We need a proper celebration when we meet her. You know that, don't you?"

"And we shall have it. It will most likely include Mr. Hawthorne as well. He's with her. How will this set with you? Your family and his have been sworn enemies for a long time."

Roman frowned. "That's what I've been taught ever since I was able to know better. It's lore not only between our families but throughout the Magiverse."

Eleanor cut her husband a sideways glance. "Have you not ever tried getting to the truth of the matter? Really dig deep and find out what happened?"

"Crystal spheres, smoked mirrors and gazing pools will only reveal to you the answers, if they want to. Many of us have tried and to no avail. The secrets and answers simply won't come. Nothing."

"After all these years? I don't understand what the secret is. I would have thought it more beneficial to clear up the misunderstanding right away." Eleanor rested her head against the high-backed chair, musing on the subject.

"Unless," continued Roman, "there is no simple answer or there's something darker at play." He looked over at his wife and rested a hand on hers. "I've been thinking about this more since we've all been separated. I'm suspecting something darker, and worse. I have a sneaking suspicion it's more than a murder out of anger. Besides, Uncle Desmond was an honorable witch. He would never do something as nefarious as harming someone. He knew quite well the consequences of breaking certain laws, and not just in the Mortal world, either."

"Would someone else have wanted to harm Clement South Hawthorne? Any Mortal or any Magical have a grudge or a bone to pick with him?" Eleanor shrugged. "Could be, you know. And poor Desmond happened to be at the wrong place at the wrong time."

"This subject is far from over. But now, back to my cousins." Roman smiled. "Before we leave Cuenca, we need to quickly go to Quito and find them. They might know something."

Eleanor smiled at her spouse. "I'll go wherever you wish, my dear."

***

To Roman and Eleanor, the seven-hour drive from Cuenca to Quito may have appeared pleasant and uneventful, but ever-watchful eyes followed them. When the couple arrived at an attractive condominium complex and parked their car in a space for visitors, they were all but inside the entrance of the building when another car parked a few spaces down.

A young man watched with interest in the rearview mirror. He pulled a small crystal sphere out of the console resting between the driver and passenger seats. When he activated the sphere, another male's face came into view.

"I followed them. They're here in Quito," said Dennis, the driver of the car. "They just went inside one of the condo buildings here."

"Were you able to get any information, who they are visiting and why?"

Dennis shook his head. "A little too secretive, I'm afraid."

"Do you think they suspect anything?" From the ball, Edouard's face showed a look of frustration.

"I can't tell. They seem pretty carefree to me."

"Trust me, I'm sure they're anything but carefree. To be so hush-hush as they are." Edouard sighed. "Try and see if you can break through any of their barriers. Surely one of them has to be somewhat careless and give us access to a vulnerable spot."

Dennis grinned. "Kind of like the dragon with the soft underbelly, eh?"

"Let me remind you," Edouard said, scowling as he spoke, "those two so-called dragons have precious treasures galore. Lest you forget, they are royalty, descendants from a long line of prominent elemental witches. That family technically is as old as time itself."

"As are all elemental claves. Doesn't time run out for all things at one point or another?" said Dennis.

Edouard laughed. "Excellent statement, my dear friend. That's why I took you and Daniel in as prominent members of Order of the Chevron. Our intent is to eradicate this family and anyone or anything else that stands in our way of becoming a leading power of the world. You both are doing good work."

"I'll keep an eye out and ears perked up."

"See that you do. We need to find out why they left Cuenca and are visiting people in Quito. And heaven knows where they are headed next."

The crystal ball went dark and ended up in its protective bag inside the console.

***

Roman and Eleanor walked across a decorative tiled floor of an attractive lobby and took an elevator up to the floor where his cousin lived. Before leaving Cuenca, he had contacted Paulo Narea, a relative from one of his father's brothers. The Narea family, as it turned out, was one of several prominent families in Quito. One night, Roman had used candle magic and a contact spell for reaching out to his cousin.

Paulo was overjoyed. *"Primo mio*—my cousin—how wonderful it is to hear from you."

The man's smile and shining eyes had made an impression on Roman, and he liked his cousin immediately. They spent a few moments with basic small-talk and the remainder of the conversation was spent sending brief messages back and forth through the magical papyrus and pen. This meeting was too important to risk anyone hearing or tapping in too much. There was an agreement that the only time they would speak out loud is when nothing important was being said.

When the door opened, a man greeted them with a broad smile. He hugged Roman and Eleanor. "Welcome, please come in." Paulo shut the door and ushered his guests into a spacious living room filled with ornate furniture and crystal chandeliers hanging from the ceiling. "Ah, it's so good to finally meet you. Please, have a seat anywhere you wish."

The condo, having been on one of the upper stories, allowed a magnificent view of the city. Roman stood with a transfixed gaze toward the window a few moments longer before selecting a seat.

"It's even more beautiful at night." Paulo grinned. "Shall I pour you some wine? I have an old vintage label that I have been saving just for such an occasion as this."

Roman glanced at Eleanor. She smiled, nodding in Paulo's direction.

"Excellent. Allow me a moment." The gentleman walked over to a small table next to a fine leather chair and picked up a sterling silver bell. The crisp clear ringing sound summoned an indigenous-looking middle-aged woman from a door located across the room.

"Noemí—*vino, por favor*—wine, please. Bring the special bottle in the wooden box. You know the one I'm talking about."

"*Si, Señor.*" Noemí bowed her head slightly in deference to her employer.

Paulo replaced the bell and seated himself in the chair. "Did you have a good trip from Cuenca? It's a beautiful day."

"We did," said Roman, patting Eleanor's knee.

"So how have you been doing?" Paulo sat back in his chair.

"Pretty well. Tending to business and my family. Trying to get my old life back in order after being away from home, family, and friends so long." Roman eyed his host, studying the strong build of the man sitting across from him. The mustache his cousin wore closed the look for an authoritative, classic face that gave off an air of one who should be taken seriously. The smile softened everything about Paulo. "And how about you, my friend? How have you been?" Roman grinned.

"The same. For me, I've been focused on managing my exports business. Always something new to deal with. You know how that goes."

Noemí entered the room with a silver tray holding a bottle of wine and three glasses. After filling each one, she gave Paulo the first glass and handed the others to Roman and Eleanor.

Paulo picked up his glass, sniffed, and took a small sip. "Ah, the finest ever. Shall we toast? To the wonderful company of family." He stood up with an outstretched arm.

Eleanor and Roman joined him. All three clinked glasses.

After everyone sat down again, Paulo asked, "Tell me a little more about you, Roman, and of your family. As for me, I have heard about a feud. It created quite a problem. What happened?"

Roman placed his wine glass on a small ormolu-decorated table situated between his chair and Eleanor's.

"The story has become a legend throughout the Magiverse. Unfortunately, the conflict between our family line and that of South Hawthorne started with my great uncle, Desmond, son of Nicholas Strondovan. Whatever happened long ago has created a negative effect. As we have been told, there has been a slow increase of power within the dark forces, and now we have reached a near climax. They appear set on taking over if something is not done. The Glanarium Supremo said that the time has come for both families to set the record straight and right the wrong."

"Ah, yes." Paulo took another quick sip of wine, eyeing his guests. "We all know quite well that darkness takes root when it finds an opening. For Magicals, there must be harmony overall. Any differences between entities must be solved. Here in Ecuador and throughout South America, there seems to be a palpable charge in the environment. Tensions mounting, and you can't quite put your finger on it. I suspect this is happening throughout the world. It's been a subtle increase over many years. I have to agree with the Glanarium Supremo. This issue must be rectified, or we will have our heritage obliterated."

"We felt it in the other countries where we stayed also," Eleanor added. "It has become more than a simple change in thoughts and mores. Now it's like we've turned a corner. I'm afraid if the issue isn't resolved, things will never be the same."

"My dear, you are so correct about this." Paulo smiled graciously at Eleanor. "What about the others in your family? Have you heard anything from them?"

Roman thought a moment, not wanting to reveal too much. Paulo may be family, but he really didn't know his cousin or how much he could trust him. They had just met. "Eleanor has reached out to her sister. We are still working on reuniting the rest of the family. Information is sketchy." He displayed a knowing smile at his host. "Tell us more about your exports business. That sounds fascinating."

Paulo smiled. "I have been selling various supplies to Magicals for a little over twenty years. As for family, my wife is deceased. We had no children."

"I'm so sorry to hear that," said Eleanor. "It's terrible when spouses can't be together any longer." She eyed Roman and placed her hand over his. "We were forced into separation for years and have now reunited. I'm sure you heard about the family being scattered and hunted down for killing."

"I have heard that," Paulo answered. "Such an atrocity, especially when none of us know the true story of what really happened. My side of the family has had to be careful, too."

Roman spoke up. "How are sales in your business these days, given the environment we find ourselves?"

"Business has never been better. Sales are booming more now, though they have always been steadily good." Paulo sipped from his wine glass.

"What is selling the best for you right now?" asked Eleanor.

"Honestly, more supplies for protection and attack spells."

Eleanor raised an eyebrow. "And who are buying these?"

"The older ones are purchasing items for protection and the younger ones are focusing on attack. It's like the senior Magicals are on defense and the younger on offense."

Roman shook his head. "What do you make of that?" He rubbed his finger over the rim of his wine glass. "Spells for protection and attack aren't unusual in and of themselves, but usually love and money spells are the most sought out, aren't they? There is an imbalance, based on what you're saying."

"Again, as we've discussed, something is about to happen. And we must be ready." Paulo viewed his guests with a look of concern. "I think we will be called to fight to save ourselves and our heritage if necessary. If we want the lives and legends of Magicals to live on, we must fight."

"Do you know of anyone who could give us more information on what is happening, what we need to do?" Roman looked his cousin in the eye.

"Follow me," said Paulo, leading his guests to a dining table located in the far corner of the room where Noemí made her entrance and exit. He sat at the head of the table. Roman sat at his cousin's right, with Eleanor sitting beside her spouse.

The host quickly uttered an incantation. His papyrus and pen sailed from a small cabinet beneath a window and landed on the table in front of him.

"My dear, would you please?" Roman smiled at his wife. Eleanor dutifully removed her husband's papyrus and pen cleverly hidden in a large purse she had carried with her.

Paulo quickly wrote:

I have been best friends with *El Presidente*—the president—of Ecuador since we were children. We grew up together and have remained close. I am part of his advisory council. He would like very much to meet you.

Roman and Eleanor watched as Paulo's words lit their papyrus. Roman wrote back:

Can you arrange a meeting? How quickly would this happen?

Paulo answered, scribbling furiously:

I will contact him. This meeting needs to happen as quickly as possible so you can be on your way, back to Cuenca or remain in Quito or go wherever you feel led.

Roman smiled, writing the following on his papyrus:

Make this meeting happen quickly.

***

The president of Ecuador sat easily in his office. A smile lit his face. He had just finished a quick contact session with Paulo, who was his dearest friend. Their friendship had endured through the ages. He was also well aware of Paulo's magical abilities, of which he had pledged a sworn oath never to reveal this knowledge to anyone. It had been their secret ever since his friend's special skills had been told to him when they were only young boys of fourteen years.

Having finished an important call to the President of the US two hours prior, the chance to meet the most renowned elemental family in the Magical world couldn't have come at a better time.

The sound of shattering glass startled him. His reverie squelched, the president stood up and cautiously made his way to the far-right window behind him. The sound of voices wafted through a gaping hole in the pane. A large rock lay among shiny, jagged shards. Narrowing his eyes, he quickly studied the floor before creeping closer to the thick burgundy curtain.

He gently pushed aside the sheer drape wide enough to peep outside. And there they were, a gaggle of people below, glaring up at him. Or upward in his direction, nonetheless. He jerked back a little to avoid further detection and decrease the chances of being hit by another projectile they might toss a second time. The dismayed looks on their faces reaffirmed his concerns.

Idyllic days of old were dying a slow, agonizing death. Like it or not, that death song started many years ago. The actualization of it in full swing hit home now. Not only his beloved country, but others around the globe were experiencing a great shift. Something wonderful or something terrible, depending on the outcome.

Another round of voices slipped through the window. He bristled in alarm and ventured another timid peek out the window. A larger crowd came marching up the street, chanting.

The president's blood ran cold. What had he expected to see this time? It was like many of the other scenes he'd viewed lately. Youth clashed with old. The older ones shook their heads. Others rebelled with cutting words. Some prayed. Protests and outbursts issued forth from citizens against each other in all kinds of places. Many charged after the ruling establishment with raised fists and anger flashing in their eyes. It was as if something evil possessed them, and he couldn't quite put his finger on the reason or the culprit.

The crowd enlarged all at once and moved at a more rapid pace toward the palace. His eyes darted toward the door. Make a run for safety? Alert someone? Press the panic button? To his relief, the palace guards had swung into full action. Whistles blew, loud voices rang out. There was a lot of shoving and commands to leave. Several minutes later, the crowd had dispersed with many scuttling off down the sidewalks and across the street.

Relieved, the president stepped back from the drapes. He had conversed with the United States President several times about this very scene he just witnessed. His fellow leader had expressed the same observations and sentiments in his country. Both knew at some point it was every citizen for themselves. Those who had the wealth would still manage.

Others would fare according to their abilities and means. Both agreed that they would do everything in their power to fight the darkness, the evil collective that had slowly taken root. They knew some would die while others survived. In his mind, the Ecuadorian president knew that if they joined forces, the United States was the body. It had the capacity to move and shake the world.

South America would function as the heart. And Ecuador was the key to the beating heart that sent life blood, energy, and vitality throughout the body. With its natural resources, location, and mystic heritage, it was the ideal country to lead. It exemplified a teaching that there was power and great in the small.

Together they would be a giant force to behold. But something else was needed—the head. A collective of knowledge, experience, and an endurance of the ages. Any place on earth could be just that. Europe, though, had the history of some of the greatest inventors, philosophers, orators, and teachers who ever lived. Their creations had endured the test of time, through wars and peace.

Yes, it was determined that strong allies from South America, Europe, and the US would be the torchbearers and warriors for ensuring the light lived on, drowning out darkness and ignorance from the world forever. In the end, all would co-exist, both Magicals and Mortals.

"Señor Presidente." A young woman had stepped into the office.

He whirled around. "Ah, Erlinda, I was preoccupied. What can I do for you?"

Erlinda gazed in astonishment at the mess on the floor. "What . . .? Do I need—?"

The president waved her off. "*Es nada*—it's nothing. The guards took care of everything." He displayed a smile of assurance. "The crowd—everyone has gone."

She nodded slowly, not entirely convinced. "What happened?"

He didn't answer. They stared at each other a few seconds, both lost on what exactly to say.

The young assistant continued, "I'm leaving for the day and wanted to know if you needed anything else."

"No. Please go ahead. You may leave." He glanced down at the gold watch on his wrist.

"I'll call someone to clean up the glass. *Está bien?* Are you okay?"

"I'll call someone myself." The president pointed to his watch. "Time for you to go. I'll be fine."

Erlinda nodded and backed toward the door.

"Oh, before you go, I do want to ask you this. Have you noticed the people who seem to be congregating more frequently outside? How do they look to you?"

Erlinda relaxed her stance somewhat and stepped forward. "They want to tear everything apart. The anger. You can feel it. Everywhere. Never did it used to be like this. Now, it scares me. I go home every night and pray."

The president nodded. He hadn't done that, but maybe he should. In one of his drawers in his private bedroom, he had a rosary somewhere. At least, he thought he saw one there the other day.

"Why would someone throw something through the window, Señor?" Erlinda shook her head, trying to make sense of it all. "That is very bold to do something like that here on the palace grounds." She moved closer to her boss. "Why wasn't this place guarded better? To allow someone to throw a rock like that?" She pointed to the floor.

He shook his head in thought. "Let's be honest. Things happen. Sometimes you can't explain it."

"It's a curse," said Erlinda. "Something dark has come upon us. We never used to worry about things we're seeing now. What will become of us?"

"We'll get through it. Just a bad time for the world right now, really." He smiled, trying his best at reassuring the attractive young lady standing a few feet away. "But do not worry. Go home and try to have a good evening, what's left of it."

Erlinda said nothing but stared at him a few seconds. Turning on her heel, she headed out the office door.

"We'll get through the best we can," whispered the president. He reached down and picked up the rock that had been well-aimed at his office window. It was the size of a baseball. The person who threw it must have had a strong arm and determination. As he held the stone, it became clear that this was no ordinary one grabbed from the ground or someone's garden.

It had been fashioned into a perfectly round sphere. The longer he gazed at it, the stone seemed to glow a soft mossy green before fading back to dull brown. He blinked his eyes. Surely nothing more than fatigue and a heightened imagination. Rocks didn't glow. Not like this one. The more he thought about it, the more he remained certain that no ordinary citizen could have thrown this so easily with such marked aim. His gut clenched. But who or what did it? Something inside compelled him to place the rock in the drawer of his desk. He didn't want to alarm anyone, but no one should see this rock—no one but perhaps Paulo and the renowned family he was about to meet. He glanced at his watch and swore. His guests would arrive at the palace in about twenty minutes.

The president strode over to his desk and contacted housekeeping. "Come quickly. I have a meeting coming up."

***

Paulo followed the palace escort, Eleanor and Roman in tow. With quick steps they walked the hallway to the president's office where the escort formally ushered them inside.

"Ah, Paulo, it's been too long!" The president stepped out from behind his desk and hugged his old friend.

"It has been a long time." Paulo smiled, shaking his friend's hand with vigor. "And please, allow me to introduce my cousin, Roman Strondovan and his lovely wife, Eleanor."

"*Un gusto a conocerle*. . . nice to meet you." The president shook Roman's hand. A large smile spread across his face. "And you, too, lovely lady." He lifted Eleanor's dainty, manicured hand and brought it to his lips, landing a delicate kiss on top. "Shall we talk?" Within seconds, they all had seated themselves at a small table at the opposite side of the office.

At that moment, Paulo spoke up. "So what's with the broken window, my friend?"

The president eyed him a moment. "I was hoping you wouldn't notice right away. But then again, it's a little too much to ignore."

"Come now. You wanted us to see it. With all the space you have here, you would have met us elsewhere, if you wanted to keep it a secret."

"Ah, Paulo, right on all counts. And as important as our nice gathering is today, I intend for us to still meet elsewhere. But not without a moment of some wine and a getting-to-know-you chat. Right?"

Paulo bowed his head politely, "As you wish."

The president pressed a special button under a table next to his executive chair. A uniformed staff member entered the office.

"*Vino para todos, por favor* . . . wine for all, please."

The gentleman nodded in respect and left the room, only to return in several minutes with a cart holding wine and crystal. After filling the goblets and offering one to each guest, he left the room.

"Tell me, Roman, what brings you to our country?" The president sipped lightly from his crystal goblet. "I hear you are someone important. And I make it a priority never to miss meeting with important people." He smiled graciously.

Roman placed his crystal goblet on the table and sat up straighter in his substantial armchair. "I come from a long line of elemental families, if you will." He spent several moments briefing the president on what had happened to his family, keeping details vague while still giving a satisfactory overview. He ended by stating, "It is our hope to help vanquish the evil that is overtaking the world, restore balance, and maintain the light."

"My friend," said Paulo speaking up, "as I said to you earlier, my cousin may be just the one to help you and other leaders. They have talents and knowledge that most don't have."

"Don't you have this knowledge?" the president looked over at his friend. "Your skills are no secret to me, and if you are related, I would think you know just as much. After all, you're cousins." He gestured between Paulo and Roman.

"Yes, we are family. But since the trouble started in his branch, it must be his familial line that rectifies the wrong. We've all had to be on our guard as well, but overall, the rest of us are strong supporters, all bringing in our talents."

The president considered his friend's words, thinking a moment. He got up from his chair and strode over to his desk, pulling out the strange stone. "Perhaps you or Roman can tell me about this. I just received it today." His guests peered at the object in his hand. Eleanor gasped. Paulo and the Strondovans quickly averted their eyes.

Picking up on something he couldn't explain, the president said, "Let's go to a special place where we can talk freely, shall we?"

Chapter Thirteen

Deep in the bowels of the palace, an escort led the president and his guests to a furnished bunker. Bright-patterned sofa pairs rested in corners of the room. In the middle stood a long mahogany meeting table with matching elegant chairs.

"Please, join me over here." The president led Paulo, Roman, and Eleanor to one of the pairs of sofas in a far corner. He seated himself on the opposite one. "We will be able to speak freely in here."

"My earlier family helped design this room, along with other rooms down here," said Paulo. He smiled and nodded at Roman and Eleanor.

"There are other rooms?" asked Eleanor. Her eyebrows raised in interest.

"We are outfitted with everything down here, just enough in case we have to stay a while. You never can be too careful. Things happen when you least expect it." The president acknowledged Eleanor with a nod.

"May I see the . . . you know?" Paulo pointed toward his friend's hand.

"You mean this?" The president held out the stone.

Paulo immediately pointed to it and launched into an incantation. "*Erupto fini!*"

The president's eyes contained a startled look. Face contorted in pain, he dropped the ball with a careless thud on the wine-colored carpet. The sphere rolled between the sofas, glowing a brighter green than before, pulsating, crackling, and ending with a solid pop. Nothing remained but shattered pieces. Unable to resist, Roman added his magical contribution by flicking his fingers toward the mess on the floor, mumbling a strange command that sounded similar to his cousin's. The remnants on the floor turned to grey ash and vanished altogether, leaving no trace of the former object.

Eleanor smiled with delight while a stunned Ecuadorian leader sat speechless. "That was beautiful," she said.

"Why did you do that?" the president asked. "I was starting to like that stone. Wanted to keep it, perhaps as a memento, though I can't honestly tell you why I wanted to." He scratched his head, perplexed.

"And that was the problem, my friend," answered Paulo. "We had to get rid of it. We could not speak freely with something like that around, especially since we don't know where it came from or why it was directed at your office." He tapped Roman on the arm. "As I was saying, just so you know, cousin, my family helped design these rooms down here. Not only do the walls have soundproofing, we also added protective stone and other elements to block psychic waves. This means even Magicals cannot penetrate these walls with some of their best communication methods. Except the one we just destroyed. That was clever, whoever created it."

Roman looked at the president and said, "Let's talk about what is going on and what needs to be done."

The Ecuadorian leader sat back and looked at his guests. "I have had talks with the President of the US, and we both agree that we will have to act soon. The Magicals from the dark forces are teaming up with Mortals who share their same goals, to take over and keep the world steeped in darkness, in ignorance, in a form of slavery, if you will. From our discussion, we both have determined that this most likely has been building for years."

Paulo interjected his thoughts. "The dark side is very clever at winning over Mortals. Mortals don't understand the power of Magicals and how enchantments and spells can be used to manipulate the mind. Mortals usually regard magic and most subjects related to that realm as mere make believe, something you see in movies or read about in books. Little do they suspect how wrong they are."

"Can you explain something to me, Roman? I simply must understand more about what this feud was between your family. Paulo says that the severity of it created a rift, affecting the Magicals and their world quite heavily. Obviously, I am not in the know when it comes to things like that. Your cousin is. Can someone fill me in on this?"

Roman smiled politely toward the leader. "I can imagine how hard it must be to understand how a simple feud between two families could disrupt an entire world, or system, I should say." He leaned forward a little, brows furrowed. "You see, there is balance in all things, mundane or cosmic. Thoughts are things. Actions reverberate. When my relative, Desmond, supposedly killed Clement Hawthorne, of course there was immediate reaction to that. Now, they never proved that Clement did it. We've never gotten to the full truth of it all. Regardless, the Hawthorne's rage and ire spread like wildfire. Jove and his clave have many allies, and they rallied around him.

"All of our allies suddenly turned against us, not wanting to have anything to do with a murderer or one purported to be one. Before we knew it, everyone was against us. Magicals were taking sides, and it wasn't ours. And worse, the few who tried to support or help us only met with wrath and baneful magic against them, too. Just the mere mention of our name set off the flames of indignation and hate so badly that forces came together and came after my family and even some of my friends.

"If we didn't escape or do something quickly, our whole line would be extinct—and it nearly became so."

The president fixed his eyes on Roman with rapt attention. "Go on, please."

"So you ask how something so minor as a feud between two becomes more, I have given you the first part. But here's the other part. Balance. You see, we are an elemental earth clave, as old as time itself. Our family line embodies a point on the pentagram, earth. And while there are other earth representations, including other cave types, our line extends from the super seven crystal cave in Brazil. Our cave produces some of the rarest and most powerful crystals."

Eleanor spoke up. "That super seven crystal cave is the only place where you find these crystals. It can only be managed by the family and the descendants who rightly come from it. Without its use and proper care, there is a hole in the fabric of the Magiverse, the 'missing piece', as you say. In a cosmic structure, everything matters. All of us, Magicals and Mortals, are important, even down to the most seemingly insignificant person, animal, plant, or mineral. Everyone and everything are important in some way. As you well know, the cosmic system rules all of the Magiverse and Mortal universe."

The president shook his head in disbelief. "Simply amazing. I didn't expect such an explanation." He grinned.

"It's a war we have. You know that," said Paulo. "Events can have a rippling effect that once started can't seem to stop. They take on a power of their own and in the case of the Magical world, the ramifications have dipped into the Mortal world. We're parallel, you know. When an evil force uses an opportunity to sport their own agenda, they become a force to be reckoned with."

"Yes, I see that." The president scratched his head. "So, what do we do about this? How do we stop it? In my city, people are protesting when things don't go their way. They are not happy with anything I do. Neighbors are fighting against each other over subjects that used to be passed off as casual conversation or an agreement to disagree. In the US, the President has mentioned the same thing. People are coming after each other with virtual pitchforks, beating each other up, storming businesses. Some are being ostracized from society. And it seems that someone or something is in a dark corner, hidden yet present and powerful."

"We're trying to reach our daughter, Larissa," said Eleanor. "She was taken from us when just a baby. We had to place her elsewhere for safety. And there's my sister, Dorenda. If we can reunite and ready ourselves for the fight, it's my hope we can straighten everything out. She and August South Hawthorne are on an expedition right now, trying to get to the bottom of what exactly occurred. Every way of discovery about what really happened has remained closed to the rest of us."

"Let's just hope your daughter and her companion succeed," said Paulo. "I think they had little to nothing to go on. It's quite a puzzle they've been trying to solve."

"Roman, do you and Eleanor have any plans of returning to the cave?" asked the president. "I would think you should be heading back there. And quickly too."

"We were headed that way but decided we wanted to stop here first. To at least meet some of our family." Roman glanced at Paulo who nodded in affirmation. "We need to get word to our daughter to meet us there."

"Before arriving here, Roman and I managed to contact her briefly. Just as we were about to tell her where to meet, we had to break contact." Eleanor looked at each gentleman.

"Had to break contact?" The president's face contorted into a puzzled expression. "Why would you have to break contact? That doesn't sound good."

"We saw something in the shadows coming behind her. Luckily, the moon was out a little, or we wouldn't have seen anything."

Paulo, impatient, spoke up, "What did the 'something in the shadows' look like, for heaven's sake? Was it an animal? A human?" His eyes squinted. "Or something else? It had to be something significant for you to break a communication with your daughter. Was that your first time ever talking to her?"

"Yes," Roman answered.

"Oh god!" Paulo smacked the palm of his hand against his forehead. "Do you even know where she was?"

Roman and Eleanor's eyes met. "No," they said in unison.

"Are you sure she wasn't held captive somewhere? Of course, I know you wanted to make sure your instructions would only be heard by her."

Roman answered, "That's true. No one needs to know that she's coming to us, except August Hawthorne. And obviously, we didn't get a chance to learn each other's location."

The president shook his head, perplexed. "I really think you need to try and contact her right away. Get back to that cave. I'm not versed in anything Magical, other than what I learn from Paulo, but I know from a Mortal standpoint, that none of us are safe right now. If there is anything I can do to help, please let me know."

"Thank you. We will do that," said Roman. He nodded also at his cousin, who signaled agreement.

Paulo made eye contact with his friend. "Señor Presidente, the world is in a shift right now. Either we fix it, or the ways we have known before will not stand, and it won't be a good thing. What do you plan to do?"

"I plan on getting my military ready. The US President and I will talk more and get other world leaders involved. I'll call him again this week, see if we can finalize a plan."

"And you," said Paulo, looking at Roman, "find a way to get word to Larissa to meet you at the cave." He smiled, "Shall I be there, too? I've never seen it before."

Roman considered the question. Paulo was family, after all. "Can you gather other family members? I know some may be much older, but it would be nice to have a reunion." He grinned.

"Excellent!" Paulo slapped his knee with emphasis. "I like that idea." He turned to the president. "I think we're finished here. We'll keep in touch."

"Yes, most definitely." The president stood up and led the way out of the bunker and back to the main hallway of the upper floor of the palace. "I hope to hear from you soon, my friend." He hugged Paulo. "And as for you two, my best wishes and service for anything you might need."

Roman and Eleanor nodded politely and followed Paulo and the escort, who had arrived, out the palace doors.

***

Dennis leaned against a tree several yards away from the presidential palace. Scowling, he pulled his jacket tighter around him and moved a leather hat on his head further downward, shielding his eyes from outward view. The last thing he wanted was for anyone, Magical or Mortal, to come up and start making small talk. Everything had gone according to plan—until it didn't. He cursed in silence.

Plans on hearing further exchanges between the Strondovan couple and to whomever they were conversing at any given moment had been thwarted once again. What else could he expect? Everyone was wizening up, especially Strondovan and his wife. Their cousin wasn't too bad, either. And now the president of Ecuador was in on it, whatever that was. The young man had tried listening in on the conversation in Paulo's condo, successful at first, until everything grew quiet. They were finding the most discreet ways to conduct business.

After that, the young man birthed a plan. A brilliant one, so he'd thought. Much of it was probably speculation and pure hope but a plan, nonetheless. He heard everything between the president and Erlinda, including the first several minutes of prattle when Paulo and crew joined in after she left. Like the condo experience, it all suddenly went quiet again.

With calculated energy, the stone hurled through the window landed into the office with perfection. But the silence signaled utter failure. Something happened to the stone. If that rock had stayed with the group, he could have heard and seen everything. Designed and charged with an enchanting spell for allure, anyone who held and stared at it long enough had no desire to get rid of it any time soon.

The rock held a recording device and magical crystal that reflected images back to him. Filled with worry, he pocketed his own receptor sphere and walked away. Telling the boss his failure in bypassing protective systems would not be fun. If he kept running into roadblocks like this, favored rank and earned rewards risked a sad ending. As he walked back to his car, Dennis noted a pocket of people gathering several yards down the street. They looked angry, sounded angry from what he could discern from the vocal tones.

From what he and his boss had discussed, it wasn't uncommon to see sights like this in the city here now. The same could be said for other parts of the world, especially the USA. He knew things would be coming to a head soon.

***

Back in the presidential office, the leader sat at his desk, studying some papers that had been placed there earlier. Out of curiosity, he opened his computer and pulled up his favorite go-to world news site.

What he saw in the headlines and accompanying pictures didn't rest easy with him. In all parts of the world, there were angry citizens. They were in open rebellion, it seemed.

He sat back in his chair musing. He didn't want to admit it, but he knew good and well that most governments and leaders didn't do right by their people. Never had, really. Hunger for greed and power by those who were in charge still lingered, even today. Nothing had changed since thousands of years when the ancients ruled. It had taken this long for things to come to a head. The people were having no more of it.

Perhaps this was it; there was no turning back. If the wrong ones took power now, things would be worse. Forever. It wasn't that he necessarily wanted things so bad for the people he governed. It's just that he, like his predecessors, liked power too. Having another group win only meant possibly nothing for him. No doubt the other leaders felt the same way. They'd be crazy not to admit it.

One thing was for certain, he and his peers would not go down without a fight if they wanted to keep the status quo for themselves. At once, he felt weary. He thought about the stone that Paulo and Roman destroyed. What was it about that stone that made them so nervous? Shaking his head in bewilderment, he got up from the desk and headed for the door. All the papers and things he had to read would wait until tomorrow. Tonight, once he was in his private quarters, he would search for that rosary that lay hidden somewhere. It was time to use it.

***

"Failed again? What is it with you lately?" Edouard glared at Dennis. "All I ask is that you eavesdrop, which should be pretty simple, and you can't even do it." He paced back and forth, running a hand through his hair. His eyes, when angry, seemed to take on a greenish glint, displaying the features of an almost crazed-looking figure.

Dennis shrank back a little, unable to completely hide his nervousness. "They're on to us, I think. There's a lot of secrecy now. I thought my stone was a brilliant idea. I even landed it right where I wanted it. And then something happened, and I don't know what."

"Things are only as good as the results they get, and no matter how brilliant you think it all was, it fell flat—no pun intended." Edouard scowled. "Daniel, I'll try you. Any other ideas you have? I'm eager to hear just about anything at this point." He sat on a red velvet-covered chair that resembled a small throne.

"I have been thinking about all this as well." Daniel got up from his chair and positioned himself between Edouard and Dennis. "I don't think gadgets and gizmos are going to cut it anymore. It all sounds pretty clever, until we keep hitting roadblocks like my buddy, Dennis, is running into. It's no fault of his or mine or yours." He gestured toward Edouard.

"Go on. I'm listening," said Edouard, rising up from a more relaxed position.

"Let's grapple with them personally. Get into their heads. Create confusion. Make them think we're on their side. When they least expect it, bam! We strip them of their magic, their powers. You see, we really can't do that. Not technically. But the power of the mind still reigns supreme. Once they are mentally weakened and side with us, they won't have the desire to fight. They just change their ways of thinking. What they used to hold dear won't matter anymore." He looked from Edouard to Dennis.

Edouard shifted in his seat. "I think I get it, and I kind of like the idea. It's kind of like what my father did with Dorenda. You see, she wasn't always like she is now. Father convinced her and worked on her enough until she decided to join us." He rubbed his chin reflecting on his words. "Father told me not long ago that he had to do some of his most baneful magic to shake her up mentally enough to come around, if you know what I mean."

"I do," answered Daniel. "When you work baneful magic, you only hope that your enemy—or frenemy—isn't on to you. You get them when they least expect it. You keep things sweet when you're in their face, but when they turn their back, you go after them." He shrugged. "Maybe not the easiest to do at times, but it works. That clave is super smart, but that doesn't mean we are dumber."

"No, of course not!" Edouard laughed. "Dennis, you have anything to say about what Daniel said. And don't for the love of the deities say you were just thinking the same thing."

"Welll," Dennis answered, "maybe? Or maybe not. I just hadn't gotten that far. I've been too busy traipsing after people to think about it any further."

Daniel laughed. Edouard turned his gaze quickly ceilingward in a look of disgust. "Listen, you two are my top people in The Order of the Chevron. Both of you are bright, capable witches. What is really important to me is that both of you have had a relationship with Larissa." He sighed and sank back in his chair. "I could say I sort of did at one time, but it's been too long. It all seemed to end just when it started. I was hoping I could rekindle the feelings again when she was here at Sulphure Castle, but now they have all escaped and only the gods know where they are headed now."

Edouard jumped up from his seat, agitated at this point. "I really thought I had her, could sway her over, but I had to go to the secret meeting, and now it's all slipping away. Something made her leave, and she took that damned god-awful August Hawthorne with her. For that I should be thankful."

"So get the romance back, Sir." Daniel walked toward Edouard and tapped him on the shoulder. "Get her back. You can do it just as easily as I or Daniel can. There's nothing in us that could lure her any more than someone as magnificent as yourself." He smiled.

"Oh, can it, Daniel. Stop the bullshit." Dennis clenched his fists. "Speak for yourself. And my remark is in no way meant as an offense to you, Edouard. You are quite magnificent in all you do. But we have all held her interest at one time or another."

Edouard regarded both men, grinning. "True—on all counts, gentlemen. But something has changed. I sense it. And I don't like it. Getting her back now will be harder, and none of us can deny it, so we need to stop fooling ourselves." He pointed at Daniel. "I rather like your suggestion, though. I've been toying with something similar but until now had no strong preferences one way or the other."

"We just need the specifics to the plan of our attack. Won't be easy, but I think we can do it and win. And dumping that goofy Hawthorne witch shouldn't be a problem at all."

"Let's talk on this more tomorrow, shall we?" Edouard stood up. "I don't know about you, but I'll sleep better at night once we get a more solid plan in place."

***

"You seem preoccupied, my dear." Roman placed his hand on Eleanor's shoulder. "Is there something about today that is still bothering you?"

Paulo had insisted that his cousin stay with him before heading to the super seven crystal cave in Brazil. They had returned to his condo from the executive palace only twenty minutes prior. Noemí and he had headed to the kitchen so dinner could be prepared to his specifications.

"We need to contact her tonight. Larissa. I feel it in my bones." Eleanor looked into her husband's eyes. "It's the night of the new moon, the time for new beginnings. What we have now is definitely that." She grinned.

"Let's do it. Take the lead. I'm sure Paulo will gladly support us."

Eleanor nodded. "I'll get everything ready."

Later that night, after a tasty meal served with Paulo's finest wine, she and Roman retired to their quarters. Paulo had kindly agreed to make himself scarce for a while, wholeheartedly agreeing to their plan. Inside their spacious bedroom, she opened a large travel bag and retrieved a rosewood box with a pentacle etched on the top.

This was her portable altar, which accompanied her on long travels. Inside she carried the basics any witch might need if something were to come up and a ritual or a spell needed to be done. She placed the box carefully on a small table, unlatched the lid, and peered inside, fingering the objects carefully stored away. There were several candles of different colors, red, gold, black, green, white, silver. Tiny jars held various herbs used in spell work. There were several gemstones, charms, talismans, sigil drawings, and even a couple of small altar cloths, ones used for planetary magic and another used for moon magic.

She plucked out a small jar filled with bath salts used for ritual cleansings on nights of new and full moons, which she did religiously. The chosen jar held the formula for protection, lemon balm, peppercorn, allspice, and a secret oil mix that was her special concoction. Wanting to keep this simple, Eleanor decided on using the salt as a scrub to set the intent of scrubbing away any barriers to reaching her daughter. Scrubbing away any interference from someone or something else. Seeing what had looked like the unmistakable form of another person, Magical or Mortal, hadn't set well with her.

Just what the reason was for their coming up behind her daughter in the middle of the night unnerved her. Where was Larissa, anyway? There could be no interference tonight. One last item, a white candle for bathing and cleansing in candlelight. She headed to the bathroom, undressed, and gazed at her naked reflection in the mirror.

With a simple ritual, she blessed parts of her body, touching the areas lightly with her fingers. After lighting the candle in one of the recesses in the neatly tiled shower, she stepped inside and recited, "The new moon opens me to all potential. I am powerful, strong, protected. Nothing stands in my way." Eleanor opened her jar, inhaled the spicy sent of the salt mixture and continued her ritual.

While his wife showered, Roman slipped into a robe and spent the rest of the time setting up their space from where they would place the crystal spere used to contact Larissa. Like his wife, he also carried a portable altar with him. On a special cloth he used for moon magic, he placed a beautiful round, flawless, quartz crystal sphere that sat on a sterling silver stand. Beside it he placed the citrine that had come out of the egg reading he received in Cuenca.

He knew they would most likely not be heading back to Cuenca any time soon, and he had quickly contacted Quri, asking if she would secure his residence there. His nerves matched the frenzy of his wife's. They must reach Larissa and give her instructions on where to meet them. Time was running out. He felt it instinctively.

Roman closed his eyes, seeking guidance from the goddess, Selene. "Mighty goddess. One who is the moon and all her light. My request I beseech you hear tonight. My daughter, the one we wish to speak. Show the paths that we might seek."

A light wind rustled through the room. From the corner of his eye, he glimpsed a rustling of the curtains covering the windows. Outside, only the faintest sliver of moon shone in the inky black sky. But he knew she was there, only hidden briefly until she'd show herself slowly as the next several nights passed until her full glow would show in full resplendent glory.

A light crackling sound emitted from his crystal sphere. Roman look on in interest at he watched the orb turn from clear to cloudy. On the silver stand now sat a sphere of perfectly polished selenite. He narrowed his eyes. What was this? He did have selenite in his altar box but didn't normally use it for communication like what would happen tonight.

"Use this to communicate with your daughter, Roman," said the soft whisper of a woman's voice.

As he watched, an ethereal outline of a female clothed in a silky transparent gown morphed into full view in front of him. She wore a crown with a crescent moon emblem firmly fixed in her hair of white flowing tresses. Her eyes sparkled like diamonds under a bright light.

"This sphere will still allow you to see and hear your daughter. She will see and hear you. But an onlooker, if there is one, will not be able to discern your identity or hear you clearly." The lady smiled.

"Ah, beautiful Selene, you are most kind and wise. For this reason, I called on you for help." Roman bowed his head lightly in respect.

"I am as old as time, from the Titans themselves. And you, dear Roman, are from a family line nearly as old. From the earth, strong and true. Enduring."

"We have not endured well. My line has nearly been stamped out by fear, hatred, and evil. Lies and deceit. That's what has fueled all of this."

"You will rise up and fight. The least sometimes is the most powerful. Is not the venom of a baby snake not as powerful as that of an adult of its species?"

He looked up at her, puzzled.

Selene tilted her head, lightly smiling. "You know exactly what I mean. Make use with what you have, be it family who remains or with others who wish to help. Nature and the cosmos always seek to restore and maintain balance." She pointed toward the selenite sphere. "Go on and do what you must do."

When Selene disappeared, Roman viewed two white candles on either side of the sphere. He grinned. She had put them there.

"Are we ready, darling?"

He quickly turned around, seeing Eleanor robed in silky white. Had it not been for the long red hair, he would have sworn for a moment that Selene herself was standing before him in human form.

"I see you have everything set up. I'll get the two chairs from over there, and we'll get started." Eleanor walked across the room. Roman joined her. Both placed the chairs in front of the altar space and sat down. "A selenite sphere?" she asked. "How peculiar."

"A suggestion from the moon herself, Selene. It's more protective that way." Roman smiled at his wife.

"Ah, then we are good. Let's get started." She snapped her fingers. The lights in the room went out. Only the two substantial white candles glowed. Taking Roman's hand in hers, she stated aloud, "Dear husband, let us take a few deep cleansing breaths, connect ourselves with her frequency, in the good fortune we find it, and we shall call out to her."

"Agreed," answered Roman.

Both breathed in, held their breaths a few seconds, and released slowly. As they performed this crucial step, each one felt the space between their eyes tingle. It was a familiar sensation telling them they had opened their pathways to spirit, to the ether, to the deities, to whatever that ultimate power was that ruled the heavens, earth, the universe.

Eleanor spoke again shortly. "With the power, protection, and love of the moon, Selene. With the power, protection, and love of the primordial power ruling over all, we ask that you grant us the presence of our daughter tonight. Open her mind, heart, and spirit that she may hear us."

Roman repeated his wife's words silently to himself, gazing at the sphere, willing the image of Larissa within the stony layers. Never had he wanted anything more right now. He wanted it. His wife wanted it. With any luck, Larissa wanted it too.

The sphere lit up. A bright light issued from it, filling the room with white. As quickly as it came, it subsided to a soft glow. From within, it looked almost like there was snow falling inside the orb. The stone took on a snowy look, went gray, lit up brightly once again, and settled back to the soft light.

Eleanor gasped. Roman sat up straighter. They saw her. Larissa.

"Mother, Father, is that you?" Larissa's head bobbed and swayed as if she were looking through a haze.

"We are here," Eleanor spoke, struggling with the tears forming in her eyes. She glanced at Roman.

"Larissa, your mother and I are both here. We had to end our contact quickly last time. Are you alone?"

"I am," said Larissa.

"Why is she looking around?" Eleanor whispered in alarm to Roman.

"Shh." Roman lightly shook his head and tightened his grip on his wife's hand. "Larissa, are you quite sure no one else is around?"

"Quite sure, Father. Allow me a few seconds, please."

The image of Larissa faded briefly, flickered back in a few times, and ended with a stable image.

"Can you tell us where you are? Are you safe?" Eleanor asked. "We are extremely worried about you."

"I'm fine, Mother. I'm in an area well beyond a place called Walnut Grove, from where we left not long ago. We have reached a resting spot until we decide what to do next. I only wanted to move to a different location to make sure no one hears us—and to get a better view of you. It's not as clear as it was the first time we talked."

Roman spoke up, "Never mind that. There's a reason for it. Your mother and I want you to come home. Meet us in our ancestral place."

Larissa's eyes lit up. "You mean where Aunt Dorenda showed me before I started out on this quest? The sup—?"

"Don't say it out loud!" Roman raised his voice a little in alarm. "You know where it is, then? The place I'm talking about?"

"I do, Father. Where are you and Mother? Couldn't I just come where you are?"

"No, dear," Eleanor spoke up. "We need to all meet at the place we are discussing. You and August Hawthorne."

"Oh," said Larissa, wrinkling her nose.

Roman and Eleanor glanced at each other. Both heard the disdain in her voice.

"When?" Larissa asked. "Tomorrow? Please tell me tomorrow. I want to see you personally. I'm so excited. I haven't been the same since our first talk. And there is so much to talk about."

"The same for us, darling." Eleanor blew a kiss toward the sphere. She turned toward Roman. "Is there any reason we couldn't all meet there tomorrow? It's not like we have to book a flight like Mortals do, you know." She rested her hand on Roman's thigh.

"I don't see why not." Roman thought a little more. "Let's make it tomorrow."

Larissa smiled. "Tomorrow it is. If I get there first, what do I need to do?"

Eleanor looked at Roman and shrugged. "Darling, you can familiarize yourself better with the place, maybe clean and arrange things? You have seen it all more recently than we have." She chuckled.

Larissa laughed. "Of course. Silly me. I'm so excited, I almost can't think. This is too good to be true. My real mother and father."

"We are real," said Roman. "And you are, too, to us. Please know we love you."

"And I you." Larissa kissed her fingers and held them out toward her parents. "Tomorrow."

"Yes," said Eleanor. "We must go now. Be careful, watch your back. You can't trust anyone."

"True," answered Larissa. "Good night to both of you."

Roman and Eleanor each held up a hand toward their daughter's image, watching sadly as it flickered and faded out of sight. The sphere flashed white and returned to its original clear quartz state, ready for placement back in Roman's portable altar. A quick breeze snuffed out the candles, which disappeared altogether.

Chapter Fourteen

Larissa, August, Phuctious, and Willem loaded their belongings inside the Vanishport. Today they would be making the trek to Brazil, to the super seven crystal cave that belonged to the Strondovan family and their earth clave ancestors since the beginning of time. She finally broke down and told her compatriots why they needed to leave today and where.

"Are you excited to meet your birth family?" Willem asked Larissa. "This must be such a momentous time for you."

Phuctious nodded in agreement, his eyes flashing with emotion.

August turned and gazed at Larissa, also waiting for her answer.

"I'm so nervous. I've only met them briefly through my crystal ball. They seemed like nice people. My father is as handsome as my mother is beautiful. They're just the way Aunt Dorenda described them." Larissa nodded.

"Nice people? Perhaps once you meet them, you won't be so matter-of-fact in your descriptions and attitude toward them as you are now," said August. He eyed Larissa with great curiosity, ignoring the nasty scowl cast in his direction.

"Ah, Heir August," said Willem, "perhaps you are being a bit unfair toward your travel mate. Let's admit it. Her parents are strangers. They were torn apart, nearly extinguished due to rumors and mere speculation."

August turned a glaring eye on Willem. "I hardly think Uncle Clement's murder is mere speculation, as you wish to call it."

"But August, this is the entire reason we are on this quest. To get to the bottom of what really happened. You surely wouldn't declare Desmond Strondovan a murderer without knowing all the facts, would you?" Willem clucked his tongue in dismay, frowning.

"I know for a fact that Desmond Strondovan raised his wand, and something happened. The death of Uncle Clement, that's what."

"Sometimes what you think you see isn't really the truth," Phuctious added.

Larissa tapped her foot impatiently. "You know, that's just like you, August, always making things about yourself. Willem kindly asked how I was feeling about, oh, only the most important day of my life. Meeting my birth family for the first time since I've been nothing but a mere orphan all my life. And you have to suddenly spin things around and make it all about you, your family, your thoughts." Her face turned red. Tears welled up in her eyes. "You'll never know what it's like to not know your history, not be loved by your parents, know who your relatives are. You'll never know what it's like to be hated and despised for something you didn't even do." She clenched her fists.

Willem elbowed August, bringing him to full attention. Phuctious shh'd him, frowning.

August floundered a moment, getting his thoughts together. "I'm sorry, Larissa. My comments were totally uncalled for. And I do apologize for that. We'll get to the bottom of what happened and try to set everything right. We'll succeed—or die trying." His words trailed off, followed by his eyes moving downward as a sign of total loss.

"Miss Larissa," Willem added, "please know that Phuctious and I are here to support you as well as August. I'm sure, if the truth be told, he's just as nervous as you are and probably too proud to admit it. Your parents, equally of royal lineage, could easily disapprove of him and find him unworthy of their beautiful daughter. So he needs to be smart and on his toes." The young wizard stole a quick glance at his master, landing a stern gaze on the young man and insinuating he would do well to mind his manners. August grimaced in response.

Larissa couldn't help but smile at Willem. "You are the only one who comes through when it comes to being a gentleman. And I thank you for that from the bottom of my heart."

"I sincerely meant every word, Strondovan Heir." Willem bowed graciously in Larissa's direction.

All four stepped inside the boundaries of the Vanishport. As usual, the boundary lines turned the familiar icy blue color that signaled take-off. Everyone held their breaths. From their location now, it would be a longer transport to the super seven crystal cave. All went black. Larissa's stomach lurched. She heard August gasp. Phuctious let out a grunt. In the darkness, Willem had grasped her hand. All seemed normal at first. But this time something strange happened. The craft suddenly beeped and stopped, jostling the occupants. The interior boundary lines now glowed pink, which usually signaled safe arrival.

"What the hell?" August staggered back into place before he toppled over.

Willem loosened his grip from Larissa's hand and stepped through the outline of a door, peeking outside. "Something tells me this is not where we're supposed to be."

Larissa stepped up beside him and peered out the door. "We seem to have landed in the woods somewhere. I just don't know where."

August spoke up, "It's a cave we're going to. Wouldn't it be in the woods? There's nothing strange about that at all." He frowned at the pair gaping outside the door. "Let's start this thing up again or unload and start walking."

"Heir Hawthorne," said Willem, "If you look at the coordinates, they are not correct. As a matter of fact, they are scrambled, illegible."

"What?" August turned in the direction of a lit screen. Sure enough, Willem had spoken the truth. The coordinates, set before take-off, glowed pink, just like the outline of the craft. The numerical digits displayed haphazard lines.

"I've never known of a Vanishport malfunctioning." Larissa's brow furrowed in thought. "This is not like cars or other vehicles that Mortals use. This is specially designed for true witches to use during travel."

"Shall we try again?" Willem asked. "Let's see if we can reset the coordinates." He walked over to the control panel and said the spell for setting the coordinates. The numbers lit up again in blue, along with the interior dimensions of the Port. "There we go." He smiled, rather satisfied with himself. "Perhaps something got a little scrambled. We'll have another go at it."

Everyone braced themselves again. The Port sailed off, only to stop in the manner it had done earlier.

"I don't like this one bit." August strode to the door, barely glancing at the scrambled pink numbers on the control panel. He peered out the door. "This looks just like where we were earlier. Damn!" He pounded the fist of one hand into the other. The young man looked at Willem. "Are you thinking what I'm thinking?"

"Something's playing with us," said Larissa, sidling up next to August.

"Worse," added Willem, "something's intent on our not reaching the crystal cave. They will not let up. Unless we try a different plan, we're trapped."

"Are you sure it's not the Anguis? After all, we didn't exactly tell them goodbye and thank them for their hospitality when we left." Phuctious let out huff.

August looked at Larissa. "Where are we, exactly?"

"I've got the Numeromancer Tiberinus gave us."

Willem's eyes lit up. "What a wonderful tool! Not many Magicals have one of those. I've only seen one once when I was very young."

Larissa grabbed her bag of magical tools and rummaged around for the box holding the Numeromancer. The object looked rather like a spinning top but contained a clear quartz panel to discern the numbers. From what Tiberinus, Lord of Lakes, had briefly instructed, this tool divined numbers for anything a user wanted. She pulled it out and walked back over to Willem.

"We didn't receive any instructions on how to use it. Would you happen to know?"

The wizard held the piece, beholding it with an admiring gaze. Curious, Phuctious tugged at Willem's sleeve to indicate he wanted a better look. "Quite a beautiful divining tool," said Willem. He turned the top-like device around in his hands. There was a stem on top, one that looked like the user could merely spin it. "I must think on how to use it."

"Wouldn't you just spin it and simultaneously call out what you're looking for?" August nibbled on a hangnail, looking on with a bemused expression. "Can't be that hard, right?"

"Glad you've made yourself useful, August. Thank you very much for that." Larissa took the Numeromancer from Willem, placed it on the ground, and spun it. "Current location," she called out. The four stared at the piece. As it spun, it gleamed a glimmering gold. Around it, numbers flashed in haphazard fashion, glowing white as they faded in and out. The Numeromancer came to a halt. Larissa picked it up.

The numbers were in latitude and longitude. They shined in flashing colors of black and red. "I have no idea what the coordinates mean," Larissa said. "Not off the top of my head, anyway."

Willem snapped his finger. A floating map popped up. "It appears we are here," he said, pointing to a location on the map.

August squinted at where Willem pointed. He straightened back up instantly. "We're nowhere close to the super seven cave. Have we even gone far from where we left?"

Larissa thought a moment. "Based on the map, we're a fourth of the way into our journey." She looked at Willem and Phuctious.

Willem the wizard gazed at his companions in silence. At last, he answered. "We will have to walk to Brazil or find another way there. Even if we used a conventional airplane Mortals have concocted, we're nowhere near an airport."

"How far to the nearest town with an airport?" asked August.

Willem reviewed the map once again and shook his head with disappointment. "Over three hundred miles and counting."

"We cannot walk that far." Larissa smacked a palm against her forehead in dismay. "There has to be another option."

"What I still can't figure out is why the Vanishport isn't working," said Willem. He walked over and grabbed his bags. "Since we can't use it, let's just find a cozy spot and think about our next plan."

When everyone stepped out of the Vanishport with their bags, it disappeared. They found a large mossy patch under a large tree and sat down. August looked glum. Larissa rubbed her temples like she was warding off a massive headache. Phuctious shook his head in defeat. Willem's face held a look of worry, which worsened when a nasty clap of thunder crashed overhead.

"Damn!" August swore. "As if we need this kind of weather."

Large raindrops fell to the ground, gathering speed with each second.

The wizard stood and lifted both hands. "*Mansionem*!"

A few feet away, a simple cabin stood with a door ajar.

"Let's go!" Willem grabbed his bags and sprinted toward shelter. August, the dwarf, and Larissa followed.

Larissa shut the door of the cabin, dropped her bags, and rushed toward the stony hearth. "*Ignis*," she said, aiming a finger toward the opening. A set of logs and blazing fire appeared. Without a word, she turned and grabbed a chair that Willem had just created simultaneously with another spell. "At least we can stay warm while we think."

August picked up a second chair, followed by Willem. In moments, all sat in front of the fire.

Phuctious spoke first. "How do we break the spell, Anguis or otherwise? But I still feel strongly that they are behind this."

Normally, Larissa would have come to Edouard's defense, but since she had seen the nasty side of him, she kept quiet.

"We are in need of help, and it's not clear to whom we should ask." Willem sat back in his chair, hands clasped behind his head. He seemed at a loss.

"Got any friends in high places?" Phuctious looked at Larissa and lightly tapped on her knee.

She didn't readily answer but kept her eyes on the fire.

"What about a spell to unbreak a spell? We do it all the time," said August.

"I'm in no mood for trial and error," Larissa answered. Her words came out in staccato harshness.

"Hawthorne Heir, our companion is right," said Willem. "Unbreaking a spell can take some time."

"I could ask Aunt Dorenda." Larissa shut her eyes a moment. "She might be able to think of something."

August sat up straight. His face flushed with indignation. "Did you not hear what I told you earlier about your aunt?"

"What else do you want me to do, August?" Larissa shouted.

Both Willem and Phuctious jumped at the outburst. August, however, merely huffed in disgust. "Oh, quit your screeching and actually be of some use. Surely, you have something in your bag of tricks to help us get out of here. I've already made my suggestions." He slumped back in his seat and crossed his arms.

Larissa thought for a moment. This was a time when parents would come in handy. Part of her wanted to contact them, let them know what had happened. Another part of her felt shame in not knowing what to do. Eleanor and Roman may be her birth parents, but they were still strangers to her. "Welll, there is something I might be able to use."

August, Willem, and Phuctious sat forward in their seats, their eyes on her.

"Out with it, then," answered August. His voice resounded with continued irritation.

"Someone offered me only one opportunity to call on him should we ever need assistance. But once this favor is granted, I cannot call on him again." She looked each of her companions in the eye. "Do you think this would be a good time to use his favor?"

"Not really, when you can ask me." A calm voice sounded from the door.

All four of them turned to gaze on Edouard Anguis, standing against the doorframe and looking smug.

"Didn't think I'd find you, eh? Didn't even wait until I returned and at least give me a proper goodbye." He eyed Larissa. "My dear, I would have never guessed you'd cut and run. Why?"

The men kept quiet.

"We needed to be on our way," she answered. "You and I had discussed that very subject before you left, and I merely found an opportune time. The fact that it was while you were gone is really nothing against you." She smiled lightly at Edouard.

"Thank you for clearing that up, because I would have always questioned your leaving if you hadn't explained it all quite nicely."

He smiled back, but Larissa knew the insincerity in his attitude. The only sincerity she caught was his being pissed off at all of them, especially her.

Edouard opened the door. Turning briefly around, he shouted a command and stepped aside. Several guards entered inside the cabin and unceremoniously marched all off them outside. The rain continued pouring down, drenching her to the bone. Glum looks on the faces of her companions dismayed her more. For the first time, she felt helpless.

"Come, my pet, let's get you back to Sulphure Hall where you can dry off and be safe. I see your companions are with you. I'll take care of them, too, mark my words." He winked and waved them all off.

It wasn't only the wind and rain that chilled Larissa at the moment.

Chapter Fifteen

August found himself back in his old prison cell once again. This time he had company, but his companions were cloistered away in nearby cells. He didn't have Larissa's gimp spell to somewhat protect him. For the first time, he felt fear for her safety just as he did for himself, Phuctious, and Willem. Her words came back to haunt him.

What were those personality traits to which she had alluded when they conversed about Edouard after first getting back together? What did she see, and why would she say such a thing? He tried to warn her, but she'd rebuffed him. And he wasn't about to reveal all that his father had told him. Why waste precious energy when she wouldn't have believed him anyway?

Phuctious paced up and down in his cell, fretting over their predicament. He chastised himself for not having seen it coming so clearly as he had other things before. How had Edouard Anguis been so slick? But that was the way it went with that clave. Sneaky. Conniving. Ruthless. He'd come up with a way to get himself and his friends out or die trying. He jumped up and down a little to warm himself. Being the free nature-loving soul that his kind naturally were, the realization of spending an unknown amount of time in a dank cell unnerved him to the fullest. He felt his energy slowly draining away.

Willem sat against a rock wall, gazing at the floor. What was happening with Larissa? If Edouard harmed her in any way, he'd deal with that devil himself. There had to be a way to communicate with August and Phuctious. They needed a plan of escape, though the means of accomplishing this looked dim right now.

"My darling," said Edouard, "I hope you are okay with your old room. You didn't seem to mind it the first time." He bowed graciously. Inside, he seethed.

"Was it really necessary to put my friends in the dungeon? Surely, you could have afforded them a room." Larissa hoped she didn't come across too rough. At this point, she knew playing her cards right meant life or death. The memory of what Edouard did to the girl who tried to spin burned hot and heavy in her memory. She would never unsee that moment until the day she died.

"Ah, my sweet, it's just that I'm a bit nervous with so much company right now. You will always be my guest, but they . . . let's just say your companions don't necessarily rub me the right way. I must be honest about that." He rested his hand on her shoulder.

Restraining herself from shaking free of his touch took far more energy than she'd thought it would. Larissa gritted her teeth and spoke, "Would it be too much for you to kindly let them have rooms? Just for me? They have not done anything. You speak of love for me. Surely you wouldn't mistreat close friends of mine."

"Come, let us walk in the garden again. Perhaps clear air, sunshine, and flowers will help us with better and clearer discourse."

The pair headed outdoors, taking the same route they used last time they were together. She still marveled at the beauty surrounding her. With all her heart, Larissa wished this quest had never started, never been needed, that she and Edouard could have been the lovers that Aunt Dorenda had wanted. From what she witnessed that day when Edouard snuffed out that poor girl, trusting him any longer remained a no-go.

"I have something very personal to ask you, Edouard, if you don't mind." Larissa sucked in her breath and turned on the charm. "It's been on my mind for a bit, and I'm hoping you can explain it to me." Her arm slipped around his and tightened. Playing this game took effort like getting along with August—maybe a little more.

"My darling, you have only to ask me anything, and I'll happily answer if I can. I want no secrets between us." His face turned to hers, imparting a grand toothy smile.

"Before you left for your meeting, I saw something that has left me . . . how shall I say it? Perplexed."

"Oh? Please go ahead and ask." Edouard motioned for her to continue.

"I saw the room full of spinning wheels. And all the girls. And then there was one that you . . ."

Edouard stopped in his tracks, stiffening at her words.

"Don't stop. Let's keep walking. I think I'm feeling better, like you said I would. Fresh air and all."

"Mmm," he answered.

They continued down a stone path.

"What were you doing, and why did you need to off that girl? Why so many spinning wheels?" She glanced up at her admirer. "I'm confused. Really, I am."

He cleared his throat. "I'm glad you asked me that, though I extend my apologies for such an unsightly scene. I am working on a secret mission, as I choose to call it, and because of its sensitive nature, sometimes I have to rid myself of those who may talk too much once I dismiss them. You know how that goes, don't you?"

"No, I really don't, Edouard. If my memory serves me, you were quite angry at her for not being able to create something for you. Something about a cloth. Am I right?"

This time Larissa stopped and faced him head on.

The young man squared up his shoulders and mustered a smile. "You know what, sweetness, I'm glad we are having this conversation, because I was going to bring it up with you anyway."

"When?" she asked, staring at him with inching defiance.

"Well, when I returned, darling, but I had an important meeting to attend. I didn't run off like you. And the truth is, I would have discussed this with you when I returned." His face showed a forced grin.

"Then out with it. Why all the spinning wheels and then killing someone?"

"Don't you think that's a little harsh?" he asked. "I told you my reasoning, but let's not argue. She didn't suffer that much."

Larissa tapped her foot in annoyance.

"Okay, here goes. I am trying to create a conjuring cloth too. Surely you know the myths and stories we hear are not absolutes, right?"

"Go on," she said.

"Under the right circumstances, most anyone could likely create conjuring cloths. I'm just trying to figure out the particulars."

"That girl seemed to come awfully close, from what I saw. Don't you think giving her a little more time might have solved your problem?" Larissa whispered in his ear, "You seemed so angry and uncontrollable Are you like that all the time?"

Edouard's jaw tightened. "Again, my apologies, dear one. I don't like admitting this, but sometimes I get so excited about something I tend to overreact a little. Really, I don't usually mean any harm." He returned her stare. "Can we let the subject of Corinne go? I understand you're upset about that, but there's nothing to be done about it. We can, however, forge forward."

"We?" Larissa answered.

"I want to consider us a team. Always. In things we do together," said Edouard. "I hope you don't hold certain things against me."

They walked on together in silence for a few moments.

"I've been wondering if maybe you could try your hand at spinning."

Larissa answered, "Why do you want a conjuring cloth so badly that you create a whole spinning room and will, um, you know? And why would someone steal a cloth from someone else . . . hypothetically speaking, if we may?"

"Darling, that's a good question. You know how we witches like to collect tools we think can amp up our power. We all do it, and we're quite connoisseurs, if I might add. That cloth is no ordinary tool like a wand or crystal sphere. Anyone should want one. Many Magicals don't know a lot about them, as they are quite rare. Honestly, I'm shocked you seem so nonchalant about it. A cloth like that holds great power, channeling energy directly from the ether and back down over the person who holds it. Their thoughts and desires manifest almost immediately. It's that strong."

He stopped and placed his hands on her shoulders. "And they are so rare. You might have the genes or the skill and never knew it to create cloths yourself. You would be the best of all since you are a descendent of Ciana's. And if you think she created a cloth . . . well, I trust your speculation on that. You're quite intuitive."

The young lady eyed him with suspicion. "I thought you implied that anyone could create this cloth. Genetics shouldn't play a part, right? Why couldn't Ciana not create a cloth for you, or try, if you asked her? Especially when it might be so valuable. Because for some reason, I have a high sneaking suspicion that she quite possibly could."

Edouard winced at her words. He recovered quickly and smiled. "That's something to consider."

"You've never asked her? You told me you have met her, and your family has helped keep her safe," Larissa stated. She linked her arm around his and started walking again.

"You have to understand that we don't know for certain that a conjuring cloth was taken. And we don't know for sure she created one. We're only discussing this now, and it's all mere speculation on our part. For us to ask your Aunt Ciana to create a cloth out of the blue would sound absurd.

My father has never mentioned asking her. I have not. We wouldn't have thought about it." He tried smiling again. A throb flared up in his temples. An overwhelming desire to lay down and rest consumed him. This conversation could escalate badly for him and his crew if he didn't answer with great care.

Lying usually didn't bother him at all, but the inability to speak honestly with the object of his desire strained him more than he would have bargained for. And he admitted privately to himself that he rather disliked Larissa's shrillness and heated temperament. At this moment, he considered that a union between the two of them would be fabulous and unmatched, if he could sway her to his side. Or they would blast each other to smithereens if they became foes. He still banked on the former.

"Honestly, Edouard, I sense you hedging, especially about Ciana, and I can't understand why. Again, why do you want a cloth? When did you decide you suddenly wanted one? What would you use it for? And taking me to see Ciana might clear up a lot of things, don't you think?"

Damn! He was in no mood to play twenty questions. The young man kept his stride as he battled with himself in maintaining composure. At this moment, he wanted to just slap her silent. He clinched the fist of his free hand.

As if on cue, Larissa unlinked her arm from his and kept walking, waiting for his answer.

"Well, dear," he said after a few moments of thought, "I've been studying the spinners for quite some time. Had we been together more over the years, perhaps it could have been a subject we studied together. Maybe we could have discovered the secret." He looked over at her and managed a light smile.

"As far as what I would do with a cloth if I had one, I would use it for creating, um, wonderful things, perhaps help Magicals and Mortals alike."

Larissa looked over at her companion. Something about him reeked with insincerity, and she needed to get to the bottom of his true intent. At that moment, the desire to be with Willem, or even August, held great appeal. Something in her wanted to run.

Edouard glanced over at her, his face solemn, his eyes cold in their gaze. She forced herself to look away and toward the towering mountains and greenery that made up Huigra, South America.

"I want to meet Ciana," Larissa said at last. "I'll ask her myself. Maybe she can teach us both." She turned her face toward his and showed her sweetest smile.

He snapped his fingers in response. "You know what just occurred to me? Your Aunt Dorenda. Why not ask her? She's easily available."

Larissa scowled. This was not the answer she expected. Her gut clenched. "Why would she know how?"

"And why not? Just a shot in the dark, like Ciana. Dorenda is one of the best learned witches I know." His eyes sparkled with emotion.

The two stood gazing at each other. Larissa had wanted to keep Dorenda's attempts at spinning a secret. At this moment, she could either lie or tell the truth. She shot back, "Since you're not inclined to speak with Ciana, I'll talk to Aunt Dorenda the next time I see her. How about that?"

"Let me know what you find out," he answered. "Because I've tried, too, and I'm missing something. Maybe we both can truly learn this mystical craft. And together we could do great things in the world." He took this moment to land a quick kiss on her lips.

***

"Where is she?" Eleanor paced inside the front room of the great super seven crystal cave. "She should have been here by now."

Roman's face remained stiff with worry. "Something's amiss. I just know it."

"Do you think she changed her mind?" Eleanor stepped up beside her husband and place her hand on his arm.

"Why would she do that? Makes no sense." Roman hoped he hadn't sounded too snappy. "Maybe she had to take care of some things before coming."

"Like what?"

"I don't know, darling. I really don't."

Both parents stood in silence. Eleanor finally kicked at a stray crystal and went back to clearing the floor. They had managed a little headway in making the cave entrance and front room presentable.

"Hellooo!"

Roman and Eleanor glanced up.

"Andrea!" Roman cried out. He ran to his sister and hugged her tight. "It's you. I've missed you."

"I've missed you, too. Oh, it's been so long." Andrea stepped back, pulling her husband, Stephan, toward them.

"Roman, good to see you again." Stephan shook his brother-in-law's hand with happy vigor.

"And who do we have here?" Roman stepped toward two young attractive ladies.

"Uncle Roman, I'm Ciela, and this is Astrid." Ciela gave her uncle a hearty hug, with Astrid following her.

"They are just beautiful, Andrea. I remember them as very little girls before we were scattered. I wouldn't have known them if I'd seen them on the street today."

"With the help of allies, determination, and calling on the deities, I got them cared for. Now they've returned to us." Andrea wrapped an arm around each daughter and smiled with pride.

"Anybody home?"

Everyone turned around.

"Yo-ho and a bottle of rum! Any drinks in the house?" A man's booming voice called out.

"Brendan, you're as loud as you've always been." Andrea laughed.

"I've missed you the most, my dear sister." Brendan winked at her and turned to deliver a hug to his brother first.

Andrea smacked Brendan's arm. "Come here, silly. Give me a hug too." Both she and Brendan fell into each other's arms, laughing.

"Oh, don't let me forget my family. Dannie!" Brendan called out to a pleasant-looking woman with long light brown hair.

Dannie, Brendan's wife, ran from hugging Eleanor and stood before Roman, arms outstretched. "Good to see all of you again. And here are the boys, Gregory and Aiden."

"Hi, everyone," said Gregory.

Aiden's eyes darted around. "This is a great cave. Will we see more of it?"

"You'll be seeing plenty of it, son." Roman laughed and patted his nephew on the back. "I'll take you on a personal tour."

"Got room for us?" A voice sounded from the entrance.

"Hey! Henry finally made it!" Brendan called out. "You're late. Where have you been? Party's started."

"You're lucky I made it at all. I despise traveling." Henry stepped into the crowd and hugged everyone. "I guess you all remember Jasmine."

Henry's wife smiled and greeted everyone in turn. "And if you don't remember, here are Paul and Samantha."

Paul stepped forward and extended his greetings, followed by Samantha.

"I swear this is just amazing," said Roman. "I really don't know some of you, but it's like I've known all of you for such a long time."

"Well, brother," said Henry, "it's the children who seem newer. They were all so young when we had to leave everything. And now they've become young men and women."

"And I'm sure more than capable witches," added Eleanor, smiling.

"From what I gather, we'll need every capable witch there is," added Henry.

"Where's Larissa?" asked Jasmine "We're all dying to see her."

Eleanor's eyes grew large. "Roman and I were just asking ourselves the same thing just before all of you arrived."

"She's not here?" Brendan squinted, confused.

Both Roman and Eleanor shook their heads.

Andrea frowned. "Interesting. I would have thought she'd be the first here or at least before we all came. Have you tried contacting her?"

"We were just going to do that," said Eleanor. She looked up at Roman with a questioning expression.

"Truth is," answered Roman, "she told us she was on her way. That's been hours ago."

"That doesn't sound good at all." Dannie spoke up. "I hope she's okay."

"Maybe the Anguis got her," Aiden spoke up in a matter-of fact tone.

Startled at the remark, everyone turned around and stared at the attractive tall, lean young man.

"And why would you say that?" asked Gregory.

"I've been hearing things for the last year or so. There's trouble brewing, and I've heard the Anguis are right in the thick of it." Aiden nodded in confirmation at his own words. "It's possible that maybe they talked her out of coming, right at the last minute. They have their crew everywhere. You never know."

"Has anyone else heard the same, about the Anguis?" Jasmine looked around at everyone.

Stephan spoke out, "I've heard about a group called something like 'The Chevron'. I'm not sure what the name is, because I've heard very little about it."

"I think I've heard about it," said Samantha. She sidled up next to her brother, Paul. "They're called "The Order of the Chevron." Paul looked at his sister and nodded in agreement.

"And I think I've heard rumor where the Anguis and Order of the Chevron are in cahoots. Whatever that is supposed to mean," added Astrid.

Roman shook his head. "How is it that you young people know more about this, and we older adults seem clueless?"

Ceila answered, "I think it depended on where you lived and the kind of people or groups you hung out with. I know where I grew up, they got you into politics and events as soon as you were in school."

"That's probably true," said Gregory, "My life growing up was more sheltered, but I still heard some of what my cousins and brother are saying."

The sound of crunching stones under foot resounded throughout the cave. Everyone stopped talking at once and listened with anticipation. Within seconds, Paulo entered the front room.

After a round of introductions, Paulo explained more of who he was and brought everyone up to speed on his branch of the family line.

"That's wonderful of you to come," remarked Stephan. "It's a shame you couldn't get anyone else in Ecuador to come with you."

"They felt it would be best to remain there and prepare. They're all getting more nervous every day." He turned to Roman and Eleanor. "And I'm like the others here. Very concerned about your daughter not showing up. That is so troublesome."

Andrea piped up. "I agree with Paulo. I'm very worried about Larissa. Roman, you or Eleanor need to get to the bottom of why she's not here. The quicker the better."

Chapter Sixteen

"Let me see her, Eustace," said Dorenda. "You've had her all these years, and you have refused to let me see her."

"I've been trying to woo her over, not bombard her with more witches. I was hoping you could figure this out yourself and we could bypass her altogether." He sighed. "So you just can't seem to get it together, eh?" Eustace gazed on Dorenda's face captured within his crystal sphere.

"I've tried everything. I come close but no cigar, as the Mortals say." She shrugged lightly.

"I've had no luck in getting her to do anything. I have the cloth we took from her, but she refuses to let us activate it. Do you think she's made others that were activated, and we don't know about it?"

"From what I've learned, each cloth that's made is activated by a fire power source. Once it's used up, another one will need to be made for its next spell. She wanted Clement to activate the cloth you have."

"Seems like it," said Eustace. He remained silent in thought.

Dorenda spoke up a few seconds later. "She came to me in a dream. She must have wanted to share something."

Eustace stared back at his lover. "That was only the one time, unless she's done it more than once, and you've not told me."

"Only the one time. It was before you and I . . . well, you know. I'm hoping the reason she came to me was to show me how to spin the cloth, maybe hoping I could also teach Larissa. Why else would she seek me out?"

"But she's not tried since that time, right?" asked Eustace.

"Oh, what's your point?" Dorenda crossed her arms in irritation. "You're so patronizing, Eustace. If you use that stance with Ciana, no wonder she won't give in."

"Calm down. You're starting to tick me off. And I assure you that's not a good thing to do."

"I'm just trying to get you to let me see her. You've kept her cloistered away. It's time for someone else outside your family. Maybe I can get some information from her. Anything."

Eustace scratched his head, thinking. "Well, at this point, I don't see how it would hurt. We've all tried to coax it out of her. She's stubborn and resolute."

"Let me see her," said Dorenda. "Maybe I can talk her into it, try a different approach. I think it's time. I can't figure it out. She won't budge with you. Nothing to lose, dear."

"Come on, then. I'll give you the location."

After being duped by Jove, whom she thought she could trust (and whom she could have liked almost better than Eustace), she needed to get her confidence built up once again. More than anything, she needed to solve the riddle of spinning a cloth. She'd come so close before. She was sure of it.

Daniel's words of warning had unnerved her, and Eustace's irritation and mild threat during this conversation worried her as well. He'd never taken that tone with her. The father of their child was running low on patience. It was now or never—or worse.

She didn't trust her son any more than her lover. Maybe at one time, but not now. Edouard still hadn't been told the truth about her, but even if he knew, he was still much like his father. That much she knew. Dorenda wrote down Eustace's instructions, packed a small bag of essentials, and took the next Vanishport to Rouen, France.

***

Dorenda had been careful about travel during Larissa's childhood. Eustace and the Anguis were powerful, but that didn't stop another Magical from exercising their skills and taking her out completely. Thus she had not visited her lover in Rouen, France. And then there was the ugly business of dealing with Priscilla. She could not afford to have Eustace's wife finding out anything about what she and he had done.

It had been Eustace's preference that Dorenda stay away and keep a low profile. It hadn't kept them from talking at times and keeping up with one another, though. As Larissa and Edouard matured, so had the Anguis's dark plans to take over the world and other dimensions. Her lover's charms and sweet talk lured her in, and now she was in too deep to back out now.

The Vanishport landed in front of the chateau, within the inner boundaries of the gate and a few yards from the main steps to a gargantuan front door. Dorenda took a moment and gazed upward, taking in the vision of towers and the steep roofline making up a quite striking dwelling. Oh, what it would have been to spend time with Eustace here. If he and Priscilla hadn't been slated to marry, she would have easily been mistress of this house.

She shook her head, focusing her thoughts on the real reason she travelled here. Forget wishing on what could have been. The older lady had a job to do and completing it had become harder than she imagined. The prospect of meeting someone like Ciana thrilled her to the marrow. Not many— maybe no one—had ever gazed on someone like Larissa's great great aunt. Perhaps her tone with this special lady might yield better results.

The Anguis could turn on the charm with the best of them, but once they lost patience, she knew all too well their ability to exact revenge. If this good lady had refused Eustace and Edouard all these years, her days may be limited. Dorenda hoped that Ciana knew this in some way. She grabbed her travel bag and walked quickly toward the front door, pulling a bell rope.

From inside, the clanging sound announced her arrival. The butler answered the door. "Miss Soltaro?" He bowed his head lightly in respect.

"Yes." Dorenda smiled. "I'm here on Mr. Eustace Anguis's request."

"I'll show you to him, ma'am."

Together, they walked down a large hallway toward Eustace's study. She didn't know which place she liked better, this gorgeous one or Katharta Castle. Too bad she'd not be visiting there anymore. Jove had gotten the best of her, and the most she could hope for was that whatever happened during their night together, he could keep a secret.

"Ah, my dear, you've made it." Eustace, draped in a fine silk embroidered dressing robe, got up from an overstuffed copper-colored leather sofa and headed her way, arms outstretched. "You may go, Jacques. We need nothing right now."

"As you wish, sir. I'll listen for the bell in case you change your mind." The refined butler bowed and turned out of the room.

"What a stunning place you have here, Eustace." Dorenda smiled at him.

"Finally, we can have all this to ourselves with no interference from anyone." He tilted his head and pursed his lips.

"When are we going to tell him the truth?" asked Dorenda.

"I've had a fit trying to conceal everything from my daughters. I was on eggshells thinking of how I would present the fact that the sweet boy who lived with grandfather was actually their brother. And that the only reason he stayed there is because their mother couldn't tolerate her son bearing less than average looks." He shook his head. "She was always a shallow one, that much is true."

Dorenda listened, lightly nodding at intervals. "We will have to tell them someday soon."

"Why do we even have to tell them at all? Sometimes things are best left a secret, don't you think?"

"Not meaning any disrespect, my darling, but I want to leave this earth with my son knowing who his real mother is."

Eustace rubbed his hand across her cheek. "All in good time, my dear. For someone so formal and proper, you have a soft spot, don't you?"

"I do. And that's not a bad thing. Good witches can harbor some compassion. We need balance in our lives."

"Ah, you sound so philosophical. Shall I pour us a drink?"

"As you wish." Dorenda smiled in agreement.

She watched as her lover walked toward a fully outfitted bar, pulled down a bottle of his most expensive wine, and filled two heavy crystal goblets. Maybe Eustace would mind his manners and not pull the stunt that Jove did. If he ever learned that she and Jove had shared a bed several times, she might leave the earth sooner than she'd bargained for.

"Come sit close to me, Dorenda." Eustace sat on the sofa and patted the empty space by his side. "Let me feel you close. I've dreamed of moments like this all the while Priscilla was alive, and even more after her death." He looked at her, taking a moment to stroke her thigh. "It's just finding the right time, you know."

"I understand. Any chance we can make up for lost time?" She grinned.

"I want to do that and more. The world is ours for the taking, Dorenda. Edouard just went to a world meeting to address those who are fighting on our side. The Mortals and Magicals are an elite group from all over the world. They want the same things we want, to enjoy every luxury and freedom we can muster up and then some." He rested his cheek momentarily against hers. "No reason we shouldn't have all that, right? Don't you agree?"

"I very much agree," answered Dorenda. She sipped her drink, letting the alcohol warm her.

"And our Edouard has your beautiful niece with him, and her, um, friends."

"Oh?" Dorenda looked over at him in surprise. "I didn't know she was with him. I haven't heard from her in a while."

"I'm sure he's entertaining her well. Just a mere brief interruption in her journey. He'll see that she gets back on track." Eustace's eyes gleamed. He took a moment and kissed her cheek, moving slowly to her lips. "You taught her well, dear woman. You taught her well. Now we'll see if our son can sway her at all. I hope he has better luck with her than I've had with Ciana."

"We shall see, won't we? But the relationship between Edouard and Larissa has to be handled delicately. We can't let things get too far out of hand but just far enough for Larissa to give us what we need. That's all and nothing more." Dorenda closed her eyes, feeling her mind surrendering to the drink in her hand.

"Larissa doesn't know you, does she? The real you. What you stand for, what you really want."

"Not a clue. I've not told her anything but merely have served as her aunt and teacher." She looked hard at her lover. "It's been hard, Eustace. Do you know how hard it's been to not break down and tell her? I've lied to her for many years. And we've been pushing a relationship that should never be, won't be. It will break her heart."

"Oh, come now." He chuckled and sat his drink on an end table. "Don't start getting all weepy on me. In this game, you do what you have to do. Just call it one of the down sides and move on. We're too close. You and I are about to fulfil our destiny, be where we should have been all along if life had not gotten in our way." He lifted her face to his. "Now, Larissa and Edouard can fulfill their roles. It's the way it's supposed to be. And you must admit that our glamour charms have worked wonders on our son."

Eustace slipped a hand into her blouse, searching beneath her bra. Dorenda closed her eyes once again, feeling the warmth of his hand as his fingers toyed with her nipple. With a snap of his finger, the locks on the doors clicked shut.

Dorenda's eyes popped wide open. She looked at the man beside her. His eyes glowed with lust. He toyed with her flesh with more urgency. With a free hand, he loosened the belt holding his dressing robe in place, revealing more of his dark skin. Between his legs, a throbbing member stood firm and erect. She'd not forgotten his ample size, and the sight of him stirred up the old memories, their clandestine trysts, the passion, the secrecy, the delectable moments when they thought no one was looking.

Inside, she sensed her body preparing itself, awakening, becoming wet, giving way to a pleasure ache that would soon drive her to the heights of ecstasy. Her frame yielded to his touch as he placed her goblet on the floor and gently but firmly pushed her back on the sofa. Dorenda didn't care that she hadn't seen him recently or had just crossed his threshold. Didn't care to think about what she must have looked like, reclining on the huge sofa, legs spread apart while Eustace slipped off her undergarments and dipped his thick silky fingers deep into her core.

She clenched her teeth, stifling a moan, undulating her hips slightly. He turned his fingers upward and stroked back and forth, nearly sending her writhing to the floor. With one quick move, he positioned himself, plunging in his stiff flesh, sighing as he did with a wide smile on his face.

"I've been fantasizing about this for a long time, Dorenda. Tell me what I want to hear, that you love me, that there is no one else but me."

"Oh . . . Eustace!" Dorenda looked deep into her lover's eyes and gasped with pure unadulterated pleasure. "Eustace, I love you. There has been no one for me but you. My love, my heart. Take me. All of me."

He moved harder and faster, his body smacking against hers. "Dorenda. For the love of the gods, you're all mine now. You're all mine." Eustace pumped his hips several times, gasped and let out a moan. He pushed hard, grunted, and inhaled a deep breath of relief.

Dorenda wrapped her arms around him, holding his body close to hers. Perhaps if she played her cards right, he'd be in better humor than she'd hoped.

***

Dorenda and Eustace gazed at each other over the breakfast table. She had not dared push further on seeing Ciana the day before, much preferring that he decide when they should meet. She hoped with all her might that their lovemaking had placed him in a much more relaxed frame of mind. Being overeager never won anyone anything, so she had chosen to play it cool and let him have his way with her.

Of course, it wasn't like she didn't revel in their union. But despite her love for Eustace, there was still something about Jove that she really liked. He had an eager fiery burning energy while Eustace had a deep heated one. Both were hot and tantalizing but with a different approach and feel. She had to forget about August's grandfather. Jove only risked muddying the water, and maybe it was best their fling ended.

"Are you ready to see her? Think you can get something out of Larissa's great great aunt?" Eustace sipped his coffee.

"What's she like? Tell me a little about her. Prepare me. What do I need to know?"

"I'll let you see for yourself. No need to go into this thing with any preconceived notions or any of my prejudices." He winked at her.

"I must admit I'm a little nervous, and I don't know why." Dorenda placed a small piece of melon from a dainty silver fork into her mouth.

"Nothing to be nervous about. Although seeing something like her is quite a privilege. It's not every day we knowingly see someone like her kind or the history to go along with it. But I got over that awe a long time ago."

The two spent several moments in silence as they finished the breakfast laid out before them.

"Come, you can have a crack at her," said Eustace. He got up from the chair and stretched out his arm toward Dorenda.

She wiped her mouth, stood up, and took a deep breath. Linking arms with her lover, she followed him through the glistening halls of the chateau and down to its depths. Eustace didn't bother knocking on the thick oak door at the end of a shadowy hall, dimly lit by small sconces.

"Ciana, you have a visitor." He lightly pushed Dorenda in the woman's direction. "She wants to talk to you."

Ciana, who was reclining on top of her bed, sat up, surprised. She'd never been granted visitation before, not that anyone would be looking for her. When she saw it was Dorenda, her eyes narrowed with disapproval. Dorenda didn't miss the expression on the Nephilim's face and tried smiling. She hoped the gesture might soften a tense situation.

Eustace continued, "I'll leave you two alone to discuss your business. And you know your way back to me whenever you're done." He aimed his last sentence at Dorenda, gently tapping her on the shoulder. She nodded and watched the door close behind him.

"So, you've come at last," said Ciana.

Dorenda stared a few seconds, taking in the woman's height. She was much taller than the average human, slender in frame, with a striking face for someone so old.

"Remember me, or have you forgotten? You came to me in a dream long ago. I still remember it."

"It's taken this long? Pity you didn't come before spreading those ample thighs of yours for the devil himself. On top of that you bore his wretched spawn." Ciana stepped closer to her visitor and whispered, "How does it feel to hold the devil's seed deep inside you and become fat with his child?" Ciana let out a huff. "And guess what? Now we have two devils controlling everything." She sat on the edge of the bed, arms crossed with displeasure.

The words stunned Dorenda into a bout of silence. Both ladies eyed each other, Ciana with heightened disapproval, Dorenda with confusion.

"I'm sure I don't know what you mean."

Ciana laughed. "Oh, you most certainly do. Don't play coy with me, Dorenda Soltaro, mother of Edouard Anguis." The lady pursed her lips in anger. "As far as I'm concerned, you are an accomplice to Priscilla's death. Worse, you are an accomplice to the ending of this world as both Mortals and Magicals know it. No one will convince me of anything else."

"Ciana!" Dorenda stepped toward the Nephilim with an outstretched arm. "I'm not sure why you're saying this."

"You know perfectly well why I'm saying this, and I speak the truth. So, what is it that you want? What is this business of which Eustace speaks, though I think I can figure it out already?"

Dorenda clasped her hands and prepared herself. This meeting was nothing like she'd ever planned. She'd reviewed all the different ways in her head about how to approach a Nephilim, her niece's great great aunt. The reaction and words to which she'd been subjected hit hard. Her heart chakra ached.

"I think in the dream, you were trying to show me how to weave a conjuring cloth. I've been practicing, hoping I could get it all down perfectly, but I'm a bit stuck at this point."

"And stuck you'll stay from any point onward." Ciana scowled. "A whore such as yourself has no business learning how to create a cloth. You're not worthy. You're a defiled liar. And let me tell you something else, Eustace cares nothing for you, just like Edouard cares nothing about anyone with whom he comes in contact. If it doesn't serve them, they will dispense with you in the blink of an eye. And you let yourself be fooled. I guess lust kind of works that way, doesn't it?"

"Ciana, listen." Dorenda lightly cleared her throat. "I didn't come to fight, and I surely didn't come to you in hostility, either. I was trying to follow up on what had been started years ago, when you came to me. You had a reason. I know you did."

"Again, that was before . . . you know." Ciana wagged a finger in Dorenda's direction. "I refuse to help the dark forces. If the betterment of humanity and witches can't be obtained in a sound, pure way, I'll not participate. Never." Her eyes glinted with pure defiance.

"Will you not give me the slightest hint? A simple suggestion? I mean, we are not dark forces, Ciana. We have our ideas about what would benefit this world to make it a greater place for everyone. Whatever convinced you to think otherwise? What you say is ludicrous." Dorenda tried staying calm.

Ciana's gaze turned colder as she stared hard at the woman in front of her. "The Light Bringers will win. You have little time left. You cannot mold the world to honor just your will and that of your evil lover and son. People have been steeped in darkness and ignorance far too long. The knowledge of the great power they hold within themselves has been cloistered away, and now it's about to be unleashed. And you and the devil are powerless to stop it."

"You can't be serious! Are you even listening to yourself?" Dorenda shook her head in despair.

"Get out!" Ciana pointed to the door.

"But . . ."

"Get out!" Ciana yelled.

Dorenda sucked in her breath and left. As she walked back to the upper levels of the chateau, her heart pounded. She knew without Ciana's guidance, her ability to come up with a cloth had ended, leaving the Dark Forces nothing. She was aware of Edouard trying to create a cloth, as Eustace had told her that much. But Edouard had made it clear, with his father's backing, that anyone associated with the Strondovan line, was to try and spin. Dorenda had been all too eager to try her hand at it, especially when Ciana had visited her in the dream. But now all hope was lost.

For the first time, she was not only in fear of what would become of her, but what would become of Ciana. She wiped away the tears welling in her eyes and headed to Eustace's study. If he allowed it, she'd take her bags and return home. Getting in touch with Larissa was a must. They had to talk, share any information they could. Things were starting to turn dire. She felt it in her bones.

***

Ciana bolted out of a deep sleep to the sound of the door opening and Eustace entering.

"Get up, Ciana. Get up right now." He strode over to the bed and yanked the covers back.

"What?" She grasped the covers in retaliation and pulled them back over her. "I'm sleeping. Go away."

"Get up this instant," said Eustace. His hot breath hit her skin. He grabbed the covers one last time and pulled them all the way down to the end of the bed. "Never mind about dressing. Your nightgown will do. Besides, our guest has gone."

"What's it to me? She was *your* guest, not mine." The woman scowled and slid her feet off the bed and onto the floor. "What do you want, Eustace?"

"Something I should have done long ago." He latched onto her arm and shoved her toward the door.

"Don't you have any manners? Pushing an old woman like me around. Have some respect, if that's even possible." Ciana tried pulling away from him, but he gripped her tighter.

"I've had enough manners with you to last a lifetime."

"I guess you like pushing me like you did your wife." Ciana looked down at him with a sneer and a knowing gleam in her eye.

Eustace stopped mid stride and glared up at her. He considered her a moment and finally smiled. "Let's go."

The pair entered a room at the opposite end of the dreary hallway. One of the house staff opened the door. Ciana looked around at the room. Other than a chair and a small table with some curious hardware on top, it was empty. A small door at the far corner remained latched. The staff member moved the chair to the center of the room. Eustace guided Ciana toward it.

"Sit down, and don't move," Eustace said. He cocked his head toward the table.

Within seconds, Ciana sat with her feet under the table and her hands shackled securely in place on top. Puzzled, she looked up at Eustace.

"You'll find out in a few seconds what your stubbornness will cost. I've been patient long enough. I decided to give you one last chance with Dorenda, and you totally blew it."

"I won't give information to you, and I surely wasn't going to give it to your whore." Ciana cast her gaze on the tabletop, shoulders slumped in despair.

"Even in this moment, you still choose to defy me." Eustace shook his head. "You've got guts, I'll warrant that."

He nodded to the male staff, who promptly walked to the small closet door and brought out an axe.

Ciana bristled at once when she saw the blade. Her stomach lurched. She glanced at Eustace's cold, expressionless face.

"Just do what I ask, and I can stop all this."

She said nothing but stared straight ahead.

"As you wish, Ciana. You can't say I haven't tried." He paced before her. "I could have you blindfolded so you don't see what's coming, but all things considered, I'll just let you watch if you're so inclined." He stepped back and signaled to the man. "Abe, go ahead."

Without a word, Abe stood on Ciana's right side, lifted the axe, and brought it down with a sure, hard blow right above her wrist, landing on his target with a sickening thud. She screamed in pain and shuddered, the breath catching in her throat. Tears instantly spilled from her eyes. Labored breaths hitched in her throat.

"The other one, Abe, and we'll be done. I'm not giving her a chance now to save the other hand."

Abe nodded and positioned himself on the other side, performing the same movements as before. Ciana screamed again, breaking the string of sobs coursing from her throat.

Eustace lifted the two severed hands dripping with hot fresh blood and placed them in Ciana's line of vision. "Take a last look at them before they are truly gone forever."

Ciana bowed her head. From the depths of her soul, she screamed out her despair, sobbing the hottest, hardest tears she'd ever cried in her life.

Chapter Seventeen

August's stomach clenched. His heart hurt. He grabbed his chest. Was he having a heart attack, and at such a young age? Had the dungeons of the Anguis finally gotten the better of him? Taking a deep breath, he stood up and paced. Something happened somewhere, and he couldn't get a grip on what.

His hands burned like they'd never burned before. Wincing, he glanced down at them. They seemed redder than normal and throbbed in time with the beating of his heart. The wrist joints ached without mercy. This was strange. He hadn't injured them trying to find a way out of the cell. He hadn't over-worked them with magic, nor had he crumpled himself into an odd position trying to find a more relaxing way to rest on the stony floor.

His eyes closed as he fought to get the pain under control. In his gut, these series of sensations was a sign, and he knew instinctively that he had to get to the bottom of it. He tried contacting Willem through a psychic connection spell but failed. Phuctious didn't respond, either. He gasped with another bout of pain and dropped to the floor, wracking his brain hard on what to do next.

With the discomfort surging through him, going through a spell or ritual would be extremely difficult. His frame of mind prohibited it. He swore under his breath. Their travel bags had been confiscated. With any luck, Larissa may have sweet-talked Edouard into letting them stay with her. August walked to the far wall and sat down. As usual, water pooled into the same place as it had before when he'd inhabited this cell last.

The reflection worked okay enough when Jove spoke to him. He'd have to use it again, this time as a gazing pool. It wouldn't be at all nice like the one back home in Katharta Castle, where he'd first visioned the wand duel between Desmond Strondovan and his uncle Clement—the encounter that started this whole mess between the Strondovans and the Hawthornes.

Without Larissa's horrid gimp spell hindering him, he used his normal agility squatted down, placing his mouth close to the small puddle. Slowly he blew over it, chanting in his head a magical mantra he'd learned as a child. His breaths created a larger puddle. He sat cross-legged and closed his eyes. The words from his spell flowed from his lips. *"Water deep, water free, show me what I long to see. Good or bad, it may be so. Show me what I need to know."*

He opened his eyes, sighing with relief when the water rippled, just as it had done with this exercise back home. A murky light filled the cell enough to illuminate August's space where he gazed. He let himself go into a trance and watched. The scene he witnessed between Ciana and Eustace sickened him to the core. The urge to vomit wracked his body, and it took great effort to prevent launching his stomach contents into the dark corner opposite where he sat.

He closed the scrying session and stood up, taking deep breaths to try and clear his head. Had Larissa felt anything odd like he did, or was it just him? If the sensations had been felt by him alone, why? Why would Ciana target such emotions his way and not a direct descendant of hers? August had to do something, act, tell Larissa, talk to Willem and Phuctious. First, he had to get out of the damned cell. And Edouard didn't hesitate throwing up that hateful barrier like before. That would be a bitch to take down . . . unless . . .

Time to summon help again. Like before, he called up his demon ritual book and searched through it. Ah, Agares! Just the spirit being who could help with more than one situation, and he needed help with two of the situations listed. He took some deep breaths, trying to clear and center himself. Reviewing the ritual, he performed the visualization exercises, gazed at the sigils, recited the invocation, and waited.

Something damp and grainy filled August's hand. He looked down in amazement and gazed on a fistful of wet sand, as if he'd grabbed it up from the beach at low tide. It all slipped from his hand, turning into white grains when it hit the cell floor. His nostrils caught the odor of what smelled like swampy water on a hot, humid afternoon. The inside of his mouth filled with a salty taste. August licked his lips and frowned.

"To what do I owe this summons, August Hawthorne?"

In the dim light, a wispy, barely discernable figure morphed into view.

"I'm so glad you answered my call, O Agares, the great and powerful one who assists with weakening magical power and authority. One who assists with communication when it seems to have been blocked. I'm in trouble and need your help."

"Yes, I gathered that," answered Agares. "On with it, then. What can I do for you?"

"That nasty Edouard Anguis has thrown me and my two friends down here in the dungeons, while he has our other companion cloistered away somewhere. I can't get a telepathic connection with Willem and Phuctious."

August boldly stepped closer toward Agares, who remained rooted in his spot, not about to move for any reason. "He's put up that crystalline shield again with these bars, and I can't seem to break through them no matter how hard I try. My energy is shot, and so it is with my friends."

Agares studied August through squinted eyes, listening to his caller. "Have you given any thought to what you will do if I help you get out of here?"

"Well." August blinked a few times, stumped at the question. It was a simple one, really. One that he didn't have entirely mapped out. "I-I don't know at the moment. I haven't talked to the others. I think something is blocking our ability to reach out."

"I would agree on that hunch. Again, what will be your purpose if I help you out? You must be able to make good use of my assistance, or it's a waste of both our time." Agares relaxed his posture.

Frustrated and worried, August paced the floor. "I need to get out of here. I need to get my friends out of this forsaken castle. I need to get *her* out of the Anguis Chateau!" He strode up to the demon. "Did you see what happened to her, Larissa's great great aunt? It's an abomination!"

"August Hawthorne, again, what are you going to do about it?" Agares's voice grew sharper. "This time you are in really deep over your head. Power of the darkness is consuming you, and now it's time for being smart, sly, and quick-witted. I'm giving you three more seconds to get your plan together, or I'm leaving."

The young man stood still. Panic set in. His mind went blank. He had never felt more helpless until now. "Ow!" The top of his head stung like someone had landed the tip of an ice pick firmly on top of his scalp. "Was that necessary?" He glared at Agares, who now looked rather amused.

"Pipe down. I didn't touch you." The demon's eyes lit up. He raised a finger above August's head. "Perhaps that might jog your memory?"

August looked up just in time to see a bright dandelion-looking frond floating above him. It disappeared once it hit the dungeon ceiling. The image of the penis pitcher plant in Greta Marvo's enchanted garden came to mind. It was the prick, the idea that he had held with him all along but merely hid in the recesses of his brain until the right moment. Now it had meaning.

"I do have an idea—and I just thought of another to go along with it."

"Good for you. Thought I might have to call this day a wash." Agares grinned. "Now that you are truly ready, let's get started on breaking through the bars and get you talking to your buddies."

August walked toward the cell door.

"Now, I will weaken the power of Edouard Anguis long enough for you to execute your ideas, but when I say long enough, I mean it. You have one hour."

"One hour?" August shot Agares a look of surprise.

"This isn't a social party, August Hawthorne. Get down to business, be quick and smart about it, and get moving."

Agares's visage glowed white. He lifted his hands toward the cell door. A red light flooded the chamber. The bars shimmered like glitter and quickly turned back to their regular black iron color. The lock squeaked and broke loose, sending the door swinging outward.

Behind the demon, August watched as a light blue glowing matrix set up behind him. A large dot of white light coursed over the pathways, sizzling as it moved. "Go. Now!" Agares pointed toward the open door and disappeared.

August darted out of the cell, surprised that none of the guards were around. But he didn't have time to think about that. He ran calling, "Willem. Willem! Phuctious."

"I'm down here," said Willem.

August ran to the wizard. "Have you tried the door?"

"Of course I have, Heir Hawthorne. But you can guess it's been locked tight. I can't beat their spell."

Exasperated, August pulled open the door. The wizard stepped out with surprise.

"Listen, Willem, trust me when I say we have a little less than one hour to get out of here, you, me, Phuctious, and Larissa. We have to find her, Ciana. She's in—"

"Let's go. What are we waiting for?" Phuctious had already discovered his door had mysteriously unlocked, walked out of his cell, and headed toward Willem and August.

"You gotta plan? Let's hear it." The dwarf's eyes were wide, intent. "I couldn't find anything magical in my cell that I could use for spell-breaking. Couldn't reach any of you either. My energy was sapped, I tell you."

August spoke up. "I need you two to get to Larissa. Tell her she'll just have to trust us, but we are leaving to find Ciana. Her aunt is in big trouble. And she needs to call on the Druids of the Desert to help. They said they would. She has the incantation with her. I don't have it. We need an army of help right now."

Willem and Phuctious stared at August.

"And what do you plan to do?" asked Phuctious.

"I'm going to get to the bottom of what that sleazy con man Edouard Anguis is up to." August grinned. "And I'll stop at nothing to get it. I will prevail. By the end of the hour, we will meet at the castle gates and get the hell out of Dodge. We'll know where to go, because I'm going to find out."

***

Edouard walked near the tree line surrounding Sulphure Hall. He turned and viewed the spacious structure he had created, marveling at his own handiwork, the design of it all. Huigra, Ecuador allowed him beauty and privacy to do his work. Pity most Mortals—and many Magicals—didn't have the wherewithal to create what they wanted. Mortals, especially, had ignored their inner power for ages.

At least this was his opinion, as it had been for many years. But Mortals were awakening. They now sought out the great teachers and organizations to help rediscover their power; many were learning to use it and use it well. He and his group had to hurry. If all went as planned, he'd have the world at his fingertips, doing his bidding. Only a small intimate group would be privy to this kind of all-encompassing power.

He saw the world changing before his eyes. Factions had formed. There was little trust between and within the groups of Magical and Mortals. Of course, there were many who wanted to fight against what he wanted, what he stood for. Like it or not, he admitted that their power railed against his, and he must stop it at all costs. Larissa was so close to seeing it his way, or so he hoped. Her words encouraged him. She wanted to talk to Ciana, and he wanted to see if she could talk some sense into that old fool. He had wanted to find the best time, that's all.

When his father Eustace confessed to him what had happened after Dorenda left his premises, Edouard was beside himself with irritation. Normally, he didn't give a damn about what happened to Ciana, for he had also grown weary of her rebellious nature, her impertinence. Going to such extreme, however, now placed his plans for Larissa meeting her great great aunt in enormous jeopardy. How would he explain this? She'd be lost to him forever upon learning the horrid truth.

He walked onward, thinking over his troublesome quandary and how best to handle it. Ciana would tell her relative the truth. If the aunt suffered through what Eustace inflicted on her, she'd most likely die for a cause she believed in. Ciana harbored a stubborn streak and showed no intention of backing down.

Edouard stopped and squinted, shielding his eyes from the sun. Several yards away, he spied a young woman staring in his direction. Who was this person? How did she wander onto his property? He'd never seen her before. And she didn't belong to the spinning entourage he held captive inside him home. The lady stood still. In the sunlight, her long maroon silk dress ruffled about her. He headed forward, watching intently and with great curiosity while the breeze playfully tossed locks of her brilliant long golden hair.

She looked antiquated and quite out of place. Edouard thought hard. He grinned and chuckled. The woman resembled a maiden character out of the medieval era. This would be interesting. Nobody dressed like this, unless there was a festival or cosplay group in the area, and that wasn't likely. He picked up his pace and ran.

"May I help you, miss?" Edouard asked, catching his breath. The run took a little out of him, but it was the face on this creature that nearly sent him reeling. The young lady's face entranced him beyond words. Shamefully, he admitted to himself that she was even more beautiful than his fair Larissa. Edouard may have lost any noble intentions toward his old flame, but he still admitted when a young lady had it made in the looks department.

"Ah, fine sir, and what do you do out here alone among the trees and fields?" The maid turned her face toward Sulphure and back to Edouard.

He took a quick breath and held out his arms a little. Standing still and straight became a problem the more he stared at his uninvited guest. Her flawless skin glowed, and her ruby lips tempted him to grab and kiss her, consequences be damned. The lady seemed to sense his interest. She pursed her lips lightly and lifted her face a little, gazing deeply into his eyes.

Edouard blinked and swallowed hard. "I was merely taking a walk to clear my head."

The lady turned her gaze toward a large amulet Edouard wore. She rubbed a dainty finger against the stone's surface, gazing at the flashes of dark pinks and greens.

"My father gave me this." Edouard glanced down at the maiden's hand touching him. "It's been in the family hundreds of years."

"Does it do anything special?" asked the young woman. She gazed into his face with curiosity.

"I, um, it . . ." Edouard shook his head, flustered. He swiped his forehead and tried stammering out some words.

The young woman's face showed a flash of disappointment. "You look troubled, my good man. What has caused you such consternation on a glorious day like this one?" She smiled lightly and touched his arm. "And for one such as yourself who wields great power?"

The touch of her hand on his arm brought him nearly to the point of fainting. Edouard gasped and staggered, forcing himself to stand upright and still. "I was told by my father of a most troubling event that recently occurred, and I want to figure a way out of it without hurting someone who may be privy to the information soon."

"Perhaps I can help. I am wise beyond my years. Pray, do tell."

"I don't even know who you are. You don't belong here, on my property, maybe not even this country. There is something about you." He inhaled the deep scent of the countryside. The sun warmed him.

The young woman's eyes glittered a rich sapphire blue. Edouard found himself smitten and locked on to her gaze.

"Dear sir, it is of no consequence my appearance or from whence I come." She rested her hand on his arm and whispered in his ear, "Tell me, darling. Tell me all I need to know so I can help you." Her lips barely grazed his cheek as she stood back, ready and listening.

He shook his head. A fog had set into his brain, and he couldn't explain what was happening. All he knew was that he wanted to kiss this strange girl, talk to her, tell her everything. Desperation set in, and he loathed the feeling. For the first time in a long time, he felt his power slipping away with no explanation.

"I am working on a project, dear lady, and one whom I hold in my chateau will not cooperate. As a result, she has suffered greatly."

"Oh, dear," answered the maiden. "Do continue, please."

"This one to whom I refer is related to another who is with me now in this castle, Sulphure. It was my hope that those two could share information to help me with my project, but I fear such damage has been done that all is lost."

"Dear sir, where is this one who will not cooperate? Perhaps I can guide you in this troublesome matter."

"My beautiful lady—and you are quite the most stunning creature I have ever beheld—this uncooperative being is in Rouen, France, secreted away in Chateau Anguis, my dwelling there. Her niece, the relative staying with me here, will be furious when she learns what occurred. I was to take her to France to meet her great great aunt."

Edouard wanted to look away from the enchanting face in front of him but couldn't tear his gaze away, not even for an instant. "I'm at a loss on what to do, and that's quite unlike me."

The maiden continued staring up at him. "This niece, is she so important to you in this project you wish to come to fruition?"

"Alas," said Edouard, "I do love and care about her, but I'm slowly discovering that perhaps our goals may be at odds, and I must convince her to see things my way. I think I may have her loyalty, though I am not quite sure anymore. I'm prepared to go on without her. If it means her downfall, so be it. If she's as stubborn and resolute as her aunt, I will not tolerate it under any circumstance."

The lady's cheeks flushed. Her eyes grew richer in hue, and she kept them fixed on Edouard. "So I see. You are a most determined man." Her grip tightened on his arm. "Let me help you. I believe I can take care of this matter for you. There will be no work for you, only the reward and desire you so intently seek."

Edouard's heart raced. "You can do that for me, strange lady? We don't even know each other. And to go out of your way—"

"Shh, don't say a thing." She placed her finger gently on his lips. "I am as good as my word. And I'm on your side. You are a most noble and powerful man. It is my sworn duty, a pledge to myself and others, to see that you get everything you deserve."

"My beautiful one, show me that what you say is true. Can you seal this declaration of which you speak, perhaps with a token of your promise?" Edouard pressed the lady's slender hand against his chest.

"I would never dream of leaving your presence without such a token. Never!" She leaned toward him and placed a kiss on his lips.

The young man closed his eyes, feeling the warmth of her flesh against his, and slowly slipped to the ground.

"There, you useless cad. I'll most surely see that your ass gets what it deserves." August Hawthorne stood looking down on the fallen Edouard Anguis, wiping his lips fervently with his hand. He glanced down at his attire, which had transformed from the beautiful maroon gown, back to his own clothing. He ran a hand through his hair, feeling the former length.

He hugged the tree line for several yards and cut across the field back to Sulphure Hall. His spell, like the rest of the time allotted by Agares, would not last. In fact, it would end quicker. August sprinted to a side door of the castle and slipped inside. As he strode down the hallway, taking care to blend in with the surroundings, he heard the sound of men's voices.

Puzzled, he stopped a moment. They sounded so familiar. He'd heard them a while back. August pressed against the wall leading to the doorway of the room from which he heard the men.

"I hope Edouard can have Larissa meet her aunt soon. Maybe he has her totally convinced and she can finally help us."

August quietly peered into the room. His heart nearly stopped. Inside, he felt his blood boil. The man who spoke was Daniel, the one who drove them to the Hall of Winds. He cursed to himself. And the other man with him was Dennis, the one they met when they visited the Order of the Onyx Night. So it seemed that Larissa had unwittingly surrounded herself with the wrong people, and all thanks to her Aunt Dorenda. There was no time to try and find his companions and risk getting seen.

Creating a cloaking spell, August turned and raced back out in the direction he came and made a mad dash to the castle gates. He prayed that Willem and Phuctious could convince Larissa to make a run for it with them.

***

"Ah, you're here! We have very little time, Heir Strondovan. Please come with us." Willem and Phuctious finally located Larissa with a quick powerful divining spell Willem cast. The castle appeared strangely quiet and empty, as if all the occupants had either retired somewhere else or had fallen asleep somewhere.

"How did you get out?" Larissa stood up from an elegant velvet covered chair in the morning salon, where she ate breakfast or sometimes dined privately with Edouard.

Phuctious answered, "August said we had less than an hour to get out. Must be a reason because he was extremely urgent about it. He didn't go into detail."

"That's just like him." Larissa wrinkled her nose.

"Please, we have to leave. Now." Willem took the liberty of taking Larissa's hand, pulling her to him.

"I understand you two are in a tizzy, but I don't understand what's going on." Larissa stood resolutely in place.

"Just trust us. We'll explain later. Have you tried contacting your parents? They have to be worried sick about you," Phuctious asked.

Larissa's face clouded. "Aunt Dorenda tried to contact me, but I didn't want to speak to her. It's not a good time. I have tried contacting my parents several times with no luck. I can't seem to reach them."

"Try again. Do you need any of your spheres, a papyrus and pen? We have to tell them that we've been delayed but will be seeing them soon. We must hurry. Please." Willem tugged on Larissa's sleeve.

She frowned. "Would you stop that?"

"Miss Larissa," said Phuctious, "please don't be angry. Where is your room? You'll need your things—and ours too. Perhaps you can try again to reach your parents. Willem and I have a sneaking suspicion you may be able to talk to them now."

Before Larissa could protest, Willem took her and yanked her toward him. "Show us your room."

Larissa led the way through the hallways back to her room. Willem and Phuctious gazed around in wonderment at the beauty and comfort of it, from a luxurious canopied bed to the oversized voluptuous chair in front of the fireplace. The room held other elegant furnishings and pieces of art. Scrambling to an armoire, she handed Willem and Phuctious their belongings, ending with removing the bags belonging to her and August.

"You're quite fortunate your dear host didn't remove these from your possession," said Phuctious.

"I've been trying to play it cool with Edouard. I've seen things that make me a little uneasy about him," said Larissa.

"You think? I assure you, he is most likely behind why the Vanishport didn't work and why you haven't been able to talk to your parents," said Willem.

"Go on, Miss." Phuctious pointed to Larissa's bags. "Try them now."

"I'd use the papyrus and pen," said Willem. "Can't hurt to be on the safe side."

The young lady pulled out a papyrus and pen, scribbled her message with quick strokes and waited:

Larissa, is that you? It's your mother. Where are you? We're worried.

Willem and Phuctious raised their fists with happy affirmation. Larissa penned back:

Have been delayed in Huigra, Ecuador at Sulphure Hall, home of Edouard Anguis. Will be en route to you soon. Will explain then.

Eleanor wrote back:

Take care and guard yourself well, my dear. We are all waiting for you. Your family is here!

Larissa wrote back an affirmation of understanding and placed the papyrus and pen back in her bag of tools. "Did you hear that? My family?" she fairly danced with delight.

"Heir Strondovan, how wonderful. You must be anxious to meet them. All the more why we need to get these bags and leave now. And that means Edouard, wherever he is, mustn't know." Willem and Larissa picked up their belongings and joined Phuctious at the door.

"To the castle gates, my friends. I think our real journey has just begun." Phuctious saluted them and took off running with Willem and Larissa fast behind him.

August paced back and forth between the castle gates. If everyone showed up like they were supposed to, they would have ample time to get into the Vanishport and sail quickly to Rouen, France. Thoughts of what happened to Ciana sickened him so much that his heart still hurt. He'd destroy Edouard, one way or another. He peered toward the castle, relieved upon seeing the vision of three people rushing in his direction.

He waved at them to come on. To his dismay, he also saw a figure staggering forward in the distance. One hand was raised in anger. The man shouted something, but it was unintelligible. "Damn him!" August punched the fist of one hand into the palm of the other. "Hurry!" he yelled to the other three. "He's behind you!"

Willem quickly turned back and saw it was Edouard. He indicated to Larissa and Phuctious they needed to run faster. Within seconds, they were all together. Willem called up the Vanishport. All four with their bags in tow hopped within its boundaries and sailed off.

Edouard Anguis collapsed to his knees swearing with all his might. His head hurt. His brain barely shook off the fog, but it had dissipated enough for him to know that he'd been had.

A guard stepped from the shadows of the trees. "Sir, are you hurt? Let me help you up."

"Let go of me." Edouard jerked his arm away. "I'm fine."

"You look a little shaken, sir. Are you okay?"

"Where were you? Didn't you see that our so-called guests had just a little too much freedom? Why didn't you intervene, alert me? And where are the other guards?"

The guard looked surprised. "I wasn't aware that anything was amiss. I assure you we kept a close eye on her. And of course, the other three were in the dungeon, securely locked away. When I saw them gathering at the gate, I called on the others for assistance. Unfortunately, they were a little too quick for us."

Edouard looked around. True to his guard's word, he saw his other men stepping out from the trees. Some headed toward him. He took in a deep breath and closed his eyes, trying to calm the anger swelling inside of him. He may have to sleep this enchantment off. From the looks of his men, something powerful had gotten a grip on them too.

The South Hawthorne dynasty was known for their fine enchanting skills, but who knew that stupid August Hawthorne would have thought of something so clever. One thing was for certain at this point, he'd never underestimate Larissa nor her associates ever again, regardless of any rumor or legend he'd heard in the past.

Chapter Eighteen

The Vanishport landed with a thud, jostling the occupants inside. Larissa grabbed the numeromancer from her bag. "I want to see where we are. This seems to be the same thing that happened the last time." She spun the device. "Location." The numbers whirred and ended on the coordinates marking where they were.

Willem glanced at the display. "Just outside of Rouen, but at least we're in walking distance."

"Walking distance? How far?" asked August. "And why didn't we land exactly where we wanted?

Phuctious squinted out the door of the Vanishport. "I think our nemesis, Edouard perhaps has awakened. He seemed rather groggy when we left, but he had some energy about him."

"We're not going to get much better than this, I don't think," said Willem. "I suggest we start walking. It's only about ten miles to the city, but we might get lucky and find somewhere to stay." He shrugged. "You never know, and luck doesn't seem to be on our side lately."

"I'm with Willem on that one." Larissa grasped the handle of her bags and stepped out the Vanishport door. After everyone followed her, the vehicle disappeared with a loud pop and a spark.

August winced. "That didn't sound good. Maybe we're lucky Anguis didn't make it explode with us in it."

All four walked for a good three miles through woods and fields until they happened upon a quaint village. They saw a building called The Cozy Quim Inn.

"How odd to find an English inn here," said August. He stopped and surveyed their surroundings.

The village contained the inn, a stable for horses, a tavern, bakery, and various charming shops.

They marched inside the inn to the desk where a rotund little older man sat scribbling in a ledger.

Willem cleared his throat and spoke up. "Excuse me, sir, but have you any rooms for weary travelers?"

The man glanced up, straightened his glasses, and spoke. "Will that be four rooms?"

Willem nodded. "Yes, please."

"Let me see." The clerk picked up another book across from him and scanned through the pages. "Yes, you are taking my last ones."

A few hours later, after scouting out the town and warding off the area with strong protection spells, everyone returned to the Cozy Quim Inn and settled in their rooms for a sound night's sleep. Only Phuctious, who didn't seem to need nearly enough rest as the others, stayed up drinking and singing old drinking songs in the nearby tavern until nearly dawn.

Still, he was the first one awake and had wandered over to the stables to check out the horses. When Larissa awakened the following morning, she was surprised to see August and Willem in the Inn's charming guest study, sitting at a table in front of the blazing fireplace with their heads close together. Each of them, she had noticed, tended to avoid having private discussions with each other, preferring to include the entire group.

For all the time Willem and August had spent together, though she knew that a grudging respect had grown between them, she thought it a shame that they had never forged a close friendship. When she appeared, they hastily stopped their conversation and turned toward her. Larissa thought she detected pity in Willem's eyes. August's expression was grim.

"We need to talk, just the three of us," August told her. "Willem and I agree that it's high time we share some intelligence—important intelligence that heretofore has only been hinted at."

Larissa frowned at August's words.

"You and Willem *agreed* on something?" she stated in a scoffing tone. "Since when do you and Willem even talk, unless it's absolutely necessary?"

"Please don't get caught up in the extraneous details of how we reached this point," Willem said curtly. "This is important, Strondovan Heir. In fact, I would recommend that you sit down before you hear it. Don't you think that would be best, August?" he added.

"Yes, I agree with Willem," August said quickly, "You may sit on my lap if you like." He patted one of his well-muscled thighs. "Honestly, I highly recommend it."

"No, thank you," Larissa said. Her words came out stone cold. "I believe I'll just remain standing. What is this news that is so important that you think I can't take it standing on my own two feet? I must confess I'm very curious."

August and Willem looked at each other for a long moment. When August nodded, Willem cleared his throat and turned back to Larissa, holding out a small oblong object wrapped in a piece of silk.

"I think it might be best if we start with this," he told her. "I will explain how August and I came by it."

Larissa took the box and unwound its wrappings. She gasped when viewing the contents.

"Where did you get this?" she whispered, staring at the smooth, dark purple gem. It was approximately two inches by three inches in size, oblong in shape, and gave off a violet glow as it warmed against her skin.

"Then you recognize it?" August commented. Turning to Willem, he said, "I told you she would recognize it."

"My Soul Stone," Larissa murmured. She continued staring at it in a dazed-like state. "But . . . but how did you come by it? It is supposed to be kept forever by my ultimate Guardian, the one who is sworn to protect me for all time." She looked up at the two men. "My Aunt Dorenda. Is she dead?"

"No, your aunt is alive and well, I'm afraid," August answered. "Very well, in fact, since she was paid a fortune to give it up to the Anguis.

Willem and I happened to get wind of the exchange. My grandfather Jove sent his swiftest carrier pigeon to bring the news to us this morning. It was the only time he could ensure we got the stone, because there was no way any of us could receive it when we were in Anguis's dungeons."

"How did your grandfather learn of all this?" asked Larissa.

August continued, "He became aware of the exchange through several channels. Our good friend Tiberinus, for one. Just to be sure he'd heard correctly, he checked out the information with his own Oracle. And believe it or not, also your parents. Since they couldn't get in touch with you, because that bastard, Edouard, used baneful magic to hinder connections, they finally decided to contact my grandfather.

Willem and I got up before dawn and intercepted the rider who was to make the exchange and deliver your Soul Stone to the Anguis. Once in their hands, they were hoping to use it to control you. Since your aunt has essentially washed her hands of all ties to you as well as obligations to protect you, she was in no position or held any desire to stop it. And trust me when I tell you, you're Aunt Dorenda has been a fraud for years."

As Larissa finally tore her gaze from the stone and looked up at them both, they noticed that she had gone completely white. Willem caught her just as her legs buckled. August quickly got up from the table and sat down on a nearby bench. He gestured for Willem to help Larissa sit next to him.

"You need to stop being so shocked, Larissa!" August said gruffly. He took her chin in his hand none too gently. "I am not as old in years as my father Jove, or as wise, but even I understand that there is no creature breathing that doesn't have its price. Your Aunt should never have been entrusted with your care. She is the mother of the devil!"

Sitting down on Larissa's other side, Willem took Larissa's hand gently in his own. "Well, they don't have it now, so they will have to find some other means to entrance and capture you. If they had acquired the stone, you would likely fall asleep one night and end up mesmerized and going to them without even knowing what you were doing." He squeezed her hand in earnest. "You must cast the stone in the fire and reclaim its essence now."

As they watched, Larissa's color slowly returned. She gazed at the stone.

"Yes, of course, you're right," she said in agreement. Sighing heavily, she got up from the bench. "I don't want to do it inside the Inn. Will you two go with me, please so we can make a birch fire in the woods? I remember seeing some trees not far from here."

Both August and Willem nodded. Leaving Phuctious to his own devices, they all three headed to a strip of woods about half a mile from the village. Soon they reached a clearing, well-hidden from prying eyes. Willem made a small fire of birch branches and waited until it was fully blazing. "I think you can feed it to the flames now, Larissa."

Walking forward, Larissa looked down at the beautiful stone one last time, recalling sweet memories of her Aunt Dorenda showing it to her from time to time and telling her it's meaning. She remembered well her aunt's words that day. "As long as I hold this Soul Stone for you, my beautiful darling Larissa, if I have this small part of you, you will always be safe. I promise I will never allow harm to come to you, and my love will protect you."

And to think those words of love had been a lie! Larissa had been a cautious and distrustful child, but she had *always* believed in her Aunt Dorenda. Until now. Willem and August's revelation cut her to the core, burned her soul. At once, the anger of hurt and betrayal consumed her. August had always tried her patience. She mostly doubted his sincerity, thinking he simply wanted to antagonize her.

But when Willem backed up what August said, there was no other choice but to believe. Torn with despair, she tossed the brilliant purple stone into the flames. They immediately roared, growing higher and turning the same violet color as the stone. Out of the flames a small phantom bird rose and made a beeline for Larissa's chest. Its tiny vaporous purple form melted into her. She gasped at the sensation.

"That was certainly interesting," August said. "Can't say I've ever seen a Soul Stone reuniting with its owner before."

The two men had watched everything with great intent. Willem and August worked on stamping out the fire.

Concerned, Willem asked, "Do you feel any differently?"

"I think . . . better somehow," Larissa answered, "Clearer in mind, body, and spirit. I can't describe it, exactly, but I think you know what I mean." She looked at her companions. "Now if you two don't mind, I would like to take a short walk in these woods by myself for a bit. It's been quite a morning, and I need to think."

Both her companions agreed.

"Listen," Willem told her, "I understand you need some time alone, but August and I will be waiting right here for you. Take all the time you need, Strondovan Heir. It is a hell of a lot to process."

Larissa nodded and headed off in the direction where she glimpsed a view of a rivulet flowing off from the Seine.

As soon as she was out of sight, August looked at Willem with disgust. "I wanted to get coffee and the giant pancakes they serve at the Inn!" he said, grumbling. "I was already tasting the mumbleberry syrup and the butter melting down the sides."

Willem snorted. "I will say this, Hawthorne Heir, and meaning no disrespect, but it is so like you to think of your empty stomach and creature comforts, no matter the circumstances."

From a much further distance than either of the gentlemen would have guessed Larissa could travel in such a short time, they heard an ungodly wail echoing through the distant canyons.

In answer to August's look of immediate concern, Willem raised a hand. "Yes, that was her, Larissa. She just needs to get it out of her system, make a bit of noise." He tapped August's arm with a knowing look. "She is strong, perhaps the strongest witch I have ever known. She will be just   fine."

Chapter Nineteen

Thousands of miles away in the United States, Dorenda sat alone at home. She tried fighting off the throbbing pain in her head. When she closed her eyes, sounds of anguished screaming in her mind created profound loneliness and deep sadness. For the first time in her life, Dorenda came face to face with despair. Larissa had tossed the Soul Stone into a fire somewhere. They were severed forever.

The older lady felt as if her heart had been ripped out of her chest. She had lived a lie for so long, betraying not only her sister, but her beloved niece. And there was love for her, the one she had watched over for many years. But a stronger love had crept in, taken hold of her, and now it gripped her stronger than ever. Greed, a desire for more, a union with Eustace Anguis and everything he stood for.

Was it all that bad, what she and her lover wanted? Mortals and Magicals want many things. Why should she be punished for wanting what she thought would make her happy? But in that moment when Larissa's cries rang out, sound waves flashed through a matrix of energy paths, leading right to her. The jolt she felt at that moment filled her with deep shame, and she was powerless at this point to stop the series of events she saw playing out in her mind.

She'd never felt more alone in her life. Jove had not contacted her, which she didn't expect him to. Contacting Eleanor, her sister, was out of the question, since the promise to care for Larissa had been utterly broken. Eustace would be no better a source for comfort, the one person she'd always thought cared for her deeply.

After her visit to France, it was clear Eustace cared nothing for her, only for what she had given him, body, son, loyalty, trust. Any words of assurance from him had only been said to appease her, to keep her from rebelling or leaving. But she knew to do any of those things would result in far worse than what happened to Ciana.

Dorenda hadn't quite bargained on what her lover did to Ciana, though it didn't fully surprise her. There was nothing she could have done to prevent the evil deed, either. She couldn't fake knowledge that wouldn't be shared with her, despite all hopes and desires that it would be. The aunt knew one thing, both she and Ciana were trapped, and neither knew how much longer they would hold out.

It was done. She'd lost her niece, one that had been almost like her child, allowing her to experience some semblance of motherhood that she never was allowed with Edouard, her real son. Rick and Amy Martin got that joy of being Larissa's parents the first half of her life, and now Roman and Eleanor had her back forever.

Throwing all caution to the wind, Dorenda got up and retrieved her crystal sphere. Centering herself and calming her mind as best she could, her eyes locked on the shiny surface and penetrated its depths. She concentrated hard, willing on a certain face to appear before her.

"Yes?" said a voice from the sphere. Edouard's face shone clearly. "Dorenda, is that you?"

"Yes, darling," said Dorenda. "You don't look well. Are you okay?"

"Um, sure. Just waking up from a nap. Do you need me for something? Is Father all right?"

"I just spent some time in your father's chateau recently. If you have a moment, there is something I must tell you. Something that your father and I have kept secret all your life. And I can't keep it secret any longer. He doesn't know that I'm telling you."

"Go ahead, dear Dorenda," said Edouard. "You know how much respect I've always had for you. Truth be known, I always wanted to spend more time around you. In Quito, we seemed strangely like a family."

"About that, Edouard. The truth is, you weren't a son from some random Magical family that gave you away. I'm your biological mother. We kept it a secret from Priscilla the Beautiful and even your sisters. Eustace, your grandfather, and I made up the orphan story just to protect you. Priscilla's death made it easy for us to let your sisters know they had a brother and for you to take the rightful place in the Anguis family. No more hiding."

Dorenda went silent after those words, watching her son's face intently. Edouard grew paler in color. His eyes turned a bright green for a moment before returning to their normal state. He licked his lips, trying to regain composure.

"I wanted to be a mother to you, dear Edouard, but it couldn't be. Your father and Priscilla had already been selected for an arranged marriage, and he couldn't break free from that. So we made the best of what times we found together. And you were the best thing that ever happened to us."

Edouard heaved with emotion. Tears trickled from his eyes. The young man swiped a hand across his cheek. "I see." His voice cracked as he spoke. "I'm glad you said something because it explains the loneliness I felt living with Grandfather Clavius all those years. I was told the orphan story too, and that Grandfather had taken me in and promised to offer the best opportunities for learning the magical arts and honing my skills as a witch. Finally, Father let me return home when I came of age, saying that it was time for me to take a leadership role in the family. But I see now he didn't reveal everything."

"Just know that I've always loved you, darling, though I could not be with you or say anything about it. There's going to be some rough times coming our way, a battle to deal with, and I wanted to take this time to tell you the truth. And do know that I love you very much. There isn't a day that goes by that I don't think about you, wishing I could hold you and talk to you, be a part of your life."

Edouard nodded. "Thank you for being honest with me . . . Mother. I must go now. This has been a lot to take in."

His image disappeared. Dorenda let out a breath of relief and placed her sphere in its stand. She went to her wine cabinet, popped a cork, and downed a whole bottle of wine before collapsing on her sofa in a deep sleep filled with fitful dreams.

***

Larissa, Phuctious, Willem, and August checked out of the inn and made their way to locate Ciana. Using the trusty numeromancer, Willem noted the location coordinates and shared it with their driver. They had found a kind person who accepted their fee to drive them close to their destination. From there, they would make their way to the Anguis chateau.

"We must plan our attack," said Phuctious. He gently tapped Willem on the knee. "If we get caught, we'll be in worse trouble. You know who is probably planning his mode of attack back on us for not only getting away but making him look like a fool to boot."

August kicked Larissa's foot. She glared at him. "Hey," he said, "I've been thinking about the very thing Phuctious is talking about. We need reinforcements, and I think I have the solution."

Larissa clenched her teeth in disgust. "You always say that. Kind of funny for someone who ends up in scrapes."

"Listen," August answered, "I'm the one who got us out and on our way here. So why are you talking to me with such disrespect?" He smacked his forehead in mock surprise. "Oh, I forgot. That's par for the course where you're concerned."

Willem stated, "Larissa, I have to agree with August on this. Without his help, who knows where we'd be. And I think you were lured into Edouard's lair, which isn't totally your fault, but still . . ."

Her face colored with embarrassment. She glanced at Phuctious, who quickly turned his face away and gazed out the window, pretending to be oblivious. She cleared her throat. "Okay, August, what magnificent plan do you have in rescuing my great, great aunt?"

"Druids of the Desert. We need an army, a great force. They should be able to keep the chateaux staff at bay while one of us gets Ciana out of that godforsaken place. We'll hide our bags somewhere. When your aunt is out, we jump in the Vanishport and pray with all our might that we reach our first desired destination." August nodded. "We use that favor Prince Elek gave us. We need it. Sound good to you, ma'am?"

"I actually like that idea," said Willem. "Between our magic and theirs, it will at least buy us the time we need." He shook his head. "And I do feel like we are living on borrowed hours every time we turn around."

"When did you want to contact them and fill them in on what's happened?" asked Phuctious. "We have to be ready and quick about this. I think they need to be at the chateau when we are, and we all perform our roles in unison."

"Exactly," said August. "Willem, what do you think?"

"Sounds good to me." He looked at Larissa.

"So glad I can count on you all to have a plan, instead of me doing all the work," answered Larissa. She didn't fail to detect the look of dismay from her companions at her snarky comment. The young lady rummaged through her magical tool bag. "I have the incantation. But you know that once we use this, it's done. They will never assist us again."

"I'm aware of that." August acknowledged her words with calm and politeness. "We'll have to figure out our moves if something worse happens, but it's highly important to rescue your relative. When we have a moment, I will tell you everything I have learned."

Larissa raised her eyebrows in surprise. Willem winced. Phuctious said nothing but twiddled his fingers in a fit of nervousness.

As promised, the driver stopped when they reached their agreed-upon destination.

"Do you wish to take my information so I can pick you up once you're finished? A ride back to the inn or another place?" asked the driver.

"Sure, but we may not need it." August smiled at the gentleman and made note of the information in a small notebook he kept in his travel bag for such occasions as this.

"If you need me, just call. I'll be only too happy to help."

All four exited the vehicle and watched the driver wave back as he sped away. Larissa did a quick forgetfulness spell on the driver, ensuring he wouldn't remember anything discussed while they were in the car.

"Looks rather safe out here." Willem surveyed their surroundings. "We're just enough out of the city, but not in the middle of a forest range so far we can't reach civilization again."

August turned to Larissa. "Contact the Druids of the Desert."

Without another word, Larissa recited the following: "*One request granted. One request asked. Please help us, O Druids with this which we're tasked.*"

They waited and watched, hoping that no car or person would venture down this lonely turnoff from the main road. Unless someone had a reason to reach the Anguis or simply chose this way in error, there shouldn't be any disturbance.

A breeze picked up, sending fallen leaves scattering along the road. Thunder rumbled lightly overhead. They all looked up in time to see a silent large lightning flash bolting overhead. In front of them a few feet away, a whirlwind spun into view, twirling in colors ranging from gray to red, pink, and back to gray. Before them, out from the swirl of colors, stood a winding staircase that stretched high into the clouds.

Numbers of Prince Elek's army trooped down the steps, headed by their leader. He wore a neat sandy-colored overcoat with several rows of brass buttons and red epaulettes. With quick steps, he headed toward Larissa and her companions.

"I am Solamine from the great Prince Elek's army. Who contacted us?" asked the commander. "We come in fulfillment of a special request. It is our obligation to grant it." He bowed lightly in respect.

Larissa stepped forward and curtsied. "I did, sir. It is Prince Elek who gave us a handsome gift of asking your assistance if we were ever in need, and now we find ourselves in such a situation."

"Ah, but you know that once this assistance is granted, per the rule, we will not be obligated to assist you again—unless perhaps our esteemed ruler wishes otherwise."

"I am completely aware of the rules, and I wish to use the gift of assistance now."

"What is it that you need, my good lady?" asked Solamine. Several of the group had come forward. Others stood a few yards back. More druids still came down the stairs.

"We are headed to the Anguis Chateau located farther down this road. It is my great great Aunt Ciana whom we need to rescue."

"The Anguis Chateau? Here?" The leader frowned.

"Surely you can help, no matter the people involved. Yes?" Willem stepped forward.

The gentleman pursed his lips in thought. He turned briefly to his men and whispered something to his second-in-command. The subordinate nodded, and they chatted for a moment.

Larissa strained her ears, hoping to catch some of their words. The breeze carried the sound in another direction. Surely, they would honor Prince Elek's command.

Solamine returned shortly. With his finger he drew the shape of a square in front of him. An image blazed into view, showing a map of a magnificent building that looked castle-like.

August and Phuctious joined Larissa and Willem, eyeing the map with great interest.

"Is this the Anguis chateau?" asked August, pointing to the building.

"It is, sir," answered Solamine. "Do you happen to know where the aunt might be? The more we know of this building and the occupants, the better we can devise a plan to help."

"I believe she is kept in the lower part of the chateau," August said.

"And how would you know that?" Larissa turned toward him and scowled.

"Trust me on this and stop questioning everything I say." August, with reddened face, turned toward Solamine. "I have it on good information shown to me from spirit guides."

"Ah, very good." Solamine nodded with approval. "Any specific direction?"

Phuctious, who had been unusually quiet much of this trip, stepped forward. "I have a sprig of goldenrod. It should be able to tell us exactly where to locate Larissa's aunt."

Solamine glanced down at the dwarf and frowned. "Mmm, I—".

"Let him do his work," said Willem. "He is quite reliable."

"Thank you." Phuctious bowed toward Willem. He opened his bag, and after rummaging quickly through it, pulled out the plant sprig. He held it toward the map, closed his eyes in concentration, and blew at the bright golden flowers.

Everyone gazed in fascination as the flowers lifted up and floated in unison toward the map. They floated around the lower part of the chateau image, and after a few seconds, decidedly landed in unison on the desired spot. With the sound of shimmering chimes, the flowers disappeared in a poof of yellow smoke, leaving a bright red x that marked the location.

"Quite clever," said Solamine. He rubbed his chin in thought.

"Thank you." Phuctious turned away with smug satisfaction mixed with some indignation at having been treated so by Prince Elek's army leader.

"We need to know who is at the Chateau now, other than Ciana." August pointed to the map. "Might help us prepare for battle in case we can't sneak the aunt away quickly enough."

"Yes, good point." Solamine looked at August. "Of course, we can always do the basics of surrounding the building, including exits and entrances. I also have a special team who can quickly disperse once they're inside."

"Will they be able to contain anyone they find?"

"If they're fast enough. We're good with our magic, but as you know, it becomes precarious when there is fighting and a battle of wills."

"True." August rubbed his lip, staring hard at the map. "We know Edouard is in Ecuador, unless he's paid a surprise visit that we aren't aware of—and won't know until we get to the chateau. From what I gathered in my information, Dorenda, Larissa's other aunt, left the chateau before . . ." The young man's face flushed, and he swallowed hard.

Larissa stared at him, perplexed but said nothing.

Solamine took in the scene between the two and nodded. "Very well. Let's assume that it's just house staff, perhaps some security guards on the property, and the owner." He glanced at Phuctious. "I guess you don't have something that could tell us who's at the chateau?"

"I'm so glad you asked," stated Phuctious. He tried containing his growing irritation. "As a matter of fact, I have some honeysuckle flowers. They should do the trick quite nicely."

"Continue," said Solamine. He motioned for the dwarf to step before the map.

Phuctious pulled some honeysuckle flowers from his bag, stood in front of the map and said, *"Show us true. Show us well. Tell us whom and where they dwell."*

All eyes viewed the map. The pistils wiggled through the flowers and out the bottoms. Using the nectar collected on their tips, they wrote names and titles of staff members on different parts of the building, noting where each one might be at any given time. Eustace's name came up in the study. Servants were located throughout the chateau—kitchen, hallways, various rooms. And as noted earlier, Ciana was in the lowest part of the house.

"It's confirmed again," cried August. "I'll go there first and get her out."

"Have you a plan on how to do that?" asked Solamine.

"There is a window where her name is written. Surely we can pry it open and help her climb through."

Larissa stepped forward. "Let's find out how high the window is from the floor. Remember, this is a chateau, and the ceilings are not like ones in regular homes. Will we need a ladder? You know, that sort of thing." She removed the numeromancer from her bag and spun it on the ground. "Height of window from Ciana's bedroom floor." The number twenty showed up.

Solamine looked away from the map and at the small crowd gathered near him. "Maybe we have a group sneak inside the castle to her room while we have others at the window trying to get her out. We can create equipment, if you will, to help in any case. We must be quick and decisive every step of the way. We'll only be able to contain the occupants only so long, and they will fight back if they can."

The leader talked for several minutes with his men. "Let's get this task completed. I will allow no more than an hour."

The four friends glanced at each other.

"Will that be enough?" August asked.

"With all due respect, sir, we are not having tea and crumpets. We break in, contain the occupants, and you get your damsel in distress and leave quickly. It's my offer. Take it or leave it."

August nodded.

Many of the army headed off toward the chateau immediately to surround and contain the dwelling, including incapacitating guards along the way.

A small group was assigned to go with August and Larissa to rescue Ciana. Willem went with another group to help guard parts of the castle. Phuctious agreed to stay outside the castle within a few yards of Ciana's window so he could call up the Vanishport and guard the bags. With swift speed everyone arrived at the chateau, ready for action.

A druid quickly distracted a guard at the entrance gate long enough for one of his comrades to knock the man out with a quick bolt of lightning. The man dropped to the ground at once. They all trailed through, nearly flying into place.

August beelined straight to Ciana's window. Larissa followed. Phuctious scrambled behind and set up his post a few yards away, placing all their travel bags next to a large tree. Several druids surrounded his area, keeping close watch to ensure no guards or staff came near.

Willem and several guards broke the lock off one of the side doors and entered the chateau.

"Just what do you think you're doing?" asked one of the cooks. He grabbed up a rolling pin and waved it at Willem with indignation. The wizard pointed his index finger at the cook, raising and lowering it quickly. The staff member didn't have time to think. The rolling pin flew out of his hand and smashed the man's head with a dull thud. Druid members wrestled with a few other kitchen staff, before leaving them crumpled on the floor.

Solamine and his group came up through the hallway from the other side, where they had managed to break through another door and made their way to the kitchen. "Follow me," he said. "Eustace Anguis is in his study. We need to go there now." Willem and his group followed Solamine and his. They quickly made their way to the study.

The activity hadn't gone completely unnoticed. Eustace Anguis's solar plexus had been aching hard the past few hours, and he was stumped as to the reason. Whatever it was, it couldn't be good. He felt that much. His faithful butler stepped through the door, not bothering to knock. The scowl on Eustace's face left in an instant when he saw the large blood stain on the man's white shirt.

"Sir," said the butler. "We have been breached. Whoever the enemy is, they are getting the better of our staff and guards." Wincing in pain, the man gasped and collapsed.

Eustace ran over to his servant and placed his hands over the wound, hoping he could heal it. No matter how hard he concentrated and tried the best incantation he knew, nothing changed.

"Sir, I don't think there is much you can do. They have made their attacks sure and swift. It's been a pleasure serving you." He closed his eyes and breathed his last.

"Damn," Eustace shouted. He stood up, only to have Willem staring him in the face.

"And damn you, too," said Willem. "You're a rotten, filthy bastard. We'll get the better of you."

"Men," said Solamine, "Contain this man." He pointed to Anguis.

At those words, Eustace held out his hands toward the druids and let out a blast of heat and electricity. The shock sent them reeling against the wall and sliding to the floor. A few of them lay in a shriveled heap.

Eustace chuckled. "You'll get the better of me, eh?" He glanced from Willem to Solamine. "I think not." With a clap of his hands, he cried out, "U*stulo*." A rain of fire showered over Solamine and Willem. The men screamed in pain. "No one will ever get the better of me." The senior witch laughed.

From another side door of the study, druids poured forth and doused the flames on their leader and Willem. The remaining druids knocked Eustace out cold.

Solamine groaned in agony but was still able to move. He scowled at his cloak, which hung in strips. "How are other parts of the chateau? Are we contained enough for us to check August and his group?"

"Aye, you'll have to be quick about it. We're running out of time," answered one of the lieutenants.

"And how are you?" Solamine looked at Willem.

"I'm so sore. My back must be toast." He ran some fingers through his hair, grimacing at the singed locks. "Boy, he hit hard." The wizard winced as he touched his head and glanced at his arms.

"We'll try and get the wounds healed the first chance we get. We must get to the lady before *he* wakes up." Solamine pointed to Eustace.

They all left the room and headed toward the lower part of the chateau.

"I'll make a ladder so you can climb up to the window," said one of the druids.

August watched as a ladder of thick vines wove itself upward. He remained in awe at the druid's steady focus, holding out his hands and moving them in a series of strange swirls. At times he clapped.

"There, you can use it now." The druid stepped aside and motioned for August to ascend.

"Please be careful, August. It's high up there. You'll kill yourself if you fall." Larissa shaded her eyes from the sun as she gazed upward.

"As if you care." August shot her a nasty scowl.

Larissa's lips tightened, startled at his words and cold stare. Hugging herself tightly with anxiety, she watched him climb the ladder.

Ciana had sensed the breach the moment it happened. Something in her heart suddenly felt liberated. For the first time since her captivity, she envisioned a ray of hope for her salvation and freedom from this dreaded chateau. But where was Eustace? Surely he'd act, do something to interfere.

A group of druids managed to unlock the door and filed quickly into the room. Ciana gasped at the sight of them.

"Never fear, fair lady. We have come to rescue you." A leading druid walked over to her, stopping midstride at the sight of her bandaged arms with two prosthetic hands at the ends. "We'll help you out."

At that moment, August managed to loosen the window and poke his head through. Ciana looked upward in shock and relief.

August called down to the druids, "Any way to lift her up here?"

Ciana looked from August to the druids. "Can't we just leave from here? Why the need for going through the window?"

Another member of the druids answered, "It's too risky. We're working hard to contain the occupants. They won't stay asleep or knocked out forever. That is, the ones who aren't dead." He shrugged lightly.

"Oh!" Ciana shrank back in horror.

Without waiting for another order or set of instructions. August had climbed through the window and, using a floating spell, gently landed on the floor. He looked up at Ciana, avoiding the sight where her hands used to be. The lady was taller than all of them. At least nine feet.

"The Druids of the Desert are our friends. They can help you up and out of here. Are you ready?"

"Yes!" she cried. "I can levitate too. I've practiced this skill and know it well."

"Then let's have at it and be gone." August smiled at her.

Ciana smiled back and closed her eyes, centering her mind. Slowly, she lifted off the floor. Using their magical skills, the druids stretched their bodies to form a ladder, each one helping her to the window. On the other side, the remaining druids helped her out of the chateau and down to the ground. When Larissa saw her great, great aunt, she ran and held her tight.

"Oh, I've dreamt of this day, just like meeting my parents." She looked up at the older lady with tears in her eyes.

"And I, too." Ciana kissed the top of her niece's head.

Larissa stepped back and surveyed her aunt's arms. Her brows wrinkled in confusion. "What . . .?"

August's voice cut through the air from the open window. "Aunt Ciana, I forgot to ask. Where did that monster do . . .?"

"Out of my room and down the hall. Last room on the left."

Confused, Larissa glanced at her aunt and back up at August. "What are you doing? We need to go."

"We're not going anywhere until I take care of one last piece of business." August disappeared inside the castle.

Solamine and Willem entered Ciana's room.

August said to Solamine, "Get Anguis and bring him down here. Have your men contain everyone else just a bit longer."

"But sir, we really don't have time for anything else." Solamine followed August out the door.

August whirled around, face tightened with determination. "I really need your help in this one last thing, and we'll be out of your hair. It would mean a lot to me and that poor woman. You didn't see what we did."

"It's true," said one of the druids who assisted in getting Ciana out. "Very startling to see, indeed."

"Very well," said Solamine. "What would you have us do?"

"Get Eustace Anguis and take him to the last room on the left at the end of this hall."

"To do what, exactly?"

Willem's face contorted into a look of dread on seeing the speaker who uttered the question.

Eustace Anguis had stepped from the hallway and now stood in the doorway, his lips twisted into a sneer. "You thought I'd sleep through all this? You may have gotten me briefly, but that's the last time."

"Go fuck yourself." August flipped his fingers toward Eustace and murmured his well-used acid spell Jove taught him long ago. Only this time, he created enough to elicit compliance instead of completely devouring his adversary.

The senior Anguis screamed in pain as the surface of his skin sizzled. The druids held their noses and turned their heads away at the acrid stench. August pushed passed Eustace and strode down the hall.

"Let's go," Willem said to Solamine. "Get this man to the room August talked about. Tell your other men to guard everyone else in the chateau until we're done."

When Willem found August in the place described by Ciana, he looked around.

"Get that table from the wall and bring it to the center, right here." August pointed to the spot. He walked quickly to the closet and located the axe, rubbing his finger over the blade. "Still nice and sharp."

"What are you going to do, Hawthorne Heir?" Willem's face turned ashen in color.

"What that bastard deserves." He looked up at Willem, Solamine, and the druids who had now entered the room, Eustace Anguis in tow.

"Place him in this chair and fasten his arms in these." August pointed to the table shackles.

Anguis tried to fight, but the druids used enough magic to bind his energy. One of them rubbed their hands together and blew a light dust of sand into his eyes. Eustace screamed and tried to rub his face, but the druids held tight.

"You can't do this!" he shouted. "You'll pay dearly for whatever you do."

August kicked the chair aside enough for the druids to guide Eustace's rear into the seat with a rough thud. "I'll take my chances, you son-of-a-bitch." He leered into his enemy's face. "What you did to Ciana is beyond the pale. I have every right to avenge what happened, and I intend to do so. Don't worry, you sorry miserable cur, I'll go fast." He grinned at Eustace as the man whimpered at the sound of shackles locking shut.

"Stand back, everyone." August grasped the axe.

With one quick strike, he managed to cut loose the pinky finger on Eustace's left hand. The young man didn't flinch when his enemy howled in distress. He merely yanked the scarf from Eustace's neck, wrapped up the severed finger, and placed it in one of his pockets. He glanced out at the others. "Now for the good stuff." He lowered his face to meet Eustace's. "Ready, partner? I am if you are."

Eustace shot out a thick wad of spittle that landed squarely on August's cheek. The young man's face reddened in anger. He wiped himself clean with the back of his hand and landed a sound hard smack on his adversary's face. "Don't do that again!" Lifting the axe, August brought the blade down on Eustace's left wrist, and without a care, did the same to the other.

It didn't matter to August that his enemy's wretched screams echoed through the room, sending some of his remaining servants, who weren't stalled by the druids, streaming down the steps and into the hallway.

"Let's go!" shouted Solamine.

Willem pulled out a talisman from one of his pockets. Swinging it in front, he called out, "*Utu doromnia.*" The Anguis staff stopped where they were and fell into a deep sleep. "Sorry, bud," he said to a weeping Eustace, "you'll have to fend for yourself until they wake up." The druids disappeared. Willem ran to Ciana's room, following August up to the window where both men were assisted to the ground.

August whipped out the wrapped finger of Eustace Anguis. "A small token of my revenge just for you." He opened the scarf, showing everything to Ciana. She viewed the finger and smiled. "I'll carry it as my talisman forever." The young man placed the scarf and its contents inside a deep pocket of her gown.

"I have the Vanishport!" called out Phuctious. "Hurry, I see guardsmen heading our way."

Willem, August, Ciana, and Larissa beelined for the Vanishport. Phuctious already had their bags loaded. Larissa selected the coordinates to the super seven crystal cave in Brazil, and the Vanishport took off, not stopping until it reached the preset destination.

Chapter Twenty

The five travelers stood staring at the super seven crystal cave entrance.

"You've arrived, Strondovan Heir," said Willem. He motioned toward the mouth of the cave. "You should go first. We'll follow."

Larissa sucked in her breath, fanning her face with both hands. She looked at her companions. "This is it. I'm really meeting my parents and family for the first time." She pinched her cheeks, straightened her dress, and fluffed her hair. "How do I look? Am I all right?"

"You look beautiful," August blurted out.

He gazed at her with a look she'd not noticed before, one of genuine sincerity and a certain fresh interest. She smiled at him for the first time she could ever recollect, nodded lightly in thanks, and made her way through the cave entrance.

They wound their way to the great front room where Dorenda had first introduced her to the elemental family home.

"Anybody home?" she called out. The room was strangely empty. Had everyone left and not told her?

"Larissa?"

Eleanor stepped out of the shadows from another entrance across the room. She gazed at her daughter several seconds.

"Mother?" Larissa returned the gaze, marveling at her parent's beauty.

"I see you've finally made it safe and sound." Roman had reached his wife and now stood tall and strong behind her.

Larissa's face lit up with a bright smile, and she tore across the great room and hugged her mother. Roman received the next hug.

"I can't believe it," said Larissa. Tears streamed down her face. "I'm seeing you for the first time. It's real, isn't it? I'm not dreaming? You won't up and disappear on me?"

"Never again, my dear." Eleanor hugged her daughter.

The remainder of the family came out and everyone introduced themselves to their new-found relative.

"And who are these fine people with you?" Roman asked gesturing to August, Phuctious, Willem, and Ciana. "You'll have to excuse us. We surely haven't forgotten all of you." He walked toward Ciana, a bit confused.

The lady spoke up, "You look so much like father. I would know that resemblance anywhere, even after all these years."

Everyone stopped chatting and stared at the woman.

Larissa walked over to her great, great aunt and wrapped an arm around her. "This is Ciana, our aunt. She is from our line. We rescued her from the horrid Anguis chateau."

Roman stood speechless and in awe of his relative. He shook his head. "What a remarkable thing that you have survived all these years." He reached out and took the great aunt in his arms. "It's an honor and a privilege to just be in your presence."

"Ah, I wish I could say I have seen many things all these years, but alas that is not the case."

"You will have to tell us your story. We want to hear it." Eleanor walked up and gently guided the aunt toward the other members of the family. "Come meet everyone."

Roman walked over to August.

August bowed lightly, taking Roman's extended hand in his. "August South Hawthorne at your service, sir. It is my great hope that we can make amends."

For all the hate August had harbored, Larissa marveled at his words.

"I have every good confidence we'll get to the bottom of this mess. It's a pleasure to meet you." Roman smiled at the young man. "And you fine gentlemen?"

"Willem Wyndom Wiles, also known as Willem the Wizard. I am at your service as well." He bowed low. "I was sent to Heir Hawthorne as his guard, but upon my word, I have guarded your lovely and gracious daughter as well. I could not have done otherwise."

Roman grinned. "I'm sure you are a most worthy guard and wizard. I've heard of your grandfather. He was quite the Magical."

Willem blushed with pleasure at hearing this, and promptly presented Phuctious. "And accompanying us is the illustrious Phuctious Hesperides."

"A dwarf, I see," said Roman. He nodded thoughtfully as he surveyed Phuctious.

Phuctious cleared his throat and put on his best smile, though deep inside he felt most uncomfortable. He'd grown weary of the constant discrimination.

"I've never shared this, but I am quite fond of your kind. Being an earth elemental, we share many things in common, if you gather what I'm saying."

"I do, indeed," said Phuctious.

"Welcome to our ancestral cave. You should find it to your liking." Roman patted the dwarf on the back.

Eleanor and Roman spent some time showing Larissa and her companions the rooms of the cave, how the special stone, the super seven crystal, was made in nature, how they collected and stored some of their favorite and powerful crystals. Ciana followed and listened to every word, nodding and smiling. Larissa marveled at the rooms, viewing swaths of bedrock bearing the super seven matrix. She still loved the room with the large crystal sphere where she'd first learned about the wand duel between her family and August's. Though the family had done their best to tidy up, arrange and make the rooms more orderly, much of it still lay in its natural state.

"Were rituals ever done in these rooms? What was the cave used for in the past?" Larissa asked her parents.

"Rituals were done here long ago. Obviously, nothing recently." Roman smiled.

Eleanor spoke up. "We will come here periodically and arrange things to our liking. What we've done in this short time are more preliminaries, basic straightening out. Your father and I have been discussing how we'd like to use this place in the future. It's something we'll be discussing." She rubbed Larissa's shoulder with affection. "Right now, we are charging ourselves with the super seven energy and selecting certain stones from our collection that will be used for the upcoming battle. And make no mistake, there is a big battle ahead."

"Well, are we ready to go?" asked Roman.

Larissa looked up at her father in shock. "Go? We just got here. Where would we go?"

"Ah, my darling daughter, you surely weren't thinking we'd be camping out in here, did you? I mean, we could, but I think it would be rather uncomfortable."

"We do have a home, you know," said Eleanor. Her face flushed. "I guess Dorenda never told you about it?" She eyed her daughter with curiosity.

Larissa winced at the mention of her aunt's name. August stared at the ground, while Ciana stood close to him. Both remained silent.

"Um, she never discussed home. Home was always Kansas, where my adoptive parents were. Rick and Amy Martin. There were wonderful, you know. But nothing ever fully takes the place of your real parents." Larissa smiled at Eleanor and Roman.

"We are eternally grateful to the Martins for taking on the task of raising and caring for you in our absence," said Eleanor. "It broke our hearts when we had to leave you. To have missed your childhood, the birthdays, the holidays and sabbats, spending time with other family members. It was such a loss for us."

"Perhaps you can now make up for lost time," said August.

Everyone turned in surprise and viewed the young man who spoke out. Larissa stared at him, speechless.

"Ah, dear August, it is our intent to do so," said Roman. His eyes sparkled as he spoke.

"Yes, all of you have the future. Make the most of it," Ciana chimed in. She looked at each of them. "It's always important to focus on what you have, what can be done in the present moment and into the future. Remember that." Her lips trembled a little as she spoke.

"And to answer your question, dear niece," said Andrea, "you have your home in the French Quarter in New Orleans, Louisiana." She grinned. "I'm sure you've heard of that place."

"I know I have," said August. "Rich in history, drinking, and good times." Everyone laughed. "But it's a magical place. I know that much too," he added.

"And right you are, son," said Roman. "Let's get the Vanishport and head to the family home."

"Do the rest of you have a place where we do?" Larissa asked.

"No," Brendan answered. "We all live in other states, but we'll never turn down an opportunity to visit New Orleans." He laughed. "I wouldn't miss it for the world."

"Let's go," said Roman.

The Vanishport was summoned, and all family members boarded. In a short time, Larissa, her cohorts, and family were standing before a spacious home on Royal Street. Her mouth fell open at the architectural beauty. "Oh, this is more remarkable than anything I could have imagined." She turned to August, "Though Katharta Castle is quite amazing."

"Apples and oranges," answered August. "And both are equally delicious."

Larissa narrowed her eyes. There was something unusual about August, and she couldn't figure out what it was. Ever since his role in rescuing her aunt, something had changed.

Roman tapped Larissa on the shoulder, "And I know you're dying to see this place. Your eyes keep wandering around."

"I'm overwhelmed. I won't lie about that." Larissa laughed.

"Do you have the key, darling?" Eleanor asked.

The door squeaked as Roman opened it. Everyone filed inside. Larissa took in a deep breath, inhaling the musty scent of antiquity. She liked the setup immediately, a style of Victorian cleverly blended with a touch of modern added to it. The hallways and stairs showed off an elegance that somewhat reminded her of Katharta Castle, though this home was extremely modest for royalty. She loved it anyway.

"Aunt Ciana, Larissa, follow me," said Eleanor. "I'll show you to your rooms. Roman, you'll show the others to theirs?"

"Absolutely, my dear." Roman smiled. "Our staff will help. There's enough for all of us."

Larissa loved her room and its elegant surroundings immediately. This was nothing like her home with the Martins, who cared nothing for antiques or elegance. She also liked the fact that her great, great aunt Ciana was in the room next door. The fact that the lady bore bandaged arms and appeared to have no hands troubled her greatly. Due to the urgency surrounding her rescue, there was no time for deep conversation.

After everyone settled in, they all followed Roman's request to meet in the large dining room because there were more than enough chairs to seat family members and guests.

Much to Larissa's pleasant surprise, there were staff members present who attended to everyone's needs.

"The best wine, please," said Roman, pointing to his family. "I know we have some fine vintages in the wine cellar. Do we not?"

"Yes, sir. We most certainly do. I'll select the very best." A pleasant-looking gentleman dressed in waiter attire smiled and headed off.

A heavier set young lady, dressed in similar attire as her cohort, busied herself placing fine cut crystal goblets in front of everyone. Another gentleman brought out hors d'oeuvres and placed them in neat order on an ornate serving buffet table. Other staff came in and out of the kitchen, setting out small decorative plates and sterling silverware on the table. After the family and guests spent time eating and getting to know each other, the staff removed everything from the table and retreated to the kitchen.

"Thank you to everyone for coming," said Roman. "What I'd like to do next is talk about some of the things in store for us in the upcoming weeks and months, what we need to be aware of, what we need to plan for. That sort of thing. Would someone like to start first and get the ball rolling?" He gazed up and down the table at everyone.

August spoke up. "I'd like to speak, if you don't mind, sir. I have some grave information to share with you, and much of it won't be pretty."

"Then have at it. Let's hear it." Roman indicated for the young man to continue.

August spent the next couple of hours reviewing everything from the beginning of their travels, all their treks, and finished at last with him and his companions being captured by the Anguis, his enchantment of Edouard, and Ciana's horrid abuse.

Larissa, along with others, sat open-mouthed with horror at the last part. What struck her most was that Ciana seemed to gravitate to August, and that he had so tenderly administered to her during the meal, seeing that she was able to get her fill and that she had everything she needed. The horrid Anguis clave at least provided her with prosthetics so she could somewhat care for herself. Another amazing notation was how August referred to the lady as "Aunt", as if it were the most natural thing in the world to do.

Ciana spoke up after August's revelation. "I must say that if it had not been for darling August, I'm not sure what would have eventually become of me. When Eustace Anguis did what he did to my hands, I screamed out for my beloved Clement. Of course, they didn't hear me do that, but I did it from the depths of my heart.

"You see, beloveds, precious Clement did not kill my brother, Desmond Strondovan. The Anguis did. They just passed the dirty deed off on Desmond so they could get away with murder. My brother watched out for me like a protective father, but he would have honored a union between Clement and me, had the Anguis not interfered. That was our plan, for Clement and I to wed."

She turned to August and kissed him on the cheek. "Make no mistake about it, dear one. You have Clement's genes, and his extraordinary handsome looks. Others may not think much of your magical abilities, but I'm here to tell you that you are quite remarkable, if you continue developing your skills." Ciana took a moment and delivered a pointed but kind look at Larissa. The young lady blushed and stared down at her coffee cup.

"Aunt Ciana," asked Astrid, "there has always been a legend about a conjuring cloth. That its power is beyond all Magical tools. Is that true, or is that just a myth that got fabricated and passed down throughout time?"

Ciana smiled. "It is said that only the Nephilim can create this wondrous cloth, or those with such specific genes, that you have to be born to do it. But that is not true. Dorenda Soltaro figured that out. It had been my intent to try and teach her. Her magical skills were beyond reproach. Unfortunately, she turned to the ways of the Anguis, and I simply could not teach someone such as her. It was my refusal when she approached me during a visit to the Anguis Chateau in France that got me in my position now." She lifted her arms a little.

"What do we do with my sister? From what August said, she has taken a baneful path." Eleanor wiped tears from her eyes. "And to think that I trusted her with the care of Larissa. The whole prospect is quite frightening."

"Dear Eleanor," answered Ciana, "She taught Larissa well. The problem is that she also knows limitations as well as her knowledge base. We'll have to strip Dorenda of her powers. Neutralize her, if you will."

"Hey, August," Aiden blurted out, "maybe you can do a neat enchantment spell and take Dorenda out." He chuckled at the suggestion.

"Aiden!" Dannie scolded her son. "That's not an appropriate thing to say."

"Sorry, Mom. But you have to admit, that would be pretty cool." Aiden shrugged.

August said nothing but raised his eyebrows at the comment.

Ciana continued speaking. "Anyway, I must tell you that the Nephilim were not a mix of human and angels, as it is often told. We were a mix of human and star beings from other places. Those from the stars were versed in ancient knowledge stemming from the beginning of time. They knew the laws of nature and the universe. They knew how to work with it to their advantage.

"There were those, over time, who sought to stifle that knowledge, keep it hidden so man would lose touch with his own inner divinity and power. We knew that man was on the brink of danger if the truth of the cosmos was kept secret. Thus, we rebelled. We fought. Because we railed against the narrative, we were shunned, kicked out of society, and eventually banished.

"We had to disperse and mingle with others in strange lands in order to exist. It was always our intent to keep the arcane knowledge alive. It is the Anguis and their allies that are intent to drive the final wedge between man and his connection with a divine lineage. If they win, humans will be lost to darkness forever. That leaves the Anguis and their intimate cohorts in control forever.

"If this happens, humans will be nothing more than robotic slaves forever, incapable of thought or creation, which would be a waste for such a magnificent species. Humans are capable of great things. They are hindered by their apathy and blind ignorance more than anything."

"Aunt Ciana," asked Ceila, "what does the conjuring cloth really do? No one has ever given a great explanation of that."

Ciana smiled. "Ah, the conjuring cloth is tricky to make, to start with. Basically, it is a magical tool that uses two-way energy to execute what the holder or user of it desires. It directly takes on etheric energy. When fully charged, it expels that cosmic energy, mingled with the user's strong intent, and hits the target. Its power is rapid and strong. There is no other tool like it. Few, if any, will have it."

"Will you teach us how to spin?" asked Samantha. "And can males do it too?"

"I'm glad you asked, dear girl." Ciana's eyes sparkled. "I want to teach you. You're my family and worthy of the knowledge, to boot. And yes, male or female, it makes no difference."

Paul asked, "If this whole mess was about stealing a cloth or our family killing someone in another family, why is there a need for such a battle, if we know the truth now. That it was Anguis and not Desmond? We just tell the Glanarium Supremo what happened, and that's it. They'll deal with the Anguis."

"It's not about killing Clement. And it's not really about stealing a cloth, which I had already made. It's something much more, far greater. The earth and its inhabitants are hanging in the balance. The fight is still necessary."

"And why our families, us and the Hawthornes?" asked Gregory. "Why wouldn't you get an army together for both sides and duke it out?"

"The Strondovans, the Hawnthorne's, and the Anguis are catalysts. Others will gravitate to either the Anguis or the Strondovan/Hawthorne team," said Ciana. She looked at August. "It's not a battle between the Strondovans and your family, darling. The Strondovans and the Hawthornes are actually a formidable team. The Glanarium Supremo had been made aware of this impending battle for centuries and using this set of events that occurred between Desmond, Clement, and the Anguis, was a means of gathering the troops."

Everyone at the table stared at Ciana in silence. Some bore looks of disgust on their faces.

"I know you feel used," she said, "but you're actually being useful. A savior, really. It's not what you planned for your life, but sometimes you learn your true purpose through a terrible misfortune. It's taken quite some time for the right people and circumstances to occur. And here you are."

"What if we're simply not that much into saving the world?" said Aiden. "Let's be honest, is anyone really into that sort of thing?" He yawned.

"Aiden, be quiet!" said Brendan. "If you can't think of something useful to say, just keep your mouth closed."

"Aiden," said Ciana, "just remember that your cousin and her friend, August, didn't want to do this, either. And here they are. The least you can do is think positive thoughts and wish them well. Any little bit helps, and it shouldn't take much effort. Remember, little things we do are powerful. And that includes the kindest of gestures."

Aiden turned red with embarrassment and nodded politely at Ciana.

"So, when is the first spinning lesson?" Jasmine spoke up.

"Very soon," answered Ciana.

After the meeting, Larissa slipped away and strolled down the streets, sniffing the air, feeling the sun warm her skin. People were everywhere. Never had she experienced such crowds. Bourbon Street held its usual cadre of customers, drinks in hand, people laughing, patrons in some of the bars tossing mardi gras beads to others below. She smiled. Never in her hometown in Kansas had she seen this. The air electrified her, igniting a new energy she'd not sensed before. The French Quarter with its architecture and antiquity struck a chord deep inside her being. There was an inexplicable connection to this place.

She glanced through the shop windows, admired the other homes, and soon she made her way to Jackson Square. As she walked, the events that occurred in her family dining room played over and over in her head. Ciana's doting over August still boggled her mind. Never in her wildest dreams had she anticipated that. And to think that August had been so intuitive as to intercept her cries of anguish and make a plan to save her.

Larissa grinned as she viewed the tarot card readers dotting the area in front of St. Louis Cathedral. There were more shops she'd have to explore, especially Faulkner House of Books, an enchanting bookstore she just passed. She beelined over to the park and sat on a bench, gazing out at the statue of Andrew Jackson and the Mississippi River.

"Mind if I join you?"

She turned in surprise. August stood behind the bench.

"If you wish. Where's Willem and Phuctious?"

"Bourbon Street got Phuctious. Willem decided to check out other parts of the Quarter."

August seated himself quite close to Larissa and stared out into the distance. "Quite a magical city, if I say so myself. I honestly have to say I love this place."

They sat in silence for several minutes. Larissa spoke first.

"I want to thank you for taking care of my aunt. That was very kind, considering how you feel about my family." Larissa stared squarely at him.

He turned his attention to her and reciprocated the light smile. "My biggest regret is not preventing it in the first place. I would have moved heaven and earth to have gotten her out of there sooner. But I simply didn't have the full knowledge until after the fact."

"You really care about her, don't you?" Larissa sat up straighter and moved her face closer to his.

"I can see how Uncle Clement would have adored her. She's . . . magical, just like this place. When I tapped into time and went back and saw what that wretched Eustace Anguis did to her . . ." August paused and wiped an eye. He shuddered; his face flushed. "I can't even talk about it. It was the most despicable thing I'd ever witnessed. I decided without hesitation that I would never leave her there to suffer a horrible death. That would have been next. I'd wager that much."

"Oh, August." Larissa, without thinking, rested a hand lightly on his knee.

August looked down where she touched him, startled.

"I'm sorry." She jerked her hand away, blushing.

"At any rate, I got him back."

Her face blanched in surprised. "You what?"

"I gave that old bastard what he deserved. Turn about, fair play, you know. He got a taste of his own medicine."

"You didn't!" Her mouth opened in horror.

"Don't worry. Ciana has his finger as a souvenir." He grinned.

"You didn't say any of this at the table when we were all there, but I did notice that Willem looked white as a ghost."

"He was quite the trooper."

Larissa continued staring at August. For the first time she allowed herself to really look at him, his facial features, eyes, nose, mouth, and a gorgeous head of wavy golden hair, which had caught her attention the first time they'd met. She averted her stare when he stopped talking and stared back.

"Will you learn to spin when Ciana teaches us? She said gender didn't matter."

"Not sure." August shook his head. "But it would give me more ammunition in my witches tool kit."

She nodded at him.

"Come on," he said. "Let's go walk around the square. I hear there's a great bookstore in the area."

Larissa smiled and got up from her seat. She also didn't flinch when August gently placed a hand in the small of her back and guided her out the park gates.

Chapter Twenty One

Inside Chateau Anguis, Edouard burned with fiery anger as he gazed at his father. Once August and his crew left, Edouard had been urgently summoned to attend to his father's request at once. Eustace sat in his study, dejected, broken in spirit, maimed beyond repair.

"That damned August Hawthorne did this to me, son. On top of that, he took Ciana and left."

"How could you let this happen?" asked Edouard. He went to the bar, poured them both whiskeys and returned, placing a glass on the coffee table in front of his father. The senior Anguis had been reduced to using prosthetic devices like his former prisoner. Magicals could do some wondrous healing. Reproducing limbs was not one of them.

"I'll kill that bastard. I can taste his blood now." Edouard tried soothing his emotions with a mouthful of the burning liquid, letting it slide down his throat without batting an eyelash. "Again, how did you let this happen?" He glared at Eustace.

"Enough of your questions. I may not have hands, but I can still do magic. At any rate, Hawthorne and his foul comrades plus the Druids simply took us by surprise."

"The Druids?" asked Edouard. His father's admission stunned him. "You mean those druids, the ones of the desert?" He studied his whiskey glass, perplexed. "We don't hear of them much. How did Hawthorne manage to get their help? That's confounding."

"That whole bunch is confounding at this point, and that's why we need to rid them from the planet. And now I think Larissa is full in the know. And I had high hopes for that girl."

"When were you going to tell me about her?" asked Edouard.

"Huh?" Eustace looked back at his son, confused.

"Dorenda. Mother." He enunciated the last word.

Eustace sank back on the sofa. "So she finally told you, didn't she?"

"She did. And when would you have stopped me and Larissa if I had won her over?"

"Oh, we would have put a halt on the love interest. Trust me on that. But turn of events took care of everything in that arena." He stared at Edouard. "And let me tell you, son, Dorenda would have made a fine mother for you and a wife for me. Know that and never forget it."

After a few minutes of silence, Eustace said, "Now it's my turn for questions. How did they escape Sulphure Hall?"

"Since we're spilling our guts here, I'll tell you. That stupid sneaky August Hawthorne enchanted me. He was so smooth and slick, I didn't see it coming." Edouard related the story to his father in full detail.

"Oh, by the gods!" Eustace raked his glass off the table, not caring when it shattered on the floor, wetting the fibers of a fine woven rug in strong liquor. "We simply can't underestimate them any longer. At this point, August Hawthorne is smarter than we think, like it or not, and Larissa is not so starry-eyed that she was interested in hanging around you for any length of time."

"Listen to us fight, father. They wove a tactical spell for that. I just know it."

"Ha! Just like you knew August was really August." Eustace managed a sarcastic laugh. "There's no spell involved, son. We have underestimated them and overshot our abilities. We will have a real fight on our hands. No doubt in my mind anymore."

***

One late evening, Phuctious and Willem had been politely asked to leave the premises and enjoy the activities of the Quarter for a while. In the topmost level of the Strondovan mansion, the family members gathered in a candlelit room. Even Aiden, for all his youthful quips, had an interest in learning the coveted art of weaving this prized cloth. The family formed a circle with Ciana in the middle.

"Listen carefully," she said, "for what I reveal must never leave this room. What you learn must be kept within each of you and used only in the direst of circumstances. The weaving of the conjuring cloth is a secret handed down from the ancients. It has nearly become a lost art. Only few remain who have this skill.

"The opportunity to teach what I know to several family members at once is truly remarkable. I do this now because my remaining time among mortals is waning."

"Are you going to die, Aunt Ciana?" asked Astrid. "Please tell us that's not going to happen so soon."

Ciana smiled. "Ones like myself live much longer than Mortals and Magicals, but we don't live forever. I will be eternally grateful to precious August for saving me. His dear Uncle Clement would be proud of his nephew's magical finesse and bravery. If he hadn't rescued me, the art of weaving the cloth would nearly be forever lost. Now, as I was saying, I'm passing my knowledge to all of you."

"How did you come by this knowledge, Aunt Ciana? Who are you, really?" Paul asked.

"I'm glad you asked. I will tell you the story. I am a descendant of the Watchers, the ones who came to earth to civilize man and educate them in ancient knowledge. They taught humanity many things over the ages. That's what my mother told me in private one day. She wanted me to know my history. One day there was a being that she encountered. He was not of this world but another. They engaged in a secret relationship, came together, and here I am. My earthly human father never knew.

"And I never met my biological father. Mother and I kept this secret between us. She knew I would discover things about myself as I grew older and wanted me to understand what they were and why. We didn't reveal such a secret to anyone. I'm telling you now so you know the truth.

"I am not a Magical, but I do possess many gifts, which may appear divine in nature. The truth is, my kind, the Nephilim, wanted to share ancient knowledge to humans, whether Mortal or Magical. The conjuring cloth is the most tight-lipped secret. Magicals, by their nature, seem to create this item much easier than Mortals. Now, how to create the conjuring cloth.

"The first thing you must know is that there are two parts to the cloth. The making of it and the activation of it. It takes two to make it work. There is unity that is involved in this process. One to guide the crafting and one to ignite its power once the cloth is ready for use. Someone, male or female, must belong to an earth clave to guide the crafting. Someone, male or female, must be a member of an elemental fire clave to activate.

"I included Jasmine and Dannie in this meeting because they have joined the clave through marriage and were chosen by their spouses because they are highly seasoned and gifted metaphysical practitioners. The rest of you are Magicals. I'm so glad Paulo was able to join us. He can take this skill back to South America with him and share with other family members."

"And I am eager to do so," said Paulo. "But I have a question? How do we determine when to share what you are teaching us? You said never do it, but that would mean the art of weaving stops with us."

"Ah, you are so correct," answered Ciana. "Let me clarify what I mentioned earlier. You only share this with a family member, if they are interested and worthy. Never is this to be divulged outside the family. That's why there are so few spinners. Not every earth family can spin. Only divinely selected earth familial lines and those taken in marriage and thus joining that line. If Dannie or Jasmine ever leave the family, their abilities leave with them. Family of the blood keeps the skills until death."

"Well, that should keep either of you from straying," said Henry, grinning at Dannie and Jasmine.

The two ladies laughed and waved him off.

Ciana continued, "In the creation of a cloth, you must first purify yourself. That's why all of you were asked to bathe in special infused waters and oils before coming up here. You may finetune your own ritual for this, but it must be done, nevertheless. What is surprising is that you do not actually weave or spin anything yourself. To do this in a physical manner in any way will always result in failure."

"Aunt Ciana," Larissa interjected, "the Anguis had a spinning room in Sulphure Hall filled with people supposedly from our family line who were made to try and spin. What they created looked convincing, the way the cloth had a certain look to it. But as you said, the piece disintegrated seconds later." She didn't share what Dorenda told her about trying this herself.

"That's the interesting thing that happens when someone tries to create a cloth without the true knowledge," answered Ciana. "It's no surprise that their spell methods can create an impressive look-alike. You can conjure or create whatever you desire, but the proof is truly in following the proper instructions in any ritual you do, any spell you cast.

"If you follow a method, you must follow it to the letter, unless there is license by the creator of the method for some creativity. Where the conjuring cloth is concerned, there is not. Absolutely not."

"Are you ready for the fun part?" Ciana turned and viewed each family member. "I will teach you the incantation to call on the ones that spin the cloth. They look like ordinary creatures you see every day. Ready?"

Everyone nodded.

Ciana closed her eyes and turned her face upward. *"Come one, come all, great moths of the air. Come gather around as I prepare. A powerful cloth so rich and bright. My desire I manifest in truth and light."*

A brief chill filled the room, dissipating quickly. All the windows clattered opened. Family members looked around at each other in great excitement as breezes blew. It was at that moment they all perked up on hearing a light tinkling sound reminiscent of an old music box. One by one through all the windows they came, the great moths like the one that visited Ciana in the Anguis Chateau.

On first sight, as Ciana had mentioned, the moths looked like ordinary plain white ones. But something wondrous happened. For several seconds, the lady intoned a monotonal sound as she stared intently at the thick white cloud gathered above her head.

"Satus telarum nunc," Ciana called out.

Everyone sat, dumbfounded, as the moths began their ritual task, flittering and floating in and out from one another. As they moved, their wings lit up, showing off the most enchanting swirls of pastel colors, pink, violet, lime, yellow, orange, blue. In and out and up and down they moved in a certain rhythmic pattern. Ciana intoned the sound she made earlier periodically throughout the weaving process. The moths moved effortlessly without missing their places, never bumping into each other. In a matter of minutes, the moths had woven a twenty-eight-by-twenty-eight square.

The cloth-like material remained suspended in the air. Within the grey fibers, an iridescent light flickered. All the moths headed to the windows and disappeared into the night. Ciana reached up for the cloth as it floated down into her prosthetic hand.

"And now it must be activated." She turned to August. "Precious one, you are the only one among us who can activate it. Say the following: *"Ego ignem cindera."*

August dutifully did as instructed. He walked toward Ciana, held his hands near the piece without touching it, and gave the command. *"Ego ignem cindera."*

The cloth ignited into white light. Within the square shape, the colors swirled brighter and with more clarity. Everyone gasped.

"Wow, that's cool!" said Aiden.

Ceila spoke up, "What are you going to do with it?"

"For practice, let's bring Phuctious and Willem home. We didn't give them a specific time to come back, so I'll have them return now. One thing to remember when using the cloth once it's ignited, the one who used the weaving spell must state their desire in the present tense, as if it is so or as if it already exists. That's extremely important, so don't forget it." Ciana held the cloth out in front of her. "Phuctious and Willem are here."

The sound of a bell rang out from below. Within seconds, a voice sounded from the doorway.

"We're back," said Phuctious. He and Willem stood watching everyone.

The cloth, having done its job, disintegrated into thin air.

Ciana gestured for them to enter the room.

The dwarf added, "The party is just getting started out there. Anyone up for a quick run to Bourbon Street?" He held up a long plastic container with an equally long straw.

"Um, Phuctious, why don't you and Willem return downstairs and we'll join you there," said Roman.

"Is that it, Aunt Ciana?" asked Samantha.

"Yes, dear. That's it. We got what we wanted." The spell of the evening had been broken. Ciana accomplished her lifelong goal. She turned to August and Larissa. "Talk to me later, and I will repeat the spell incantations so you can add them to your grimoires. There is a secret code used to write them so no one but you understands it. And if everyone will excuse me, I'm heading off to bed. It's late."

"I'm in for joining Willem and Phuctious," said August. "Who else wants to come?"

Henry got up. "I think I want to join those guys. Anyone else?"

Soon the only occupants of the mansion were Larissa, her parents, Ciana, and house staff.

"You didn't want to go out, dear?" asked Eleanor. "If I were younger, I'd be out there too." She wrapped an arm around Larissa and kissed her on the forehead.

"I was hoping to talk to you and Father for a little while. I really haven't had a chance to be alone with you."

"Let's go downstairs for some tea," said Eleanor.

In a cozy study, Larissa sat with her parents.

"Anything on your mind?" asked Roman.

"I do have some questions," answered Larissa. "I'm really struck by how kind you've been to August."

Her parents looked at her with surprise.

"How else would you expect us to be, darling?" said Eleanor. "He's been with you for a while now, and he's our guest. We wouldn't dream of treating him unkindly."

"You treat him like you've known him all along, like he's a member of this family." Larissa shook her head in frustration. "I can't quite describe it. And Aunt Ciana practically adores him, dotes on him."

"August has been extremely kind to our relative, risking his neck to rescue her, see that she's taken care of. He's congenial with all of us. What's not to like, Larissa? He conducts himself like a gentleman, at least around us." Roman stared at his daughter as he sipped from his teacup.

"What's your experience with him?" Eleanor narrowed her eyes.

"He's arrogant and obnoxious. And he despises us. He's even said so. As you might expect, he's been much nicer since rescuing Ciana."

Roman studied Larissa, slowly tilting his head from side to side in consideration of his daughter's words. "Have you ever thought for a moment that whenever he made that declaration he has since changed his mind? I don't get a sense that August is an enemy or that he's trying to get one over on us in any way. I do understand that being thrown together and knowing little of what transpired was a big shock to both of you. And who knows what August was told about the history of the feud between our families."

"What do you think of Willem?" Larissa asked. She looked at the faces of her parents, trying to read their reaction. "I think he's such a gentleman, kind, sensitive, trustworthy. He's been a joy. Saved my sanity on several occasions. We've become close."

"He's a non-royal," said Roman. His lips tightened as he stared at his daughter.

"And why would that matter? Dannie and Jasmine aren't royals."

"Dannie is a priestess of her own coven, though it's comprised of Mortals. Jasmine is a grand master of a renowned order. They are at least leaders in what they do."

Larissa frowned.

"Look, dear," continued Roman, "We royals either marry other royals or at least high-level metaphysical practitioners. And when I say high level, I mean heads of groups, covens, orders, you name it. They are more than mere initiated members. They have worthiness in their practice, so to speak. Willem is most likely a good wizard. Just because his father was well-known doesn't mean he is. He didn't pursue a leadership role, only a serving one, not that that's bad, mind you."

Larissa opened her mouth to object when her mother spoke up.

"Darling, you know that we expect you to marry a royal, especially since you are our only child." Eleanor reached over and placed her hand over Larissa's. "We must continue the royal lineage."

"I was only asking, that's all." Larissa grimaced. "Why do the Hawthorne's have Katharta Castle, and we don't have such a place like that? I'm told we're on par with August's family. I would think we would own something as magnificent." Larissa flushed with embarrassment as she uttered those words. "I adore our home here, though. It's quite lovely."

"You have to remember, dear, that all we owned was destroyed by those who wanted us gone. We once had such places. We were able to salvage this home because of kind friends who were willing to help us. They used the house for other enterprises while we were gone. Those ventures ended on our return."

"And one other thing," said Larissa, "where are August's parents? All I've ever heard about is his grandfather Jove, who was most kind and gracious to me when I visited."

"Did you and August not talk at all?" Roman asked.

"To be honest, we've mostly been at odds." Larissa picked up the silver teapot and poured another cup of hot tea.

"By who's part, yours or his?" Eleanor smiled lightly in Larissa's direction.

"Maybe both of us. I think he's tried a time or two to win me over, but I wouldn't budge."

"You're a stubborn one, and I mean that comment with great love." Eleanor nodded in thought. "The truth is August's parents were killed in a freak accident involving interdimensional travel. Jove kindly took his grandchildren under his wing."

Larissa looked at her parents in surprise. "He's never said anything about that to me. Not one word. Not one hint."

"He was two years old when it all happened. Most likely there's not much to remember," said Roman. "You two are quite similar in that regard. We were robbed of enjoying your childhood, and August was robbed as well, not knowing his parents."

"He's so proud, he'd never admit such a thing." Larissa tapped her fingers on the arm of her chair.

"Well, it might be something you two can talk about," added Eleanor. "Larissa, you really need to break down your barriers where August is concerned. You might find you two have more in common than you think."

"I discovered he actually likes to read. Found that out when he followed me to Jackson Square the other day."

"How nice," said Roman. "It's sounds like you two might be breaking the ice. Better late than never, yes?" He smiled at his daughter.

"I guess so." Larissa said nothing else. She would have to ask more about the Strondovan history another time when it wasn't so late. After kindly excusing herself, she headed to her room and crawled into her luxurious bed.

August, Willem, Phuctious, and the rest of her family still hadn't returned for the evening. In the French Quarter, people were known to keep all kinds of hours. The way her parents brushed off Willem disappointed her greatly. It was as if they held no regard for the kind young man, preferring, like Ciana, to dote on that odious August Hawthorne.

Or was he really that odious? She had now seen parts of August's skill and magical finesse that intrigued her. Tapping into time and learning information, calling on spirits and deities for assistance, responding to telepathic cries for help and having empathic skills to feel another's pain. On top of everything, he enchanted Edouard Anguis and devised a plan to rescue her aunt.

His exacting such horrid revenge on Eustace Anguis impacted her senses the most. She didn't know whether August should be declared a monster, too, or be regarded as a valiant warrior. Warriors sometimes had to do awful things, and it seemed like August Hawthorne had the balls to take matters into his own hands and set a record straight.

She relived their moment on the bench that day in Jackson Square, how he'd teared up when talking about Ciana, how they looked at each other when discussing such intimate details that he dared only share with her, even though they could be awful. The touch of his hand in the small of her back created a feeling that left her greatly conflicted. There was no way she could be changing her feelings for August. No way. Her love for Willem was too strong. Wasn't it?

At once she perked up, filled with an uncanny desire to join the others. Dressing quickly, Larissa left her room and slipped out of the house. Sounds from the crowd and music met her ears as the front door clicked shut. Closing her eyes, she tuned in to the energy of her family. Intuitively she walked to Bourbon Street, where everyone still congregated. August spied her from a distance. "Hey, over here," he shouted.

Brendon kindly purchased her a drink, and the group made their way all through the Quarter, stopping to grab a bite at a café, chatting with others, and finally taking a walk by the river in Jackson Square. August somehow stayed close, taking her hand at times so they wouldn't get separated from the family. Phuctious humored all of them with witty quips. Willem stayed strangely quiet.

Later, they all returned to the Strondovan mansion. Tired from all the walking and a little hazy from the drinks she'd consumed, Larissa headed straight to her room, followed by August. They both looked at each other awkwardly.

"Mind if I join you?" he asked.

She struggled to clear her head from the haziness of alcohol and fatigue. They had spent so much time together since they'd started on this quest. Strangers no longer, confronting everything from near-death experiences, battles, and dreadful secrets, the two had been through so much. And there was more to come.

Surprising herself, Larissa said nothing but indicated for him to follow her to bed, where they undressed and slipped between the sheets. The moments after that became hazier. Was it excitement from learning a wonderful secret from her aunt, food and drink, or had she, too, fallen under an irresistible enchantment spell from August Hawthorne? Tonight, she threw caution to the wind, banished her prejudices, and willingly surrendered.

The next morning, Larissa awakened to the sound of talking in the hallway. She rolled over and viewed the empty space next to her. Deep inside her body tingled and burned with the paradox of pleasure and discomfort. Those sensations nudged her memory of August and his lingering effects. From the sounds slipping through the door, it seemed like the family was slowly awakening and starting their day. Someone knocked on the door.

"Come in," she said. It didn't matter to her that she was naked and tucked away beneath her warm covers.

"Good morning. Care to get some coffee with me?"

It was August Hawthorne, looking dashing as ever in his form-fitting jeans and a sports shirt. He didn't look hung over or otherwise affected from the former nightly romp.

"Am I late for breakfast? Is everyone downstairs?"

He shrugged. "Some are downstairs in the dining room. Others are snoozing away. It's eight in the morning. If you hurry, we can make it to CC's and beat the crowd."

"I guess. Give me a few. Meet you downstairs."

August nodded and closed the door. How strange, thought Larissa. She didn't expect him to search her out again so soon. Everything they had done until now was out of obligation or in fulfillment of a mission. Unless her parents had suggested it? Perish the thought! Part of her still rebelled a little. She pulled herself out from under the covers, cleaned up, and threw on some clothes.

Inside CC's Coffeehouse, they seated themselves at a table and dove into their coffees and croissants.

"You're up early after being out all night." Larissa sipped from her coffee cup and gazed at August.

"We didn't get back that late." August licked his finger, salvaging a piece of his food.

She asked, "What do you think about last night?"

"Definitely the most interesting thing I've ever seen. And it worked. Fast."

Larissa nodded. "And the way it all came together. Just beautiful."

August added, "I have the perfect plan on when to use something like that. We'll talk about it later."

"Why didn't you ever tell me about your parents?"

"Huh?" August placed his cup back down on the table. The expression on his face showed extreme shock and annoyance. "Why would you ask me such a thing? And who mentioned anything to you?"

"What's the big secret, August? And it's nothing to be ashamed of. So your mom and dad had a bad accident. It happens. Unfortunately, you've had to live not knowing your parents." She leaned toward him. "You could have told me. It's something we have in common, whether you like it or not."

"I don't get to spend time with my parents because they're not coming back." He sank down in his chair.

The young man's words snapped at her as if someone wielded a whip against her skin.

"I'm sorry. I didn't mean that to be unkind in any way. Mom and Dad told me last night."

"To be honest, Larissa, you haven't been the most congenial on this journey, let alone amenable to chats. Look, I'll admit my part in it, too, but when I have tried in small ways, you might as well have just slapped me." He snapped his fingers, "Oh, you know what? I think you've done that. More than once. Correct me if I'm wrong."

Larissa held out her hand. "Oh, by the gods, August. I never meant to pick a fight with you this morning. I know you probably thought we'd have a peaceful breakfast, and I've rained on the parade. I'm so sorry."

"Really?" he asked. His eyes blazed.

"I am. I'm not trying to make fun of you, either. And again, I haven't been very nice." She glanced down at her food. "Even my parents alluded to that fact."

"I like your parents. They are very refined and intelligent witches. It would do you well to listen to them." August bit off some of his croissant.

"You really like them, August? And I'm not asking that to be facetious."

"I do like them. And like I've said before. I adore your aunt. You're extremely lucky to have all of them. I'm envious, if you want to know the truth.'

Larissa stared at him but said nothing and continued eating. After several minutes in silence, August spoke up, "We have got to get on the same team. It was a rocky start, but we need to come together if we're going to beat whatever is thrown our way."

"I know. It's going to be big, and I'm not sure how it's all going to come about."

"Me, either. I suspect the Glanarium Supremo will direct us." August swallowed down the rest of his coffee. "So you do think about me from time to time. I mean, especially if you're talking to your parents about me."

She chuckled at the comment. "You're so silly. Truth is they really like you a lot and clearly told me so."

"Like I said, you need to listen to them more." August looked around. "Let's walk around the Quarter. I saw some shops I want to visit."

Again, Larissa didn't object when her companion placed his hand between her shoulders and guided her out into the streets. They stopped at Bourbon French Parfums, a lovely perfume shop, where August kindly purchased her a small bottle of a wonderful scent she liked. Later, they went to the Vampire Café and indulged their palates and their sense of humor with red cocktails cleverly packaged in little blood bags, like the kind found in hospitals. They sat at a table outside and sipped their drinks from the tubing attached to the bags and chatted amiably as if they did this every day.

"Missed me?" said a voice.

Larissa stifled a yelp at the ball of fur that appeared in her lap. "Sophie!" She hugged her kitty, her familiar. "I have missed you. Where have you been?"

"Trying to get away from that loathsome aunt of yours, Dorenda. She's been trying to have me spy for her, but I won't do it. I dodged a spell to hold me captive, bit her, and ran off. So here I am." The cat grinned in only the way cats can do when they're feeling proud of themselves. Sophie turned toward August.

"Hey, fleabag. So you told the old broad off, eh?" August grinned.

"I agree with her," answered the cat, angling her head in Larissa's direction. "You are silly. And I've thought about you, too. Pretty impressive work you've done." Sophie jumped down from Larissa's lap and made her way to August, hopping up to his shoulder where she rested as the pair chatted more and later wandered around the Quarter.

Several yards away, unseen, Willem watched. He had seen everything.

Chapter Twenty Two

"What does it say?" asked Larissa. Standing behind August, she tried reading the letter he held. "And why did you get it and not me?"

"Oh, by the gods! Does it matter? I saw the postman slipping mail through the slot." He turned around and added with a smirk, "Besides, your father told me to make myself at home and that included grabbing up the mail."

Larissa grimaced and looked at the letter. "Go on. Read it." She smacked August's arm. "Out loud!"

He laughed. "Okay, here I go:

The time has come for the families of North Strondovan and South Hawthorne to appear before the Glanarium Supremo. Events are transpiring rapidly and deserve attention and action. We wish to discuss this in further detail in a grand meeting of the council. Please report to us on the thirtieth day of this month so our task may be accomplished.

Sincerest Wishes,
Glanarium Supremo

"Thirtieth of this month? How long do we really have?" Larissa frowned.

"About two weeks," answered August.

"What was that, again?" Roman walked into the room, followed by Eleanor.

"The Glanarium Supremo wants to meet with us. I think things are about to happen." August handed the letter to Roman.

"That's in about two weeks," said Eleanor.

"Yes, it is." August glanced at Larissa and patted her gently on the back.

"Do you know how these meetings go?" Larissa looked at her parents.

Eleanor answered, "They are formal, straight to the point, no mess, no fuss." She nodded in thought. "Don't get me wrong, the members are not unkind, it's just that they mean business, like any other members of an overseeing group."

Larissa shivered. "Now I'm really nervous. This adds such a high dose of reality to everything we've done."

"It does." August stared off as she spoke. "You and I need to think about what things we can do to ward off Anguis and his crew. Whatever the plan, everyone is going to bring their toughest spells and fiercest moves."

"One thing's for certain," said Roman, "we'll definitely know everything better after the next two weeks. In the meantime, we really need to pick Ciana's brain as much as possible. Not sure how much she will know, but whatever insight she can provide, it will be golden."

***

The Glanarium Supremo met in an undisclosed interdimensional space. No one could accurately trace the location because it changed each time the council met with non-Supremo-initiated members. As a group, they tried not to be dictatorial but supportive. At times, they had to give orders if it meant for the greater good of all involved.

Larissa's nerves fired off as she looked at the scene around her. Light from the stars and sun had been captured and placed in crystalline globes that swirled beneath a high ceiling. Their flashes illuminated the room in a mix of gold and silver. Stone archways lined the sides. All around, council members seated themselves in their assigned galleries. Honored senior memlbers were seated on the main floor.

"You okay?" August whispered.

She looked over at him and smiled a little. "As best I can be."

"We'll get through this." August squeezed her knee in reassurance.

She rested her hand on his. As of late, being closer to him filled her with a sense of calm, which was a totally new experience for her after all they'd been through, after all their warring and bickering. When Willem stared in their direction, she averted her eyes.

Trumpets sounded. Everyone watched as the majestically dressed head witch of the Glanarium Supremo made her way up the main aisle to the front of the room and seated herself on a white marble throne. Decked out in a regal gown of black silk, covered by a burgundy flowing cloak, she mesmerized the eyes. Another beautiful witch in robed attire entered the room, walked down the aisle, and stood behind a selenite podium.

"Come to order, one and all. It is time for the meeting of all meetings." The Mistress of Ceremony's voice rang out loud and clear in the great hall.

On the right side of the Mistress of Ceremony, Roman and Eleanor joined their daughter and August, along with Jove. Because Ciana was the victim in this case, she also joined the family. On the left side of the Mistress of the podium sat Edouard, Eustace, and the two sisters, Malevolinda and Carnetta. The other Strondovan members were present, along with Paulo. They sat in nearby seats marked for family. Willem and Phuctious sat in the guest section. Much to Larissa's surprise and relief, Tiberinus, Greta Marvo, Gamal Emara, Ivey (Mistress of the Hedgerows), and Remington Allwine joined them.

"What's he doing here?" Larissa quickly whispered to her father. She gestured to Allwine.

"Ah, I called him up one night and we had a big chat. I got him to take our side. After all, he has the keys to the deities. Luckily, the Glanarium Supremo made a huge exception, like they did with Ciana, and allowed him to come." Roman tapped his forehead with an index finger. Larissa smiled.

The head leader stood behind the podium as the Mistress of Ceremony stepped aside and seated herself on a second throne of white marble.

"Greetings one and all, dear Magicals and other esteemed guests. I will waste no time with pleasantries. This meeting is called to address a great upcoming challenge that will change the world, for better or for worse. Even we know not the winner. We do not seek to interfere but wish to maintain ourselves as guides, offering support and advice when needed. On occasion, we do send out mandates to protect our members of the Magiverse. We strive to be fair, remain impartial, and facilitate the good for all, both Magicals and Mortals.

"As the story goes a precious relic was stolen from a North Strondovan family member. But that's not all. At the time the relic was stolen, a murder occurred during a wand duel between two witches, one from the North Strondovan line and the other from South Hawthorne. It has always been the assumption that the North Strondovan member killed the other while dueling. In the process, the relic was taken from a second North Strondovan family member who was present at the event.

"It was the murder, however, where Magicals held their focus. In our duels, it is merely a contest to see who out bests the other, not killing someone as in the case of duels between Mortals. This occurrence set up division between the two families, of course. Worse, it created division in the Magiverse, such was the outrage by others when it was discovered what happened. As it turned out, the South Strondovan line was nearly eradicated, which was most unfortunate, as the North Strondovan and South Hawthorne lines are revered families, royal in lineage, and favored by most Magicals.

"It has been brought to our attention over time several details about this event and what happened. Some of it might be truth. Some of it might be mere speculation. We have been diligently collecting information and investigating. It was hoped that the two families would resolve this issue and that the relic that was stolen would be returned to the rightful owner.

"Current heirs from each family were designated throughout the years to rectify this issue, all to no avail. It is the heirs we see now who have truly risen to the occasion and have brought this matter to a head. But first, we want Ciana Strondovan to voice what really happened on that fateful day. Will you come forward?" The leader gestured to Ciana.

The lady nodded and headed toward the podium. Edouard and his family shifted nervously in their seats, glancing at each other with a look of disgust on their faces.

Ciana spoke. "Thank you, great leader and Glanarium Supremo members for allowing me to set the record straight on this whole unfortunate affair. I have waited a long time to speak the truth, and in all honesty, if it weren't for the valiant and resourceful August Hawthorne, I would most likely not be here." She turned and briefly glared at the Anguis family. "For the sake of time, I will get to the point.

"It was not my brother, Desmond Strondovan, who killed my beloved, Clement Hawthorne—for that is who Clement was. My beloved. It was a member of the Anguis clave. The moment Clement hit the ground, that clave moved quickly to take me captive and steal a conjuring cloth I had just woven. It was my intent that Clement would be the one to activate it."

Murmurs scattered throughout the Supremo members. The leader, who had taken her place on the other marble throne, whispered something into the Mistress of Ceremony's ear.

"I have spent until these past several weeks imprisoned in the Anguis Chateau in Rouen, France." Ciana held up her hands, showing off the prostheses. "This is finally what they did to me because I would not spin for them or allow them to activate the cloth."

Everyone in the hall gasped.

"Dear council members, I am a Nephilim and a spinner. I am not a witch, though I have my own divine powers. To ensure this highly secret art of spinning continues, I have taught the Magicals in my family. Though worthy high-level practitioners of metaphysics can learn this, it is Magicals who are the most amenable to this skill.

"Note that the hour of the witch spinners is at hand, and that the Anguis seek nothing more than to use any precious cloth to their advantage to wreak havoc on the world." Ciana looked around the hall. "This is what I have to say. This is my warning to all of you. A catastrophic event will occur if the Anguis spread their influence. That is all." She stopped speaking and returned to her seat.

The Mistress of Ceremony stepped up to the podium. "To the South Anguis clave, this charge is most serious and alarming. What say you to those words, to the story of Ciana Strondovan?"

Edouard rose, but Eustace pushed him down and strode to where the Mistress of Ceremony stood. From behind the podium, he faced the crowd. "Members of the Glanarium Supremo, I will also get to the point. The South Anguis clave has ideas we think will benefit the world. We wish to implement them. Ciana Strondovan may seek to disparage us, but her beloved Clements's descendant did this to me." He also showed his prosthetic hands.

Everyone in the hall murmured in what appeared almost like approval, much to the chagrin of Eustace Anguis. "So now I'll set the record straight. We, the Anguis, hereby declare war on the North Strondovan and South Hawthorne claves. They refuse to be our ally and stand in the way of everything we desire for the world. One's disagreement on a matter is the other's chief goal regardless. Whether or not we have a cloth to help us matters not. We will prevail. Our decision stands and is non-negotiable."

Eustace glared defiantly out at the audience, turned on his heel, and returned to his seat. The Anguis members nodded and smiled in agreement with their father's words.

"Very well," said the Leader. She had returned to the podium. "It appears that the South Anguis have made a declaration of war. We are all witnesses to this and are powerless to stop these events that were set in motion long ago. We've waited a long time as well. There was no other choice but to hold the status quo until this moment came, a part of time and history that cannot be stopped but must be fought for and a winner declared, for good or for evil.

"These claves will, therefore, be told the time, date, and location where the great battle will be fought. It will happen in a dimension that won't directly affect Mortals, but they will be informed of some events that will occur as this war takes place. Leaders from around the world will speak to their people.

"We, the Glanarium Supremo, will remain ever watchful of the events. Our place in the Magiverse and our future interactions with Mortals hang in the balance. The outcome of this future event will either bring light and harmony or ignorance and darkness. I wish we could say may the best clave win, but alas, this is not that kind of competition nor that kind of situation. To the claves involved, you will receive instructions soon. This council is adjourned. I thank everyone for coming."

The Anguis didn't stick around to mingle. Without another glance or word to the others, they filed out of the hall.

"They have a lot of nerve," said August. "I mean, to blatantly declare war like that?"

"What did you expect, August? An invitation to a tea party?" Larissa grimaced. Edouard had flashed her an if-looks-could kill expression before he left. And to think she had been in love with him.

"Oh, Larissa, there is something else I need to tell you about your old flame, Edouard Anguis," said August. "He's really your cousin, the son of Eustace and your Aunt Dorenda. My Grandfather learned this from Tiberinus. It was Dorenda's plan to have Edouard sway you over to his side. Consider yourself lucky that any further romance between the two of you was nipped in the bud due to circumstances."

Larissa held her cheeks in horror as she listened to August's words. Jove came up beside them. "Is it true, Jove, about Dorenda . . . Edouard . . . what Tiberinus told you?"

"I'm sorry, dear girl," said Jove. "It's the nasty truth, and the moment I learned this, I had to tell August."

Larissa stared at the floor humiliated, her face crimson. She looked up at August. "I really must have looked like a fool. I was played for one. And to think . . ."

"Shh." He wrapped an arm around her in sympathy. "Look, things like this can happen even to the best of us. Now you know. But, you need to start trusting me a little more." He pulled her close for a hug.

She returned his gesture. "As odd as this is for me to admit, maybe I should."

***

As it turned out, the world readied itself for the most imposing battle in Earth's history. At this time, the worlds of both Magicals and Mortals nearly mirrored each other. There had reached a point where a great shift was occurring, the death and destruction of old ideals with the incoming of the new. Old foundations were being torn down in how the world functioned, and new systems and beliefs were taking root. The outcome would save or perish all inhabitants. Each country had people supporting those of the light and those of the dark. Regardless of which side a leader of a country chose, the speech to their citizens was the same, and all made by that leader's clone. The world had, it seemed, fallen into a uniformity like no other time in history.

Each country had determined the time and date on sharing a rehearsed script to the people. On that chosen date, it was the moment of the big announcement, the cover story that would be spoon-fed to the press and the public to explain what would appear to be the most startling and pervasive atmospheric disturbance ever recorded in the entire history of mankind.

It would be "spun" so that none of them would ever guess that the course of civilization would be forever altered by its outcome. Only Magicals, Occult Creatures, Morphemes, and Realm Rulers would be aware of the true nature of the events to take place, events foretold in nearly every religion by oracles, prophets and seers, and outlined in fastidious detail in their sacred manuscripts.

It was the Battle of the Lightbringers versus the Shadowbringers, the final battle between the forces of Darkness and the powers of the Light. For the President of the United States, it was always unnerving to step out of his dressing room and come face to face with his clone. He had gotten to know "Larry", aka his Apex Replicant, but he was not a stupid man. He knew that there were likely not just one, but several clones of himself in existence.

The powers that controlled the United States Government as well as most of the world had been clever in their strategy. He'd been shown films at one point to convince him that he would be ruined if he did not cooperate with the political puppeteer known only as "Umbra".

The films, starring various cloned counterparts of himself, showed him in various illegal and reprehensible situations: cheating on his wife with two young women, engaging in the torture and sodomy of a young woman who was weeping and begging for her life, and the bell ringer of them all, a video showing him molesting young children.

Though he was innocent, he would never be able to prove it against the damaging and un-doctored video testimony. So, his decision was a simple one. Do whatever they wanted him to do. Umbra's henchman was his Chief Advisor, Phil Cranston, so Umbra literally always had the President's ear.

He watched Larry, his clone, who had studied all his mannerisms, walk out to take his place at the podium. The only thing the replicant scientists and doctors could not get quite right was the voice of the clone. Thus, he would be reading the prepared speech from off stage into a high-powered microphone. Larry would lip sync it from the teleprompter.

After waving and waiting for the final strains of "Hail to the Chief" to die down, Larry began the speech.

"Greetings to my American family." His voice boomed loud and inclusive. "I know you are eager to hear this announcement, and I hope that this speech will reach the ears of every living American through social media and other communication modalities.

"The first thing I want you to know is that you are in no immediate danger, and as long as you adhere to the precautions outlined by the Department of Homeland Protection, you will remain safe. We have worked with the global community of scientists and meteorologists, and although there are some minor disagreements as to how the coming weather patterns will play out, one thing is quite clear.

"Due to a myriad of factors, including global warming, environmental pollution, and tectonic plate shifting, we will be experiencing a weather event of cataclysmic proportions. Fortunately, we will have an onset date, and we still have time to make sure that all Americans are adequately sheltered with several days of food and water in order to be protected from the worst of it.

"Since the disturbance in the upper atmosphere will influence other weather factors, evacuations for hurricanes, tornadoes, and tidal waves will start tomorrow for those residing in low lying coastal planes. Many of our Federal Uniform Camps, our FUC's, have been in place to house thousands of American citizens who must seek refuge from the most threatened areas.

"I am confident that the same sense of unity, tenacity, and bravery that has characterized all Americans since the founding of our great country will carry us through! Please join me and the Army National Guard chorus in singing, "God Bless America", and then keep updated on bulletins we will be sending out as the atmospheric disturbance approaches. Thank you, and may God bless us all."

Paulo had returned to Ecuador where he had the honored pleasure of standing beside his leader. The president's clone made a similar speech for his people. But his contained an element not mentioned by others of the world. And the gentleman only remarked on it because Paulo, under the direction of the Glanarium Supremo, had told him to do so and provided him the wording.

"Dear citizens," said the president. He gazed over the crowd gathered in front of the presidential palace. "As I end with parting words, sharing with you what I have been told and how we are going to protect you, I want to add one more thing. Ecuador is a chosen country. We are chosen not only for the heart of its people and the beauty and history of our land, but we are chosen because we have some of the greatest biodiversity and human diversity of all. We have character and power.

"We may be a small country, but remember one thing, we carry great power. Any circumstances occurring on our land or in our air space on any level or dimension will be supported through our energy that is concentrated and boundless. We are strong, resilient, and valorous. That is all. May all of you go and live in peace."

Though everyone who heard the president speak thought his ending words most uplifting and encouraging, only people like him and Paulo knew the true meaning behind what was said.

Chapter Twenty Three

Back in his sanctuary of Sulphure Hall, Edouard prepared for what was to come. Like the others, he had also listened to the president of Ecuador's speech. He'd remained hidden in the shadows and would not have missed the speech for anything. He had talked Dorenda into coming to Ecuador to stay with him. Her support lifted his spirits in so many ways that his father simply couldn't do. The attack by August Hawthorne had left the older man brooding and angry.

Inwardly, Edouard sighed with satisfaction. They would win. He was sure of it. He envisioned a changed world, the world that would forever establish his family as the supreme omnipotent rulers and himself as the most powerful Magical of all. A world in which all-natural light had forever been extinguished. A world in which a black holed sun, ringed with a corona of infrared fire, would burn eternally and cast its hazy crimson glow over all that remained.

A world where only the Lords of Darkness and the vanquished remained, where the Lightbringers were kept only as broodmares, food for some of the Night creatures, and slaves. A world where all life dependent on the sun, including all plant life, was gone.

A world of rock, and dry winds and desert as far as the eye could see, bathed in the red light that had been at one time reserved for developing film with chemicals in darkrooms. An austere and exquisitely desolate world where nothing grew.

***

The Glanarium Supremo worked out the final details for the great battle. It would be fought in the interdimensional air space above the lovely country of Ecuador, South America. The president there had alluded to the reason when he addressed his people. But this country also had strong ley lines from which the battle fighters could draw strong energy and support their movements and their magical attacks.

On the main fighting plane, it was decided that Larissa, August, Willem, and Phuctious would represent the Strondovan/Hawthorne claves. Edouard, Carnetta, Malevolinda, and Eustace would represent Clave Anguis.

Outside the main field, other clave members and allies would position themselves and fight in alliance with their clave or chosen side. Their battles would be no less fierce or less important. And thus it all began the moment the Glanarium Supremo dropped the Magical flag.

Nothing as momentous as the final battle between the Lightbringers and the Darkness Dwellers could have been hidden from the global inhabitants of the Earth, and though it wasn't, all the news reporting services misinterpreted it to a startling degree.

The Skyborne Battle would rage for three days and be termed a "Huge Scale Atmospheric Disturbance." During that period of time, Wi-Fi was spotty, and there were rolling power outages in every major city. Having survived a pandemic and many electrical signal disruptions in the past, not everyone—in fact, practically no one beyond the small population of prescients, clairvoyants, Magicals, and spiritually-attuned beings—recognized it for what it truly was:

It was the Final Battle between Good and Evil.

On the ground, each side had their cheerleaders and advocates, but none of them were destined to rise and join the ongoing battle in the skies during the three-day struggle. It began with a gathering of an immense bank of broiling black and green lightning-streaked thunderheads rolling in from the west. Behind the nimbus vaporous front line, the edge of the Onyx Curtain was trailing, ready to be hoisted like a shroud and encircle the sky surrounding the earth as soon as the last Lightbringer was vanquished. Or at least that was the plan of the Darkness.

The other half of the sky, emanating from the East, and also further up in the atmosphere, was filled with the light of both the sun and the light of millions of stars that were also suns in other galaxies. In between the darkness in the western hemisphere and the light in the eastern portion of the sky, just overhead, was a spectacular blood red sky through which falling stars streaked down like furls from a huge fireworks explosion.

Some thought the sky was falling and scurried off to take shelter. Only Magicals could ascend to the battlefield, where both demons and angels and every phylum in between would be waging war. The final prize of the battle would be the Earth realm, and the side that conquered would reign over it.

Their fate unannounced, and as yet undecided, the inhabitants of all the countries of Earth went on about their business, even though they were aware of all the buzz surrounding the unusual atmospheric activity. The explosion of long dormant volcanoes in the so-called "ring of fire" that encircled the Pacific rim was speculated to be the cause of the heavy dark clouds occupying part of the heavens. But still no weather experts were willing to step forward and give a definitive explanation for what seemed to be the atmospheric event of the Millennium. All planes were grounded worldwide.

At the start of the battle, on the first day, Larissa and August, along with Willem and Phuctious, waited tensely in their Launch Silo for a signal to ascend and take their battle positions. The rest of the world outside of the Magiverse had been guarded by a huge Spell Net against knowing what was about to transpire. Linear time as they knew it had been suspended for the duration of the battle.

After waging war for two days, this was the third and final day. Each time, the Glanarium Supremo had given the signal to start the battle once again. Larissa fidgeted. She was so exhausted. Nausea had set in. She sucked in her breath, trying to calm herself. Willem reached over and took her hand in sympathy. He felt sadness emanating from her, and it worried him. An emotion like this would affect her conjuring abilities during the conflict. Every witch and wizard knew that strong emotions could drain one's energy field.

"I know it is a tall order, but Larissa, as I've said before, you are not responsible for the decisions your relatives made long before you were born, not the bargains with the Darkness your Aunt Dorenda made using you as a pawn, a sacrificial lamb.

"She showed her hand when she tried to seize that opportunity to transfer her energy into *your* young body and shove you out of your soul seat. No act is more reprehensible than that, save wholesale murder."

"I know, I know, Willem," Larissa replied softly, "but even though I feel like I never truly knew her, I grieve the loss of the one essential Magical relative in my life. She taught me everything I know—everything. I would not be able to fight this battle without using the defensive spells she taught me."

"Oh, speaking of Magical skills," August interjected. "Do you have it with you, next to your heart? Ciana said if you keep it next to your heart, then no one can take it."

Larissa sniffed. "Of course, I have it safely with me. Next to my heart." She felt rather hurt he would not trust her to bring their most valuable defense weapon. "And at the ready to bring forth when needed, like we talked about. But I hope we won't have to use it. I was able to come up with two Conjuring Cloths. After all, they disintegrate once they achieve a desired outcome. And we surely wouldn't have time to create one on the battlefield."

August nodded. "True. Look on the bright side, though. After all this is over, there should be no bad guys to snuff out, and we just let the little moths live their life in peace. Yeah? Or we do just the opposite and form our own hit squad. There are Magical and Mortals who would hire us."

Willem snorted, resisting an impulse to laugh out loud. Not because he thought August's remark clever or funny, but because he thought it silly and inappropriate timing. It was his experience that August had a knack for saying the wrong thing, especially in sensitive circumstances.

He marveled again that it seemed August and Larissa were destined to be a couple. In his opinion, they made a volatile match at best. Never mind that he caught private moments of civility when they thought no one was looking.

Ciana appeared. Though she was not a Magical, The Glanarium Supremo allowed her to be present near the battlefield, along with other special ones who were vital to the cause. "Time is nigh," she told them, "And the last day of this battle begins momentarily. Make certain to garb yourself in protective spells before ascending and may the Light be with you. The fate of humankind rests within your hands."

On the way out, as Larissa walked between August, who led the way, and Willem, who brought up the rear, she felt time suspend momentarily as a vision enveloped her. She knew it was from Willem, and her heart went out to him as a panorama of images floated through her mind. They were not "memories" in the usual sense, because these were the never-to-happen visuals of Larissa's life with Willem, which was never destined to be.

She saw their first kiss, which *had* actually happened, but all the rest had been created from Willem's fantasy yearning for her. She saw their marriage, a simple ceremony in a woodland meadow with a dwarf officiating. She was garbed in a simple white gown with a crown of flowers and colorful ribbons on her brow.

She saw Willem carrying her over the threshold of a simple, yet adorable cottage festooned with hyacinths and roses. She felt their passionate lovemaking, with Willem being both tender and determined to make sure that she had experienced pleasure before he took his own.

She saw them welcome the birth of a son, born with abundant curly brown hair and with her eyes. The visions were visceral. She could feel every iota of sensation and pleasure as they enveloped her. Her eyes teared up, and she knew he heard her when, without even turning around to look at him, she said, "You know I love you. I always have and always will."

It was the truth, a truth she had never felt free enough to be honest about. But at that critical juncture she thought he deserved to know, because she was certain that at least one of them would die during the final conflict.

They reached the launching roof of the Catapult Battlement Tower. Like the two days before, dozens of bodies ascended into the sky, many in battle garb, some other diaphanous beings like ghosts or specters. Some were recognizable as witches of great renown. There were also intelligent creatures that were thought by mortals to be mere legends represented during this war. Larissa had gasped at the sheer number of them the first day she saw it all. Many of her favorites such as phoenixes, unicorns, and golden griffins shot up into the atmosphere.

Yet their ascension was eerily silent, befitting a moment of both gravity and import, a sacred moment that would determine whether Earth would continue to shine and prosper and heal, or be plunged into darkness as the final Curtain of Darkness was drawn closed around it.

When they reached the battleground level, once again they found themselves part of a huge front line facing off against another massive front line, populated by both the profane and the beautiful. Creatures that slithered, grotesque giants with hideous features carrying massive, spiked clubs, and demonic fifteen-foot-tall entities with extra twitching limbs and hoofed feet all scowled menacingly at them.

In sharp contrast to their fighting cohorts, dark angels with strikingly beautiful faces and golden hair, dark fairies with gauzy segmented wings, wicked pixies with long pointed ears rising above their heads all made chittering sounds at them, as though they were jeering the Lightbringers.

Hovering above both groups were those creatures accustomed to attacking from above, flying in dizzying circles as they took in an aerial view of the armies on both sides. For the Dark Army, every creature that could slither out of a hole had been amassed, including giant spiders and scorpions, poison lizards, and even peridragons, whose numbers had been neatly split between the Darkness and the Lightbringers, resulting in their being represented on both sides.

Seven Angels sounded the loudest horn blast ever heard across the heavens from seven trumpets, and a mighty chorus of war cries erupted from both sides as they cleared the distance between them and began to engage one last time.

Larissa had originally intended not to use her amplituner, a kind of last-minute powerful gift from Jove. She'd long since used up her first one, given by Dorenda, in the Hall of Winds when she first made contact with Ciana. On viewing the impressive ranks of the enemy on display, she quickly changed her mind. Today, she had to use it. Out of the corner of her eye, she noticed Archangel Michael once again fighting alongside her. She had always harbored a crush on God's chief warrior angel. Seeing Michael's magnificence gave her the power boost, confidence, and gumption she needed to make swift work of removing a particularly ugly and loathsome smelling giant from the ranks of the Dark Forces, a snarling three-headed demon, a vicious Cerberus Hell Hound, and a ravenous giant arachnid.

She tried keeping both August and Willem in sight. Willem fought from behind on purpose, attacking anything that attempted to creep up on her. August, a few yards away, killed off a persistent hoard of Cerberus Hydras, slicing off heads with the precision of a skilled butcher. Since his sword was enchanted and imbued with extra spells, he managed to cut off the powerful and magical middle heads of the creatures.

The fang of a giant serpent that had gotten too close grazed her shoulder, but fortunately the wound was so slight that no venom had entered her bloodstream. Nevertheless, the drop that had managed to land on her skin caused a momentary feeling of wooziness.

To her vast relief, August, who had obviously been watching her as closely as she had been watching him, was right there in an instant, his tall muscular body partially shielding her from any further attacks until she could regain her composure. Just his proximity, the clean pine and ocean scent of him as he pressed his body to her own, seemed to restore her clarity.

On the side of the Lightbringers, Larissa stood firmly holding the line with August. A determined Phuctious at her side dealt with the crawlers that seemed to rise all around them, and they included serpents, snakes, spiders, and even giant centipedes. Phucky was indefatigable. Since he operated at a lower level, he could meet them head on and destroy them before they landed their venomous bites.

Surprisingly Remington Allwine had formed a triad of singular fighting power with Greta Marvo and Gamal Gamara, and all three were firing off Lightning Arrows and Flicker Throwing Stars. The Throwing Stars were enchanted. As soon as they reached a target, they were unstoppable. They whirled in a corkscrew motion around the outside of the hapless creature and landed on them, slicing off their skin or bony covering until their innards were exposed.

Since Allwine held the keys to the deities, he had summoned Athena to help strategize and direct their positions and use of weapons. Miss Ivey helped capture groups of the opposition by throwing up labyrinthine hedgerows in strategic places. The unfortunate beings trapped withing the mazes couldn't find their way out and thus met a horrid end. Tempest, true to his word, also joined in. He contributed, slicing and dicing anything in his path or that of his cohorts.

Larissa caught sight of her Aunt Dorenda across the Battle Plain and for a moment their eyes met. Despite her aunt's betrayal, there was the little girl part that had enjoyed her aunt's affection, company, and the many treasured memories as a result. Larissa hoped that somehow her aunt would forsake the Darkness that she had always served.

But as their eyes met, Larissa shivered. What she saw in her aunt's eyes was cold, stony ambition and a determination to finish what she had started. What she perceived was that Dorenda was hellbent on finishing what she had started, a plan that she had woven like a giant spider web around the young girl, in order to groom her so that Larissa's gifts could be harvested for the Darkness. And so that Larissa could be offered to the Dark Ones as a living sacrifice.

At that moment, her last hope that Dorena had ever truly loved her was extinguished, along with her memories, and she found herself thirsting for bloody vengeance, not really for herself but for the innocent child that had been raised for slaughter.

Larissa's heart sank again as she also saw Dennis and Daniel joining with Eustace. And to think she had liked them not long ago. In their various positions, each did their best to drive the Lightbringers back. On either end of the designated Battle Plain, which would forever afterwards be referred to as "Ager Sanguinis", the legendary "Field of Blood", there was a sheer drop off, an abyss that had no bottom.

Whichever side was driven back to the edge of the cliff would find themselves falling forever, caught in a wormhole fissure that existed outside the space-time continuum. It was actually one of the Seven Hells.

Willem, guarding Larissa from the rear, felt an eerie sensation, a premonition of impending danger. He whipped around to see the source. His blood ran cold. Somehow, a trio of Ghouliaths had circled around the perimeter of their position and now marched right up through the center of their ranks. The Ghouliaths were huge, at least fifteen feet tall. They were armed with giant iron swords, using them to cut down Lightbringer soldiers three at a time. After severing heads from bodies with little effort, the horrid creatures erupted in laughter from their hideous twisted lips.

Larissa turned and saw the Ghouliaths. She had only ever been aware of one, whose name was Horreum. He had been on a list of well-known Mercenaries for Hire, and she knew from her aunt's teachings that Ghouliaths had no loyalty and would murder for or fight for the highest bidder. Their sheer size was daunting. Willem, who had been at her side just seconds before, seemed to have disappeared. This worried her immensely.

As the monster's shadow fell over her, Phucky darted out and swung his ax, chopping off the giant's big toe on his left foot. It was the awful Horreum himself, who let out a blood-curdling howl. As Larissa looked up and up, due to the creature's enormous height, she was shocked to see that Willem had somehow crawled up on the monster's shoulder.

He caught her eye and smiled a lovely smile. Raising his sword, he aimed and plunged it into the side of Horreum's neck. At the same time, a giant boulder flew through the air—it had been conjured and aimed at Horreum—and hit him dead center in between his wide-set eyes. The Ghouliath crashed to the ground. To Larissa's relief, Willem leapt from the monster's shoulder. His sword remained planted in Horreum's neck.

The wizard scrambled up quickly, running toward her. She watched, viewing the scene as if it were in slow motion. Horreum, in one last defiant act, raised his bloody face and swung the sword he still clenched in his out-stretched hand. At that critical moment, time stood still as an unidentifiable object flew forward, catching Larissa in the solar plexus. She collapsed to the ground.

With the wind knocked out of her, she gasped for breath and struggled to sit up. Looking down into her lap, she could do nothing but stare. At first her mind couldn't make sense of what she saw. Willem was staring up at her from her lap. Not all of Willem, though—just his head. Larissa shrieked in horror. August heard her cries and raced to her side.

In another foul blow to the Lightbringers, a wicked poison lizard sneaked up behind August and shot out its tongue, landing the barbed end into the young man's side. Larissa gasped as she heard her companion scream out in agony and drop to the ground. His face turned ashen. She knew that the venom from these special lizards meant sure death, as there was no Mortal medical treatment. Magicals also had a difficult time curing anyone who had been attacked by one of these wicked creatures, and success was rare.

"I got him!" yelled Phucky. He hacked down the hateful lizard, smiling as the animal's eyes clouded white with death. "Do something quick, Miss Larissa. You have to move. Do something now!" The dwarf turned his attention to an oncoming fire dragon, barely missing a thin precisely aimed stream of fire.

Larissa took in a deep breath and wiped her brow. Her brain teemed with ideas on what to do before it occurred to her. Two of her companions had been brought down by the opposition. She held one last solution, which came to her in a flash of intuition. The puzzle box. This special box was given to her by a Mr. Whitelock, a mysterious person, whom they had met on their travels to Ichor Barony. King Bello, of the Stygian Labyrinth, had told her during their feast together that he knew what was in it but couldn't reveal the nature of the contents. Something told her without a doubt that inside the box lay the answer.

She whisked out the box from inside her bag of tools brought for battle. Under her breath, she swore, wracking her brain on how to open the box.

"Just lift that piece right there," said a deep voice. A finger pointed to the place.

Larissa looked over, relieved to find King Bello himself kneeling next to her.

"Do it quickly. We can only cover you so long. Your help is greatly needed." Bello bowed his head in respect, stood up, and tore off running to vanquish an onslaught of nasty pit vipers.

With shaky fingers, she pried out the middle piece, a puzzle part with a ruby gem on top. The gem glowed bright red on removal. The lid slid off and inside a velvet-lined interior was a cut crystal vial. A note dangling from it read: "Elixir of Life: *Save a life. Take a life. You must choose wisely no matter the strife.*"

"I have to choose?" Larissa clapped a hand against her forehead and groaned. She glanced up. In the distance Ciana, gazed at her with clasped hands and an imploring expression. This elixir may heal Willem, make him whole again. It would bring back August as well.

Ciana and her parents would never approve of Willem, no matter how kind and gentlemanly he was. August won their hearts from the outset, and there was no turning back. She had seen all his sides, arrogant, funny, serious, impertinent, valiant, brave—and loving. She twisted the wax-sealed cap off the vial and whispered to Willem's head with tears in her eyes, "I will always hold a special love for you. Nothing will ever change it."

She scrambled over to where August lay, pried his mouth open and poured out the contents from the tiny vial. The color of his face pinked up immediately. His eyes flew open. Larissa moved back to Willem so their eyes would meet for the last time. From his lips he said to her, "It was always you."

Chapter Twenty Four

A strange silence fell upon the Battlefield. August jerked Larissa to her feet, snatching her away from a macabre reverie. She looked wordlessly into his face and saw that he was weeping. During all their time together, she had never seen August weep.

"Willem is gone!" His words came out in a harsh strangled voice. "We must continue to fight, Larissa, because if we are not fighting, we are losing. Do it for us, for our future, and for Willem. He gave his life for you."

Larissa found her situational awareness returning, and strangely enough, she had the odd sensation that Willem was still wrapped around her, hugging her from behind. There was a warmth, and she could feel his arms. That was enough to give her the strength to kill one of the other Ghouliaths, screaming as she catapulted up the giant's body and stabbed her longsword into the front of the hideous creature's throat.

"For Willem!" she yelled in triumph.

The battle raged on, and both Larissa and August fought as though they had nothing to lose. When they wearied of swinging either the sword or the enchanted axe, they sent out Blinding Webs, a version of the Conjuring Cloth she had brought for such a moment. As he ventured forward after the steamrolling Blinding Webs, August was surprised to find himself face to face with a half blind Edouard Anguis.

Edouard, in severe pain, couldn't make out whether the figure blocking his path was friend or foe. In a feeble act of bravery, he plunged ahead, readying his sword. He shouted in a commanding tone, "Speak or be silenced!"

Behind him, he heard screams and the scent of burning flesh. He didn't know that some of the Wyverns, having been blinded, had run amuck among their own Dark comrades, screeching and haphazardly throwing out plumes of flame. Unfortunately, this ended up with Magicals and Creatures catching on fire.

"I believe we've met before." August stood within two feet of the once proud and now disheveled Anguis heir. "I am August South Hawthorne, grandson of Jove. And I am going to kill you now."

While August quickly debated whether killing a blinded Edouard was a righteously moral act, Edouard let out an outraged cry and plunged forward with his sword. The tip of it caught August in his solar plexus. Edouard, sensing he had made contact, grasped his sword with both hands and pulled it upward, thinking that he was gutting his opponent. August quickly decided that whatever he did next was only in self-defense, and it needed to be done quickly.

His hand was on his own sword, but he found himself wanting to end Edouard's life in a more personal manner. If time hadn't been of the essence, he would have delighted in strangling the life out of the Anguis heir. But lacking the time, he opted for an attempt to stab Edouard in the throat with a bejeweled dirk.

August not only lacked time, but luck wasn't on his side, either. Edouard had somehow sensed that his sword maneuver didn't yield quickly the results he wanted. He drew his blade back and started to plunge it into his opponent's gut.

Larissa charged toward August, simultaneously shoving him aside and placing the pointed end of the labradorite phurba against Edouard's chest. "*Tenibrio vincata!*"

On hearing the sound of his former love interest's voice, Edouard's face contorted with fear and horror. He opened his mouth to say something, but the only thing that came out was an agonizing cry of pain. He dropped to the ground, paralyzed. From his body rose a black wisp of smoke and the ugliest contorted face Larissa and August had ever seen. The grotesque figure gyrated and swung in their direction, nearly hitting them but veered again and rose upward, vanishing forever.

Elbowing August, she said, "Go for it. I've removed evil from him. He's basically harmless now, but I want to see him dead."

August obliged and shoved his sword into the helpless Edouard. The blood that gushed forth cast a satisfying spray over August's handsome face. He watched Edouard's eyes glaze over. A burbling sound emerged from the dark-haired foe.

The young man whipped out a handkerchief and wiped his face. Both he and Larissa stared at the fallen Anguis. "You killed him," she said quietly.

August did a mock bow. Reaching down, he jerked a heavy chain away from Edouard's neck. It was the huge amulet he saw on the day Edouard fell prey to his enchantment. He hadn't counted on it being so potent. He grinned at the memory of it all. August handed the gaudy trinket to Larissa. "Put this away for later," he told her. "Whatever it is, it must be powerful, because it was handed down to Edouard from his father and has been in their family for hundreds of years. Now it is yours, my lady."

Larissa's eyes shone as she took it, shoving it into her horseman's bag that was tied to the belt at her waist. "Thank you, August," she said.

"Oh, by the gods, here they come!" August squinted through the sun.

In the distance, Carnetta, Malevolinda, and Eustace came running toward their fallen family member. The glint in their eyes expressed every hate-filled word and emotion welling up from the depths of their depraved souls.

"I think it's time to use it, Larissa. You know what I mean." August nodded toward her bag.

As soon as Larissa removed the folded iridescent grey square material from inside the bosom of her dress, she held it up into the air in the direction of the oncoming opposing forces. In accordance with Ciana's instructions, August uttered the activation spell. Larissa called out the desire: "The Anguis Clave and all their allies are destroyed forever."

The cloth lit up in a bright light of swirling colors. Instantly, thick waves of violet fog glinting with silver rapidly spread over the killing field. It enveloped the opposing forces, temporarily blinding everyone in the front line of the Darkness Dwellers. It was a weapon they had desired but could not possess. They were not prepared for such power and its effects.

The scene was horrid to watch. Members of the enemy clawed at their dripping eyes. Some had managed to rip them out completely. Others left them hanging on by their main connecting nerves. Many gnashed their teeth as blood ran out of their mouths, coating their battle armor. Yet others coughed up green phlegm and gagged on their own vomit. One by one, they all staggered blindly to the edge of the abyss where they dropped from sight.

August pulled Larissa against him, acting as her shield. The wind howled. The dust blew up. Still the violet fog prevailed. They inhaled the scent of spilled blood in the air and heard the cries of the retreating Darkness Dwellers echoing around them as they subsequently fell to their deaths off the edge of the battle plane they had so desirously kissed.

All knew that the Lightbringers had prevailed. The Darkness Dwellers were vanquished, and if any stragglers still managed to survive, they would be taken as prisoners and swiftly dealt with. When the cloth had disintegrated and the violet fog cleared, the Lightbringers knew they could finally celebrate. August was thinking of celebrating the hard-won victory between Larissa's lily-white thighs.

Roman slipped up behind August and his daughter, wrapping an arm around each. "Well-fought, my children. Well-fought."

Ciana embraced Larissa. Red-eyed with tears, she whispered, "You made the right choice, my dear niece. It was so hard, I know. But you made the right choice."

Remington Allwine, Gamal Emara, Greta Marvo, and Miss Ivey all came running up to the Strondovan Clave members who had joined up with each other.

"What a fight, my friends. A well-earned victory." Remington Allwine smiled at everyone.

"Thank you for helping us, Mr. Allwine. You did well in assisting us." Roman clapped a hand in a show of approval on the man's back.

"Ah, sir, I could do nothing else once you convinced me to see the bigger picture. If any of you need anything in the future, you have only to ask."

"And I as well," said Gamal Emara. He turned to August and said lowly in his ear, "I think that little exercise you two did a while back will come in handy. I feel it."

August's face lit up with a smile. He said nothing but turned a light shade of pink.

"Miss Larissa," said Ivey, "I hope you feel differently toward me. I know you weren't happy before."

"You fighting with us won favor like nothing ever will. You risked your life, Ivey. I will always have benevolent feelings for you." Larissa hugged the older lady. "And you! Thank you for your help and hospitality. It was a most interesting visit when we saw you last." Larissa embraced Greta Marvo.

"You and your, um, friend will need to visit me again. I would love to be your hostess." Greta winked, turned, and struck up a conversation with Mr. Allwine.

"Well, that was a fight like no other." Tiberinus, Lord of Lakes, had swirled up from his kingdom below. "I don't normally come up to these dimensions, but I had to congratulate all of you. Jove, you have a most extraordinary grandson."

Jove, who had slipped up to the group, said with pride, "It took some time, but as a true South Hawthorne, he has grit. And his magic abilities are becoming rather quite stunning, if I say so myself."

"Let's all go home," said Roman. "Paulo, come spend some more time in New Orleans with us."

"I'd be delighted," answered Paulo.

Eleanor kissed Larissa on the cheek and walked with her to the Earth dimension landing site.

Tired from a hard-fought battle, everyone left the field and made their way to the Earth plane or other dimensions whence they came.

***

It had been a horrid scene beyond Dorenda's worst nightmare. Even in her darkest depths of despair before this war, nothing compared to the emotions roiling inside her now. She had managed to slip away undetected. Everyone dear to her was gone, Eustace, Carnetta, Malevolinda, and worst of all, her beloved son. Never would she be able to enjoy motherhood in the proper way she had hoped. Her niece and August Hawthorne had grotesquely butchered Edouard, and it had pained her beyond words. She made her way back to the Earth plane and returned to Sulphure Hall. It was important to remain out of sight. Being caught meant sure death.

She wasn't ready to leave it all behind. It was a huge world with many places to run and hide. As much as she enjoyed her son's home in Ecuador, it wasn't her desire to remain here. Just as she started to enter the gates of the Hall, a sudden commotion sounded from behind, a loud pounding of hooves.

Dorenda turned around. Horrified, she recognized the huge horse galloping forward. Why would Arion seek her out after all these years? True, she had blinded the poor creature in a fit of rage, but that was long ago. Why had he returned now? The huge beast didn't stop until he reached her. The lady let out a scream. Arion reared up and knocked Dorenda to the ground.

With flaring nostrils and a wild look in his eyes, he trampled over her body until every bone broke with a resounding snap. The horse looked down at her inert figure and snorted, "Karma is a bitch, Honey."

***

Back at the beautiful mansion on Royal Street, August casually followed Larissa to her room, where they each showered. She said nothing as they both tumbled into her soft warm bed for a deep sleep.

Larissa stirred and suddenly startled awake. Even though the Battle of Light and Dark had been over for hours, the sounds of war still thundered in her head. She realized that August was no longer beside her and wondered where he was. She felt a gentle tap behind her shoulder. When she turned, August was already on one knee, which was all by itself, astonishing. As he gazed up into her lovely face; his eyes were positively incandescent.

"When we met, I thought you were a spoiled uppity little bitchtress from a ruined witch clave," he began.

Larissa wrinkled her nose. In true August style, already his words were winning him exactly zero points as far as she was concerned.

August continued, "And you *are* uppity, but I understand now that your pride in your heritage matches my own. And pride is always a source of strength, no matter what anyone says.

"You are beautiful, Larissa, truly beautiful. Of course, I was attracted to you from the start. It surprised me that you were not an easy conquest, as I am used to having my way with ladies. But the fact that you were having none of it only presented more of a challenge, and I was determined to have you.

"I wasn't worthy of you. I am still not. I know your courage, skill, and determination. But I am as hell-bent as only another prideful witch from one of the preeminent witch claves can be to win you. My time with you changed me. I know how to love now. I understand that I have opened my heart to you and in doing so, it has made me entirely vulnerable.

"You can destroy me, yet I choose to open myself completely, holding nothing back. My hope is that you will do the same. I believe our love will be extraordinary and imbued with a powerful magic all its own.

"I offer everything I am and everything I have to you, if you will agree to accompany me on the rest of our journey in this realm together. I'll even sign a prenup. Such as I am, will you take me?"

Larissa's last modicum of resistance ebbed away as she gazed at the beautiful diamond ring nestled in the white velvet box August showed her. She extended her hand, marveling at the size of it. He slipped it on her finger.

"Yes," she told him, "I will marry you, Hawthorne Heir, with just one stipulation."

"And that is?" August asked. He smiled because it didn't surprise him that if Larissa agreed to marry him, she would make a negotiation out of it, the way she did about everything.

"If we have a son, I want to name him after the bravest male we have ever known," she told him.

August feigned a look of surprise. "You want to name our firstborn son Phuctious?"

Larissa grimaced. "No, of course I don't! I want to name him Willem." When she realized August had been teasing her, she punched him. Unfortunately, her aim landed somewhat lower than she'd intended.

August yelped in pain, cupping his slightly injured balls. "You might want to watch that. And I also have an added request."

"Go on," said Larissa.

"That if we have a girl, I want to name her Laurel, after my mother."

"Oh, August. Yes, Laurel will be her name. Absolutely."

Larissa, throwing the past behind her, kissed him. As they fell together on the bed, he reflected that even though she could be rough, stubborn, argumentative, and possessed the legendary Strondovan temper, he knew that his life with Larissa would never be boring.

***

On her wedding day a month later, Larissa prepared herself for one of the most important moments of her life. She fussed with her gown, ensuring everything looked perfect. Once they had made their mind up, she and August had decided to marry immediately, not wanting to stall. Someone knocked at the door.

"Come in," she answered.

"Hey, Larissa," said a lady's soft voice.

When the young girl turned around and saw Rick and Amy Martin standing in her room, she cried out for joy.

"You made it!" Larissa said. She hugged them both, the two parents who reared her with discipline and love. They would always be part of her life.

"Wouldn't miss this for anything," said Rick. "You'll always be our daughter too."

"We were devastated when you left," said Amy. She stroked Larissa's hair. "Finally, we learned the truth, your whole history, mission, everything."

"Quite a story," added Rick. "But it explained a lot of what happened at home."

Eleanor and Roman entered the room.

"We are grateful for everything you did. Thank you. It took a load off our mind knowing she was well-cared for," Roman said.

Eleanor added, "It's true. You are just as much her parents. We're so glad you came today."

"We enjoyed it," said Amy. "Larissa filled an empty space in our lives, a real dream come true."

Later that afternoon, everyone gathered in St. Louis Cathedral in Jackson Square on that brilliant sunny day for the wedding of the century. To outsiders, it passed as a normal Mortal occasion. But to the Magicals and their associates, this was an important union. Quri, along with Paulo, came from Ecuador.

"I wouldn't miss this for anything," said Quri.

"You were his guardian while he lived in Cuenca," answered Paulo. "You definitely should be here."

Quri smiled. "When I got my invitation, I danced with joy. I even did a special ritual celebrating this union."

The music started. Everyone stood up and witnessed a beautiful Larissa North Strondovan, clothed in a luxurious white gown, as she walked down the aisle with both her fathers. At the altar, a nervous but elated August Hawthorne smiled, feeling his heart would burst from excitement. Phuctious, his best man, also smiled, grateful to have been invited to share in this whole journey.

Larissa and August joined hands and said I do. Upon that declaration and presentation as husband and wife, everyone stood and clapped for the happy couple.

The End

About the Authors:

Scarlet Darkwood:

Scarlet Darkwood wields a mighty pen, or at the very least, delivers mighty punches to the computer keys when she's typing furiously on a story. She likes dark and twisted, and the weirder, the better.

Always preferring Avant Garde themes, her stories take the reader on unusual adventures, exploring the darker parts of the human psyche as she whips out cunning prose wrapped in provocative themes. Sometimes she veers from her beaten path and takes a happy-go-lucky romp in the brighter sides of life, kicking up her style into sharp, snappy dialogue and clever descriptions.

Writing in several genres unleashes her imagination so she never grows bored. From a young age, she's enjoyed writing and keeping diaries, but didn't start creating novels until 2012. She's a Southern girl who lives in Tennessee and enjoys the beauty of the mountains. She lives in Nashville with her spouse and two rambunctious kitties.

You can visit her BLOG at: www.scarletdarkwood.com
Follow her on Instagram (scarletdarkwood), Facebook (Scarlet Darkwood Author)

P. Mattern:

P. Mattern is a USA Today Award-Winning author, an Amazon #1, top 100 best-selling and award-winning author. Born with a stylus clutched in her tiny hand, she's been producing stories since she was in utero and hasn't looked back. She is the author of the Strident House and Full Moon Series, as well as other entertaining novels, short stories, and novellas. Always the weaver of enticing plot lines, she wrote stories to entertain classmates in elementary school and won awards for fiction and poetry in college. After being laid off from her professional job in mental health, she began writing down all the stories she had carried in her head and made outlines in earnest for her vibrant characters.